# PRAISE FOR **AND THE WORLD CHANGED**

"This first-ever anthology showcasing English-language creative writing by Pakistani women is a timely reminder of the intellectual strength, imaginative power, moral significance, and political pertinence of the female voice from a part of the world that has often been seen as oblivious to its gender inequities and devoid of the struggles for women's rights that other countries . . . have experienced. The dignified and informative Introduction by Muneeza Shamsie contextualizes the stories by giving a brief historical account of the sociopolitical conditions that have determined the course of English-language writing by Muslim women in the Indian subcontinent. . . . I can see this becoming a regular text for university courses in South Asian and postcolonial literature, woman studies, and third-world feminism."
—Waqas Khwaja, associate professor of English, Agnes Scott College

"This . . . anthology . . . often surprises, as the best stories feel charged with undercurrents or submerged histories. Female and minority protest against conditions in Pakistan often coexist in these stories with a desire to assert being Pakistani. Muneeza's Shamsie's Introduction provides useful comments on Pakistani politics and how they have increasingly disadvantaged women. Shamsie is a major source of knowledge about Pakistani English writing. This is an anthology I am glad to have."
—Bruce King, *Wasafiri*

"This landmark collection of Pakistani women's writing in English is of immense historic, political, and literary significance. Its authors address themes ranging from the politics of gender, religion, and colonialism to poverty, Partition, and Pakistani national identity. These words will change us as they invent worlds we thought we knew."
—Sunaina Maira, author, *Desi in the House: Indian American Youth Culture in New York;* associate professor, Asian American studies, UC Davis

"I could not put this book down! *And the World Changed* is a ground-breaking collection that has the potential to propel contemporary writing by Pakistani women to the center of postcolonial literary canons. Encompassing multiple generations, and national/diasporic cultural landscapes, these poignant, often bittersweet narratives of Pakistani womanhood offer insight, analysis, surprises, and pure delight. A book to savor, to think upon, and share with everyone."
—Chandra Talpade Mohanty; author, *Feminism Without Borders: Decolonizing Theory, Practicing Solidarity*

"Muneeza Shamsie's impressive new anthology . . . encompasses a remarkably wide range of voices that complement, contradict, and qualify each other to show the variety of ways in which the women of Pakistan speak about their rapidly changing world. Collectively, the stories include . . . the resourcefulness of peasant women in rural Pakistan; the plight of the urban underclass of maidservants in Karachi; out-of-work fishermen who trawl city streets for employment; and children orphaned in feudal wars, looking for dignity and hoping to find love. [These stories also describe] the sheltered lives of the privileged and the powerful, second-generation immigrants struggling to conform to parental expectations, as well as others who vociferously resist those expectations or who have shrugged off that baggage and demand to be accepted on their own terms. In short, this splendid anthology engages with history, old and new, with colonization and the great wars of those times, as well as their aftermath that took the form of civil wars, Partition, migration, neocolonization, urban warfare, and militant religiosity. [It shows how] history has impinged on the lives of Pakistani people, at home and in the diaspora. Shamsie's selections . . . will strengthen the growing claims of English-language fiction from Pakistan to a distinct identity and place in the wider literary world."
—Ira Raja, department of English, Delhi University; coeditor, *The Table Is Laid: The Oxford Anthology of South Asian Food Writing*

"Muneeza Shamsie's gem-like collection is once personal, autobiographical, and national. The stories suggest that the tiniest personal moments connect, directly or obliquely, to the traumas of national and political identity formation. Living in new geographic and cultural contexts, characters recognize, through the crucible of experience, the haunting of the present by forgotten histories. The violence of the past bleeds into epiphanies and losses of everyday life: the deaths of mothers, grandmothers, marriages, and friendships, the killings of Hindus, Sikhs, Muslims, and Christians, of [Zulfikar Ali] Bhutto, and, much later, of Benazir Bhutto. The loss of home and homeliness runs through all the stories: the mother who, after leaving her autistic child, wakes up in pain 'as you might expect of someone who has had an arm amputated to save the rest' might be read as a metaphor for the larger amputations of loss that resonate, not only through other stories, but through Partition, nation-building, and diaspora. The multiple references in each layered story suggest the richness of this valuable contribution to subcontinental and world literature."
—Zohreh Sullivan, professor of English, University of Illinois at Urbana-Champaign

"*And the World Changed* is a pathbreaking anthology; a feast of women's writing that challenges stereotypes of Pakistani women since Partition. It is essential reading for anyone interested in this emerging literature."
—Janet Wilson, professor of English and postcolonial studies, The University of Northampton; editor, *Journal of Postcolonial Writing*

# AND THE
# WORLD
# CHANGED

# AND THE
# WORLD
# CHANGED

*Contemporary
Stories by
Pakistani
Women*

Edited and with
an Introduction by
Muneeza Shamsie

The Feminist Press
at The City University of New York
New York

Published in 2008 by The Feminist Press at The City University of New York,
The Graduate Center, 365 Fifth Avenue, Suite 5406, New York, NY 10016

Library of Congress Cataloging-in-Publication Data

And the world changed : contemporary stories by Pakistani women / edited and
with an introduction by Muneeza Shamsie.
    p. cm.
  ISBN-13: 978-1-55861-580-9 (pbk. : alk. paper)
  ISBN-13: 978-1-55861-591-5 (cloth : alk. paper)
  1. Short stories, Pakistani (English) 2. Short stories, Pakistani (English)—
Women authors. I. Shamsie, Muneeza.
  PR9540.8.A53 2008
  823'.010892870954910905—dc22
                              2008009270

Text and cover design by Lisa Force

This publication was made possible, in part, by public funds from the New York
State Council on the Arts, a state agency.

State of the Arts

NYSCA

13 12 11 10 09 08      5 4 3 2 1

Printed in Canada

# CONTENTS

৪৩

# CONTENTS

# CONTENTS

# CONTENTS

# INTRODUCTION

&

What you hold in your hands is the only anthology of creative texts written originally in English by Pakistani women, ever. This may come as a surprise, since from the creation of Pakistan in 1947, there has been a tradition of English writing by Pakistanis, and English has remained the language of government. The fanning out of migrants into the English-speaking diaspora, accompanied by the facility of travel and the growth of the electronic media, has provided an impetus to Pakistani English literature; it reaches a broad Anglophone audience but in Pakistan has a much smaller readership than indigenous languages and literatures, which are much more widely spoken and read.[1] Thus, Pakistani women who employ English as a creative language live between the East and the West, literally or figuratively, and have had to struggle to be heard. They write from the extreme edges of both English and Pakistani literatures.

Although many of the writers included here are well known, the goal of this pioneering anthology is to reveal how Pakistani women, writing in a global—albeit imperial—language, challenge stereotypes that patriarchal cultures in Pakistan and the diaspora have imposed on them, both as women and as writers. In selecting stories for this volume, I have tried to include as wide a spectrum of experiences and voices as possible. Also, I made a deliberate attempt to include new, young writers. I gave preference to short stories, but I included some extracts from longer works, provided they could stand on their own; in some instances these were given titles specifically for the purpose of this anthology, with the permission of the author. In the call for stories, I did not specify the subject matter because I did not want preconceived parameters to limit contributors. I wanted to discover what their texts might yield. I wanted literary merit to be the prime criterion. I think this has given the collection its diversity.

Contemporary English writing by Pakistani women, which is the subject of this volume, began with Bapsi Sidhwa and the publication of her first novel, *The Crow Eaters,* in 1978[2]; hers was also the first English novel by a resident Pakistani since Partition to receive international recognition, regardless of gender. However, the history of English-language fiction by Pakistani women, being a colonial legacy, must be looked at in the context of Indo-Anglian[3] women's writing in British India, which dates back to the late nineteenth century.

In traditional society, whether Hindu or Muslim, men and women were segregated. Women observed the veil—*parda*—and lived in the women's apartments—the *zenana*—within an extended family. Toru Dutt (1856–1877), who is widely regarded as the first Indo-Anglian woman writer, was a glaring exception. Her Anglicized wealthy Brahman family had converted to Christianity, and her literary uncles were famous for their creative writing in both English and their native Bengali. She was educated in France, traveled to England, wrote an acclaimed poetry collection, and was the author of the Indian English and Indian French novels, *Bianca* or *The Spanish Maiden* (1878) and *L'Journal de Mademoiselle Anvers* (1879), both written by the time she was 21 and published after her death at that age. Dutt's English poetry, as well as the work of a privileged milieu of Anglicized Indian men, emulated the Romantic English poets who, in turn, had been influenced by the copious translations of classical Indian texts—Sanskrit, Persian, Arabic—by British scholars in India.

In 1837, English replaced Persian, the language of the Mughal administration, as the language of government, but in the lower courts, Persian was replaced by vernacular languages. This led to a two-tiered educational system, English and vernacular, that persists in South Asia, perpetuating huge social schisms. English became the language of the Indian elite, a means of advancement and employment and of communication with the colonial rulers. Indian reformers such as the Bengali Brahman Ram Mohan Roy (1772–1833) also advocated English, believing it to be a window to new ideas, new technologies—and progress (Rahman 2002). Muslims, who identified more strongly with Persian—because it was the language of the Mughal court and thus a symbol of Muslim power in India—shunned English until the dynamic educationalist and reformer Sir Syed Ahmed Khan (1817–1898) galvanized public opinion among Muslims in favor of English. He inspired a social transformation, propagating reform among the Muslim elite who redefined their identity as modern Indian Muslims. His ideas were pivotal to the genesis and ethos of Pakistan (Jalal 2001).

After the establishment of the British Raj, when Queen Victoria became Empress of India in 1858, British hubris and power in India were at their height. Among Indians, nationalist sentiment grew, which the vernacular press disseminated widely, although by the late nineteenth century, English-speaking Indians played a pivotal role in conveying this nationalist, Indian point of view to the British. Thus English became the "link language" in the political debate between the representatives of India and the Raj. Meanwhile The Indian National Congress was established in 1885, and then the Muslim League in 1905, to voice the concerns of India's Muslim minority (Jalal 2001) in a new, unfamiliar, social and political order. The complex relationship between these two political parties spiraled into bitter disagreements, sometimes fostered by the colonial power. In 1947,

3

this led to the Partition of India and the creation of Pakistan as a separate Muslim homeland. The founding fathers of both countries—Gandhi and Nehru in India, Jinnah and Liaquat in Pakistan—had been educated in British universities, used English as fluently as a first language, and pressed the demands of their electorates in the legislatures of British India.

For much of the nineteenth century, the acquisition of English remained gender specific and education was largely restricted to vernacular languages for most Indian women. Reformist debates on women's education "focused more on what and how much they should be taught, rather than whether they should be taught in English" (Mukherjee 2002). The gap between well-traveled Anglicized men and their cloistered mothers, wives, and sisters grew. Sarojini Naidu (1879–1949), a poet, nationalist, and women's rights activist, was the most celebrated Indo-Anglian woman writer of her generation. She belonged to a Hindu family closely associated with Hyderabad, a very large Muslim princely state that was the size of France. There, in 1881 her father set up one of the earliest schools for girls (Pernau 2002). Others followed suit. Instructors began to introduce English to their students, but among Muslims in particular, a secluded life in *parda* and private education, with or without the addition of some English, continued to be the norm for the well-born woman.

At the same time, Urdu, which came to be regarded as the language of Muslim identity, had its own reform movement. The earliest Urdu women's magazine dates back to 1886 and was a platform for early women writers. They included the convent-educated, Muslim intellectual Atiya Fyzee (1877–1967), who migrated to Pakistan in 1947. She wrote beautiful English in her timeless book on musicology, *The Music of India* (1914), but she published her articles and a travelogue in Urdu in order to reach Muslim women with her liberal, egalitarian ideas. The women in her family were among the first Muslims to discard *parda* (Karlitzky 2002).

## MUSLIM WOMEN WRITING ENGLISH FICTION

During the early half of the twentieth century, fiction writing by Muslim women in English remained a rarity. Among the few exceptions was Rokeya Sakhawat Hossain (1880–1932), who grew up in Calcutta (now Kolkata) where she received a traditional education in Urdu, Arabic, and Persian, and with the support of her husband, taught herself English and Bengali— now the national language of modern Bangladesh. In 1905, she wrote her first and only story in English, the 12-page "Sultana's Dream" (Hossain 1988, The Feminist Press): one of the most radical of early feminist writings.[4] She went on to write in Bengali and attack the *parda* system and traditional attitudes toward women. She set up schools for girls, but continued to observe *parda* to allay Muslim parents' great fear that education would encourage their daughters to discard the veil. Other Indian women writers of English fiction in the early twentieth century included India's first woman lawyer, Cornelia Sorabji (1866–1954), and her sister, Alice Sorabji Pennell (1870–1951), a doctor. Both were educated in England and belonged to an eminent Parsi family that had converted to Christianity.

In 1921 women gained the right to be elected to the legislatures. Educated Muslim women began to discard *parda* and participate in political life. They included the Muslim League activists Jahanara Shahnawaz (1896–1979) and Inam Habibullah (1893–1974), my grandmother. Interestingly, my grandmother had a private education, learned English after her marriage, but used Urdu when she wrote a travelogue and children's books. Shahnawaz, on the other hand, graduated from Queen Mary College, Lahore, and wrote an Urdu novel, but much later recorded her life and times in an English memoir, *Father and Daughter* (1963).

The presence of mission schools for girls in British India, where "progressive" families began to send their daughters, spurred the use of English for Hindu and Muslim women alike, since these schools taught entirely in English. However many families remained more conservative and feared that if young women were exposed to alien religious and cultural influences at these institutions and were not secluded, sexual and social anarchy would follow.

In her memoir, *From Purdah to Parliament* (1963), the bilingual writer Shaista Suhrawardy Ikramullah (1915–2000), a member of Pakistan's first Constituent Assembly and later, a diplomat, recalled the agitation in her family when her Anglicized father insisted she attend an English mission school, and her traditional mother, egged on by vocal relatives, opposed it bitterly. But a decision that caused such conflict in her home soon came to be the norm, Ikramullah notes:

> In 1927, my going to an English school was looked upon with much disfavor and yet by 1947 every girl of good family was going to school. What my father had said had come to pass and in another twenty years' time women were taking part in processions, had been to gaol, were working in refugee camps, and were sitting in legislatures and participating in international delegations. It seems incredible, but it has happened. (1998, 32)

In British India, English was the language of instruction in all universities. Ikramullah, Ismat Chughtai (1915–1991), and gynecologist Rashid Jahan (1905–1952), were among a small number of pioneering university-educated Muslim women of their time. Ikramullah, the first Muslim woman to earn her Ph.D. from London University, wrote Urdu fiction and English nonfiction[5]; Jahan and Chughtai, who became literary icons, channeled their extensive reading in English of British, European, and Russian literature into revolutionizing Urdu fiction.

However, even with the growth of writing in English by Muslim women, a major problem persisted: the lack of readership. There was little encouragement to write as well. Since many Anglicized intellectuals in India looked to England's classical literature to define the literary style of English-language writing, they had little patience with the stylistic difficulties that contemporary creative Indo-Anglian writers, regardless of gender, had to grapple with: how to find a modern voice in English that would transpose the authentic experience of the subcontinent without pandering to Western exotica. These Anglophiles disparaged Indo-Anglian poetry and fiction, propounding the belief that Indians should not write creatively in English because they "could not get it quite right." Muslim women with a sufficient command of English, who were few in number, suffered this dismissal acutely. Furthermore, while the work of nineteenth-century Indo-Anglian writers had emulated that of British writers, by the 1930s, Indians were expected to use English creative writing as a nationalist vehicle that would "explain" India to the British colonizers. Thus, in vernacular fiction, a truthful portrayal of harsh realities was acceptable and praiseworthy—but in Indo-Anglian creative writing, such writing became a betrayal.

In the pre-Partition years, the only English novel by a Muslim woman appears to have been the satirical *Purdah and Polygamy: Life in an Indian Muslim Household* (1944) by Iqbalunissa Hussain.[6] She uses irony to comment on the power of the mother-in-law in an extended family and lampoons callous, self indulgent, and hypocritical men:

> It is a well known fact that man is superior to woman in every respect. He is a representative of God on earth and being born with His light in him deserves the respect and obedience that he demands. He is not expected to show his gratitude or even a kind word of appreciation to a woman: it is his birthright to get everything from her: 'Might is right' is the policy of the world. (quoted in De Souza 2004, 508)

Thanks to her supportive husband, the Mysore-born Hussain learned English and graduated from college in 1930, two years before her eldest son (507). She went on to work for the education and welfare of women.

As the subcontinent moved toward independence, activists considered women's emancipation an integral part of the freedom struggle. Jahanara Shahnawaz's daughter, Mumtaz Shahnawaz (1912–1948), a Muslim League activist and a novelist, describes this very clearly in her only book, *The Heart Divided* (1959), which is probably the first South Asian English novel about Partition. She died in an air crash, leaving behind a first draft that was published unedited by her family. Despite many flaws and a narrative heavy with politics, reportage, and polemics, the book has great historical and sociological importance. The plot revolves around the love story of Habib, a young Muslim man in Lahore, and Mohini, a Hindu girl and a close friend of his sister, Zohra. Political divisions intensify the conflict of religion. At first, Zohra joins the Indian National Congress, while her sister Sughra is committed to the rival Muslim League. The two sisters attend the historic 1940 Muslim League meeting in Lahore:

> 'Shall we sit behind the *purdah*?' Zohra asked curiously.
>
> 'Of course not,' said Sughra. 'What made you think that?'
>
> 'I just wondered.'
>
> 'Lots of women sat outside at the Patna session and two of them addressed the open session.' (quoted in Shamsie 1997, 37)

Through her characters, Shahnawaz debates independence, Partition, and the emancipation of women. She stops short of the Partition riots.

‰

8

Widespread Partition riots occurred in August 1947 and led to cataclysmic violence and one of the great mass migrations in history. No one knows exactly how many people were affected, but many estimate that there were around ten million refugees and one million dead. This trauma, which marked the retreat of the British Empire and the birth of an independent India and Pakistan, continues to haunt both countries. Since Hindus, Muslims, and Sikhs were both perpetrators and victims of the horrors of Partition, this has led to a collective guilt that South Asians find difficult to confront. In politics this guilt has taken the form of India and Pakistan blaming each other for the resultant conflict, violence, war, and suffering from the time of Partition to the present day, but in South Asian English literature it has largely materialized in a tendency to sidestep ghastly details, which is why, compared to the magnitude of the event, novels about the Partition massacres are relatively few (Shamsie 2001).

In 1947, Ra'ana Liaquat Ali Khan, the wife of Pakistan's first Prime Minister, called upon educated Pakistani women to help with relief work in the refugee camps: They came in great numbers despite virulent criticism and abuse from orthodox clerics who believed that women should stay at home. A one-time professor of economics, Khan motivated and galvanized educated women to focus on every aspect of women's welfare, including female literacy. Her efforts spearheaded the women's movement in Pakistan. But the emphasis on nation building in the newly created country meant that social activism was considered a more praiseworthy occupation for privileged, well-educated, English-speaking women than the reclusive act of writing fiction.

In his informative book, *A History of Pakistani Literature in English* (1991), Tariq Rahman shows that by the 1950s writers in Pakistan began to agree with "the prescriptive dictum that their work must have an extra-literary purpose, namely to 'serve the society' . . . this propagandist and chauvinistic view of literature was one which gained official support later." By then, all English creative writing by Pakistanis was disparaged as pointless, elitist, and a colonial hangover. The paradox was that Pakistan's English-language press flourished, but it was run and staffed by men; women reporters and editors were not even considered.

Author of a collection, *The Young Wife and Other Stories* (1958), Zaib-un-Nissa Hamidullah was the only woman writing English fiction of note during that era; her stories revolved around social pressures in the daily lives of women. Hamidullah (1918–2000) was also Pakistan's first woman columnist. Beginning in 1948 she wrote for *Dawn*, Pakistan's most important and influential English-language daily newspaper, but the day she commented on politics, she was hauled up by the editor and told she must not stray from "women's issues," in other words, domestic matters. She resigned and set up a magazine, *The Mirror*, a popular glossy that recorded social happenings. Few in Pakistan remember that she utilized it to write fearless political editorials, which led to a ban on the magazine in 1957. She challenged this ban in the Supreme Court and won (Niazi 1986), becoming the first Pakistani woman to win a legal victory for press freedom in the superior judiciary. In the late 1950s and 1960s magazines such as *The Mirror*, as well as *Woman's World* and later, *She*, run by Mujib-un-Nissa Akram and Zuhra Karim, respectively, provided a platform for English-language writing by women.

In 1958, Pakistan experienced martial law for the first time, under the rule of General Iskander Mirza, soon followed by General Ayub Khan. Dissent was ruthlessly crushed, and the press was censored. None of this was conducive to English-language writing, which had a handful of practitioners and a tiny audience, unlike vernacular literatures, which had a long literary tradition, replete with rich metaphorical poetry that could be recited orally or set to music for popular songs.

Two events of great significance in Pakistan's women's movement marked Ayub Khan's rule. Women activists persuaded Khan to defy the orthodox and promulgate the

1961 Family Laws Ordinance, with clauses that discouraged polygamy, regulated divorce procedures, and introduced a minimum marriageable age. Khan, who had little interest in fostering political freedom, established a quasi-democracy and held elections in 1964 to legitimize his rule. Fatima Jinnah, sister of the nation's founder, stood up as his political opponent to widespread support and became the first woman in Pakistan to head a political party and compete for the position of the executive head of state. Ayub Khan won his election but was ousted from power in 1968.

A brief spell of democracy preceded another period of martial law. There were two wars with India. The refusal of the military and some West Pakistani politicians to accept the election results of 1970 led to brutal civil war in 1971 and the loss of a large portion of the country—East Pakistan—which declared its independence as Bangladesh. In December 1971, Zulfikar Ali Bhutto assumed power in a truncated Pakistan where he held the majority vote. In 1977 General Zia-ul-Haq overthrew Bhutto, and tried and executed him. Zia-ul-Haq ushered in a new era with religious extremists as his allies, ruthlessly pushing aside the liberal, modernizing precepts of the nation's founders.

As part of his campaign to "Islamize" society, Zia ul-Haq introduced the 1979 Hudood Ordinance, which did not differentiate between rape and adultery. He also passed new blasphemy laws. Both the Ordinance and the blasphemy laws victimized the weakest and most vulnerable—women and minorities. All this, together with blatant miscarriages of justice, provoked educated, professional women in Pakistan, particularly lawyers, welfare workers, and journalists. They formed the legendary Women's Action Forum and came out into the streets to protest. Pakistan's English-language press provided them with strong backing, and some of Pakistan's finest women journalists emerged during this decade. Still, it took three decades to pass a watered-down Women's Protection Bill in 2006, which was full of compromises for fear of alienating Pakistan's right-wing lobby and clerics (who were defeated in the 2008 polls).

Despite political restrictions, in the 1980s a university education became the norm for many young women from professional families in Pakistan, and a number of careers opened to them, including ones in the civil service. At the same time, in Pakistan's low-income groups, education remained—and still remains—a privilege, not a right, regardless of gender, but boys were and are far more likely to be sent to school than girls, although schools for girls have grown and expanded, particularly in urban areas. The disadvantages of the tiered educational system, inherited from colonial times—one in English, the other in Urdu, and a third in provincial languages—created schisms in society that have been continuously and fiercely debated since 1947, but Zia-ul-Haq's attempt to do away with English as the medium of instruction met with great resistance. Instead, the demand for English grew: It became the language of global power, global knowledge, and the new electronic media.

In 1988 Zia-ul-Haq died in a mysterious air crash, ushering in an era of civilian rule. In 1989, Benazir Bhutto (1953–2007) was elected Prime Minister and became the first Muslim woman to hold that office anywhere in the world. Bhutto campaigned while pregnant with her first child. When her second child was delivered, she became the first elected leader of a modern nation to give birth while in office. Her assertion of womanhood while serving as the executive head of state in a conservative patriarchal country was an important milestone for women everywhere. Bhutto used English to great advantage in her writings, and her posthumously published book, *Reconciliation: Islam, Democracy and The West* (2008), has received much critical praise.

Today an increasing number of upper- and middle-class families in Pakistan have allowed their daughters to receive the same educational opportunities as their sons. Several women have graduated from prestigious international universities and a large number of careers are now open to them. At the same time Pakistanis from the most impoverished regions have had close contacts with relatives in the diaspora. The dynamics of this interchange have profoundly influenced Pakistan and Pakistani migrants in the West, rich or poor—a theme that emerges quite clearly in Pakistani English literature.

Meanwhile in the West, during the late 1960s and early 1970s, the anti-Vietnam protests, the civil rights movements in the United States, the student revolution in Europe, and the feminist revolution impacted English literature, as did the presence of increasingly assertive migrant communities. Soon it was apparent that some of the most important new English writing was coming from Britain's erstwhile colonies where women's writing forged new narratives that challenged both imperial and patriarchal myths.

The beginning of this century has seen women firmly assert themselves in Pakistan as leading English-language editors, journalists, and publishers. In turn, publishers have begun to actively seek out new writers of Pakistani English fiction and poetry, many of them women, almost all of whom are represented in this anthology.

### AND THE WORLD CHANGED: THE AUTHORS

This anthology developed as a consequence of two previous ones that I put together. The first, *A Dragonfly in the Sun: An Anthology of Pakistani Writing in English* (Oxford University Press, 1997), a collection of poetry, fiction, and drama, was a retrospective commissioned to celebrate Pakistan's fiftieth anniversary. This volume was the first to bring together English-language writers living in Pakistan and in the diaspora. It also raised issues of identity: Did diaspora writers of Pakistani origin "qualify" as Pakistani? My answer was, unequivocally, yes. To explore this further, I put together a second collection of fiction and non-fiction, *Leaving Home: Toward a New Millenium: A Collection of English Prose by Pakistani Writers* (Oxford University Press, 2001), which looked at issues of home, homeland, and belonging through Pakistan's diverse experiences of migration.

An anthology on English-language writing by Pakistani women seemed the next logical step, but only emerged after my

13

chance meeting with the Indian publisher Ritu Menon at a 2004 Sustainable Development Conference in Islamabad. She suggested the book. A year later, at the next Islamabad conference, I handed her the completed typescript on disk. I was delighted at the warmth with which the people in India received the collection, and to find that, subsequently, in Pakistan, Oxford University Press reprinted the same version twice. At the request of The Feminist Press I have altered the original compilation to replace most of the novel extracts with short stories from the same authors. In this version, I have also included the work of the young Pakistani American writer, Bushra Rehman. New headnotes for the American edition introduce the authors and the texts, and in some instances, I have quoted the insightful comments that the authors provided me in my correspondence with them.

All the women included in this volume have been educated in English, which remains the language of instruction in universities and the best secondary schools in Pakistan. Many of the writers went to the mission schools and colleges that were established in colonial times, although other prestigious private schools teaching in English have also emerged. These institutions are the training grounds for resident Pakistani English writers. Some of these writers belong to families where English is spoken at home as a dominant language. While there is comparatively little working-class literature in English from Pakistan, or indeed any South Asian country, migration to the English-speaking diaspora has introduced that dimension. In these countries Pakistani/South Asian migrants do not belong to the mainstream, regardless of income, education, or class. Their voice and that of women migrants in particular belongs to a minority struggling to be heard. Among the writers included here, there is another category: those women who have attended a variety of English schools in different countries because of relocations due to their parents' professional assignments.

In this anthology, the authors have been arranged in chronological order based on their birth years to reveal the development of women's writing in English across two generations and also to create a sense of historicity. Their stories reflect similarities and contrasts between avoidance of and engagement with a changing world.

The decision to include creative work written in English—and not to include translations—highlights a language acquired by Pakistanis as the result of the East-West encounter. By including only these English-language texts, this collection is set apart from other Pakistani literatures. Almost all the writers included here live, or have lived and been educated, in Pakistan as well as a country in the West. Their choice of English as a creative vehicle has highlighted this duality, and their work is often multilayered. In most instances no clear signals emerge from the texts to indicate which authors are residents of Pakistan. Sometimes, the writers who live in Pakistan explore themes of migration to the West; often the writers who have left Pakistan set their stories in their homeland. Both groups present stories of reclamation, a charting of territory across two worlds. All their work is united by their sensibilities as women of Pakistani origin writing in English.

After I had assembled this collection based on my interest in literary quality, I wanted to explore whether there were any links among the works that I accepted for the volume. What relationship did so many well-traveled women have with Pakistan? How did the acquisition of English as a creative vehicle influence their responses? The recurrent theme of quest, in many different guises, emerged very strongly as a recurring thread in many of the contributions. I found that a number of the themes in the stories, and several of the authors, had crossed paths at one point or another.

Opening the anthology is a moving story about the Partition riots, suffering, and forgiveness, "Defend Yourself Against Me," by famed novelist Bapsi Sidhwa. In 1947, Sidhwa, who is Parsi, was a child but she has retained memories of the fires and the violence in Lahore where she lived; in her writing, Sidhwa gives equal space to communal violence on both sides of the Indo-Pakistan border without sentimentality. In "Defend Yourself," which is set in Houston, the Pakistani-Christian female narrator encounters an old childhood friend, who is Muslim, from Lahore. The other characters are Hindu and Sikh, and the story thereby represents the three main groups who savaged each other during Partition. The plot folds back into the past to reveal a great horror, drawing particular attention to the silence of women as victims of war and conflict.

Following Sidhwa is the Karachi-born Roshni Rustomji, who also belongs to the Parsi community. In her memoir "Existing at the Center, Watching from the Edges: Mandalas," Rustomji observes Partition as Hindu friends leave and Muslims from India enter her childhood city. Her narrative of adaptation in a world rife with prejudice and conflict stretches across several countries and six decades from Partition in August 1947 to the assassination of Benazir Bhutto on December 27, 2007. Throughout she retains a sense of herself as a woman who will never belong to the mainstream but who regards every country in which she has lived as her homeland—her *desh*—and identifies with its suffering.

There is a direct link between the sensibilities of women writers in Pakistan and the stories they have written about Pakistan's minorities, such as Christians, Hindus, and Parsis, because both they and their subjects belong to marginalized groups whose rights can be easily eroded. Representing another minority experience is Sorayya Khan's story, "Staying," about a Hindu businessman who chooses to remain in Lahore, despite the Partition riots. Khan looks at the importance of August 1947 by moving beyond the political rhetoric that has defined India and Pakistan to portray events as they must have appeared at the time. The story also comments on the claim of geography—rather than religion, politics, or ideology—and highlights the relationship between the colonizer and the colonized, and the burning desire of the latter to occupy the space vacated by the former.

These are among the themes that I have also explored in my story, "Jungle Jim," set shortly after Partition in a former princely state in India. "Jungle Jim" tells of empire, colonialism, prejudice, and division, and links up three events, which radically changed social structures—the two World Wars and Partition. The story also looks at the huge gap that developed in colonial times between Indian men's Anglicized lives and the cloistered worlds that women continued to occupy.

Later in the anthology, stories by Sabyn Javeri-Jillani and Sehba Sarwar explore the repercussions of the continuing conflict between India and Pakistan. In "And Then the World Changed," Javeri-Jillani encapsulates the relatively carefree mood of a multicultural neighborhood in post-Partition Karachi. The 1965 war with India alters that ambience and divides the community, laying the ground for the urban warfare of later decades, while "Soot," by Sarwar, moves beyond the wars and hostilities that have so bitterly divided India, Pakistan, and Bangladesh for sixty years, and shows the Pakistani narrator's growing interest in learning more about India and Bangladesh and her concern with the deep poverty that all three nations share.

The permeability of languages, countries, and culture runs through the work of several writers represented in this volume. While living in England the expatriate Rukhsana Ahmad was so disturbed by events in Pakistan during the period of martial law under Zia-ul-Haq that she began to write articles protesting conditions in Pakistan for *The Asian Post* in London, thereby launching her writing career. Her story, "Meeting the Sphinx," questions the certainties of history, words, and narrative in British academia through the relationship between a white, distinguished Egyptologist and a feminist of Asian origin who challenges his assumptions.

Ahmad also published *We Sinful Women* (1991) a collection

of Urdu feminist protest poetry that she translated in English to great acclaim. The volume included the work of Fahmida Riaz, who had authored Pakistan's first book of feminist poetry in 1973, thereby opening a new dimension for women writers. Though Riaz only occasionally writes in English, she wrote "Daughters of Aai" specifically for this volume: It is a haunting tale of innocence, sexual abuse, and the resourcefulness of women in a Pakistani village. She shows that in Pakistan's peasant cultures, women perform hard labor and do not observe *parda* or the veil, unlike "respectable," wealthy, or urban women.

Tahira Naqvi, who lives in the United States, writes English fiction and, like Ahmad, has also translated Urdu feminist writing, particularly the fiction of Ismat Chughtai, the pioneering and uncompromising pre-Partition writer. Naqvi's translation of Chughtai's 1940 novel *Tehri Lakeer*—later translated into English and published by Women Unlimited in India and The Feminist Press in the United States under the title *The Crooked Line* (2007)—includes an introduction in which Naqvi draws parallels between Chughtai's fearless portrayal of female sexuality and Simone de Beauvoir's pioneering work, *The Second Sex* (1949). The influences of Chughtai and the other Urdu women writers that Naqvi has translated have seeped into Naqvi's English writing. Her story, "A Fair Exchange," explores with great subtlety the complex psychological and sexual compulsions that impel a well-educated woman in a traditional but professional family to misinterpret her dreams and resort to superstition. Naqvi's use of suggestion to express repressed, unidentified, and chaotic emotions strongly echoes themes in Urdu women's fiction.

Myths and stories are immensely important to gender roles. In the West, the feminist revolution led to the excava-tion of matriarchal narratives and legends portraying women. In Britain, Shahrukh Husain culled lore about women from the world over for a series of books for adults. In this volume, her story, "Rubies for a Dog," which belongs to an Islamic tradition, revolves around a Wazir's daughter who embarks on a long and dangerous quest across distant lands to avenge her father's honor. Husain says:

> Fairy tales from the Islamic world are often stories of a quest which entail extraordinary courage, and often also include strong elements of wit and wisdom. The *wazir's* daughter . . . represents redemption or delivery in one way or another. . . . The fairy stories which form such an important part of the heritage of India and Pakistan were shared with Iran and Afghanistan and may include *paris,* jinns . . . or they might simply be about human, though extraordinary, journeys. (Shamsie 2005, xvi)

"Rubies for a Dog" is another example of the crisscrossing of linguistic, geographical, and cultural boundaries that were intrinsic to Islamic culture and are a part of modern Pakistani life.

Interestingly, among the stories submitted for this anthology, only two revolved around arranged marriages, "The Optimist" by Bina Shah, and "A Pair of Jeans" by Qaisra Shahraz. I decided to include both because they complement each other and describe the crisis of immigrant Asian young women who, at the insistence of their parents, assent to this time-honored custom. The stories clearly reveal the conflict between first- and second-generation migrants and the desire of the older generation to cling to age-old traditions in an alien land. In "The Optimist" Bina Shah employs two different narrators, a Pakistani young man and his Pakistani British bride. He decides to marry her because he falls in love with her photograph, without any perception of her as an individual, or her world and her aspirations; she has accepted the marriage, reluctantly, under great moral blackmail.

In "A Pair of Jeans" expatriate Qaisra Shahraz describes a daughter of Pakistani parents in Yorkshire, who, dressed in jeans, runs into her future in-laws: They have seen her only at social occasions in Pakistani dress. To them her boots and jeans symbolize all that is Western and decadent. Both stories reveal how the system of traditional arranged marriages has evolved and developed huge fissures under the pressures of modernity.

In marked contrast "Runaway Truck Ramp" by Soniah Kamal takes a critical look at American notions of freedom and free choice through the love story of a white American woman and a Pakistani man in the United States. Both are aspiring writers but are so conscious of belonging to different cultures that they cannot look beyond confused notions of sexual mores.

Kamal's story has a very different rhythm to the contemplation of cultural duality and exclusion in "Variations: A Story in Voices" by Hima Raza (1975–2003). She combines poetry and prose to portray the solitude of a woman who reflects upon her thwarted relationships and that of friends and family, across generations, cities, cultures, and countries.

Different cultures coexist with greater ease in *Meatless Days* (1989), a creative memoir by Sara Suleri Goodyear, who teaches at Yale University. She provides a lively insight into her dual inheritance as the daughter of a Pakistani father and a Welsh-born mother and knits together the public and the personal, past and present, across Pakistan, Britain, and the United States. Her first chapter from *Meatless Days*, "Excellent Things in Women," reprinted here, revolves around the personality of Dadi, her paternal grandmother, but the kernel embedded within is the quiet presence of Suleri Goodyear's mother and the spaces she negotiates. The whole is interwoven with small, telling glimpses of family life, particularly Suleri Goodyear's relationships with her sisters Tillat and Iffat, who act as both foil and echo to her own personality. The unity of sisterhood across the patriarchal structures of family, nation, race, and creed is a familiar theme in women's writing worldwide.

Another U.S.-based academic of Pakistani origin, Fawzia Afzal Khan uses creative prose interspersed with poetry to universalize her experiences in the memoir, "Bloody Monday," which contrasts the intense passions and fervor of a Muharram procession in Lahore and a bull-run in Spain with daily domestic life in the United States, but suggests a multitude of subtexts on gender and myth. Her use of poetry and prose creates a multiplicity of images that reflects her desire to cross boundaries and break down barriers.

Maniza Naqvi's story, "Impossible Shade of Home Brew," is an assertion of diversity as unity. The rich multicultural fabric of Lahore, its street life, old traditional buildings, and colonial monuments provide a vivid contrast with touristy Epheseus in modern Turkey. In both these cities, however, the intermingling of East-West narratives, literature and lore, and the theme of "twins" and duality becomes a metaphor for the narrator's subversion of gender definitions and gender roles.

Talat Abbasi has written many intense, feminist stories set in Pakistan, which have been extensively anthologized and used as texts in the United States. Her poignant and haunting tale of a mother and her handicapped child, "Mirage," reprinted here, won first prize in a BBC short story competition and explores with great honesty a dimension of pain that is seldom discussed.

In the last decade, Pakistan has been strongly affected by political events in neighboring Muslim lands, including the rise of the Taliban and al-Qaeda, the politicization of religion, exacerbated by Western rhetoric of Crusades, and the clash of civilizations. Humera Afridi's story, "The Price of Hubris," set in New York on 9/11, and Bushra Rehman's, "The Old Italian," which takes place in Queens, New York, in a working-class, diverse immigrant neighborhood, both touch on ideas of religion, identity, and otherness.

With great clarity, another contributor, Feryal Ali Gauhar, brings to light the disadvantaged lives of the poor in Pakistan, due to powerlessness and an inequitable legal and social system in her poignant story, "Kucha Miran Shah." She portrays the ancient tribal custom of killing of women in the name of honor, a victimization sanctioned by a village *jirga*—an informal gathering of village elders (men) who mete out a rough-and-ready punishment—and which exists in rural areas as a parallel system to the laws of the state and its courts of law. Aamina Ahmad further explores the diminished rights of the poor in "Scar," where a young maidservant is falsely accused of theft and has no recourse to justice.

The works of major novelists such as Sidhwa, Suleri Goodyear, and Kamila Shamsie have created important landmarks in Pakistani English literature, regardless of gender. Sidhwa, who wrote her first two novels in virtual isolation in Pakistan because she had no other contemporary English-language writers there, made an enormous breakthrough with the international recognition her novels have received. Suleri Goodyear's creative memoir, which employed the techniques of a novel and divided chapters according to metaphor, was another milestone, as was the quality of her prose. The thirty-five-year-old Kamila Shamsie has published four critically acclaimed novels of remarkable diversity, breadth, and vision so far; her fifth novel will be published in 2009. Her story, "Surface of Glass," though an early work, makes an incisive comment on Pakistan's stratified class system and the circumscribed life of a servant woman, who believes her enemy, the cook, has put a curse on her.

Kamila Shamsie speaks for many aspiring young writers in Pakistan when she says that she had great difficulty as a child placing Pakistan within a literary context because at school in Karachi, she had no exposure to English literature beyond that of the United States and England. This changed when she read Suleri Goodyear and then Sidhwa as a teenager, but she had to go all the way to college in the United States to discover the wider world of English writing—and her own voice.

The critical acclaim that Shamsie and another young writer included here, Uzma Aslam Khan, have received, has generated tremendous interest in the possibilities of a literary career among a younger generation. An increasing number of young, published writers have given readings in schools and colleges, and have conducted creative-writing workshops, which were rare in Pakistan until recently. Aslam Khan, who grew up in Karachi during the turbulent 1980s and 1990s, vividly captures a sense of the city's festering violence in her story "Look, but with Love," which simmers quietly with an undercurrent of desperation and ethnic tension. Her work also comments on gender roles in Pakistan.

In 2004, the British Council in Pakistan held a nationwide competition for students as part of the "I Belong International Story Chain" project, to select five writers for a creative workshop in Karachi, conducted by Kamila Shamsie. Nayyara Rahman's story, "Clay Fissures," was one of the winners. Though a student work, it has been included for its originality, its promise, and its vision of the future.

Reflecting on the texts included in this anthology, I have become particularly fascinated by how one story touches upon or fleshes out ideas in another, creating a flow, a unifying cycle that reveals many dimensions of Pakistani life through the perspective of women.

I have found that Sidhwa's description of the Partition riots in her story, "Defend Yourself Against Me," is reflected in Sorayya Khan's Partition story, "Staying," and in Rustomji's memoir account, "Watching from the Edges," which links Partition to the divisions and suffering she has seen across the world. In Uzma Khan's story, "Look, but with Love," the painting of a voluptuous woman in an all-male subculture has obvious associations with male myths about prostitution and red-light districts, which Feryal Ali Gauhar attacks in her story. The sexual exploitation of women implicit in Ali Gauhar's narrative becomes explicit in Fahmida Riaz's "Daughter of Aai," while the recourse to magic and superstition in a village finds an echo in very different stories by Kamila Shamsie and Tahira Naqvi. Kamila

Shamsie's and Tahira Naqvi's portrayals of a maidservant and a middle-class woman, respectively, revolve around a crisis of self, as does Humera Afridi's "The Price of Hubris." My story of a postwar migration to Britain and the intermarriage between an Indian and an Englishwoman in British India provides a contrast with the cultural commingling in Sara Suleri Goodyear's "Excellent Things in Women," about her Welsh-born mother and Pakistani grandmother, which also contains the composite history of Pakistan within it. The interpretation of history is central to Rukhsana Ahmad's story, "Meeting the Sphinx," set in multicultural Britain, while Fawzia Afzal Khan's "Bloody Monday" gathers up popular culture and religious ritual across three continents to make a comment on gender and sexuality. Maniza Naqvi takes this a step further in "Impossible Shade of Home Brew" to question gender definitions altogether, and also explores parenthood and loss, themes which are equally central to Talat Abbasi's "Mirage." Prejudice and division of culture and gender run through two stories that describe the Pakistani experience of "America": Bushra Rehman's "The Old Italian" and Soniah Kamal's "Runaway Truck Ramp." On the other hand, "A Pair of Jeans" by Qaisra Shah and "The Optimist" by Bina Shah describe cultural misunderstandings between people ostensibly from the same community. Hima Raza's "A Variation in Voices" describes bridges that cannot be crossed, and the poignant "Scar" by Aamina Ahmad centers on the impermeability of class barriers. The stories of Sehba Sarwar, Sabyn Javeri-Jillani, and Nayyara Rahman reflect a younger generation's desire to think back on historical divisions, nationhood, and identity. I included Shahrukh Husain's mythical "Rubies for a Dog," about a daughter's determination to prove herself equal to a son, for its transcendent symbolism. The amassed texts also reveal two sets of mothers and daughters: Rukhsana Ahmad and Aamina Ahmad in Britain; myself and Kamila Shamsie in Pakistan.

This anthology testifies, with its variety of voices, that Pakistani women writing in English have come a long way since their pre-Partition ancestors. Today Pakistani women write creatively in English because that is the language in which they wish to express themselves; theirs is a literary tradition that has been long in gestation and is finally coming into its own. They no longer work in virtual isolation. They draw on the traditions of other English literatures as well as the vernacular languages of Pakistan. They are a part of the new world literature in English that gives voice to experiences beyond the traditional canons of Anglo-American literature. In this anthology their stories describe a myriad of experiences to reveal the richness, complexity, and multiculturalism of Pakistani life—and the wider world with which it is so inextricably linked.

Muneeza Shamsie

Karachi

March 2008

## NOTES

1. The official languages of Pakistan today are Urdu and English, but provincial languages, such as Balochi/Brahvi, Pashto, Punjabi, and Sindhi, are also important. There is also a host of minor languages.

2. *The Crow Eaters* was self published in 1978 and then was published by the British publishing house, Jonathan Cape, in 1980.

3. The English-language writing by South Asians has been known as Indo-Anglian, Indian English, or South Asian English. I am using the older term "Indo-Anglian" to describe pre-Partition work and thus distinguish it from the modern, post-Partition term, "Indian English," which excludes Pakistani English literature, whereas South Asian English is the collective term for the work produced in the independent countries of India, Pakistan, Bangladesh, Sri Lanka, and Nepal.

4. In "Sultana's Dream," Hossain reverses gender roles in a futuristic country, Ladyland, which is ruled by women. Her spare, terse prose was years ahead of its time, as was her description of a world where people can harness energy, travel by air, and use solar missiles.

5. Ikramullah's groundbreaking doctoral thesis on Urdu fiction was written in a modern English and published as *A Critical Survey of the Development of the Urdu Novel and Short Story* (1945); One of its most remarkable features is

the sensibility that Ikramullah brings to her critical assessments, as a woman. She also devotes a chapter each to women novelists and women short story writers, including Rashid Jahan.

6. Iqbalunissa Hussain's birth and death dates are unknown.

## WORKS CITED

De Souza, Eunice, ed. 2004. *Purdah*. New Delhi: Oxford University Press.

Hossain, Rokeya Sakhawat. 1988. *"Sultana's Dream" and Selections from The Secluded Ones*, edited and translated by Roushan Jahan. New York: The Feminist Press.

Ikramullah, Shaista Suhrawardy. 1998. *From Purdah to Parliament*. Karachi: Oxford University Press.

Jalal, Ayesha. 2001. *Self and Sovereignty: Individual and Community in South Asian Islam Since 1850*. Lahore: Sang-e-Meel.

Karlitzky, Maren. 2002. "The Tyabji Clan—Urdu as a Symbol of Group Identity." *Annual of Urdu Studies* 17: 187–207.

Mukherjee, Meenakshi. 2002. *The Perishable Empire: Essays on Indian Writing in English*. New Delhi: Oxford University Press.

Niazi, Zamir. 1986. *The Press in Chains*. Karachi: The Royal Book Company.

Pernau, Margrit. 2002. "Female Voices: Women Writers in Hyderabad at the Beginning of the Twentieth Century." *Annual of Urdu Studies* 17: 36–54.

Rahman, Tariq. 1991. *A History of Pakistani Literature in English*. Lahore: Vanguard.

———. 2002. *Language, Ideology and Power*. Karachi: Oxford University Press.

Shamsie, Muneeza, ed. 1997. *A Dragonfly in the Sun: An Anthology of Pakistani Writing in English*. Karachi: Oxford University Press.

———. 2001. "At the Stroke of Midnight." *Dawn Books and Authors Supplement*. Karachi, April 14.

———. 2005. Introduction. *And the World Changed*. New Delhi: Women Unlimited.

# DEFEND
# YOURSELF
# AGAINST ME

&

## *Bapsi Sidhwa*

Bapsi Sidhwa (1938– ) is the author of five novels, which have been translated into many languages. She was born in Karachi and brought up in Lahore. Stricken with polio at a young age, she was educated at home until she was 15. She later graduated from Kinnaird College, Lahore. She married at 19, did social work, and represented Pakistan at the 1974 Asian Women's Congress. Sidhwa also served on the Advisory

Committee to Prime Minister Benazir Bhutto on Women's Development from 1994 to 1996. She has taught in the United States at Columbia University, the University of Houston, Mount Holyoke College, and Brandeis University; and in England at the University of Southampton. She moved to the United States in the 1980s and lives in Houston. She is the 2008 winner of Sony Asia TV's South Asian Excellence Award for Literature.

Sidhwa's first novel, *The Crow Eaters* (self published, 1978; Jonathan Cape, 1980), pioneered contemporary English fiction by Pakistani women. It was also the first major novel about the Parsi community, the ancient but small religious minority of Zoroastrians to which Sidhwa belongs. The novel's ribaldry was also rare for South Asian English fiction. Sidhwa went on to write *The Bride* (Jonathan Cape, 1983); *Ice Candy Man* (Heinemann, 1988; later published as *Cracking India*, Milkweed, 1991), which was made into a film *Earth* by Canadian director Deepa Mehta; *An American Brat* (Milkweed, 1993), which was performed in 2008 as a stage play in Houston; and *Water* (Penguin Books India, 2006), which was adapted from Deepa Mehta's screenplay of that name. Sidhwa has also edited an anthology, *City of Sin and Splendor: Writings on Lahore* (Penguin Books India, 2006). Among the many honors she has received are the Bunting Fellowship at Radcliffe/Harvard and the Lila Wallace-Reader's Digest Writer's Award in the United States, the Liberaturpreis in Germany, the Sitara-i-Imtiaz in Pakistan, and recently, the Italian Premio Mondello award for *Water*.

In "Defend Yourself Against Me" Sidhwa brings together a group of expatriates of South Asian origin with an apparent commonality of language and culture, but as the story unfolds the reader learns that these people belong to different religious groups: Christian, Hindu, Muslim, and Sikh. Using a Pakistani Christian narrator named Joy, Sidhwa develops themes that run through most of her work: minority identity and multiculturalism. Sidhwa looks at the dimensions of human compassion, the will to survive, and the capacity to forgive. In the sidelines of this story, when Sidhwa introduces Kishen's white American wife, Suzanne, she further comments on adaptation, mutation, and change that encompass both the migrations of 1947 and the movement of South Asians into the diaspora.

• • •

"They are my grandparents," says Kishen. I peer at the incongruous pair mounted in an old frame holding an era captive in the faded brown and gray photograph. I marvel. The heavy portrait has been transported across the seven seas; from the Deccan plateau in India to the flat, glass-and-aluminum–pierced horizons of Houston, Texas. The tiny sari-clad bride, her nervous eyes wide, her lips slightly ajar, barely clears the middle-aged bridegroom's ribs.

"Your grandfather was exceptionally tall," I remark, expressing surprise; Kishen is short and stocky. But distracted partly by the querulous cries of his excited children, and partly by his cares as a host, Kishen nods so perfunctorily that I surmise his grandfather's height cannot have been significant. His grandmother was either exceedingly short or not yet full grown. I hazard a guess. She could be ten; she could be eighteen. Marketable Indian brides—in those days at least—wore the uniformly bewildered countenances of lambs to the slaughter and looked alike irrespective of age.

We hear a car purr up the drive and the muted thud of Buick doors. The other guests have arrived. Kishen, natty in a white sharkskin suit, tan tie, and matching silk handkerchief, darts out of the room to welcome his guests loudly and hospitably. *"Aiiay! Aiiay! Arrey bhai,* we've been waiting for you! *Kitni der laga di,"* he bellows in a curious mix of Urdu and English that enriches communication between the inheritors of the British Raj, Indians, and Pakistanis alike. "I have a wonderful surprise for you," I hear him shout as he ushers his guests inside. "I have a lady friend from Pakistan I want you to meet!"

I move hesitantly to the living-room door and peer into the hall. Flinging out a gleaming sharkskinned arm in a grand gesture of introduction, Kishen announces: "Here she is! Meet Mrs. Jacobs." And turning on me his large, intelligent eyes, beaming handsomely, he says, "Sikander Khan is also from Pakistan."

Mr. Sikander Khan, blue-suited and black-booted, his wife

and her three sisters in satin *shalwar kameezes* and heavy gold jewelry, and a number of knee-high children stream into the living room. We shake hands all around and recline in varying attitudes of stiff discomfiture in the deep chairs and sofas covered, *desi* style, with printed bedspreads to camouflage the stains and wear of a house inhabited by an extended Hindu family.

Kishen's diminutive mother, fluffed out in a starched white cotton sari, smiles anxiously at me across a lumpy expanse of sofa and his two younger brothers, unsmiling and bored, slouch on straight-backed dining-room chairs to one side, their legs crossed at the ankles and stretched right out in front. Suzanne, Kishen's statuesque American wife, her brown hair falling in straight strands down her shoulders and back, flits to and fro in the kitchen. As comfortable in a pink silk sari with a gold border as if she were born to it, she pads barefoot into the room, the skin on her toes twinkling whitely, bearing a tray of potato samosas, fruit juices, and Coke, the very image of dutiful Brahman wifedom. A vermilion caste mark spreads prettily between her large and limpid brown eyes.

I know her well. Her otherworldly calm and docility are due equally to her close association with her demanding and rambunctious Indian family, and the more private rigors of her job as a computer programmer in an oil corporation.

I make polite conversation with Mrs. Khan's sisters in hesitant Punjabi. They have just emigrated. The differences from our past remain: I, an English-speaking scion of Anglican Protestants from Lahore; they, village belles accustomed to drawing water to the rhythm of Punjabi lore. They know very little English. Tart and shifty-eyed, their jewelry glinting like armor, they are on the defensive; blindly battling their way through cultural shock waves in an attempt to adapt to a new environment as different from theirs as only a hamburger at McDonald's can be from a leisurely meal of spicy greens eaten in steamy village courtyards redolent of buffalo dung and dust-caked, naked children.

Observing their bristling discomfiture and the desultory nature of the conversation, Sikander Khan moves closer to me. He is completely at ease. Acclimatized. Americanized.

Our conversation follows the usual ritual of discourse between Pakistanis who meet for the first time on European or American soil. He moved from Pakistan eleven years ago, I two. He has a Pakistani and Indian spice shop on Richmond uptown, I teach English at the University of Houston downtown. Does he have U.S. citizenship? Yes. Do I? No, but I should have a green card by December. Mr. Khan filed his mother's immigration papers two years ago: They should be through any day. One of his brothers-in-law will bring Ammijee. It will be his mother's, Ammijee's, first visit to the United States.

Mr. Khan speaks English with a broad Pakistani accent that is pleasant to my ears. "I went to the Dyal Singh College in Lahore," he says courteously when he learns I'm from Lahore. "It is a beautiful, historical old city."

All at once, without any apparent reason, my eyes prickle with a fine mist, and I become entangled in a web of nostalgia so intense that I lose my breath. I quickly lower my lids, and the demeanor of half a lifetime standing me in good stead, I maintain a slight smile of polite attention while the grip of sensations from the past hauls me back through the years to Lahore, to our bungalow on Race Course Road.

I am a little child playing hopscotch outside the kitchen window. The autumn afternoon is overcast with shadows from the mighty *sheesham* trees in the front lawn. There is a brick wall to my right, a little crooked and bulging in places, and the clay cement in the grooves is eroded. I keep glancing at the wall, suppressing a great excitement.

Spellbound, I sit still on Kishen's lumpy sofa, my pulse racing at the memory. Then, clearly, as if she were in the room, I hear Mother shout: "Joy, come inside and put on your cardigan."

Startled by the images, I snap out of my reverie. I search Mr. Khan's face so confusedly that he turns from me to Kishen's

31

mother and awkwardly inquires of her how she is.

I have not recalled this part of my childhood in years. Certainly not since I moved to the United States. Too enamored of the dazzling shopping malls and technical opulence of the smoothly operating country of my adoption, too frequent a visitor to Pakistan, I have not yet missed it, or given thought to the past. Perhaps it is this house, so comfortably possessed by its occupants and their Indian bric-a-brac. It takes an effort of will to remember that we are in the greenly shaven suburbs of an American city in the heart of Texas.

Bending forward with the tray, smiling at my abstraction, Suzanne abruptly brings me to earth. "Joy," she asks, "would you like some wine?"

"I prefer this, thanks," I say, reaching apologetically for a glass of Coke.

"I used to know a Joy . . . long, long ago," says Mr. Khan. "I spent one or two years in Lahore when I was a child."

Suzanne has shifted to Mr. Khan. As his hand, hesitant with the burden of choice, wavers among the glasses, I watch it compulsively. It is a swarthy, well-made hand with dark hair growing between the knuckles and on the back. The skin, up to where it disappears beneath his white shirt sleeve, is smooth and unblemished.

There must be at least a million Sikanders in Pakistan, and several million Khans. The title "Khan" is discriminately tagged on by most Pakistanis in the United States who generally lack family names in the Western tradition. The likelihood that this whole-limbed and assured man with his trim mustache and military bearing is the shy and misshapen playmate of my childhood is remote.

But that part of my mind that is still in the convoluted grip of nostalgia, with its uncanny accompaniment of sounds and images, is convinced.

Having selected a glass of orange juice, Sikander Khan leans forward to offer it to a small boy whimpering halfheartedly at his feet. I glance obliquely at the back of Mr. Khan's head. It is as well formed as the rest of him and entirely covered with strong, short-sheared black hair.

My one-time playmate had a raw pit gouged out of his head that couldn't have grown hair in a hundred years! Still, the certainty remains with me and, not the least bit afraid of sounding presumptuous, I ask, "Was the girl you knew called Joy Joshwa? I was known as Joy Joshwa then."

Holding the glass to the child's lips, Sikander looks at me. My body casts a shadow across his face. His dark eyes on me are veiled with conjecture. "I don't remember the last name," he says, speaking in a considered manner. "But it could be."

"You are Sikander!" I announce in a voice that brooks no doubt or argument. "You lived next to us on Race Course Road. You were refugees. . . . Don't you remember me?" My eyes misty, my smile wide and twitching, I know all the while how absurd it is to expect him to recall the sharp-featured and angular girl in the rounded contours and softened features of my middle-ageing womanhood.

"Was it Race Course Road?" says Sikander. He sits back and, turning his strong man's body to me, says, "I tried to locate the house when I was in Lahore. . . . But we moved to the farm land allotted to us in Sahiwal years ago. . . . I forgot the address. . . . So, it was Race Course Road!" He beams fondly at me. "You used to have pimples the size of boils!"

"Yes," I reply, and then I don't know what to say. It is difficult to maintain poise when transported to the agonized and self-conscious persona of a boil-ridden and stringy child before a man who is, after all these years, a stranger.

Sitting opposite me—if he can ever be said to sit—Kishen comes to an explosive rescue. "You know each other? Imagine that! Childhood friends!"

Kishen has squirmed, crab-wise, clear across the huge sofa and is sitting so close to the edge that his weight is borne mostly by his thick legs. Halfway between sitting and squatting, quite at ease with the restless energy of his body, he is radiant with the wonder of it all.

"It is incredible," he booms with genial authority. "Incredible! After all these years you meet, not in Pakistan, but on the other side of the planet, in Houston!"

Triggered off by the fierce bout of nostalgia and the host of ghost memories stirred by Sikander's unexpected presence, the scenes that have been floundering in the murky deeps of my subconscious come into luminous focus. I see a pattern emerge, and the jumble of half-remembered events and sensations already clamor to be recorded in a novel I have just begun about the Partition of India.

Turning to Sikander, smiling fondly back at him, I repeat, "You're quite right: I had horrible pimples."

Since childhood memories can only be accurately exhumed by the child, I will inhabit my childhood. As a writer, I am already practiced in inhabiting different bodies; dwelling in rooms, gardens, bungalows, and space from the past; zapping time.

Lahore: Autumn 1948. Pakistan is a little over a year old. The Partition riots, the arson and slaughter, have subsided. The flood of refugees—12 million Muslims, Hindus, and Sikhs fleeing across borders that define India and Pakistan—has shrunk to a nervous trickle. Two gargantuan refugee camps have been set up on the outskirts of Lahore, at Walton and Badami Bagh. Bedraggled, carrying tin trunks, string cots, and cloth bundles on their heads, the refugees swamp the city looking for work, setting up house on sidewalks and in parks—or wherever they happen to be at sunset if they have wandered too far from the camps.

A young Christian couple, the Mangat Rais, live on one side of our house on Race Course Road; on the other side is the enormous bungalow of our Hindu neighbors. I don't know when they fled. My friends Sheila and Sam never even said goodbye.

Their deserted house has been looted several times. First by men in carts, shouting slogans, then by whoever chose to saunter in to pick up the leavings. Doors, sinks, wooden cabinets, electric fixtures, and wiring have all been ripped from their moorings and carried away. How swiftly the deserted house has decayed. The hedges are a spooky tangle, the garden full of weeds and white patches of caked mud.

It is still quite warm when I begin to notice signs of occupation. A window boarded up with cardboard, a diffused pallid gleam from another screened with jute sacking as candles or oil-lamps struggle to illuminate the darkness. The windows face my room across the wall that separates our houses. The possession is so subtle that it dawns on me only gradually; I have new neighbors. I know they are refugees, frightened, nervous of drawing attention to their furtive presence. I know this as children know many things without being told: But I have no way of telling if children dwell in the decaying recesses of the stolen bungalow.

Although the ominous roar of slogans shouted by distant mobs—that nauseating throb that had pulsed a continuous threat to my existence and the existence of all those I love—has at least ceased, terrible new sounds (and unaccountable silences) erupt about me. Sounds of lamentation magnified by the night—sudden unearthly shrieks—come from a nursery school hastily converted into a Recovered Women's Camp six houses away from ours. Tens of thousands of women have been kidnapped and hundreds of camps have been set up all over the Punjab to sort out and settle those who are rescued, or "recovered."

Yet we hear nothing—no sound of talking, children quarreling or crying, of repairs being carried out—or any of the noises our refugee neighbors might be expected to make. It is eerie.

And then one afternoon, standing on my toes, I glimpse a small scruffy form through a gap in the wall (no more than a slit really) where the clay has worn away. I cannot tell if it's a boy or a girl or an apparition. The shadowy form appears to have such an attuned awareness that it senses my presence in advance, and I catch only a spectral glimpse as it dissolves at the far corner of my vision.

Impelled by curiousity—and by my loneliness now that even Sheila and Sam have gone—I peep into my new neighbor's compound through the crack in the wall, hoping to trap a potential playmate. A few days later, crouching slyly beneath the wall, I suddenly spring up to peer through the slit, and startle a canny pair of dark eyes staring straight at me.

I step back—look away nonchalantly—praying the eyes will stay. A stealthy glance reassures me. I pick up a sharp stone and quickly begin to sketch hopscotch lines in the mud on our drive. I throw the stone in one square after another, enthusiastically playing against myself, aware I'm being observed. I am suddenly conscious of the short frock I have outgrown. The waist, pulled by sashed stitched to either side and tied at the back, squeezes my ribs. The seams hurt under my arms and when I bend the least bit I know my white cotton knickers, with dusty patches where I sit, are on embarrassing display. Never mind. If they offend the viewer, I'm sure my skipping skills won't. I skip rope, and turning around and around in one spot I breathlessly recite: "Teddy bear, Teddy bear, turn around: Teddy bear, Teddy bear, touch the ground."

And again, I sense I'm alone. I rush to the wall but my phantasmal neighbor's neglected compound is empty.

The next few days I play close to the damaged wall. Sometimes the eyes are there, sometimes not. I look toward the wall more frequently, and notice that my glance no longer scares away the viewer. Once in a rare while I even smile, careful to look away at once, my lids demurely lowered, my expression shy: trying with whatever wiles I can to detain, disarm, and entice the invisible and elusive object of my fascination.

It is almost the end of October. The days are still warm but, as each day takes us closer to winter, the fresher air is exhilarating. People on the streets smile more readily, the tonga horses snort and shake their necks and appear to pull their loads more easily, and even the refugees, absorbed into the gullies and the more crowded areas of Lahore as the camps shrink, appear at last to be less visible.

One such heady afternoon, when the eyes blocking the crack suddenly disappear and I see a smudge of pale light instead, I dash to the wall and glue my eye to the hole. A small boy, so extremely thin he looks like a brittle skeleton, is squatting a few feet away, concentrating on striking a marble lying in a notch in the dust. His skull-like face has dry, flaky patches, and two deep lines between his eyebrows that I have never before seen on a child. He is wearing a threadbare *shalwar* of thin cotton and the dirty cord tying the gathers around his waist trails in the mud. The sun-charred little body is covered with scabs and wounds. It is as if his tiny body had been carelessly carved and then stuck together again to form an ungainly puppet. I don't know how to react; I feel sorry for him and at the same time repulsed. He hits the marble he was aiming at, gets up to retrieve the marbles, and as he turns away I see the improbable wound on the back of his cropped head. It is a raw and flaming scar, as if bone and flesh had been callously gouged out, and my compassion ties me to him.

Suzanne is in the kitchen and Kishen is flitting between the dining table and the kitchen filling stainless-steel glasses with water and arranging bowls containing a variety of pickles. He places a stack of silvery platters, their rims gleaming, next to the glasses. The smell of mango pickle is strong in the room and, seeing our eyes darting to the table, Kishen's mother says, "We have made only a vegetarian *thal* today." She sounds apologetic: as if their hospitality would not stand up to our expectations. I know how much trouble it is to prepare the different vegetables and lentils that add up to the *thal*. Glancing at his sisters-in-law, Sikander says, "The girls refused to eat lunch when they heard you were serving the *thal*, Maajee." The sisters-in-law solemnly nod. "I've been looking forward to the food all day," I also protest.

Turning from me to Kishen, who is folding cutlery in paper napkins, Mr. Khan declares, "I say *yaar*, you're such a well-trained husband!" and at that moment, involuntarily, my hand reaches out to lightly feel Mr. Khan's hair. Startled by the unexpected touch, Sikander whips around. He notices my discomfiture—and the unusual position of my hand in the air—and passing a hand down the back of his head, dryly says, "I'm wearing a wig. The scar is still there."

"Oh, I'm sorry. I didn't mean to . . ." I say, almost incoherent with embarrassment. But Mr. Khan grants me a smile of such indulgent complicity that acknowledging my childhood claim to his friendship, I am compelled to ask, "What about the other scars . . . are they still . . . ?"

Wordlessly opening the cuff button Sikander peels his shirt sleeve back. The scars are fainter, diminished, and on that strong brown arm, innocuous: not at all like the dangerous welts and scabs afflicting the pitiful creature I saw for the first time on that mellow afternoon through a slit in the compound wall. With one finger, gently, I touch the arm, and responding to the touch, Sikander twists it to show me the other scars.

"You want to see the back of my head?" he asks. I nod.

Sikander turns, and with a deft movement of his fingers lifts up part of the piece to show the scar. It has pale ridges of thick scar tissue, and the hair growing around it has given it the shape of a four-day-old crescent moon.

Sikander smooths down his hair and notices that, except for the children shouting as they play outside, the room has become quiet; even Kishen has come from the dining table to peer at his famous scalp.

"I think I'm out of cigarettes," Sikander says, patting his empty pockets with the agitation of an addict desperately in need of a smoke. "I'll be back in ten minutes, *yaar*," he tells Kishen, getting up.

While Sikander is out, Kishen and his mother sit close to me, and Suzanne, drawn from the kitchen by the hushed tone of their voices, joins them in pressing me with information and plying me with questions. Could I tell them what Mr. Khan looked like as a little boy? Do I know what happened to Ammijee? No? Well, they noticed Mr. Khan's reticence on the subject and stopped asking questions. . . . But they suspect she has been through something terrible. . . . Except for Mr. Khan, her entire family was killed during the attack. . . . Do I remember her? Was she pretty?

The focus of interest appears to revolve around Ammijee. They have known Sikander for a long time and his mother's anticipated arrival has caused a stir. I search my memory. I dimly perceive a thin, bent-over, squatting figure, scrubbing clothes, scouring tinny utensils with mud and ash, peeling squashes and other cheap vegetables, kneading dough, and slapping it into chapatis. . . .

The ragged cotton chador always drawn forward over her face, the color of her form blended with the mud, the ash, the utensils she washed, the pale seasonal vegetables she peeled. This must be Ammijee: a figure bent perpetually to accommodate the angle of drudgery and poverty. I don't recall her face or the color of her dusty bare feet; the shape of her hands or whether she wore bangles.

All I knew as a child was that my little refugee friend's village was attacked by the Sikhs.

I did not understand the complete significance of the word "refugees" at the time. I thought, on the nebulous basis of my understanding of the Hindu caste system, that the "refugees" were a caste—like the Brahman or *achoot* castes—who were suddenly pouring into Lahore, and it was in the nature of this caste—much as the *achoots* or untouchables were born to clean gutters and sweep toilets—to be inexorably poor, ragged, homeless, forever looking for work and places to stay.

Sikander had described some of the details of the attack and of his miraculous survival. His account of it, supplied in little, suddenly recalled snatches—brought to mind by chance associations while we played—was so jumbled, so full of bizarre incident, that I accepted it as the baggage of truth-enlivened-by-fantasy that every child carries within. Although I realized the broader implications of what had happened, that the British Raj had ended, that there were religious riots between Hindus, Muslims, and Sikhs, and the country was divided because of them, I was too young to understand the underlying combustibility of the events preceding Partition that had driven my friends away and turned a little boy's world into a nightmare.

But I had heard no mention at all of Ammijee's ordeal. Excited by my ignorance, and the spirit of instruction burning in us all to remedy this lack, Mrs. Khan and her three sisters also move closer; those who can, dragging their chairs forward; those who can't, settling on the rug at my feet. The entire ensemble now combines to enlighten me in five languages: English, Punjabi, and Urdu, which I understand, and Kannada and Marathi—contributed by Kishen's mother in earnest but brief fusillades—which I don't.

The boys and some of the men in the village, I am informed, were huddled in a dark room at the back of a barn when the Sikhs smote the door, shouting: "Open up. Open up!"

And, when the door was opened, the hideous swish of long steel swords dazzling their eyes in the sunlight, severing first his father's head, then his uncle's, then his brother's. His own sliced at the back because he was only nine years old, and short. They left him for dead. How he survived, how he arrived in Pakistan, is another story.

"Ammijee says the village women ran toward the Chaudhrys' house," says Mrs. Khan in assertive Punjabi. Being Ammijee's daughter-in-law, she is permitted, for the moment, at least, to hold center stage. "They know what the Sikhs would do to them . . . women are the spoils of war . . . no matter what you are—Hindu, Muslim, Sikh—women bear the brunt. . . .

"Rather than fall into the hands of the Sikhs, the poor

women planned to burn themselves. They had stored kerosene
. . . but when the attack came they had no time. Thirty thousand
men, mad with blood lust, waving swords and sten guns!"

Mrs. Khan casts her eyes about in a way that makes us draw
closer, and having ascertained that Mr. Khan is still absent,
whispers, "Ammijee says she went mad! She would have killed
herself if she could. So would you: So would I. . . . She heard
her eleven-year-old daughter screaming and screaming . . . she
heard the mullah's sixteen-year-old daughter scream: 'Do anything you wish with me, but don't hurt me. For God's sake don't
hurt me!' "

We look away, the girls' tormented cries ringing unbear-
ably in our ears. Suzanne and the youngest sister brush their
eyes and, by the time we are able to talk again, Mrs. Khan's
moment is over. The medley of languages again asserts itself:
"God knows how many women died. . . ." A helpless spreading
of hands and deep sighs.

"Pregnant women were paraded naked, their stomachs
slashed. . . ."

"Yes-*jee* and the babies were swung by their heels and
dashed against wall."

Much shaking of heads. God's help and mercy evoked.

"God knows how many women were lifted . . . but, then,
everybody carried women off. Sikhs and Hindus, Muslim
women. Muslims, Sikh and Hindu women."

A general clucking of tongues: an air of commiseration.

"Allah have mercy on us," says Mrs. Khan, and in resound-
ing Punjabi again asserts her authority as chief speaker. His
mother had a bad experience. Very bad. Ammijee never talks
about it, but those who knew her when she was recovered, say
. . ."

Mrs. Khan stops short. Having second thoughts about dis-
closing what her mother-in-law never talks about, she makes a
deft switch and in a banal, rhetorical tone of voices says, "She
saw horrible things. Horrible. Babies tossed into boiling oil . . ."

Sikander Khan, having bought his pack and smoked his cigarette outside, quietly joins us.

Halfway through dinner two handsome, broad-shouldered Sikhs in gray shirts join us. I gather they are cousins. Their long hair is tucked away in blue turbans, and their beards tied in neat rolls beneath their chins. Again there is an explosion of welcome: a flurry to feed the latecomers and a great deal of hand-slapping and embracing among the men. Considering what I heard just a few moments ago, I am a little surprised at the cordiality between Sikander Khan and the young Sikhs. I hear one of the men say in Urdu, "Any further news about your Ammijee's arrival?"

His back is to me: But the sudden switch from Punjabi to Urdu, the formality in his voice, and his node of address, catch my attention. There is no apparent change in the volume of noise in the room, yet I sense we have all shared a moment of unease: an incongruous solemnity.

And then the Sikhs move to greet the women from Mr. Khan's family in Punjabi, inquire after their health and the health of their children, and indulge in a little lighthearted teasing. The unease is so dispelled, I wonder if I have not imagined it.

"You haven't invited us to a meal in almost a month, *Bhabi*," says the stouter of the two men to Mrs. Khan. "Look at poor Pratab: See how thin he's become?" He pulls back his cousin's arms the way poultry dealers hold back chicken wings and, standing him helpless and grinning in front of Mrs. Khan, asks, "Have we offended you in some way?"

"No, no, Khushwant *Bhai*," says Mrs. Khan, "It isn't anything like that. . . ."

"She's concerned about your health, brother," pipes up the eldest of her three sisters, "You're too fat and fresh for your own good!" She must be in her mid-twenties.

Khushwant releases his counsing good-naturedly and the sisters, hiding their smiles in their *dupattas*, start giggling. They have perked up in the presence of these young men who speak their language and share their ways, their religious antagonisms dissipated on American soil.

On surer ground, the same sister says, "What about the picnic you promised us? You're the one who breaks promises, and you complain about our sister!" Her face animated, her large black eyes rouguish, she is charming: And I suddenly notice how pretty the sisters are in their pleasantly plump Punjabi way.

"When would you like to go? Next Sunday?" asks Khushwant Singh gallantly.

"We'll know what's what when Sunday comes," says another sister, tossing her long plaited hair back in a half-bullying, half-mocking gesture. She has a small, full-lipped mouth and a diamond on one side of her pert nose.

"I'll take you to the ocean next Sunday. It's a promise," says Khushwant Singh, "But only if *Bhabi* makes *parathas* with her own hands."

"What's wrong with my hands?" the pert sister asks. "Or with Gulnar's hands?" she indicates their youngest sister who promptly buries her face in her *dupatta*. Gulnar is the only sister not yet married. I guess she is sixteen or seventeen.

"Have either of you given me any occasion to praise your cooking?" Khushwant asks.

"They'll give you occasion on Sunday," intervenes Mrs. Khan. "But tell me, brother," she say, "what will you feed us? Why don't you bring chicken korma to go with the *parathas*?"

"No chicken korma till you find me a wife."

"Lo!" says Mrs. Khan. "As if you'll agree to our choice! There are plenty of pretty Sikh girls, but you fuss!"

"I want someone just like you, *Bhabi*," says the handsome Sikh, and turns slightly red. "A girl who knows our ways."

"That's what you say, but you'll end up marrying a white-washed memsahib!" At once realizing her folly the pert sister springs up from her chair and, abandoning her dinner, hugging Suzanne and holding her cheek against hers, says, "Unless it is someone like Sue *Bhabi*: She's one of us. Then we won't mind."

Suzanne takes it, as she accepts the smaller hazards of her marriage to Kishen, in her twinkle-toed and sari-clad stride. She told me about a year back, when we were just becoming friends, that she felt content and secure in her extended Indian family. She tried to describe to me her feeling of being firmly embedded in life—in the business and purpose of living—that she, as an only child, had never experienced. Suzanne comes from a small town in New England. Her father teaches history at a university. I haven't met her family but I gather they are unpretentious and gentle folk.

It is the Sunday of the picnic. Kishen and Suzanne give me a ride to Galveston beach. It is a massive affair. Innumerable kin have been added to the group that met for dinner at Kishen's. Mr. Khan, in long white pants and a blue T-shirt, staggers across the hot sand with a stack of *parathas* wrapped in a metallic gray garbage bag. Khushwant Singh and Pratab have brought the food from a Pakistani restaurant on Hillcroft.

Later in the sultry afternoon, exhiliarated from our splashing in the ocean and the sudden shelter of an overcast sky, we converge on the dhurries spread on the sand. Mrs. Khan and her three sisters flop like exotic beetles on a striped dhurrie, their wet satin *shalwars* and *kameezes* clinging to them in rich blobs of solid color.

The *parathas* are delicious. Sikander heaps his plate with *haleem* and mutton curry and, crossing his legs like an inept yogi, sits down by me. I broach the subject that has been obsessing me: I would like to use his family's experience during the Partition in my novel.

As we eat, sucking on our fingers, drinking Coke out of cans, I ask Sikander about the attack on the village: trying, with whatever wiles I can, to penetrate the mystery surrounding Ammijee.

I gathered from the remarks Mrs. Khan let slip on the night of the party that Ammijee was kidnapped. But I want to know what Mrs. Khan was about to say when she checked herself. I feel the missing information will unravel the full magnitude of the tragedy to my understanding and, more importantly, to my imagination. Instinctively I chose Sikander Khan, and not Mrs. Khan, to provide the knowledge. His emotions and perceptions will, I feel, charge my writing with the detail, emotion, and veracity I am striving for.

Sikander's replies to my questions are candid, recalled in remarkable detail, but he balks at any question of Ammijee.

I don't remember now the question that unexpectedly penetrated his reserve; but Sikander planted in my mind a fearsome seed that waxed into an ugly tree of hideous possibility, when, in a voice that was indescribably harsh, he said: "Ammijee heard street vendors cry: 'Zenana for sale! Zenana for sale!' as if they were selling vegetables and fish. They were selling women for 50, 20, and even 10 rupees!"

Later that evening, idling on our dhurries as we watch the spectacular crimson streaks on the horizon fade, I ask Sikander how he could be close friends with Khushwant and Pratab. In his place I would not even want to meet their eye! Isn't he furious with the Sikhs for what they did? Do the cousins know what happened in his village?

"I'm sure they know . . . everybody I meet seems to know. Why quarrel with Khushwant and Pratab? They weren't even born. . . ." And, his voice again taking on the hard, harsh edge he says, "We Muslims were no better . . . we did the same . . . Hindu, Muslim, Sikh, we were all evil bastards!"

Mr. Khan calls. His mother has arrived from Pakistan. He has asked a few friends to dinner to meet her on Saturday. Can I dine with them? Ammijee remembers me as a little girl!

I get into the usual state of panic and I put off looking at the map till the last hour. It is a major trauma—this business of finding my way from place to place—missing exits, getting out of the car to read road signs, aggravating—and often terrifying—motorists in front, behind, and on either side. Thank God for alert American reflexes: for their chastising, wise, blasphemous tooting.

I find my way to Mr. Khan's without getting irremediably lost. It is a large old frame house behind a narrow neglected yard on Harold, between Montrose and the Rothko Chapel.

Sikander ushers me into the house with elegant formality, uttering phrases in Urdu that translated into English, sound like this: "We're honored by your visit to our poor house. We can't treat you in the manner to which you are accustomed. . . ." and presents me to his mother. She is a plump, buttery-fleshed, kind-faced old woman wearing a simple *shalwar* and shirt and her dark hair, streaked with gray, is covered by a gray nylon chador. She strokes my arm several times and, peering affectionately into my face, saying, "*Mashallah*, you've grown healthier. You were such a dry little thing," steers me to sit next to her on the sofa.

Through my polite, bashful-little-girl's smile, I search her face. There's no trace of bitterness. No melancholy. Nothing knowing or hard: just the open, acquiescent, hospitable face of a contented peasant woman who is happy to visit her son. It is difficult to believe this gentle woman was kidnapped, raped, sold.

The sisters line up opposite to us on an assortment of dining and patio chairs carried in for the party. The living room is typically furnished, Pakistani style: an assortment of small carved tables and tables with brass and ivory inlay, handwoven Pakistani carpets scattered at angles, sofas and chairs showing a lot of carved wood, onyx ashtrays and plastic flowers in brass vases. The atmosphere is permeated with the sterile odor of careful disuse.

Kishen, his mother, and Suzanne arrive. Suzanne looks languorous and sultry-eyed in a beautiful navy and gold sari. There is a loud exchange of pleasantries. Kishen notices me across the length of the entrance lobby. "You found your way okay?" he calls from the door, teasing. "Didn't land up in Mexico or something?"

"Not even once!" I yell back.

Some faces I recognize from the picnic arrive. A Kashmiri Brahman couple joins us. They are both short, fair, plump, and smug. They talk exclusively to Suzanne (the only white American in the room), Kishen (husband of the status symbol), and Mr. Khan. The sisters, condescended to a couple of times and then ignored, drift to the kitchen and disappear into the remote and mysterious recesses of the large house. I become aware of muted children's voices, quarrelsome, demanding, and excited. The sisters return, quiet and sullen, and dragging their chairs, huddle about a lamp standing in the corner.

Dinner is late. We are waiting for Khushwant and Pratab. Mr. Khan says, "We will wait for fifteen minutes more. If they don't come, we'll start eating."

Hungry guests with growling stomachs, we nevertheless say, "Please don't worry on our account . . . we are in no hurry."

Conversation dwindles. The guest politely inquire after the health of those sitting next to them and the grades of their children. We hear the doorbell ring and Mr. Khan gets up from his chair saying, "I think they've come."

Instead of dapper Sikhs, I see two huge and hirsute Indian fakirs. Their disheveled hair, parted at the center, bristles about their arms and shoulders and mingles with their spiky black beards. They are wearing white muslin kurtas over the white singlets and their broad shoulders and thick muscles show brown beneath the fine muslin. I can't be sure from where I sit, but I think they have on loose cotton pajamas. They look indescribably fierce. It is an impression quickly formed, and I have barely glimpsed the visitors, when, abruptly, their knees appear to buckle and they fall forward.

Mr. Khan steps back hastily and bends over the prostate men. He says, "What's all this? What's all this?" The disconnected tone of his voice, and the underpinning of perplexity and fear gets us all to our feet. Moving in a bunch, displacing the chairs and small tables and crumpling the carpets, we crowd our end of the lobby.

The fakirs lie face down across the threshold, half outside the door and half in the passage, their hands flat on the floor as if they were about to do pushups. Their faces are entirely hidden by hair. Suddenly, their voices are moist and thick, they begin to cry, "*Maajee! Maajee!* Forgive us." The blubbering, coming as it does from these fierce men, is unexpected, shocking; incongruous and melodramatic in this pragmatic and oil-rich corner of the Western world.

Sikander, in obvious confusion, looms over them, looking from one to the other. Then, squatting in front of them, he begins to stroke their pricky heads, making soothing noises as if he were cajoling children, "What's this? Tch, tch. . . . Come on! Stand up!"

"Get out of the way." An arm swings out in a threatening gesture and the fakir lifts his head. I see the pale, ash-smeared forehead, the large, thickly fringed brown eyes, the set curve of the wide, sensous mouth, and recognize Khushwant Singh. Next to him Pratab also raises his head. Sikander shuffles out of reach of Khushwant's arm and moving to one side, his back to the wall, watches the Sikhs with an expression of incredulity. It is unreal. I think it has occurred to all of us it might be a prank, an elaborate joke. But their red eyes, and the passion distorting their faces, are not pretended.

"Who are these men?"

The voice is demanding, abrasive. I look over my shoulder, wondering which of the women has spoken so harshly. The sisters look agitated; their dusky faces are flushed.

"Throw them out. They're *badmashes! Goondas!*"

Taken aback I realize the angry, fearful voice is Sikander's mother's.

Ammijee is standing behind me, barely visible among the agitated and excited sisters, and in her face I see more than just

48

the traces of emotions I had looked for earlier. It is as if her features had been parodied in a hideous mask. They are all there: the bitterness, the horror, the hate: the incarnation of that tree of ugly possibilities seeded in my mind when Sikander, in a cold fury, imitating the cries of the street vendors his mother had described, said, "*Zenana* for sale! *Zenana* for sale!"

I grew up overhearing fragments of whispered conversations about the sadism and bestiality women were subjected to during the Partition: What happened to so and so—someone's sister, daughter, sister-in-law—the women Mrs. Khan categorized *the spoils of war*. The fruits of victory in the unremitting chain of wars that is man's relentless history. The vulnerability of mothers, daughters, granddaughters, and their metamorphosis into possessions; living objects on whose soft bodies victors and losers alike vent their wrath, enact fantastic vendettas, celebrate victory. All history, all these fears, all probabilities and injustices coalesce in Ammijee's terrible face and impart a dimension of tragedy that alchemises the melodrama. The behavior of the Sikhs, so incongruous and flamboyant before, is now transcendentally essential, consequential, fitting.

The men on the floor have spotted Ammijee. "*Maajee*, forgive us: Forgive the wrongs of our fathers."

A sister behind me says, "Oh my God!" There is a buzz of questions and comments. I feel she has voiced exactly my awe of the moment—the rare, luminous instant in which two men transcend their historic intransigence to tender apologies on behalf of their species. Again she says, "Oh God!" and I realize she is afraid that the cousins, propelled forward by small movements of their shoulders and elbows like crocodiles, are resurrecting a past that is best left in whatever recesses of the mind Ammijee has chosen to bury it.

"Don't do this . . . please," protests Sikander. "You're our guests . . . !"

But the cousins, keeping their eyes on the floor say, "*Bhai*, let us be."

The whispered comments of the guests intensify around me.

"What's the matter?"

"They are begging her pardon . . ."

"Who are these men?"

" . . . for what the Sikhs did to her in the riots. . . ."

"*Hai Ram*. What do they want?"

"God knows what she's been through; she never talks about it. . . ."

"With their hair opened like this they must remind her of the men who . . ."

"You can't beat the Punjabis when it comes to drama," says the supercilious Kashmiri. His wife, standing next to me, says, "The Sikhs have a screw loose in the head." She rotates a stubby thumb on her temple as if she were tightening an imaginary screw.

I turn, frowning. The sisters are glaring at them: showering the backs of their heads with withering, hostile looks. And, in hushed tones of suitable gravity, Mrs. Khan says, "Ammijee, they are asking for your forgiveness. Forgive them." Then, "She forgives you brothers!" says Mrs. Khan loudly, on her mother-in-law's account. The other sisters repeat Mrs. Khan's magnanimous gesture, and, with minor variations, also forgive Khushwant and Pratab on Ammijee's behalf.

"Ammijee, come here." Sikander sounds determined to put a stop to all this.

We shift, clearing a narrow passage for Ammijee, and Kishen's mother darts out instead looking like an agitated chick in her puffed cotton sari. She is about to say something—and judging from her expression it has to be something indeterminate and conciliatory—when Kishen, firmly taking hold of her arm, hauls her back.

Seeing his mother has not moved, Sikander shouts, "Send Ammijee here. For God's sake finish it now."

Ammijee takes two or three staggering steps and stands a few paces before me. I suspect one of the sisters has nudged her forward. I cannot see Ammijee's face, but the head beneath the gray chador jerks as if she were trying to remove a crick from her neck.

All at once, her voice, an altered, fragile, high-pitched treble that bears no resemblance to the fierce voice that had demanded, "Who are these men?" Ammijee screeches, "I will never forgive your fathers! Or your grandfathers! Get out, shaitans! Sons and grandsons of shaitans! Never, never, never!"

She becomes absolutely still, as if she would remain there forever, rooted, the quintessence of indictment.

They advance, wiping their noses on their sleeves, tearing at their snarled hair, pleading, "We will lie at your door to our last breath! We are not fit to show our faces."

In a slow, deliberate gesture, Ammijee turns her face away and I observe her profile. Her eyes are clenched shut. The muscles in her cheeks and lower jaw are quivering in tiny, tight spasms as if charged by a current. No one dares say a word: It would be an intrusion. She has to contend with unearthed torments, private demons. The matter rests between her memories and the incarnation of the phantoms wriggling up to her.

The men reach out to touch the hem of her *shalwar*. Grasping her ankles, they lay their heads at her feet in the ancient gesture of surrender demanded of warriors.

"Leave me! Let go!" Ammijee shrieks, in her shaky, altered voice. She raises her arms and moves them as if she were pushing away invisible insects. But she looks exhausted and, her knees giving way, she squats before the men. She buries her face in the chador.

At last, with slight actions that suggest she is ready to face the world, Ammijee wipes her face in the chador and rearranges it on her untidy head. She tucks the edges behind her ears and slowly, in a movement that is almost tender, places her shaking hands on the shaggy heads of the men who hold her feet captive. "My sons, I forgave your fathers long ago," she says in a flat, emotionless voice pitched so low that it takes some time for the words to register, "How else could I live?"

On my way home, hanging on to the red taillights of the cars on the Katy Freeway, my thoughts tumble through a chaos of words and images: And then the words churn madly, throwing up fragments of verse by the Bolivian poet, Pedro Shimose. The words throb in an endless, circular rhythm:

Defend yourself against me
against my father and the father of my father
still living in me
Against my force and shouting in schools and cathedrals
Against my camera, against my pencil
against my TV-spots.

Defend yourself against me,
please, woman,
defend yourself!

# EXISTING AT THE CENTER, WATCHING FROM THE EDGES: MANDALAS

∽

## Roshni Rustomji

Born in Bombay (now Mumbai), Roshni Rustomji (1938– ) grew up in Karachi and was educated there at the Mama Parsi High School and the College of Home Economics. She graduated from the American University at Beirut and earned further degrees at Duke University, and the University of California at Berkeley.

Rustomji lives between the United States and Mexico and is a professor emerita from Sonoma State

University, where she taught from 1973 to 1993. She has been an adjunct faculty member at the New College of California, San Francisco, since 1997 and was a visiting scholar at the Center for Latin American Studies at Stanford University from 1997 to 2005.

She has coedited the anthologies *Blood into Ink: South Asian and Middle Eastern Women Write War* (Westview, 1994), *Living in America: Fiction and Poetry by South Asian American Writers* (Westview, 1995), and (with Elenita Mandoza Strobel and Rajini Srikanth) *Encounters: People of Asian Descent in the Americas* (Rowman and Littlefield, 1999). She has also written a novel, *The Braided Tongue* (TSAR, 2003).

"Existing at the Center, Watching from the Edges: Mandalas" knits together the many cultures and countries in which Rustomji has lived to describe the war, prejudice, and violence that she has experienced across half a century. The memoir begins in Mexico, framed by the image of *la llorona*, the timeless weeping woman of Mexican lore and Rustomji's own tears at the news of Benazir Bhutto's assassination in Pakistan. Rustomji sets two of her entries against the horror of the twenty-first century's savage new weapon—the suicide bomber. Other entries include Rustomji's childhood memory of Partition in Karachi 1947, which becomes a metaphor for the conflicts that Rustomji has experienced during her many migrations. She cleverly interweaves the images of the anti-Vietnam protests and popular culture of that era with references to the battles of ancient Greece and India—and of the great discourses of Hindu philosophy in the sacred text and epic, the *Mahabharata*, between the God Krishna and the warrior Arjun, who reluctantly fights his kinsmen on the field of Kurukshetra. "Mandalas," the word of Sanskrit origin in the title signifies both the universe and the quest for unity, while Rustomji's friend, Mama Glafira, is an important maternal figure in Oaxaca, who embodies humanity and compassion. Rustomji says, "Mama Glafira is a very real person and this is the title that I and many others use for her. She is also known as *madrina* [Godmother] or Doña. She is a woman held in great respect and affection by many people in Oaxaca because of the care and support she gives to nearly everyone she knows."

The USIS is the United States Information Service, the overseas version of the United States Information Agency that fostered cultural activities and cultural exchange, and was once very active in Karachi.

• • •

*For the last fifteen years I have been writing down notes and sketches of some of the wars I have lived through and yes, often with a survivor's guilt. Notes on the back of receipts, scraps of paper, note cards, letters, books, bookmarks, whatever has been at hand. I find it difficult to put them together in any formal, traditional format as I attempt to make some kind of sense of the unending wars I have watched and lived through. Wars that have taken the shape of an adult's slap on a child's face, of the red, orange, green, blue, and yellow flames engulfing the body of a monk or the body of a woman, of the stooped shoulders and traumatized eyes of a man or woman whose dignity has been broken through conquest and poverty, and of the corpses, the obscene slaughter of human beings and the earth in the name of God, truth, revenge, and justice. Seeing, hearing, smelling, tasting, and touching war, sometimes from the very center and sometimes from the sidelines, that leads to a pattern of war existence that seems terrifyingly close to that of walking within a mandala. It continues to be a journey without any detachment or insight that might lead to any kind of understanding, wisdom, and action against the very nature of war and toward the essence of peace. Wars remind me of age-old hauntings begging to be exorcized from the body of our planet.*

**OCTOBER 31, 2001**

*EL DÍA DE LOS MUERTOS.* THE DAY OF THE DEAD

The two little girls sat beside me, laughing, as we made silly sentences out of words. They in English and I in Spanish. When we came to the words, ghosts and *fantasmas*, they became very serious. They asked me, "*Tía*, why does that ghost woman make awful noises and carry away children so that we can never see our families again?" One of their teachers had gone in for a multicultural Halloween. She had turned off the lights and told them the story of *la llorona*—the weeping woman who haunts so much of Mexico and the southwest of the United States, which was of course taken by force from Mexico, which was of course taken by force by the European conquistadors, which was of course taken by force by—and so on and so forth.

According to the accepted legend, *la llorona* wails as she wanders all over the countryside and through desolate places in towns, searching for naughty children she can take away. She cries and looks for children because she has, through pride and insanity, killed her own. I have heard men talk about how they, too, have encountered *la llorona* when staggering home from an evening of drinking. Some survived, others never reached home again. One of the men who had seen her told me, *"Una guerra. Una mujer contra todos los hombres."* Why, I asked, was it a war? Why did he say that she was a woman against all men? Because, he said, one man dishonored a woman and made her so *loca*, so insane, that she killed the children she had had by him.

The summer after the Zapatista uprising, a Zapoteca selling shawls across from my *mamacita's* house in Oaxaca stopped me. She asked me if I had heard the cry of *la llorona* the evening before. I told her that I had heard the woman who sold tamales crying out her wares late into the night throughout Colonia Jalatlaco, the *colonia* where the house is located. Her cry, "tamaaaaleees, tamaaalees" was so *triste*, full of sorrow and anxiety, that it reminded me of the laments of women all over the world as they try to sell what little they have, what little they can make in order to feed their children. The woman selling shawls told me her version of the *la llorona* legend. It is a version I have not yet encountered in any book.

According to the woman, it was the rich and powerful European lover of the beautiful Indian woman, she who was later called *la llorona*, who killed the two children she had borne him. He had done it to prove his love to his European *novia*. To prove that the two children and "that" woman were of no importance to him. As far as the storyteller was concerned, *la llorona* had never raised her hand against her children. When I asked her about the version where *la llorona* killed her children rather than see them slowly starve to death, the woman shrugged and said, "It may have been a blessing. Have you ever seen a child slowly die of hunger?"

I tried to tell my two little companions this version of the story. They were still afraid. It did not matter who killed the children, the children were still dead. And *la llorona* was still searching for children to carry away to the land of ghosts, never to see their families again. One of the girls remembered a priest telling her about the children's crusade, "many hundreds of years ago" and how brave those children were. The other little girl described the children soldiers she had seen on TV, "nearly as old as we are." Before we continued to create more sentences, the two girls decided that no one had killed *la llorona's* children. They had just run away and hidden so that they wouldn't have to go and live in a war. "In wars," said the older girl, "people are hungry. They die. By bombs, by being hungry."

**1947**

I was moving toward my ninth year. One evening, the bells of the Hanuman Temple—at the end of the road, across the *maidaan* where the dust rose and blew toward all our houses in summer—stopped. Just like that. They stopped and I haven't heard them since. A silence without a past, present, or future.

The next morning, the past and the future became the now. The "there" of the rumors of a savage war became the "here" of refugees. People, strangers, suddenly appeared, flooding the streets of Karachi. My mother said, "To count them as if they are numbers is wrong. Each one is a single person. Think, Roshni, think what each person must be feeling!" I saw tears in my beloved grandmother's eyes as she spoke of orphans, children born of rape, women who would die of rape or be forced to live with the memory of violence and the reality of abandonment. I tried very hard to understand. Looking back after nearly fifty odd years, I don't know what I understood. I did realize that now we were independent. The land had been divided and there was bloodshed.

My friend Asha told me about how her favorite aunt had wept as the red *tilak* on her forehead and the red *sindhur* in the parting of her hair were rubbed off when she was widowed. All that red of marriage and of families joining together turned to blood across the land. One morning, Asha didn't come to school. I asked when she would come back. Was she ill? Had she gone to visit her grandparents in Lahore? The teacher just shook her head. Asha disappeared from my life. I learned about a new flag, and we were given sweets in school for our newly won independence and the birth of a new country.

A week later, about lunchtime, my grandmother and mother spread their much-cherished white damask tablecloth, elegant with its finely darned patches, across our big dining table. A few years ago, I went to Karachi to empty out the old house because the landlord had sold it to be demolished for a parking garage. I refused to watch as the dining table was taken away. I remembered the day my grandmother and mother spread that tablecloth and asked me to sit at the table on a chair that could be seen from the front door. My grandmother sat at the head of the table and could also be seen from the front door. We were to carry on conversations with imaginary people on the table. I already had a reputation for holding long conversations with myself and with people no one else could see. My mother and father went to the front of the house and spoke to the crowd that had gathered there. "No, she isn't here," they said. "She didn't come to work today. She spoke about leaving for India. We can't help you."

I felt someone's head against my legs and my grandmother warned me with her eyes not to raise the tablecloth. I reached down and felt the head and face of Dossa, one of my favorite,

58

most-loved older persons. She had come to our house every morning to sweep the floors, and she and my grandmother were the only people in the house I wasn't allowed to question, answer back, or tease. A few days earlier, she had arrived at our door with two policemen. Karachi was under curfew from night to dawn. When the policemen tried to stop her from coming to the house early in the morning, she wouldn't stop walking. When one of the policemen tried to explain "curfew" to her, she beat him up with her broom and lectured him on the sanctity of work. They accompanied her to the door to protect her from any harm. And now she was hiding, her face pressed against my legs, trembling as her pathetic, alcoholic son led a group of men to our door demanding that we give him his mother so that she, too, could be converted and not have to leave their land. After all, he said, God was God no matter what He was called.

I felt something break inside me when I saw Dossa crawling out from under the table and through the back corridor, as my grandmother walked behind her to shelter her until they both reached the back door. I saw my grandmother bend down and help Dossa stand up. My uncle who was right outside the back door nearly picked up Dossa as he led her away to what we hoped was safety in India.

A month later, I stood at the same back door holding my father's hand. We were facing a man holding the hand of his daughter. The man was begging my father to find him some space for his family. My father was explaining that he couldn't. The girl was younger than me but I knew we could be friends. She looked as if she liked reading and listening to stories and making them up. The man wept as he turned away. The girl turned around and we waved at one another. My father was crying. His beautiful dark face looked as if someone had smeared dead gray ashes across it. Many years later I learned that my father had turned the top floors of the school where he was the Principal into a place of sanctuary for refugees.

My mother told us about the horrors that the refugees

*[handwritten in margin: if she wants to stay she will have to become muslim]*

who were now citizens of Pakistan had lived through. She was among the many citizens of Karachi—old and new—who set up work places where women who had become refugees could work and make new lives for themselves. There was agony but there was also hope. One of the first Pakistani patriotic songs I heard (I think it was the National Anthem for a brief time) was composed on our piano. People question that but I remember sitting quietly in a corner listening to the different variations of the melody and the words. But the wars continued and my mother got tired of trying to explain to me why people kill one another, why people hate, why we didn't stop such things and other such questions. One day she said, "Find the answers for yourself."

## 1958–1961

I used to imagine that Nasima and Arjuman, who had traveled with me from Pakistan to Lebanon, were somehow two parts of the little girl at our back door. It was their gift of friendship and laughter and serious discussions about the what and the why of Pakistan that made Pakistan truly one of my lands, a *desh* for me. I don't quite understand the concept of nations. Lebanon was the heartbreakingly beautiful land where I saw a boy, his face masked with blood, leap from a balcony moments after men in uniforms had entered the building. I stood below, surrounded by the aroma of strong coffee and the smell of freshly shaved wood, a loud thud interrupting the sounds of Fairouz singing as the boy fell to the sidewalk. That day I learned about the cruelty of men toward boys who could be their sons. It was the first time I heard the indescribable scream of a woman as she watches her child being killed.

Beirut was the city where I passed a wall of lemon trees on my way to the lighthouse and saw two women embracing and weeping. I wanted to console them but didn't know how and for what. One of them turned to me and said, "*Binti*, daughter, we cry for our lemon trees we will never see again in our home. Our Palestine." The other woman showed me the key to the house she had left behind. The house, she had just learned, didn't exist anymore. I didn't have any words, so I did what I had seen a woman do to another woman who had lost her husband, her two children and her old father on their way to Karachi from Bombay. She had wiped the grieving woman's face with her bare hands. Six months later, I tripped and hurt my knee. I went to the student health services and the nurse who treated me was the woman with the key.

The campus of the American University of Beirut was where a young woman was pointed out to me on my first day at the University. I was told, "She was there. She watched as her father was hanged. She insisted on going. She is carrying on the fight." I don't remember her face but she had a body that said, "I refuse to break." And yes, I often saw her laugh and smile. And then there was the funeral of a classmate that I didn't attend. One of my friends told me that the mother had screamed at the corpse of her son, not only for dying but also for having killed other mothers' sons. Later, I heard the same story during the Nicaragua war between the Sandinistas and the Contras, and then during the Zapatista uprising for justice.

**1962–1963**

From the Cedars of Lebanon where the gatekeeper Humbaba fought Gilgamesh and his beloved companion, Enkidu, to Durham, North Carolina, and a campus graced with "ye olde Europeanne" buildings that reminded me of the castles and churches of my childhood fairy tales. A beautiful campus with a glorious library. I boarded a bus to go to the house where I had been invited for tea. Being a rather nervous rider, I sat in one of the first rows of the nearly empty bus. The driver pulled over, came to me, and said quite gently, "Don't you know the rules?"

I shook my head. He bent down, picked me up, 78 pounds of a sari-wrapped bewildered graduate student, and placed me most carefully on a seat at the back of the bus. The books and movies at the USIS in Karachi and the professors from the United States in Beirut had not told me about segregation. I told my hostess about the incident. She said, "Oh dear, I am sorry. Only colored servants take that bus." I showed her my brown hand. She smiled, shook her head, and remarked that she was surprised that the bus driver hadn't realized that I was a foreigner. Foreigners were to be treated with the same respect as whites. Otherwise there would be international incidents.

One Sunday afternoon, late in the summer of my year in Durham, I stood on a sidewalk on the main street next to an African American family—a grandmother, a grandfather, a father, a mother, and two boys. Both boys had their grandmother's smile. The mother admired my sari and asked me if it was handwoven. We carried on a conversation as we watched a phalanx of policemen approach the group of young people trying to enter a restaurant across the street. When the first "thwack" of a baton against human flesh reached us, the grandma moaned and nearly fell over. The mother held her up. The four men stood still, their fists so tight that their arms were shaking. I remembered standing on the terrace in my mother's home in Mumbai (that is how my grandmother always pronounced the city), watching the police beating up processions of people calling out for freedom, calling out Gandhiji's name. Neither the people being beaten up in that procession in Mumbai, nor the people on that street in Durham raised a hand against their attackers. I haven't yet decided if that is really the only right way to defend ourselves.

When I ended up at the Duke Hospital after completing my thesis, the bus driver who had placed me so gently but firmly at the back of the bus came to visit me with a bunch of hand-picked flowers. He said that I should get well soon and that he was very sorry to hear about the war between India and China. I told him that my paternal great-great-grandmother was Chinese, and ever since I heard about the war, I had chilling nightmares about dragons and tigers tearing at one another.

## BERKELEY, CALIFORNIA
Memories for stories

1. Demonstrations against the War in Vietnam. I meet a man at a party who has walked in all the antiwar demonstrations in Berkeley. At the same party, his son tells me with great delight that whenever a woman teacher in Mexico was mean to him and his other American friends, they would call her "an ugly *puta*." According to him, they should know that Americans are to be respected. Disrespect toward Americans would earn them the title "whores."

2. People in Karachi have a difficult time believing my letters about Berkeley. Especially when I write that there are *gora*, "white" young men and women in ragged clothes (some deliberately torn or patched) begging in the streets around the University.

3. Coming out of the library one evening with no one around, I see a lone policeman enter the lane. He lobs a canister of tear gas at me and laughs. The horrific sound hastens the notorious "Rustomjis always get deaf as they age" process for me.

4. Entering a women's restroom in Dwinelle Hall at the University of California late one evening, I find a woman with a mop in her hand. She has tears on her face. She turns to me and asks, "How is this going to help end the war? I won't be paid extra for this extra work. The war won't end. My boys will die in that place while you march and dance in the streets." She points to the row of toilets. They are filled to overflowing with garbage, with rotten fruit, newspapers, old clothes, chicken bones, even pages torn out of books. Angry students have filled up the toilets as a sign of protest against the war-mongering authorities.

The woman throws down her mop and walks away.

4. Bumper stickers. "Mary Poppins Is a Junkie." I have to have this one deciphered for me. "Question Authority." I am confused. Is this a car driven by a person who is an authority on questions or is the person telling us to question people in authority? I am told that Berkeley is a War Zone.

5. Sitting in a professor's office translating the *Gita* with other students as a car comes hurtling down across the green lawn and stops just short of plowing into the office window.

6. Walking down University Avenue in a sari. A young woman stops me and says, "Free yourself. Get rid of all those yards of clothing." The woman is wearing a long skirt from India. Is she a friend or foe?

7. Listening to Joan Baez and Bob Dylan at Jock and Emily Brown's house where I live. Jock Brown goes to Vietnam to protest the war his country is waging against Vietnam.

8. Reading James Baldwin and learning more about the war I saw in North Carolina.

9. The smoldering anger, fear, frustration in Lebanon turns further inward. Civil War. One more motherland that has nurtured me in flames. Blood doesn't put out fire. I read: The Worst Wars Are Civil Wars. And later: All Wars Are Civil Wars. I still wonder at the different uses of the word "civil."

10. I watch televised images of the American war in Vietnam as I learn to translate the *Mahabharata* and *Iliad*. Women from both fighting sides stream onto the battle field of Kurukshetra, mourning their dead. Achilles mourns the death of his beloved companion and drags Hector around in the dirt as his old parents watch in horrified grief, and Vietnam is transformed into a blazing fire of trees and human flesh. There must have been sounds with those images but all I remember is silence as the pictures flashed across the screen while I translated, word by word, the stories of other times, other places where fires of wars raged, the innocent and the guilty were killed and glorious words were spoken. One night, after completing a very long

paper, I dream that I am running with the women on the field of Kurukshetra, I am screaming, my hair is unbound, I wear no ornaments. Hecuba appears calling for her son. A woman stops me and says, "Who are you on this land? You were not walking with us to Oklahoma."

**1975**

A student sat in my office at Sonoma State University. He looked like a grown-up version of a Renaissance cherub. There was a sweetness to him that needed protection, yet there was nothing childish about him. He told me the following story. After his first tour of duty as a Marine, he had volunteered to go to Vietnam again. He couldn't remember what fired his zeal. Yes, he said, he had seen war, both the inhuman and the human side of it. Toward the end of his second tour of duty, he and his buddies were pulling out bodies from a village set on fire by the Americans. He said, "We burned it by mistake and we were now trying to save as many of those villagers as we could. We were carrying the burned but alive bodies to the boats. I was carrying someone very light. I looked down and saw that I was carrying an old woman. She looked exactly like my grandmother back in Michigan. Old, wrinkled, wiry, and beautiful. She died in my arms. I went out of my mind. I was sent back home."

He made me realize how some people eat war and grow fat and greedy for more, how others eat war and are killed and how some transform the poison of war into *amrit*, nectar, not only of immortality but also of peace. And then he and his wife gave me a beautiful silkscreened banner with the image of our Lady of Guadalupe. They had decided to earn their living making and selling banners with the symbols of all the world's religions.

The last time I saw the student, he had graduated and was selling his banners on Telegraph Avenue. He no longer reminded me of a cherub. He had the detached, loving look of a bodhisattva.

**1987**

My mother died. The day after the funeral we found out that the Karachi policemen had towed away the cars parked outside our house during the funeral. The mourners weren't happy but they will most probably recall the day my mother was taken to the *dukhmo*, the Tower of Silence, as the day the police towed away their cars, and hopefully they will smile even as they shake their heads.

As I touched my mother's wedding ring and her glasses—I had never seen her without the ring and seldom without her glasses—I could hear her talking to me. And what struck me was how often she had spoken to me about the utter horror and uselessness of war and the evils of injustice. She never said, "That's how the world is." She always implied that our lives would be rather worthless if we didn't work against evil. I was six years old when the United States dropped the bombs on Hiroshima and Nagasaki. I looked at my mother. Her calm, rather stern face was absolutely still. Absolutely without a trace of emotion. I remember thinking that this was how my mother would look when she died. My mother was born in Japan.

**SEPTEMBER 2000**

We shouldn't have been office mates. We are far too committed to one another as friends, and much more interested in the histories of our families than in some of the academic work we need to complete. After all, we are both Indians and are comfortable enough with one another to make jokes about it. About Columbus refusing to ask anyone the way to the real India, about blankets and sheets and such nonsense. We both love literature. She is completing her dissertation and I read some of the chapters. She is a storyteller telling stories about stories and storytellers in her family, her community, her world. I read her

narrative about her family, the journey on the Trail of Tears and
the final arrival in Oklahoma. She writes about the nuanced
and multilinear, many-circled techniques of storytelling used
by her grandmother. I read about how her grandmother was
sent out with food for the wounded warriors hiding in a cave
when she was a very little girl. I catch a hint that my friend's
grandmother had seen a man die of his wounds when she was a
child. Wounds received in defense of his land and his family.

But I don't know how the story really ends. Did her grandmother ever tie up all the threads of the stories about her family, people deprived of their ancestral lands, made invisible in
their own land? Can a grandmother's stories be tied neatly—
for the sake of an academic dissertation—into the stories of the
indigenous women of Bolivia fighting for their land and their
lives? And my friend, whom I call Damyanti, the Victorious
One—says, "Roshni, there isn't an end to that story." And I
realize that as I live in the Americas, I, too, am implicated in
the story of the rape of this land and of the continual attempts
at the destruction of the first peoples in this country. I understand the woman in my dream. I had not been forced to walk
with my friend's family to Oklahoma. And I feel the pain I felt
when I saw Dossa crawl away from our house in Karachi. I don't
know if she arrived somewhere safely. I leave the office, drive
home, walk to the edge of the Pacific Ocean, stand on the sand,
and pray the ancient Zoroastrian prayer of health and safety for
everyone who dwells in these lands. I wonder if it will work.

## SEPTEMBER 20, 2001

Thursday, a week after. A dear friend whom I call *hermanocito*
sent me an email. He had barely escaped being beaten up. He
was threatened because he has a beard and wears a turban. Just
before I received the email I had been talking with my neighbor

whose wondrous eight-year-old daughter asked, "But why do those people hate me, Mummy? I'm American." And then I turned on the TV and saw what is now Afghanistan for me. Food was being distributed. Names were being called. The names were of adult males. But most of the adult males were dead or gone and so the children were coming up to collect the food allocations. No women. There were a few little girls. A name was called out. Silence. No one came up. And then one of the men smiled sadly, went to the group waiting for food, and called out a tiny girl. She had wild curly hair and the beautiful eyes of childhood. It seemed as if she were too young to recognize her father's name, who most probably was already dead or fighting toward death. She came forward and picked up the bag they handed to her and began dragging it. Someone showed her how to sling it over her shoulder. And she did. The bag was as big as she was. Maybe bigger. And then they put a cardboard box in front of her. She stood there looking at it and tried pushing it with her feet. The man who had brought her forward smiled sadly again and gestured that he would bring it to her house later. It was that small gesture of compassion, and the tiny girl-child going back into the crowd with her bag over her shoulder, that shattered me. I sat screaming, bleeding from the womb that my body hasn't possessed for over thirty years.

It may be good to write about the horrors we bring upon ourselves. Writing, after all, is a political act. I understand that peace and justice are what we have to keep working toward in our own way to keep from shriveling up in body, mind, and spirit. Compassion. I am haunted by the image of the little girl carrying the bag of food over her shoulder. War—and yet the hope of peace.

**AUGUST 2004**

Innana is the name we hear. She is—we are told—the Queen of Heaven and Earth. Her older sister, widowed Ereshkigal,

Queen of the "Underworld" recognizes the descent of Innana for what it is. Our bombs have torn the skin off the Earth and Ereshkigal emerges to wander across the land searching for shattered, unburied lovers and murdered children.

The image of the little girl in Afghanistan and the presence of Ereshkigal merge into the woman in the documentary. There is nothing contained, nothing stylized about her grief. It is the scream of the mother who has seen brutal death. She is grandmother, mother, sister, sister-in-law, aunt, daughter, *binti*, *hija*, *beti*, neighbor, *sakhi*, *amiga*, companion who has walked with us since we were born. She curses all of us, the Americans, who have brought death and destruction to her family, her friends, her neighborhood, her city, her country of Iraq. Sitting in the air-conditioned comfort of a theater in an enormous multiplex cinema complex located not that far from San Francisco, once hailed as the City of Flowers, peace and love, we are stunned into silence. The munching of popcorn and chocolates, the bubble of sodas, the soft shuffling of bodies are silenced. I see the woman in front of me trembling violently. We know that we are once again implicated in the creation of sorrow and furious grief. A very old woman enters the theater. She is late and can't see well enough in the dark to find a seat. She begins to wail softly, "I can't find a place. I am lost." She stops near me and I reach over to help her to the seat next to me. She says, "Oh my, I missed the beginning of the film. Why is that woman screaming? Is that Arabic? Is she mad?" Someone behind her tells her to be quiet.

Mad? In all the senses of the word. As I see bombs falling from the sky and listen to the young men and women ready to unleash their terrifying technology onto those they dare not think of as being human, I am reminded of the history of this particular war. The steady march of greed and the brilliant manipulation of words and ideas that have at last culminated in this war. A war that is once again shrouded in lofty words and promises. I remember the words of Euripides: "Those whom the Gods wish to destroy, they first make mad." I know that the woman's curse is on me as it is on all of us who have not yet found a way to stop the insanity called war. War in all its forms.

A few months later, a student stops me before we enter the classroom. She apologizes for having missed one of the classes and explains that she had to go home to her family to take care of her mother. I nod and say, of course, these things happen and one does have to take care of family. I begin to move away. She stops me. She says, "It is because my father died at this time last year." I look at her and realize that her father couldn't have been much older or much younger than me. Before I can express my condolences, she says, "He committed suicide." And again before I can say anything, she says, "He was a Vietnam vet. He had been attempting suicide even before he left Vietnam. Years before I was born."

As I hear about the women in Mexico sending their sons to fight in Afghanistan and Iraq so that they can get the citizenship promised them in exchange for their bodies, and as we continue to call down Peace upon our Prophets—the sung and the unsung ones—the children, the women, the men—I think of the old man who stopped me near my home in Karachi when I was moving toward my ninth year. The air was alive with the sound of the evening *azaan*. The man was a stranger and I never saw him again. He was weeping and he said, "*Beti*, may Allah have compassion on all of us. On all of us. Friends and enemies—there is no difference."

DECEMBER 22, 2007

OAXACA, OAXACA

I have been trying to read Francisco Goldman's *The Long Night of the White Chickens*. It is difficult reading. The Guatemala of the book is Pakistan to me. Pakistan of military rule supported by U.S. tax dollars. As I walk through Oaxaca, I am haunted by the sardonic words of one of the characters in the book: *Guatemala does not exist. I know. I have been there.*

I am tempted to write on the page of the novel (in pencil of course):

*Guatemala does exist. Pakistan exists. They exist to remind us of what is happening not only in Guatemala and in Pakistan but also in Mexico, in Palestine, in Israel, Iraq, Iran, Burma, France, Germany, the United States, Africa. In our world. Lawyers, students, teachers, human rights activists, men, women, children beaten, killed, disappeared. Nothing new—anywhere in the world. Nothing new except the horrifying intensity and acceleration of violence and just as horrifying an intensity and acceleration of apathy by those who think they are untouched by, not complicit in this violence.*

I do not write in the book because it belongs to the Oaxaca Lending Library.

### DECEMBER 27, 2007

#### CALLE ALIANZA, COL. JALATLACO, OAXACA

Chuck/Carlos who has been watching the news wakes me up. "Breaking news. Bad news," he says. "Benazir Bhutto has been assassinated."

I feel as if my whole living self were filled with horror, despair, anguish. He says, "Why are you shocked? Didn't you think that something like this would happen to her?" No, I did not expect this murder. I try to meditate. To calm myself, to calm the world that Benazir and I have inhabited. The people and the *tierra*, the *desh*, the *vataan* that in this time of our history is named Pakistan. All I can do is shout, "Stupid. Stupid. Stupid. We have all become inmates, all of us—of an insane asylum." I am still muttering and crying as I run two blocks to Casa Arnel to phone my cousin in California. Benazir has been murdered in Rawalpindi but her city—my city—Karachi is blowing up. My cousin in California hasn't heard the news yet. She promises to call her sister in Karachi immediately. The images of the murders, mayhem, and chaos in Karachi that I had just witnessed on television are with me as I call my friend and mentor, Ijaz Syed, in California. I can't finish the message of outrage and grief that I leave on his voice mail. English, Gujarati, or Urdu can't express what I feel and think.

Benazir had returned to Pakistan in the fall of 2007. In the first attempt to assassinate her, she survived but 170 people died. After this I received emails discussing, beating, detailing Benazir's history, her personality, her political and personal goals.

I had stopped respecting Benazir Bhutto early in her first term as Prime Minister of Pakistan. I had actually been wary of her since a brief encounter I had with her in the 60s. She was about twelve years old. I was about twenty-five years old. A friend of my parents who was a supporter and admirer of Zulfikar Ali Bhutto had invited me to go with him to the Bhutto residence in Karachi where he had to deliver some papers. He told me that he would like to introduce Benazir Bhutto to me. "She will be our Prime Minister one day," he said. He did not add, "Inshallah." The future Prime Minister of Pakistan, Benazir Bhutto, came into the room where we had been left standing, looked me straight in the eye and said not a word in response to my greetings or to the greetings of my companion. She had the coldest eyes I had seen in my twenty-odd years. Her eyes, her refusal to greet or thank us, made it clear that she was not interested in "unimportant" people such as us.

Many years later in Oaxaca, on December 28, 2007, the wonderful lady many of us know as Mama Glafira tried to console me after Benazir's murder. According to Mama Glafira, what made Benazir beautiful were her beautiful eyes. I realized that since her father's assassination, Benazir's eyes—in all the pictures of her I had seen in magazines and on TV—had lost the haughty, cold look. But even if she had retained those cold eyes and her disdain for "unimportant" people, even if she did prove to be a very disappointing and frustrating politician, the threats of violence against her and her cruel, calculated, violent death can never be justified or condoned.

It is January 2, 2008, and as I walk down Macedonia Alcala toward the *zócalo*, I remember that today is my parents' seventieth wedding anniversary. But I am still in mourning for what has happened in Pakistan, what is happening in Pakistan, the senseless and horrifying violence that is consuming our world. I bend down to thank the old, blind man who has been singing on this road nearly every evening for twenty-odd years. About ten years ago, my friend Ofelia and I had accompanied him— off-key of course but with great gusto—as he sang "Naila." Others had joined us. We had sung the song twice to the great amusement of the singer. On this January day of cold, dry air that reminds me of winters in Karachi, he senses the tears in my voice and says, *"No llores, amiga"* and begins to sing the song of the dying mother to her daughter. The mother who tells her daughter that lamentations and tears will not help. If the daughter cries, the mother is sure to die and remain dead. But on the other hand, if the daughter sings in the face of death, the mother will never die, she will always be alive. It is a song that has always haunted me.

I know—with sorrow—that I will be searching until the day of my death for a melody, a few lyrics that would exorcize the violent deaths, the injustices, the cruelty from our world.

# MIRAGE

&

# *Talat Abbasi*

A short story writer, Talat Abbasi (1942– ) was born in Lucknow, and grew up in Karachi. She was educated in Pakistan at St. Joseph's College, Karachi, graduated from Kinnaird College, Lahore, and later the London School of Economics, UK. She moved to New York in 1978 where she lives still. She worked for the UN Population Fund until her retirement in 2004, working on gender and population issues across Asia.

Abbasi has published a collection of her short stories, *Bitter Gourd and Other Stories* (Oxford University Press, 2001), in which "Mirage" originally appeared. Her short fiction is set mostly in Pakistan and revolves around class and gender; it has been published often in U.S. college texts.

"Mirage" was first broadcast as the prize winner of a BBC World Service short story competition in 2000. In this story, Abbasi provides a moving account of a mother's heroic struggle to look after her severely handicapped child, and her complex emotions on leaving him in an institution. Abbasi says:

> The title "Mirage" was taken from [an] enduring image in my head . . . this shining pool of water on the road driving from somewhere to somewhere in Pakistan in blazing heat—spectacular until of course it turned out to be just that—a mirage. A promise ending in disappointment simply because you were temporarily fooled by the deception. A commonplace occurrence most people will have experienced, the tricks life plays on you. Nothing more, nothing less.

• • •

"November twentieth," says Sister Agnes.
*November 20, I write.*
"Nineteen eighty," says Sister Agnes.
*1980, I write.*
There's something very practiced about the way she says it. Perhaps they all falter at this point, the last thing after all on the last form they'll sign. Scores of parents over the years have come through the front door of Hope House to hand their children over to Sister Agnes because they're mentally retarded, schizophrenic, autistic, epileptic, or have cerebral palsy. Hardly the complete list of reasons, just a sample. Young parents on the whole, many still in their thirties, because Hope House is only for ten-year-olds and under. Many coming alone, on their own, as I have with Omar.

Mind you, I'm not faltering, not me. Not one bit. If I'm

behaving like a puppet it's because I'm drained, exhausted. I was exhausted at least mentally even before we left home today. I'm always tense, in quite a state when I have to take him out in public and, of course, today I was worse than usual. He sensed it and acted up. I must've flung a bag of candies into his mouth by the time the diaper was done. A dozen pieces of candy at a time every time he bared his teeth to shred it. Understandable, of course, his reaction to a diaper at his age. It isn't always needed, but I have to, just in case. It's candy corn, the sticky kind he can't just swallow, is forced to chew, gives me time.

"Candy corn's bad for his teeth."

The pediatrician says that every time I take him to get the prescription refilled for his tranquilizer. But not very seriously. He doesn't expect me to give up on the candy corn. Then I zipped him into his jeans, fastened his belt which he doesn't have the skill to undo. That's why it's jeans, not pull-on pants. And then to keep his hands as well as his mouth really busy for what he hates most of all—his harness—I gave him half a bag of potato chips, his greatest weakness, the salted kind with lots of MSG. It hasn't occurred to the doctor to tell me that MSG is also bad for him.

Then all of a sudden I threw myself on top of him, pinning down both his arms with my elbows, taking him by surprise. Rammed the spoon between his teeth and held it there to keep his mouth open until he'd swallowed every drop of his tranquilizer, until it had all gone down. I realized that I had gritted my teeth so hard, I'd bitten my own tongue! I cried a bit so there was no time left to cut his nails. The taxi driver was buzzing me from downstairs. He was parked across the street two blocks away from the apartment building. That's another reason I'm exhausted. Just the thought of traffic lights and having to cross the street with him before they turn green!

He hates his harness. And that, too, is understandable. A full-grown energetic ten-year-old in a toddler's harness. Imagine being allowed to walk but in leg irons! Still, I have to use that harness when I take him out just in case he decides to stage a sit-in in the middle of traffic. He did that only once before I thought of a harness and believe me, it wasn't easy, dragging him by the collar of his shirt, inch by inch, like a dead weight across the road. And on top of it—

"Pair of loonies!" yelled the driver who had to brake suddenly.

"Who let you out?"

He meant both of us. And who could blame him? Who could blame them all for staring? Unexpected, let's face it, even for New York.

Still he was wrong about me. Not a loony, not me. But always at my wits' end, it's true, no matter what. Cooped up with a hyperactive frustrated boy in the bare two-room apartment. I lined the floor with mattresses, quilts and foam after receiving warnings from the landlord about the neighbors complaining of "a herd, at least, of thumping, marauding elephants up there." They too were wrong, of course. No threatening elephants. Just a small exquisite bird trapped in the room, flying in panic from wall to wall, hurling itself against them, hurting only itself, incapable of harming others. Watched in silence by the mother.

I thanked God it was at least a corner apartment, no neighbors on the bedroom side. Imagine having to line the walls too with mattresses, I thought, as I watched in empathy. Then as the weeks grew into months, even a year and more, and the frightened bird still found no peace—neither smashed itself against the walls nor found a way to fly out—I watched in rage and self-pity.

And becoming melodramatic at the end, likened myself bitterly to a Pharaoh's slave buried alive with him. Nothing happened this time though, thank goodness. The taxi's brought us without incident to Hope House, Omar's home.

But "Omar's home" sounds wrong. How can he have a home apart from me?

Am I faltering now?

Maybe I am.

Only ten and strikingly pretty. His black hair, which I am stroking to soothe him, keep him quiet on my lap, is amazingly still baby soft though the curls are showing signs of straightening out. His fine features are in perfect proportion, chiseled on a small delicate face. Strangers have always been drawn to him, impulsively reaching out to pet him, complimenting me. In fact only last month I took him to the pediatrician. He had had his tranquilizer and so he was sitting quietly by my side. I didn't notice this woman, being in quite a state myself as I usually am when I have to bring him out in public—there I go, repeating myself—especially to small enclosed places like the doctor's office. Yes, there can be trouble even with a tranquilizer! But suddenly she's there before me, chapped red lips parted in a smile, hands reaching out to fondle his curls.

"What a beauti . . ."

That's usually how far they get! Then they all stop, awkward, embarrassed, because close up they all see something. It's the eyes, of course, under those fantastic long eyelashes they were all set to coo over. They're not blind eyes, seeing nothing. They're seeing as well as you and I, but what they're seeing is nothing you and I can understand. That much they tell you as they confront you in one long, unblinking stare before they go back to darting constantly, nervously, from left to right and back again, never at rest.

And then they notice other little things about him which can be quite off-putting. The perfectly shaped lips—which I can tell you have rarely parted in a smile—are twitching uncontrollably, quite unprettily. And the ceaseless whimpering sound can be quite unnerving. It's very soft, barely audible, a call which seems to come from miles below.

And I understand the disappointment of strangers at being thus tricked. I, too, have been taken in by a mirage.

But as I said, there can be trouble even with a tranquilizer! So now, in a flash, the pen which I am passing back to Sister Agnes is knocked out of my hand and I am looking up at Omar from the floor where somehow I have landed. He's lunging toward the forms to tear them up with his teeth. But Sister Agnes is quicker. Scores of children, after all, who have a taste for paper!

There's nothing left but my face and to this he turns. I wince as he rakes my cheek, and grab his hands. He bares his teeth but I'm holding him as far from myself as I can. There's absolute hatred in his eyes. He cannot speak of it, he can speak only two words. One is *pani*, the Urdu word for water, which he learned late as a toddler in Karachi, where he was born. The other is *na*, which can mean both no and yes. He's saying neither now and suddenly he's neither scratching nor biting. His nails though are biting into my arms as he clings to me, face hidden against my chest. He's shaking, his eyes will now be filled with terror.

"I meant to cut his nails, Sister. I'm so sorry, Sister."

In fact I'm so sorry about his nails that I am close to tears. She must see that because she comes over, presses my shoulder. Another practiced gesture! The touch is sympathetic but brief. Scores of parents, after all! Perhaps those others too all remember something that makes them feel as guilty as I do about his nails. I never do hand him over to her. She simply lifts him off my lap, stands him up on the floor. He doesn't resist. Puppets, both of us, now.

"He won't need this anymore," she says gently, removing his harness and handing it to me.

The harness goes into the garbage chute as soon as I get home.

Also the foam and plastic which line the floor. Then the mattresses and quilts are disposed of. The freshly vacuumed Bokhara at last flaunts its buried jewel colors in the sunlight as the blinds are raised for the first time since I moved into the apartment. And a curious neighbor runs to her window to see at last, then turns back in embarrassment and disappointment, both. An apartment, then, just like any other.

An apartment, moreover, where knives, kitchen shears, scissors, nail cutters have found their rightful places. They've emerged from an old battered attaché case hidden under the kitchen sink. It makes me smile now, that battered attaché case, as I think of that wretched burglar caught red-handed by the super with it, holding razor blades as he stood dazed by his catch—what a treasure! He took too long over it, it looked so promising, a locked case hidden under the kitchen sink. I didn't see the funny side of it then but I'm beginning to now. I have a mad urge to write and commiserate with him. Dear Mr. Burglar, I want to say, what you must think of me, hiding knives, scissors, razor blades in a locked attaché case like a treasure!

Mad for sure, you must think, eccentric at best. And who can blame you?

I go to bed early and sleep right through the night because the lights don't suddenly go on, off, on again at one a.m., the taps don't run and flood the bath at three, and I have absolutely no fear that the stove will turn itself on. So in the morning I wake up, rested and at peace, and yet in pain as you might expect of someone who has had an arm amputated to save the rest.

# JUNGLE JIM

&

# *Muneeza Shamsie*

Muneeza Shamsie (1944– ) was born
in Lahore, educated in England, and
has lived in Karachi for most of her
life. From 1975 to 1982 she taught
music and mime as a volunteer at a
special-education school in Karachi.
She is a founding member of The Kid-
ney Centre, a Karachi hospital.

   Shamsie is a Pakistani critic,
short story writer, and the editor
of three pioneering anthologies: *A
Dragonfly in the Sun: An Anthology of*

*Pakistani Writing in English* (Oxford University Press, 1997), *Leaving Home: Towards a New Millennium: A Collection of English Prose by Pakistani Writers* (Oxford University Press, 2001), and this volume, *And The World Changed: Contemporary Stories by Pakistani Women* (Women Unlimited, 2005; The Feminist Press, 2008). She is the managing editor for a work in progress, *The Oxford Companion to the Literatures of Pakistan* and is also currently writing a critical book, *Hybrid Tapestries: The Development of a Pakistani Literature in English* (working title). Shamsie is on the editorial board for the bibliographic issue of *The Journal of Commonwealth Literature* (UK) and contributes to *Dawn* and *Newsline* (Pakistan), *The Daily Star* (Bangladesh) and *The Literary Encyclopedia* (online). She has spoken at many literary forums, and was a fellow of the 1999 Cambridge Seminar.

"Jungle Jim" is a literary rendering of Shamsie's view that the colonial construct is patriarchal, as is its emulation by South Asia's Anglicized elite. For this ruling class, English is connected to power, governing, and control, while the arts by their very nature are related to freedom of expression and are thus subversive. The conflict inherent in this becomes apparent in the portrayal of Uncle Jim. His drawings of World War I war victims, his opinions on the *shikar*, and his scandalous marriage to an Englishwoman challenge the foundations of Empire and its narratives. The plot, which cuts across three generations, also shows the tenacity with which Jo's grandmother, Nani Jaan, and her sister tie down Uncle Jim to an incompatible arranged marriage in an attempt to subvert modernity.

The tale that Jo hears at her school in England and the racist interpretation that British society gives to to the story of Uncle Jim and Frances embody the imperial stereotypes and notions of Otherness, which are integral to Jo's nightmares and her paintings.

The backdrop of the two World Wars and Partition shows the way in which the latter was inextricably linked to the former and the painful choice Indian Muslims confronted in 1947 when the division of the subcontinent led to the unforeseen division of families.

The story brings out another colonial subtext, that because all the people who lived in the British Empire, anywhere in the world, were considered British subjects, they traveled on British passports. Jo's father, who deplored independence, exercised the option of remaining British in 1947. He assumed that because he spoke fluent English, had adopted English ways, and was a World War II veteran and an aristocrat, he and his family would be regarded as equals in Britain. The loss of their social status in London is contrasted with the family's privileged standing in Amarkot, where the one-time ruler, His Highness the Nawab of Amarkot (HH for short) is an ex-classmate, and his wife, Her Highness the Begum of Amarkot, a cousin.

• • •

I paint. That's all I do. That's all I have ever done. But no, I don't talk about my paintings much, because I don't know how to. I suppose the best I can do is to tell a story—about myself, Raynard's Wood, and Amarkot.

## 1. 1956

My sister Lalla and I joined Raynard's Wood School in the autumn of 1956. My father, Commander Syed Mohsin "Mo" Ali Baig, drove us down, through the narrow winding roads of Hampshire flanked by overlapping trees. Begum Sitara Ali Baig exclaimed over the autumn colors, the school grounds, and the splendid white Wyatt building. I thought she was overdoing her enthusiasm—we had been there before.

There was a hub of voices, a crush of parents, girls, suitcases, and trunks, but the moment we entered a hush fell. Everyone stared. My mother was in an emerald green coat and pale silk sari; my father, in a dark overcoat, a hat in his hand. The majority of parents were in casual tweeds, sheepskin jackets, thick sweaters, and sturdy shoes: One woman was in gumboots. We stayed close together, the four of us.

An elderly woman in a white coat—the school matron— bustled toward us. She announced in a firm, confident voice. "More new girls, Lalla-Rook and Marja-Been." (Not surprisingly we came to be known as The Margarines.) Someone whispered, "Aren't they sweet?" Another voice said, "I wonder if they can speak English?" I was shocked, the color rising to my ears.

At supper, in the dormitory, in the classroom, I had to answer numerous questions about myself. No, I hadn't come from a foreign country, I said. I lived in London. I had been to a day school in Kensington. I spoke English at home. I seldom ate curry. Everyone called me Jo, which was short for Majjo, which was short for Mahjabeen. My sister, Lalla Rukh was just Lalla. I was eleven. I listened to other girls talk about fathers and brothers. I chipped in: One of my uncles—called Jim—had been to Sherborne and Oxford, too, and my father to Dartmouth. "During the war Daddy was almost captured by the Japs in Singapore," I said.

The school was haunted. I discovered this quite soon.

My newly made friends, Sarah and Lucy, said we were not allowed to talk about it because the "little ones" got really frightened. She meant the junior-most girls, to which group Lalla belonged. Mandy, who shared my bedside locker, said ghosts did not exist. But in bed, after lights, we told ghost stories. One day Cilla with the auburn hair, began: "Once upon a time, long long ago, Raynard's Wood belonged to a man with a wooden leg—"

Goosebumps ran all the way up my arm.

I knew his name: Sir Roger Allis.

"He was a bit soft in the head and didn't have any friends," said Cilla. "He thought England shouldn't fight Germany, and the British Empire was all rubbish. He had some friends in India or Africa or somewhere. They brought home this native boy. The man didn't have anyone else to talk to. He took him in and treated him like a son. Everyone said no good would come of it."

My heart was beating so loudly that it seemed to echo in my head. I knew she was talking about Uncle Jim.

"Well, he had a daughter called Fanny—"

The room was pitch black; not even a faint light seeped through the curtains opposite. I longed to cry out, to protest, but I couldn't.

"The next thing everyone knew was, this native and Fanny wanted to marry! Well! That woke the father up. He threw him out. She was very beautiful—quite The Deb of the Season. She got married in no time. But the native wasn't going to let go just like that. Oh, no. He began to meet her secretly. Her husband caught them. He divorced her for adultery."

Adultery!!

Uncle Jim and Aunt Frances had committed adultery.

"She wanted to keep her children but the judge refused, quite rightly. Daddy says it was all in the papers. It was a huge scandal. Her father blamed himself, of course. He died quite soon—on October 10. Ever since, on that day, at midnight, his ghost roams the corridors with his wooden leg going thump, thump, thump. And his voice floats across crying, "Fanny! Fanny!""

I stopped breathing. Voices and gasps washed over me.

"How terrible!"

"How awful!"

"What happened to her?"

"That's the worst part. He took her away from England to some far-off country. They didn't have proper doctors there or anything and he didn't bother with her, anyway. So she caught typhoid or cholera or some local disease and died."

I couldn't sleep.

## 2. 1952

Uncle Jim impinged himself on my consciousness when I was seven and Lalla was five. My parents in England were going through a difficult time financially. They left us with our maternal grandmother, Nani Jaan, for some months in India. She lived in Amarkot, an erstwhile princely state which had merged with India at Independence.

At first, Uncle Jim was merely one of our many relatives. The only difference was that he didn't fuss over us (which was both a relief and a disappointment) and nearly always spoke in English or an awkward Anglicized Urdu. To me, he looked quite the English gentleman in his *sola topi*, tweeds, and pipe.

One morning, dressed in my new red dungarees, I perched myself on the white balustrade with my back to the lawn. Nani Jaan was attending to the household accounts, beyond the fluted arches that divided the covered verandah from the brick terrace. Her metal-rimmed glasses were angled on her pointed nose and her gray hair was tied into a neat bun. A shawl fell over her rounded shoulders. I thought she looked quite like a fairy godmother.

There was a slight winter nip in the air. I swung my feet between the curves of sunlight and shadow created by the balustrade. I breathed in the lovely, smoky smell of peasant fires. To my right, where the verandah led away from the terrace, I glimpsed Lalla in a pink smocked dress (the one I loathed and refused to wear), half-merged with the roses in the rose garden. Our nanny, An'na Bua, was helping Lalla feed the the goldfish in the lily pond. Another maidservant shuffled past with a tray full of sweet, white, fluffy *batashas*, an offering at our private mosque beyond the guava groves.

There were signs of straggly grass and damp on the walls that caused Nani Jaan to sigh and lament the changing times, but I hardly noticed. I thought Amarkot was much nicer than living in London with its black, half-bombed buildings, drizzle, and rationing.

Suddenly, there was the loud and uneven tooting of a car horn. Uncle Jim hurtled down the drive in his shining green Bentley. Dozens of servants scurried around. I was whisked off the balustrade. Nani Jaan exclaimed in Urdu, "If he has to drink, he should stay at home. He shouldn't inflict himself on decent people."

Before I knew it Uncle Jim had maneuvered his car at an angle, pressed down the accelerator, and zoomed up all five steps, right onto the terrace! His car whirred and screeched. He drove around and around that enclosed space. He paused to wave and shout, "I've done it! I've done it! I bet a thousand rupees that I could!" He drove his car down the steps in the most terrifying manner, swung it to the left with split-second timing, and roared off toward the tall wrought-iron gates in a crunch of gravel and a cloud of dust.

In retrospect, I realize it was a rather skilled piece of driving. I don't suppose Uncle Jim was drunk at all. I picked up the servants' gossip. What did the servants mean when they whispered that Uncle Jim's wife, Shahla *Momani*, complained that he couldn't control himself when he was "in the mood"? I asked Nani Jaan. What did this have to do with the odor of whiskey? Why did this result in the servants feeling sorry for her? And what did it mean that she was fertile and had borne three sons, while his English wife, Aunty Frances, had been barren? How were children born anyway? And was it true that after Aunty Frances died he wanted to marry my mother, not Shahla *Momani*?

Nani Jaan was not in the habit of telling children half lies. Either she told the truth or she commanded them to stop pestering her. In this particular instance she summoned all the servants, admonished them in no uncertain terms, and forbade them from discussing Uncle Jim ever again.

My interest in Uncle Jim grew.

**3.**

In Amarkot, Nani Jaan knew few children for Lalla and me to play with. Her friends and family had served in HH the Nawab of Amarkot's administration, but had now been replaced by minor Indian government officials. The brutalities and the exchange of populations at Partition, the exodus of Muslims to Pakistan and the influx of Hindu and Sikh refugees meant that many of her neighbors were strangers. Two of her sons had migrated to Pakistan; her third was posted in Delhi. Uncle Jim's children and HH's were away at exclusive boarding schools in the hills.

One day, Lalla and I were playing in Nani Jaan's mango groves beyond the lawn. Our plump and bosomy An'na Bua settled under a tree, cracked her knuckles and looked on. Lalla was a beautiful, blond princess caught in a wicked witch's spell; I was the gallant tawny-haired prince battling through forests with a huge sword. Leaves rustled above my head, twigs crackled under my feet as I galloped to Lalla's rescue.

Uncle Jim was taking his evening walk. He emerged from a pathway and growled, "I am a fierce and fearful tiger. I am coming to get you!" Lalla and I squealed and giggled. We ran from tree to tree. He chased us around and around until he caught us and tickled us. "Oh, if I had a daughter, what wouldn't I do for her!" he exclaimed in accented Urdu.

"Then why do you have so many sons?" Lalla asked.

"Because it is God's will," said Uncle Jim, "unfair though God might be."

"Jim Sahib," exclaimed An'na Bua. "For the fear of God, never say such a thing!"

He laughed. He took our tiny hands in his large, strong ones and allowed us to lead him through the mango grove. We emerged by a field. A bullock was chomping grass beside a rusty well. A peasant woman in bright swirling robes collected cakes of cowdung and heaped them onto the fire outside her hut. We watched silently. Somehow Uncle Jim seemed to know that we were more fascinated by the cakes of cow dung than anything else in India.

We were torn between the temptation to pick them up (after all, the peasants did) and our polite upbringing. Lalla became restless and ran off, with An'na Bua panting behind. "Lalla *Bibi*! *Thero*! Lalla *Bibi*! Wait!"

Uncle Jim and I strolled back. I asked him the one question that had been bothering me for some time. "Uncle Jim," I said. "Why, when we like it so much here, do we have to go back to London?"

"Don't you want to go back?"

I shook my head.

"Well," he said. He lit a pipe. "The English were here for a very long time. Now they have left."

"Like Aunty Frances," I said. I knew I was venturing into forbidden territory.

"No. Aunt Frances—or Fanny as I called her—died of tuberculosis. The best doctors in India, England, and Switzerland couldn't do anything for her. There was no cure. In any case, she was my wife so she was one of us."

Uncle Jim and I walked through leafy shadows. He puffed his pipe, thought a bit, and began again.

"You see, Jo, the English ruled us for many years. Now they don't. Now we are independent. But the country has been divided. Many, many people have been killed. My sisters, your uncles, and many others, have left for the new Muslim country, Pakistan. I, like your grandmother, wish to live and die here, where I was born. Your father, on the other hand, thinks very highly of the English. He's decided to settle in England."

Somehow this did not seem a very satisfactory explanation, but I soon realized that it was all I was going to get. Besides, Uncle Jim had seen Nani Jaan approaching. He became boisterous again. He rumbled and roared like a tiger and chased me until I sought refuge in Nani Jaan's silk sari.

"Jim *Mia*, will you never grow up?" Nani Jaan said.

"Never," he declared.

"Never?" I asked. "Like Peter Pan?"

He laughed and ruffled my hair. "Yes, Jo. Like Peter Pan."

Of course this was quite wrong, I decided, because Peter Pan had only been a boy while Uncle Jim was quite grown up. He was even older than my mother and father, though he was much more fun than either of them. And he knew about Peter Pan.

**4.**

"Uncle Jim," I said. "Have you ever been to England?"

Uncle Jim gave a short laugh that made me think I had said

something very stupid. But then he smiled and said, "Yes, Jo, I've been to England."

He had invited us to tea. We hardly noticed the peeling paint and faded surfaces in his stately colonial home. In his wood-paneled study, leopard and cheetah-skin rugs lay at our feet; antlered heads gazed at us from the wall with shining glass eyes. A wood fire warmed us.

"England?" said my grandmother. "Why he was almost born in England."

"Were you?" asked Lalla.

Lalla was half swallowed up by a leather chair, her hair tightly scraped into two neat bunches, hands very white and small against the armrests.

"No," he answered. "No, I wasn't."

An elderly servant in green and white livery served crumpets, sandwiches, scones, and sponge cake in silver dishes. Uncle Jim's pallid wife, Shahla *Momani*, poured tea. Lalla and I were almost afraid of being too boisterous in her presence in case she fainted, or of bumping into her in case she fell. She seldom contributed to a conversation, unless it revolved around her misfortunes.

"If his father, the Judge Sahib, had had his way, probably he would have been born in England," said Nani Jaan. "The way he carried on, you would have thought anything Indian was a sin. He had to have English governesses, English food, English furniture. . . ."

"Then what happened?" I asked

"What do you think happened?" she said "He sent him to school in England in 1912. When he was nine."

Uncle Jim's mother, Nani Jaan, and my father's mother had all been sisters.

"Then why don't you live in England?" asked Lalla.

"Yes," Shahla *Momani* suddenly spoke up. Her small beady eyes danced; her thin bloodless lips compressed into a feline smirk. "Ask him why."

Uncle Jim didn't answer.

Instead, he took us off to his piano. His strong, manicured hands pounded and slithered rapidly over black and white keys. We sang with him, clapped our hands, and did a twirl or two.

Lalla and I began to visit him often.

Uncle Jim taught us to play chopsticks. He helped us fly kites. He sketched us. He used an easel where I, too, liked to stand and draw. He encouraged me to portray the jackals I had glimpsed near the waterfall at the far end of his garden, or the hyenas I heard after dark. He would hold my attempts up for scrutiny, pointing out minor improvements I could make. But he warned us, these were wild animals. They lived in the snake-infested vegetation and tangles beyond the shrubbery, though there had been beautiful cane fields and secluded walks there, once. The government had taken the land away from his family, after Partition, but it was too boring to explain. He showed us the water colors he had painted some years ago, of the trees and arbor and stream, as well as squirrels, flowers, and birds. Oh yes, he said, the paintings in the house of Shahla *Momani*, their sons, HH's pink palace, the bazaar, and fort, were all done by him.

Suddenly Shahla *Momani* loomed in the arched doorway. "It is six o'clock," she announced.

"Oh," said Uncle Jim. "Right. I'd better get these children home, hadn't I?" He added in a conspiratorial whisper, "Your grandmother's a stickler for time, you know."

In time, he introduced us to his favorite trophy: an enormous stuffed tiger with a fierce snarl, pointed teeth, and glistening green eyes, which stood in a large, musty billiard room. "Isn't it beautiful?" asked Uncle Jim. Lalla and I were paralyzed. How were we going to get past without being devoured?

Uncle Jim laughed.

"It's not real," he said, "look." He stroked the tiger, touched its teeth, and put his hand into its mouth. He persuaded us to do likewise.

"It's very special, you know," he said.

"Why?"

"Because it was a man-eater. It had eluded capture for many, many years, but I finally caught up with it. It had killed lots of people in the villages my father owned."

"Did it eat them, too?" I asked with held breath.

"Yes, I am afraid it did."

"Then why didn't it eat you?" Lalla asked.

I blushed at her lack of tact and discretion.

"It very nearly did," Uncle Jim answered. "Twice, when I thought I'd caught it, I discovered I had shot some harmless animal. In the end I tracked it down. I had calculated it was a little ahead of me when I almost walked into it. I saw it just in time. I stood absolutely still. It looked at me like a satisfied cat just before it sprang. I brought my gun very, very slowly into position. I shot it, and in that moment it leaped."

After that, Uncle Jim became our hero. We loved to hear about his exploits. We learned about distinguishing pug marks, the importance of wind direction, the individual habits of a tiger. Uncle Jim said the tiger was the most magnificent of animals. It stood fearless in the jungle, until men intruded into its territory with guns, elephants, and beaters, and shot it down in cold blood from a tree. Uncle Jim had vowed that once he caught up with his man-eater, he would never hunt again.

He showed us the bullet marks that had killed the tiger. He pointed out the wound and the broken teeth that had made it difficult for it to find food and had turned it into a man-eater. We played around and around the tiger—and our favorite game became Jungle Jim and the Man-eater.

## 5. 1953

"Well, Sitara, Mo. What do you think of your children? Haven't they grown up?"

Uncle Jim was among the first to greet my parents, along with Nani Jaan, Lalla, and me, that sweltering summer morning when they alighted from HH's limousine, which had motored them down from Delhi.

"You have been so kind to them, Jim *Bhai*," said my mother. My mother had had her hair cut and permed; her eyebrows were plucked into a fashionable arch; she wore bright red lipstick, as always.

Lalla hurtled toward her, but I was conscious that I was too big for that now. I flung myself on my sturdy, comforting father instead.

"Hello, Old Girl," he said and hugged me. My mother gave me a kiss on each cheek and was soon chatting away with relatives in the drawing room. I kept trying to interrupt, to show her my paintings of tigers and jackals, jasmine and double jasmine, of peasant huts, but my mother said, "Jo, can't you see I'm conversing?"

She was regaling her cousins, the Begum of Amarkot and Shahla *Momani*, with an account of the chiffon saris you could buy on Jermyn Street.

"Sitara, the child is pleased to see you," Uncle Jim interceded, "she wants a little attention."

My mother turned toward me and smiled valiantly. "Yes, Jo," her face creased in lines of concentration. "What do you want?"

I was so confused I couldn't think of anything to say. I had forgotten how we taxed her patience in London and how often, in our sparse, dark, and creaky Kensington flat, she would break down and cry, "I can't cope. Oh, I just can't cope."

The ceiling fan whirred overhead. I could hear the zap and snap of the cotton-lined bamboo blinds being unrolled by servants on the verandah outside to block the midday sun. I shuffled sideways to a space somewhere between Uncle Jim and my father. I tried to tell my father about the Man-eater.

"Man-eater?" my father said. His dark hair was slicked close to his head; his feet were planted squarely on the ground and a signet ring glistened on his finger. "What Man-eater?"

Uncle Jim was stuffing his pipe, but golden strands of

tobacco scattered on the rich blue Persian carpet. Suddenly, I was conscious of the gray that peppered Uncle Jim's hair and the lines etched on his face. Nani Jaan pressed him to stay for lunch, but he left shortly.

Nani Jaan kept telling everyone how well Uncle Jim had looked after Lalla and me.

"I don't see why that gives him license to tell them tall stories," my father said.

"Mo!" protested my mother.

"His father was a great hunter," my father rocked on his heels, his hands in his pockets, "I doubt if Jim has shot anything but a partridge."

"That's not true!" Lalla and I chorused.

I didn't want to go to England with my parents, I wanted to stay in Amarkot. I said as much the next day.

"Jim *Bhai* has really spoiled these girls," my mother said to my grandmother that afternoon. I was half-dozing beside Lalla on an old-fashioned divan with silver legs. My mother was reclining against a bolster. We were in the wide passage that divided Nani Jaan's portion of the house from the half she had decided to rent. At the far end, a matting of tall, sweet-smelling reeds, *khas ki tatti*, blocked the large window. Outside, a man sprinkled water to keep it wet. A large electric fan fitted in the center blew in the cooled air. "He loves children," Nani Jaan said. "His own don't respond to him as yours do. Shahla encourages them to scorn his English ways in the name of nationalism." I could hear the click and chop of her silver cutter as she dexterously cut betel nuts into tiny pieces.

"I don't know why you chose Shahla for him," my mother burst out.

"He said he wanted a girl with a pale skin, beautiful feet, and a mole on her chin. We were lucky we found anyone."

"He said it as a joke! He was shattered when Frances died, he didn't want to marry again."

"What difference does that make?" Nani Jaan said. "He

never had any consideration for anyone's feelings. No one in our family has married an Englishwoman—and that was bad enough, but to bring all the scandal and shame upon us! No one would receive him in England. No English official would receive him in India. He ruined his chances of joining the Indian Civil Service, which was his father's dearest wish. Can you imagine what his poor parents went through? His education, honor, everything—thrown to the winds."

"Civilized English people met him," my mother answered, "as did enlightened Indians. We all knew that if there had been any justice, he should have been allowed to marry Frances in the first place. Instead, they encouraged her to marry that awful man with his titles, horses, dogs (and an American mother's fortune), who beat her black and blue and wanted heirs, even when childbearing became a grave risk for her."

"Poor Frances," my grandmother sighed. "She was too good for this world, so kind and gentle. But if his mother wanted to find him a suitable Indian bride from our own family in Old Delhi and with the same background as us, who can blame her?"

"He was speechless when he heard you had proposed to Shahla on his behalf and her family had accepted," my mother said. "He felt honor-bound to go through with it."

"He had his eye on you."

"Of course he didn't! I was 14 or 15, just a naïve little girl to him, barely out of *parda*. He was comfortable with me, that's all, because I had been close to Frances and used to play badminton and tennis with her. Anyway, I had been betrothed to Mo since childhood."

"That would hardly have been an impediment. He had no regard for any Indian custom."

"Oh, Mother!!"

The conversation died. The afternoon wore on. My head grew heavy with the heat. I sipped cool water. Suddenly, a breathless servant charged in. "Begum Sahib, Begum Sahib, a terrible thing! A woman has been killed and eaten by a tiger near Jim Sahib's house!"

I sat up.

"Nonsense," said my mother. "There isn't a tiger within miles."

"My brother saw it," the servant took in a great gulp of air. "He heard its roar and he heard her screams. In the cane fields—that belonged to Jim Sahib once. There's a secluded stream that people visit."

"Visit?"

"They use it as a latrine," Nani Jaan explained.

My mother rang Uncle Jim. He said the tiger had escaped from a reserve thirty miles away and somehow found his way, crosscountry, to Amarkot. Oh no, Uncle Jim said, the animal was nowhere near his house, he wasn't in any danger. But his best advice was for everyone to stay put. There was utter confusion outside. People, mostly young men, had come out with sticks and stones to combat the animal. One look at the mangled woman and the sound of another roar, and they had fled. Within a few minutes the story had spread. Everyone wanted to see the tiger, they were converging on the cane fields.

"Dear God," my mother said. "What do they think it is? A fun fair? Where are the authorities? The police?"

She called my father from his room. Lalla, too, woke up. The servant wheeled in the tea trolley but no one looked at it. My father donned a *sola topi* and walked up to Nani Jaan's gate with us. Two jeeps appeared with the Chief of Police and the local MP, accompanied by HH in safari dress. HH had been at Aitcheson College in Lahore with my father. He said, "Hello, Mo, old chap. Want to join us?" My father hopped into the jeep despite my mother's protests. The jeep's loudspeaker blared: "There is a tiger in Jim Sahib's old cane fields. Do not go near. Keep away. Keep away! We have everything under control."

This had quite the opposite effect. Soon, the avenue was

crammed with people heading toward the fields. Vendors of sweet drinks, cigarette, and *paan* jostled along with the curious mob, advertising their wares with loud singsong chants. There was a distant rumble and screams. A movement of people, pushing, shoving, running. A passerby told us that the frenzied animal had leaped at the crowd and killed one more woman.

My mother returned to the house with Lalla and me. Rivulets of sweat ran down her flushed face and ours. We retreated into the dark, cool passage and gulped down iced water. Nani Jaan tried to ring Uncle Jim but the line was busy. Some of her servants slipped away to join the melee; others supplied us with bulletins. No one quite knew what was going on. We huddled next to my mother.

Someone reported that the mob had reassembled. The police had moved in with jeeps, rifles, and megaphones, asking people to clear the area. No one had budged. Instead, onetime hunters, political workers, and everyone who possessed, or could aim, a gun had turned up. Suddenly, Shahla *Momani* ran in, screeching, "*Hai! Hai*, Allah! Do something. Jim has disappeared with his rifle."

"God preserve us!" my grandmother began to pray. My mother sat there with her hands wrapped around her head saying, "Where is Mo? Where is Mo? I wish he was here."

What happened next was pieced together by conversations between grown-ups and eyewitness accounts. Uncle Jim was seen striding through the field with his gun. He pushed his way to the front of the crowd that had encircled the tall, unkept cane where the tiger had retreated. He came across some boys laying bets on whether the Chief of Police or HH would kill the animal. Apparently Uncle Jim said, "I will kill it." The boys gawked. An old family retainer crept toward him and tried to wrest the gun away. A shot rang out. The tiger sprang from its hiding place at its attacker—Uncle Jim. In that split second Uncle Jim aimed and fired. The animal sank to the ground. Half a dozen other bullets went off from all directions. The brief silence that followed was shattered by another loud bang.

Uncle Jim had shot himself in the head.

## 6. 1956

In our London house there was a photograph of Uncle Jim. He was standing under a tree with Frances outside their elegant summer home in the wooded hills of Nainital. He was looking directly at the camera with a wide, confident smile. A center parting divided his hair into two bouncy waves. The open collar of a white sports shirt clung to his neck and its tip rested casually against his cleanshaven chin. A tennis racquet dangled from his hand, almost as if it were an extension of his long, sinewy arm. Frances had an air of such fragility that it almost seemed as if, but for the small, pale hand anchored in the crook of his arm, she would have wafted away. The impression was reinforced by the gentle billow of her skirt against her knees, the fine strands of translucent, sunlit hair that had escaped from her perm and the tautness with which she held her long neck high, at a slight angle, her eyes fixed firmly on him.

I still wonder how or why it was possible that my mother, who seemed to know everything imaginable about Uncle Jim and Frances, should not have known or recognized the name, Raynard's Wood.

Of course we didn't talk much about Uncle Jim any more, but my mother was always going on about Rajas and Nawabs, Lord This or Lady That, or her ambassadorial brothers, one Indian and one Pakistani.

"What are we?" I asked her.

"We are British," she said. But whenever I said this to people, the British looked blank and Indians and Pakistanis laughed— one or two pinched my cheeks and said, "How shweet."

By this time my father's business in real estate had prospered. Our new house in Richmond was filled with light, gleaming parquet floors, and subdued colors. One day my mother declared that she could send us to "a proper school" at last. School prospectuses flooded in, but on further inquiry no school had a vacancy. One day, Lady This-That, an ex-colonial friend, suggested Raynard's Wood School and wrote a letter of recommendation. Despite this august introduction, the principal, Mrs. Fotheringay, wanted to meet us to ascertain our "standard of English" and our "ability to adapt to English ways." My mother exclaimed, "Oh really, how absurd!"

She dressed carefully and stylishly in gray, beige, and blue that icy spring morning, and we drove to Raynard's Wood. We turned into the wrought-iron gates, down a drive lined with cedars. There, before us, rose a white edifice topped with faux battlements and a central tower. My mother clasped her hands together and gasped, "Isn't it beautiful, Mo?"

A thin woman let us into a wood-paneled hall. A huge animal skull sat on a wooden chest. Hunting trophies, including antler heads, looked down at us from a great height. A tiger head was mounted and spotlit against false jungle foliage in a glass box by the marble stairs. Lalla blanched. I felt nausea rising. My father placed a soothing hand on my shoulder and took Lalla's hand. Mrs. Fotheringay, a large regal woman, sailed down the stairs toward us.

My mother seemed transfixed by a row of oil paintings, dominated by one of a slim, handsome man in the khaki uniform of the First World War. "They are rather fine portraits, aren't they?" said Mrs. Fotheringay. "That's the previous owner, Sir Roger Allis. And those are his three children, Godfrey, Hugh, and Frances, with Lady Caroline, their mother. Sir Roger sold the house to a South African businessman during the Great Depression. No one has lived here since. We found the pictures in the garage."

"How sad!" my mother said. "How sad!"

My father steered her firmly by the elbow into Mrs. Fotheringay's study. There he put on his plummiest English accent (which was too round and too pronounced to be really English) and trotted out the usual, "During the war when I served in the Royal Indian Navy," or "When I was at Dartmouth," which always seemed to break the ice with the English. My father and Mrs. Fotheringay discussed The Two Wars for some time. She showed us the Great Hall with the Allis coat of arms emblazoned above the fireplace. We saw dormitories, classrooms, common rooms. My mother kept exclaiming, "Oh, how beautiful! How beautiful!" at every vista of evergreens, bare trees, or terraced lawns as we wandered across to the tennis courts, the hockey pitch, and the swimming pool.

Mrs. Fotheringay duly indicated that there would be a vacancy for us in the autumn. My mother squeezed Lalla's hands and mine in the car and said, "Well done. You behaved impeccably." She was in a curious mood, a mixture of elation and silence. "Can you imagine, Mo, what it must have been like in the old days," she said, "when Jim *Bhai* was here?"

"At a girl's school?" I asked. "Uncle Jim?"

I could talk about him now without tears. "Of course not! Jim *Bhai* was at Sherborne. This was the family home of Aunty Frances."

### 7.

That evening my mother pulled out entire folios of Uncle Jim's watercolors and drawings from a steel trunk. My father was amazed. He had no idea that she had carted all that paper all the way from India, but even I could tell the work was really good: It was signed with Uncle Jim's real name: Zulfikar Ali. There was Frances as a young girl, wispy and blue-eyed; Frances's mother "among the first women in England who learned to fly" in goggles and baggy trousers, her elbow resting possessively on the wing of her aeroplane; Frances's gaunt father, "wounded in the First World War," propped up on crutches, not at all the proud and stately man with the shining leather boots in the portrait we had seen at Raynard's Wood. He had been "a bitter critic of the war," but "had served his country with honor and lost a leg." My mother told us that Uncle Jim had lived in England throughout "the terrible days" of the First World War. He used to spend his school holidays next door, at The Vicarage, with a family known to his in India. She showed us a watercolor of Raynard's Wood (I knew I had seen it somewhere before, she said) with that familiar building against a backdrop of blazing autumn trees. My mother said a part of it had been turned into a convalescent home. Uncle Jim and Frances, childhood friends, had helped out with first aid there. Sir Roger and Uncle Jim used to go out sketching together, with Uncle Jim pushing his wheelchair. They drew war-wounded patients too, but some were rather frightening pictures and my mother wasn't going to show us any of those. "Can't see any point in paintings like that," said my father.

My mother told us that Uncle Jim wanted to be an artist, but his father forbade it. He had done a wonderful picture of Frances with her two little girls. I looked at my blond aunt with short, shingled hair, a pearl necklace, and her two blond children. I thought that almost made me blond too, not dark, curly haired, and big-nosed.

"Oh," I said. "Does that mean I have English cousins?"

"Don't be silly, Jo!" my mother cried. "Don't be so stupid!"

"She's only a child, Sitara," my father said.

I didn't know what I had said that was so wrong.

My mother shut the folios. She said, "He gave them to me long, long ago. He said they belonged to his Old Life. He didn't want them any more."

My father ruminated: "There are still a good many people in England who remember Frances and Jim."

"Yes," my mother said. "Yes, I know what you mean." She twitched a fine, plucked eyebrow. Lalla and I knew this meant that something had to be said, or not said, to us.

"The point is," my father continued, "if you girls go around saying your aunt lived in that huge mansion, people will just think you're showing off. We don't want that, do we?"

Lalla and I shook our heads.

"Good," he said. "So there's no need to mention Jim or Frances again."

My father didn't know about the need that every English boarding school has to have a ghost, or the power of stories and images of a man with a wooden leg going thump, thump, thump along drafty corridors, crying "Fanny! Fanny!" They would be enmeshed in my nightmares and my being, along with white faux battlements and a tower, the face of a snarling tiger, a mangled woman, gunshots, the bier of Uncle Jim covered with a white cloth amid the wailing of Shahla *Momani*, my mother and Nani Jaan, crying and crying, and Lalla bawling, "But if he killed the Man-eater, why did he die?" and the silence of his ashen boys, my father, the Chief of Police, the MP—and even HH who, by tradition, had not shouldered any bier except his father's—as they carried him away from us, from me, from Lalla, forever, amid whispers that truly Jim Sahib had saved the town from a ferocious Man-eater and died a hero.

Those are the imploding dreams I try to exorcise through my paintings. As for my three dominant colors, why do people ask? Isn't it obvious? Red for blood, white for blindness, blue for sorrow.

# A FAIR
# EXCHANGE

৪৩

# *Tahira Naqvi*

Tahira Naqvi (1945– ) grew up in
Lahore and was educated at the
Convent of Jesus and Mary, Karachi, Lahore College, and Government College, Karachi. In 1972, she
moved to the United States with her
husband and earned her masters at
Western Connecticut State University. She taught English for twenty
years, then Urdu at Columbia University and now New York University. She is known for her English

translations of the works of Ismat Chughtai, including *Tehri Lakeer* (*The Crooked Line*) (Women Unlimited, 1995; The Feminist Press, 2006) and *Ajeeb Aadmi* (*A Very Strange Man*) (Women Unlimited, 2007). She has also translated Urdu stories by the Pakistani woman writer Khadija Mastur, which were published in *Cool, Sweet Water* (Oxford University Press, 1999). Naqvi is currently working on another Mastur collection. Naqvi has just finished her own English-language novel set in Pakistan, as are many of the stories in her two collections, *Attar of Roses and Other Stories of Pakistan* (Lynn Reinner, 1997) and *Dying in a Strange Country* (TSAR, 2001).

"A Fair Exchange" evolved from a true story that Naqvi heard in the 1970s, "of a woman who made a *mannat* [a religious vow that entails self sacrifice] like this and then fulfilled it, forcing her husband to marry the maidservant." However, Naqvi's story developed its own trajectory. She says, "I don't like seeing female characters give in without a fight, and sometimes I want them to openly rebel. Hence the change in plot, the twist at the end. The story encompasses so many of the ideas inherent in our society." Naqvi brings out the great social importance that is attached to marriage and provides a fascinating insight into a woman's sexuality and her inability to confront her suppressed desires, which would be considered shocking, disruptive, and self indulgent by the community. Naqvi explores the crisis and confusion that lead Mariam to offer her maidservant Jeena to her husband, and then change her mind. Mariam's subsequent resolve to find Jeena a suitable husband of a higher social status instead and provide her with a generous trousseau reveals the widespread belief (reinforced by the *maulvi* in Naqvi's story) that for rich people to arrange and finance suitable marriages for poor girls is an act of great charity and piety.

Mariam's first dream introduces the traditional power of a mother-in-law and the powerlessness of the bride's mother (and thus the bride) in a marriage. Red, the traditional color of bridal attire, is also a symbol of fertility; gold and bangles are also marital symbols but in Mariam's dreams they merge with images of a black trunk (a coffin) and graying hair.

In mentioning the border town of Sialkot, Naqvi brings to the fore a strategic place where Pakistani troops amassed during the two major wars that India and Pakistan fought against each other in 1965 and 1971. Naqvi provides a precise date for her story with the reference to the famous singer Noor Jehan and her patriotic songs, extolling the country's heroic soldiers that were broadcast in 1965.

• • •

Mariam was beset by ominous dreams.

In one she wore a red, heavily embroidered suit and moved among a throng of women. Some of them, dressed in glittering finery, were relatives, others wore faces that seemed familiar but remained nameless. Mariam spotted her husband's mother, dead for three years now, her hawk-like eyes darting back and forth as if in eager search of prey, and crouching in a corner, not far from where her sister-in-law sat chewing betel leaf like a cow, she could see her own mother who, much as she did in real life, had tried to make herself unobtrusive in the shadows.

In another dream that followed on the heels of the first, someone came up from behind and threw a *dupatta* over Mariam's head while she was going through clothes in a large, black trunk that did not appear to belong to her, and which seemed to contain newly stitched clothing—everything neatly folded, the gold embroidery on the garments shining like a trail of glitter on a bride's hair. She couldn't determine the identity of the person who had surprised her from behind, nor could she make out the exact shade of the *dupatta* even though she could see it clearly in the dream.

The most disturbing of all her dreams was the one in which she saw herself as a bride. Looking resplendent in a dark red *gharara* suit that could easily have come out of the unidentified black trunk in her other dream, she heard the jangling of shimmering gold and glass bangles on her wrists and saw garlands of crimson roses and pale-white *chameli* buds adorning her long plait. The worst of it was that her hair appeared in the same state as it was now, streaked lightly with gray, dry and thin, not at all as it had been ten years ago when she was a new bride.

Mariam knew better than to be fooled by these dreams. Aware that they were not what they seemed, she had little doubt in her mind that they spelled some dreadful misfortune about to befall her. When she awoke from seeing herself as a bride and remembered the details of the wedding scene, she shivered with fear. Quickly she recited the *Ayat-ul-Kursi*, the verse most apt for warding off evil and misfortune. As she came to the end of her recitation her eyes fell on the emptiness of the bed next to hers. In the half-darkness of the room the white bedsheet took on a ghostly aspect and Mariam felt a tremor rack her lean frame once again. The bed had been empty since her husband left for the front six months before. The war with India had escalated. Every day fatalities were reported on the radio, every day young women were waking up to find themselves widows. Turning away from the bed that had suddenly presented itself to her as an apparition, Mariam again murmured the words of the *Ayat-ul-Kursi* under her breath.

Was her husband's life in danger?

A few minutes later she rose and, walking over to the children's beds, bent down to peer closely at the faces of her son and daughter. Now that her husband was not at home she had brought their beds into her own room. The children had slept in their parents' bedroom till Razia was six. That was when Mariam's husband insisted that she and her brother be moved to the small room adjoining theirs. Mariam was uncomfortable with this arrangement. To her husband she expressed concern about the children waking up in the middle of the night, scared. In her heart she knew their presence in the bedroom was to her advantage since it made it difficult for her husband to come to her bed whenever he wished.

Her husband did not know of her reticence. Not once had she made a display of her real feelings when he silently came to her in the stillness of the night, touched her, stroked her breasts, placed his weight upon her. Her eyes shut tightly, she would take her mind elsewhere, to the kitchen, to the children's room, in a place where she would be standing alone under a clear, star-studded heaven. Bound by ties of devotion to her husband, she conceded him every privilege; she submitted to his nightly embraces, never allowing him to guess how something inside her grew cold at his touch, never allowing her love and devotion to be affected by these feelings, which were only natural for a woman, she was sure.

The children's presence had helped the subterfuge. However, her protests went unheeded and the children stayed in their own room. Now they were in her room again.

Holding her breath, Mariam listened intently to the sound of their breathing. Then, certain that they had not come to any harm, she adjusted their blankets and moved toward the door of her room. Once or twice in the past her husband had awakened to the sound of her bed creaking and, having followed her to the children's room, had caught her with her ear to the children's faces. Alarmed the first time that had happened, he came over hastily and was annoyed to discover that Mariam was just checking to see "if they are alive." Shaking her, he had propelled her back to their bedroom, mumbling that she allowed morbid reflections to rule her life.

Slowly Mariam made her way out of the room and, crossing the entire length of the silent courtyard, approached the water pots against the west wall of the room that had belonged to her mother-in-law when she was alive. The June night was warm and muggy.

There was no breeze, no rustling of leaves. The sky was the color of a faded blue *dupatta* that has seen innumerable washings, and stars glimmered sharply as though cut out of silver tinsel. Mariam picked up the wooden ladle from the mouth of the earthen waterpot, dipped it in, and swished it about a few times before drawing out the water.

Where was her husband now? she wondered idly as she raised the ladle to her mouth and drank. All she knew was that he was on the Sialkot border, very close to enemy guns. Was he inside a trench, or tending to wounds in a makeshift hospital unit? Did he find time to say all five prayers, or even one? As a rule he never missed a prayer. When he was at his clinic, besieged with patients, and the time for *namaz* came around he excused himself if the problem wasn't life-threatening, and if he couldn't get away he said all the missed prayers together, later. But this was war. He probably didn't even have time for the missed prayers.

She splashed the remainder of the water over her face, the cooling moisture dripping onto her shirtfront, and looked up at the sky again. A shooting star, like the tail end of a small firecracker, streaked across the sky and disappeared as if never there. My God, what do you want of me? Mariam whispered, her gaze held upward still. She desperately sought an answer.

There wasn't any doubt in her mind that her prayers were not adequate. Something else was required of her. A sacrifice perhaps, but not just an ordinary one, for she had already had a goat slaughtered last week to counteract the first bad dream that had plagued her. And she had also made up for the six days of fasting she had missed during the month of Ramazan on account of her periods. The hundred rupees and the three suits she gave away to her sweeper for her daughter's wedding didn't have the desired effect, either. The dreams continued unabated. God wanted something more from her in exchange for her husband's life. But what?

Back in her room she picked up her prayer beads and began to recite the *Surah-al-Hamd*. Carefully and with precision she let a bead slip from her fingers with every recitation, her eyes closed as she got into bed and leaned against the pillows. "I begin in the name of Allah who is most merciful and beneficent/Praise be to Allah. . . ." Wide awake with the first noisy chirping of birds, Mariam sat up in bed and tried to remember if there had been another dream. At first nothing presented itself to her. The morning light seemed to have dissipated whatever feelings of gloom nighttime fantasy had filled her with. Then, as she struggled to get out of bed, her newest dream spilled out in its entirety. Like water gushing out from a shattered earthen pot.

She was a bride again. But this time her mother-in-law was asking for the ring on her right hand. This was the ring Mariam's husband had given her on their wedding night. Mariam gripped her head with both hands. Gifts from the deceased are welcome, indeed they are good omens. But a solicitation from one who dwells in the beyond augurs the most dreadful of possibilities. The woman, bless her soul, was asking for her son! No doubt she was lonely without him. In life she had begrudged Mariam her time with him, and surely in death she was tormented by envy as well.

Had she given the ring? A cloud of fuzziness enveloped that part of the dream. She remembered fingering it, thinking, This is too precious to give away. May God forgive her! What was she to do? She rose from her bed, washed, and said her prayers as usual. But again and again her mind drifted to the dream and she couldn't concentrate on the words of the *namaz*. Afterward she sat back on the prayer mat and, pushing everything out of her mind, shutting her eyes tightly, she said: *Allah, what must I do to ensure the safety of my husband? Ask me for anything, I will give without hesitation.* Having asked the question, she waited, straining with all the intensity she could muster, her body trembling as if it were a reed in the wind. "Mariam *Apa*, we're out of tea, could you give me some from the storeroom?" Jeena stuck her head through the bamboo jalousie on the door.

Jeena was the young woman who helped with the housework, did some cooking, washed everyone's clothes, and scrubbed pots and pans after every meal. An orphan from Mariam's mother's village, she was a girl of ten when she had first come to live in their house as a young ayah for Mariam's newborn daughter. Now she was twenty. Since Mariam and her husband were all the family she had, it was up to them to find her a suitable husband and be responsible for the expenses incurred at her wedding.

Her beads still dangling from the fingers of her right hand, Mariam silently nodded. She would have to continue this later, she decided. "I'll be there," she told Jeena and, bending over, began folding the prayer mat toward herself.

It would have to be something as precious as her husband's life, a fair exchange, Mariam mused as she poured hot, steamy milk into Ahmer's glass.

"It's hot!" her son wailed, the words muffled by the mouthful of *paratha* he was chewing.

"It will cool off in a minute," Mariam said, absently patting six-year-old Ahmer's head. Was it something she would have to relinquish?

"Amma, I don't want milk today," Razia mumbled.

"Drink, drink, don't make a fuss." Something so dear to her, giving it away would be the hardest thing she had ever done. "And be careful, don't spill." Her life?

"Ohhh . . ." Razia whined.

"Shshsh, don't act like a baby, Razia, you're setting a bad example to your brother." No, that couldn't be—her life was for her children, they couldn't be deprived. What then?

"Mariam *Apa*, shall I bring your tea now?" Jeena's voice broke into her thoughts. The young woman stood by the stove, one hand poised expectantly over the teapot.

"Yes, Jeena, and make sure it's really hot." Mariam looked at Jeena as she poured tea into a cup for her mistress. The luminescence on the red, green, and gold bangles on her slim, dark wrists glimmered tremulously. Like the disturbed reflection of light on water. A strand of sleek, black hair had fallen over one ruddy cheek and caressed it lovingly. When the young girl bent down to retrieve a spoon that had slipped from her hands to the floor, Mariam was astonished to see how her breasts swelled. Strange that she had not noticed the fullness before, or the young girl's skin that was smooth like a baby's and shone like burnished gold, or even her long-fingered hands, which worked with such artful agility around the stove.

She should be married soon, Mariam told herself. An unmarried woman in the fullness of youth is like a cow let loose in a pasture; there's no telling where she might wander off to and with whom. Jeena handed her her tea. "Would you like some *paratha*, too? I can make it in two minutes, the pan is still hot."

"No, the tea is all I want, Jeena." Something that is difficult to surrender, to give up, Mariam thought, cautiously taking a sip of the scalding hot tea.

The sun had already begun to broadly streak the floor of the verandah when the children left for school. Mariam stood at the front door and watched them through the opening in the screen as they half-ran and skipped down the gulley. Ghulam Din, the old caretaker who accompanied them to school, tried to keep pace as fast as his wobbly legs would carry him. On a shop radio in the street outside, the singer Noor Jehan's voice rose in a deep, resonant lilt. *"O chivalrous young men of the nation/ My songs are for you alone."* The morning began with patriotic songs these days and then came the news with special bulletins that made even the strongest hearts flutter in apprehension. Mariam closed the door when, coming to the end of the lane, the children turned a corner and disappeared from view.

In the kitchen Jeena was waiting for her, the spinach for the midday meal, broad-leaved and thickly veined, washed and ready for chopping. Mariam would dole out portions of ghee and spices in appropriate measures, Jeena would sauté the onions and brown the beef, and Mariam would take over from there. The two women always followed the same ritual.

When Mariam handed Jeena the plate in which she had placed tiny heaps of ground red chilli and golden yellow turmeric, along with several cloves of garlic and a knotted clump of ginger root, she glanced at the woman's face again. How dark her eyes were. Almond-shaped, bordered by thick, sooty-black lashes that gave them a sleepy look. Dressed in clean, well-starched clothes, her hair combed neatly into a plait, Jeena looked nothing like a servant. In fact, she could easily be mistaken for a member of the family by a stranger who walked into the house without warning.

"Be sure to grind this properly, don't leave any lumps."

"Yes, Mariam *Apa*."

That night Mariam slept fitfully. If she dreamed, the dreams remained lost in her unconscious because she couldn't remember anything when she was awakened suddenly by a feeling of being weighed down. As if a large blanket had been thrown over her. Gasping for air she sat up in bed, her heart pounding in her chest like a bird darting against the walls of its cage, seeking release. After a few seconds she began reciting the *Ayat-ul-Kursi* with desperate, urgent force, unmindful of the sleeping children who might be disturbed by the loudness of her recitation.

A half hour later, still reciting, but calmer, she pulled off the prayer mat from the back of the chair next to her. This was no time for a regular *namaz* but she had to pray, she had to find an answer, and her bed wasn't the place for it.

*Allah*, she pleaded, *what do you want?*

The quietude of the night was broken only by the sound of her children's soft, rhythmic breathing. Not even a dog barked anywhere. The silence seemed to grow heavier until it became a curtain before her eyes, thick and unrelenting. She thought of her husband, tried to picture him in a ward, or in the field with a wounded soldier, his face dusty and ashen, his hands bloody as he cleaned a wound. He seemed too far away, too distant. Mariam's heart lurched with fear.

Was she wasting precious time?

*Allah*, she whispered, hot tears running down her cheeks, burning her skin as her purpose yawned before her like the sudden darkening of a stormy sky, *I'll do what you want, I vow, I pledge.*

૪૦

In the last week of October, just when summer was edging its way out, four months after Mariam had made her vow and begun her spell of unfettered, carefree sleep, her husband returned from the front. The war had ended. The danger had passed.

On the day of his return, Mariam made several attempts to bring up the subject of her vow. It wasn't easy. The children were eager to talk to their father, there was all that mail that had accumulated, and also a steady stream of visitors to inquire about the doctor's well-being and congratulate him on his safe return—husband and wife were afforded little chance to be alone for any length of time.

When he came to her bed at night she knew this was no time to talk of serious matters. But later she wished she had broached the subject then. Unable to help herself, she placed her arms on his back as he lay on top of her, felt the tautness between his shoulder blades, and a feeling stirred inside her that she had never known before. His warm skin responded to her touch. Shame engulfed her and reticence tangled her in a web, but her blood raced as if it were a torrent. Her heart beat violently, wildly. She forgot what it was to be shy. Her skin tingled, her arms tightened around her husband's body. The warmth between her legs filled her with strange pleasure and her mouth opened in a moan. She forgot she did not like to be visited in the night by her husband, that she had always allowed it only because it was something that he seemed to need and want.

All those feelings of revulsion that she struggled with when he touched her in the dark vanished. Tonight the world was shut out, and everything else with it. A few days of waiting would cause no harm, she told herself the next morning.

The second night and the one after that, Mariam lay in her husband's arms and banished the vow from her mind. On the third night, some time after she had fallen into a deep and tranquil sleep, the dreams returned. They unfolded simultaneously, all of them mixed up this time, as if some essential component that had kept them in sequence were missing. At the end came a new dream in which her mother-in-law was pulling Mariam's ring from her finger, and the two women tugged and pushed until the ring came off and disappeared into the voluminous folds of Mariam's dark red bridal *dupatta*. There was more, much more, but on waking this was all Mariam could remember. Her heart sank. What had she done?

"I made a *mannat* when you were away," Mariam began tremulously the next morning. "I was so afraid something . . . something terrible might happen." Mariam addressed her husband while he was tying his shoelaces and she couldn't see his face. There wasn't much time. He would be leaving for the hospital soon.

"Oh? What was it? Why didn't you take care of it already? You know one shouldn't delay these things." He straightened and looked at her.

Mariam hesitated. Would he think less of her when she told him?

"There was no other choice, there were such bad dreams," she murmured, turning away from his stare to smooth the wrinkles in the bedsheet.

"You're always paying too much attention to dreams. Anyway, what is it?" He stood up and adjusted his tie.

"I'm to give you Jeena." The words fell out. Like saliva that's been kept in the mouth too long.

Mariam's husband stopped what he was doing. His face darkened. A frown gathered on his forehead.

"Are you mad, Mariam?" He glared at her as if she had surprised him with disobedience.

Her chest constricted. Her ears vibrated with echoes that sounded like jumbled screams. "The dreams wouldn't give me any peace, the danger was lurking in the shadows, it had to be something that was difficult to surrender, what's a sacrifice that doesn't hurt?" Mariam blurted out the sentences hurriedly. She was on the other side of the bed, a pillow held tightly against her chest. "Islam allows more than one marriage, doesn't it? I'll give my permission." Her voice cracked.

"I don't want your permission," her husband thundered. "You are not seriously suggesting that I marry . . . this girl." He sat down, the muscles on his face quivering in anger. "You are definitely mad. I go away for a few months and this is how you conduct yourself!"

"You cannot say no, it's a *mannat*, it's a question of your life. I don't mind, I really don't mind, and Jeena . . . well, she's like a younger sister and she's pretty and I'll be here as well, I'm not going anywhere . . ." She edged forward like a beggar, her hands extended, her tone pleading.

"Be quiet, Mariam, be quiet this minute! I don't want to hear another word. I'm late for work, and when I return I don't want to hear any more of this nonsense." He raised a finger in warning, scolding her as if she were a child.

What she could do, she had done. Was it her fault that her husband would not relent? In the days that followed Mariam did not talk of Jeena or her *mannat* and was relieved that her husband did not either, although he seemed somewhat pensive, somewhat quieter than usual. He is just recuperating from the experience at the front, Mariam told herself. It takes time to forget the horrors of war.

She noticed that sometimes when Jeena removed the dishes from the table or was helping Razia or Ahmer with their clothes in the morning, her husband glanced at the girl as if seeing her for the first time. As if she were a stranger in their house. Mariam caught a look in his eyes that she couldn't understand. She blamed herself. She had made her husband uncomfortable by mentioning the *mannat* to him. He was only looking at the young woman to see what his wife had been thinking, and why. Perhaps he wished to understand Mariam's motives.

Once, when Jeena bent down to tie Ahmer's shoelaces and her *dupatta* slipped from her shoulders, the fullness at her shirt-front was revealed and, just then, Mariam became aware that her husband had seen it too. Quickly, he looked away and Jeena straightened up and adjusted her *dupatta*, all in the matter of a few moments, but Mariam realized she had to redeem her pledge, the *mannat*. The dreams were gone, at least for now, but Mariam was not so foolish as to let the *mannat* go unheeded. Without offering specific details, stressing that due to unforeseen circumstances the vow could not be executed as pledged, she consulted the *maulvi* sahib who came to instruct the children in the reading of the Quran. Stroking his beard thoughtfully, his eyes lowered in deference to a woman's presence, he listened patiently as Mariam outlined the details of her dilemma.

"Such vows should not be undertaken lightly," he admonished gently, "but Allah understands."

He put Mariam's mind at ease. Give money to a needy person or perform another act of charity, making sure it is a fair exchange, he explained. Mariam already knew that was what she should have done, but receiving the *maulvi* sahib's approval made her feel better. And she also knew what that act of charity was to be.

"We should think of Jeena's marriage," she informed her husband one night, a week after her conversation with the *maulvi* sahib. He had just eaten dinner and was getting ready to say his nighttime prayers.

At first he looked up in alarm, perhaps suspecting that she was planning to bring up the *mannat* again.

"She's old enough and too much of a responsibility," Mariam continued, ignoring the expression of disquiet on her husband's face.

"Hmm," he mumbled.

"Ghulam Din's son has a job as a clerk in the telephone department. He's educated and I've seen him, he's not at all bad to look at. I know our old caretaker will be happy that we're approaching him for his son. He knows we'll give Jeena a good dowry." Mariam spoke with authority, as if Jeena were indeed her younger sister and hence her responsibility.

Mariam's husband had no objections. Why should he? Her

spirits lifted, Mariam began making arrangements soon thereafter. She had already spoken to the old caretaker, he had humbly and joyfully expressed his gratitude. True, his son was an educated boy, a clerk in an office, yet he would never have found a girl like Jeena who, even though she was a servant in this household, was nevertheless treated as a member of the family. No doubt this connection with a family of such high status would continue even after she was married. And she was young and beautiful. He brought the groom-to-be to meet Mariam's husband, who seemed satisfied after his interview with the young man. What was most important was that the young man had a government job and would also receive living accommodation once he was married. A wedding date was immediately agreed upon.

In addition to the five suits that Mariam specially had embroidered in gold thread and sequins for Jeena, she rummaged through her own things and brought out a dark red brocade suit that was too heavily ornamented with gilded trimmings and sequined designs for her own use, and added that to the young woman's dowry. The bridal *dupatta* that went with it was heavy with shimmering gold-and-silver-tasseled edging on all four sides. That, she decided, would be Jeena's wedding suit. She bought her a gold necklace and earrings, a lightweight set, but one that gave the impression of being heavy because of the way the design had been wrought. Jeena helped with embroidering tablecloths, bedsheets, and pillowcases, and stitched all of her own clothes herself on Mariam's sewing machine with Mariam's guidance at every step. There was no skimping on Mariam's part. She was no fool. Pledges made to Allah could not be taken lightly.

A week after Jeena's wedding, on a night that Mariam had slept in her husband's arms longer than any other night she could remember, the dreams, each one clearer and more disturbing than the one before it, returned.

# DAUGHTERS
# OF AAI

ও

# *Fahmida Riaz*

Fahmida Riaz (1946–  ) was born
in Meerut into a literary family that
migrated to Hyderabad, Pakistan,
at Partition where she learned Sindhi, Persian, Urdu, and English.
She earned her masters degree from
Sindh University.

Riaz is a distinguished Urdu
poet, feminist, and human rights
activist. To date, no woman writer
in Pakistani English literature has
written either poetry or fiction with

a voice as powerful, fierce, and outspoken as Riaz. The recipient of the 1997 Hammett-Hellman Award from Human Rights Watch, she has published many collections of poetry and prose; including *Badan Dareedah* (Maktaba-e-Danyal, 1973), which was Pakistan's first book of feminist poetry and forged new directions in women's writing in Pakistan. Her use of the feminine gender for a poetry form that was usually written in the male gender caused a furor, and Riaz was accused of publishing eroticism.

In the 1980s Riaz was persecuted by the military regime of General Zia-ul-Haq, which led to many years of political exile in New Delhi. Here she began writing an English novel because she felt cut off from Pakistan's familiar Urdu milieu. Later she developed and published extracts of the novel as English short stories.

The English translations of Riaz's work include a poetry collection, *Four Walls and A Veil* (Oxford University Press, 2004) and her famous trilogy of autobiographical novels, *Zinda Bahar Lane* (City Press, 2000), *Reflections in a Cracked Mirror* (City Press, 2001), and *Godavari* (Oxford University Press, 2008), all translated by Aquila Ismail; Riaz has recently translated the poetry of Jalaluddin Rumi into Urdu. Riaz lives in Karachi, runs a feminist publishing house, WADA, and occasionally writes fiction in English.

In "Daughters of Aai," a story told to her by her sister, Riaz explores a disturbing, worldwide, and little-discussed issue: the sexual exploitation of the mentally challenged. However, Riaz's tale, set within the sociocultural context of rural Pakistan, assumes its own dynamics. Contrary to popular myths of cloistered, helpless women she describes a "typical village" where women retain a strong sense of gender and self, despite the patriarchal system within which they live. Her reference to the women's *chunri* head coverings, gauzy materials with vivid patterns created by them with an age-old tie-dye technique, hints at their inherent creativity. The contrast between female ingenuity and male notions of what is permissible or not runs through the story.

Riaz juxtaposes the lack of modern institutional support, training, and facilities for the mentally challenged Fatima—and the sexual threat to her—against the act of great love and faith that enables Aai and the village women to find refuge in ancient superstitions and create a space and shelter for the innocent and the guileless who do not conform to society's norms. Riaz also explores Muslim laws of inheritance and the mandatory *iddat*, the prescribed months of seclusion that a widow must observe immediately after the *Qul*, the final funeral prayer, has been read on the third day of her husband's death. The *iddat* ensures that if the widow is carrying a child, no one can dispute paternity, but in Riaz's hands, this seclusion leads to quite a different twist. The reference to Tolstoy transposes Riaz's story, across the centuries, from the culture specific to the universal, because Tolstoy belonged to a similar feudal, patriarchal society and through the translations of his work, influenced many literatures, including Urdu.

• • •

There they sat weeping, their heads buried in their knees, sometimes glancing at me with bloodshot eyes.

They were sitting in my courtyard, the women of her village and Aai. Her daughter wasn't there, it would have been difficult to bring her. Perhaps she was in hospital, perhaps in a mental asylum. Even if she were still at home, it was difficult to bring her all the way to Karachi. She was pregnant again.

The village women had come to seek assistance from me. They sat on the floor gazing at me wildly. Their heads were covered with green, blue, orange tie-dye *chunries*. We sat gazing at one another: me, looking at their dark feet, their thick silver anklets, arms full of clinking glass bangles, and the glimmering, glinting nose-pins and heavy nose-rings.

"Why are you weeping?" I wanted to ask. "Is it only for Aai's daughter that you cry?"

"What do you mean?" My sister, Shahbano, was wide-eyed, puzzled.

Aai bit her lips and wrung her rough hands. She worked at Shahbano's house. My sister was married to a landowner. She lived in the farmhouse, surrounded by mango orchards, by the Asthla Canal. Beyond its tranquil cool waters, as far as the eye could see, stretched green fields. The colorful huts of these peasant women were scattered on the canal bank.

Aai lived in one of those huts. How old was she? No one could tell. Could be 35 or 40. Not a wrinkle on her smooth fair face. Slim and tall, with tight round breasts jutting out of her kurta. Hard physical labor had kept her fit. Her husband was a drug addict and did very little. Theirs was a typical village when, in the months between sowing and harvesting, all the hard labor was done by women. Once when Shahbano had taken me for a walk through the fields, I had been amazed at the sight of all the men relaxing on their cots. I exclaimed, "These men, what kind of work do they do?"

A woman, her bangles chiming on her wrist as she balanced a large bundle of dry twigs on her head, said, "Madam, the men halal the chickens."

They all burst out laughing. I too had laughed. How could I forget! It always took a man to say, "*Allah-u-Akbar*," to decapitate a chicken or goat, to make the meat halal. Women could not perform this important religious task.

Aai had seven children. Her eldest daughter was severely handicapped mentally, the rest, simply malnourished. What cruel tricks fate plays: a female child and mentally handicapped! Fatimah was a beauty, growing up so fast the hand-me-downs from the landlord's house could hardly keep up with her filled-out curves.

Fatimah could not speak; she could only mumble like an infant. If you saw her you would never think that this village beauty was not like any other young girl. But when she walked you noticed the disharmony in her movements. She veered and lurched, vacantly smiling, spit dribbling from the corner of her full red mouth.

When she was fourteen Fatimah began to menstruate. Aai and the other village women tried to teach her to use cotton pads, but she only laughed and tried to play with them. Aai wept bitterly. The village women shared her grief. They made it their collective responsibility to cope with Fatimah at her time of the month. They couldn't let her wander around in that state. The men would see her soiled clothes: They would laugh their obscene laughter, point to her, and look at other women meaningfully. This would humiliate all of them. Since all the women went out to work seven days a week, the one working closest to Aai's hut would take Fatimah inside and change the cotton pad as she would an infant's nappy.

(What dirty, disgusting details! But I remember what Leo Tolstoy says in one of his essays. "Write down everything, however shameful, however painful, because it is all worth writing about." But Tolstoy was not a woman, otherwise he would have known better.)

Between Shahbano's house and Aai's hut wild reeds grow in abundance. Aai would leave her children to play there and cross the reeds to come to work. One day she came weeping and told my sister, "Fatimah is pregnant."

"Who did it? When did it happen?" Shahbano was shocked and in tears. She slipped out of her house and went to see Fatimah. Several village women had gathered in that modest dwelling. All aghast, whispering quietly.

Aai had beaten Fatimah mercilessly, questioning her, "Who was he? Who did this?" The village women were caressing Fatimah's bruises, rubbing hot mustard oil and turmeric on her swollen limbs, and weeping, weeping quietly.

Fatimah mumbled and smiled.

It was decided quietly that the pregnancy be aborted at once. Aai took a week's leave and went to the next village with Fatimah to pray at the shrine of a saint—this is what they told the men in the village: It was important that they not have an inkling of the catastrophe that had befallen Fatimah. It would be a matter of their honor. They would come out with their axes and there would be several murders. The last time an illegitimate pregnancy was discovered here, two clans had fought for a year. There were several killings, leaving behind widows and orphans and prolonged court cases that had drained the last rupee from the village.

Aai came back with Fatimah after the abortion.

"Madam, please send her to an orphanage," she wept and pleaded with Shahbano.

My sister kept visiting me in Karachi, insisting, "*Baji*, you are a writer and so many people know you. Send her to the right institution where she will be safe."

I held my head in my hands. Yes, I am a writer. I also know a few things about these institutions. "Where?" I would ask. It is well known that women in such institutions are sent out for prostitution. Normal women! And she, this unfortunate mentally handicapped girl! How would I guarantee her safety from sexual abuse?

The village women prayed. They prayed to Almighty God for a place, any corner in the world where a mentally handicapped girl who cannot speak would be safe from rape. In this great creation of the Almighty they needed men who, when they saw a beautiful, young, mentally handicapped woman in a lonely place, would not begin to lust after her body or use the first opportunity to drag her into the reed grove to satisfy a passing whim, who would look at her with compassion, would lovingly feed her, give her clay toys to play with, would hold her hand, cross the reed grove, bring her safely home—and leave.

In this great wilderness, where were those men? *Ya* Allah! Where were they? Or did You, in Your great wisdom, forget to make them?

Not a year had passed and here they were again, the village women—sitting in my courtyard. Fatu was pregnant again.

Dear God! Who was this monster? He satisfied his lust with this helpless creature and did not care a whit for the consequences. After all, did her child not have his genes, his *nutfa*? What could we do now?

"Another abortion?"

"It is too late. . . . She is perhaps seven months gone by now."

"Why didn't you do something earlier?"

"We never found out. Her time of the month has been irregular since the abortion. She wears such loose, big clothes. She was vomiting a few months back. We thought it was a stomach upset. Everyone had gastroenteritis in the village. The water is so polluted."

Aai wept inconsolably.

"If the child is born how will we bring it up? The whole village will inquire about the father."

"After the first abortion, why didn't you take her to the family planning lady? She visits the village once in a while."

"I did," said Aai. "Unmarried women are not operated upon. It is illegal."

Shahbano was wiping her tears as she told me, "The administrator in the mental asylum agreed to take her but on the condition that she would first have an abortion—even though she is seven months—and an operation to end all chances of future pregnancies. They said they simply could not afford the nuisance of childbirth inside the hospital."

I sat there, trying to hold back my own tears.

Aai began to slap herself and beat her breast, screaming, "Why does she not die! Why? I will kill her myself."

The village women were startled. They held Aai's flailing arms. One of them said, "Don't talk nonsense. Why hurt Fatu? She is sinless. She is above this world of sin and dirt. God has cast His holy shadow over her. Let the child come. We shall see."

Surrounded by the women, Aai went back to her village.

I kept pondering over what those women had said. In their artless innocence and ancient vision, they regarded Fatimah as pure and holy. She was holy and pregnant.

What my sister later told me was like a Hindi film story. She said that it was during this period that a big landlord in another district happened to die. A year before his death, Noor Mohammad Shah had taken a second wife, a young girl from a poor family of his tenant farmer. No sooner was the recitation of the *Qul* over on the *Soyem* of Noor Mohammad, than his sons and his first wife began plotting to throw the second wife, Mumtaz Begum, out of the house.

Noor Mohammad's lands and houses were to be divided among the family, but to deny Mumtaz Begum her inheritance they claimed that her marriage was never solemnized: She was merely the landlord's mistress. Mumtaz Begum's only hope lay in having a child by Noor Mohammad. She had to observe four months and ten days in isolation as *iddat*; her late husband's first wife and family hardly ever saw her. In sheer desperation, Mumtaz Begum (whom everyone called Mummo) pretended to be pregnant and shocked her stepsons into silence. It was then that she heard of an unwanted pregnancy in Shahbano's village, from a woman whose daughter was married to a man of her clan, who lived in Noor Mohammad's village and worked as the driver of her Toyota Corolla. Mummo saw Fatu's plight as a ray of hope. She sent an urgent secret message to Aai to wait for her.

After her *iddat* was over, Mummo drove down to Shahbano's village with her mother and elder brother. They had Mummo's name registered in the maternity home of a nearby town and rented a flat for their family and for Fatu. For the last two months of her pregnancy, Fatu was treated like a princess. She was given the best food and drinks and was very well looked after. When the child was born, a baby boy, Mummo brought Fatu back to Aai and whisked away the baby, protected by a birth certificate from the maternity home that said in a quaint scroll, "Son of Noor Mohammad Shah and Begum Mumtaz."

"Incredible!" I exclaimed when I heard the whole story.

"Yes," said Shahbano. "Life is stranger than fiction in our village."

"Did the village women know about this contrivance?" I asked.

"Yes," Shahbano laughed. "Many were active collaborators. They had to explain Fatu's sudden departure and reappearance in the village."

The village women did not abandon Fatu. When she returned from the town she was much weakened and her breasts ached horribly. They fomented her breasts and declared to all and sundry that she had been possessed by a Djinn and was a Holy Woman. They built a seat of bricks and cement for her to sit on by the village well under an old banyan tree. Now Fatu sits there all day, leaning against soft pillows, surrounded by children and visiting men and women, who come to her for solace and blessings. They bring her food and leave coins and rupee notes for her in a tin cup embedded in the ground. Fatu plays with the coins sometimes, but sometimes she gets tired of sitting and tries to walk away. The women gently bring her back again. When she has to go to the fields, one woman leads her there, washes her, and brings her back to her seat. By sunset Aai returns and takes her home along with the *nazrana*—the offering—jingling in the cup.

"So the village women are pretending that she is possessed by the Djinn?" I asked.

"No," said Shahbano. "They really believe she is God's woman, an *Allah-wali*. For them she is not beyond, but above, Reason and therefore pure and sinless."

I was confused. While the brave new world had so little to offer Fatimah, the old superstitious one could still make room for her!

Shahbano reflected sadly. "At least for the time being. . . . What will happen to her eventually no one can really foretell. She is restless and fidgets all the time. Sometimes she bays like an angry wolf. In her condition, perhaps the best hope is an early menopause. Aging would be bliss for her. Then she can walk around in the reeds as freely as she used to before all this happened."

"Aging is bliss for every woman in our part of the world,"

I muttered. "Perhaps then people will stop talking about her 'morals.'"

Shahbano smiled.

"Till then," I added, "a kind of solution has been invented by these daughters of Aai."

I meet them sometimes when I visit my sister. Early in the morning you can see them in their colorful dresses, streaming out of their shanty huts like so many fluttering butterflies, crossing over the bridge on the canal, jumping over small shrubs, picking flowers to sell in the market, reaping grass, hoeing the fields, separating the chaff from the corn, singing at their work, tying innumerable bundles, large or small.

This story would have become great in the hands of Leo Tolstoy. He was a great writer. What difference does it make that before turning to religion for redemption and taking up the toilsome life of a cobbler to replicate Jesus Christ, he had sexually exploited a serf woman in his house, made her pregnant, and abandoned her, completely destroying her life? On this subject he has written a heartrending novel, which is now a world classic.

# MEETING
# THE SPHINX

৪০

# *Rukhsana Ahmad*

Rukhsana Ahmad (1948– ) was born in Karachi, attended schools in many Pakistani cities, and earned degrees at Punjab University and at Karachi University. After marrying, she migrated to Britain and earned further degrees from Reading University and The University of the Arts.

Ahmad is a novelist and playwright. She has also translated into English a volume of women's protest poetry in Urdu, *We Sinful Women*

(Women's Press, 1991), and an Urdu novel, *The One Who Did Not Ask* by Altaf Fatima (Heinemann, 1993). In 1984 she joined The Asian Women Writers Collective in London. Her short stories have been anthologized extensively. She has published a novel, *The Hope Chest* (Virago, 1996), and is working on her second, *Sins*. She is particularly well known for her many plays, including the recent *Mistaken . . . Annie Besant in India* (Aurora Metro Publications, 2007), and for her work adapting plays by other writers for BBC Radio, such as Jean Rhys's *Wide Sargasso Sea*, Nawal El Saadawi's *Woman at Point Zero*, Salman Rushdie's *Midnight's Children*, and Nadeem Aslam's *Maps for Lost Lovers*. These have achieved nominations and short lists for many prestigious British awards, including the Commission of Racial Equality Award, the Writers' Guild Award, the Sony Award, and the 2002 Susan Smith Blackburn Prize. To promote Asian women playwrights, in 1990 she cofounded the Kali Theatre Company in London with actor Rita Wolf. She is the chair and founding trustee of the South Asian Arts and Literature in the Diaspora Archive in the United Kingdom (www.salidaa.org.uk), and an advisory fellow for the Royal Literary Fund at Queen Mary's College, University of London.

"Meeting the Sphinx" challenges the certainties of British narratives around notions of "academic objectivity." The resentment that Sam, a distinguished white British Egyptologist, harbors against Happy Dossa, an Asian woman colleague, illuminates structures of race, class, and gender in British academia. Ahmad's story specifically challenges many assumptions in David Mamet's play *Oleanna* (1993), which revolves around a university professor accused of sexual harassment by his female student, Ahmad says,

> Understandably, Happy reminds Sam of Oleanna but my story is an attempt to avoid the somewhat stark polarities of the play. It was prompted by a student lockout following a long-running dispute between leftists and fascists on a campus in North London. The row was reported in the press briefly. Despite that subject matter it is not a story about campus politics but an exploration of the roots of prejudice and our encounters with the Other.
>
> I thought I was writing about our own hesitation

in dealing with someone like Happy whom we cannot place easily in terms of social or racial geographies. Although Sam and Happy echo similar power relationships to the duo in the play I do believe Happy is not in the least like Oleanna, who, in fact, symbolizes rather well the Western liberal's paranoiac vision of a feminist ("harpy") with access to real campus power through her political machinations. For me, that play was a landmark in the turning of the tide against "political correctness." Attacks like that soon became a convenient way of undermining the women's movement and union power. Hopefully, the tide will turn again one day.

Ahmad's symbolic use of the Sphinx both as an ancient stone artifact and as the embodiment of an enigma and a mystery also turns Sam's notion of himself and Happy Dossa on its head.

• • •

"Here, let me help you with that, Sam! You look as though you're in pain!" she smiled, as she leaped up swiftly, standing on tiptoe to make it up to his six-foot-two as she held up his coat for him. Bending like a clumsy fledgeling giraffe he winced, turning and twisting his body imperceptibly to avoid the sharp twinges of pain in his shoulder and, slipping in his left arm first, violating age-old habit as a concession to pain.

It had been an afternoon of concessions. A cool, superficial smile curled his unwilling lips. Only a part of him was grateful.

"Thanks," he muttered, more embarrassed than touched by this extravagant courtesy from a woman much younger than him, who had been battling with him moments ago as if they were sworn enemies. And that had been her stance in all the academic subcommittee meetings that year, through several long drawn-out fractious afternoons.

Hypocritical . . . um . . . bitch! His mind gave up the search for a less vicious epithet. She had exhausted him with her crab tenacity . . . and a level of aplomb quite alarming in someone that young. She wasn't an ally. Never conceded an inch, wasn't afraid of taking on his academic might, didn't really care for him as a person nor respect what he stood for as a professional. He resented having to thank her now for this pointless gesture. Quite pointless! Everything that happened between them at meetings confirmed that their differences could never be reconciled; they stood on either bank of an endless Nile, divided by its length and breadth, unable to hear each other or even to see each other's faces clearly.

As he walked out of the meeting the Nile foamed angrily in his imagination, flowing as always at the center of his professional life. Egypt had been his field as a historian but also his love, his passion, his obsession, he reminded himself. He was the one who had formulated the theoretical framework for the course when the department (or more accurately, the university) had needed the injection of a glamorous new package on the prospectus to attract more students.

A course spanning several disciplines—art and sociology, history and literature—a broad sweep but one that would nevertheless carry within it, safely and securely, the kernel of Egyptian philosophy, a worldview well worth preserving and remembering. It took all his patience and self-control to now have to defend each choice, argue for every recommendation on the syllabus against this . . . this . . . woman, a nobody with her degree in politics from some dismal northern polytechnic. It was painfully obvious that she was driven by only one obsession, a simplistic sort of feminism which she flaunted tirelessly and practiced, in the main, through questioning the givens. Everything, always.

The subtle undertone of the questioning inevitably framed him as the prime suspect with a sinister motive behind each choice. More and more clearly he saw her strategy. She was the crazy girl from *Oleanna* with all her hang-ups and the same parasitic vulnerabilities . . . and he was fast becoming her victim, the professor rendered powerless by the power of the students' union! Here was a parallel too real to ignore.

But the very next moment he was struggling to allay his own fears. Mustn't dramatize. That was only a play, the girl was crazy. This young woman is not. On the contrary, she is firmly rooted, seems reasonable, and is much too strong to crumble quite like that. He tried to recall her face as he came out of the campus—once again perturbed by the fact that he could never picture her in his imagination when she was not there, even though he had observed her closely, for minutes together sometimes, while she argued against him with great lucidity and passion. An unusual failure for someone with a visual memory as sharp as his.

What is it about her eyes that is so striking? They're strange . . . green, or perhaps hazel? Wrong somehow, with that skin color. Icy, disturbing, and yet, tantalizingly familiar. Unlike her voice, which is definitely annoying, a touch metallic, almost alien. Sometimes modulated to persuade rationally; at other times, vibrant with the tinsel glint of passion. Whinge, whinge, whinge! God, what a moaner! It has an edgy, raspy feel to it, a determination to accentuate their differences, to stay discrete, complete with its hint of . . . a . . . foreign accent. Funny how the educated Asian voice can become a double-edged weapon, insinuating a polite reasonableness as if it were trying to negotiate approval by attempting the utmost in correct pronunciation, even as it firmly draws a magic circle around itself, defining the boundaries of how far vowels might bend and to what degree consonants may unroll.

He wondered about her background once again. . . . Whenever people commented on her unusual name (whoever heard a name like that: Ms. Happy Dossa?) she would waffle on about it for fifteen minutes nonstop, without actually revealing anything at all about herself. If someone asked her more directly about her antecedents she responded playfully, "Well, you know . . . Happy, because that's what I always am and always have been, a happy sort, and Dossa, because I used to be such a dosser!"

But Sam Jennings had come to his own conclusions about her. He decided that she was one of Idi Amin's Asians. She had the same sallow coloring and friendly extrovert manner which he associated with the Patels from their own corner shop. A kind of dogged tenacity fought through the air of long-suffering endurance and fatigue which always hung over the shop and around them. She had that quality about her, too. Certainly there was more energy about Happy, even more anger, perhaps.

Bloody . . . he thought, bloody . . . bloody . . . women! He was surprised at the venom coiled around the smoke that rose from an early cigarette cocked between his lips to shake off the tension as he walked down the corridor. Suddenly it struck him that it was not her Indian-ness that had battled with him and failed to capitulate that afternoon, but her femaleness. She had not been playing the race card today. Gender was the issue. Yes, bloody women.

He had promised Penny he would try to be home early that afternoon to see to the children's meal so she could get away for her school's open day. Now he would be late. "As always!" she might add if she had been someone else, but she wouldn't. He could already see her shrug of resignation, reproach withheld, in the face of his preemptive murmured apologies. He felt a sudden gush of warmth for her, a pride in the generosity of spirit that emanated from her lovely face with its fine bone structure, the flawless white of her complexion, the elegant tilt of her head. Thank goodness for Penny, for women like her!

Fortunately, the children alleviated the testiness of the moment with their gleeful demands for a bedtime story. He stacked the dirty dishes in the kitchen sink and led them upstairs, trying to underscore a mental note to himself about remembering to do them later, before his evening's quota of television and alcohol.

Mr. Green was making a nuisance of himself, climbing onto the cabinets, jumping on and off beds, scratching the furniture and rugs, screeching in his ugly grating voice. Each mia-ao-oow stretched across the room like a howl of bereavement. He certainly knew how to annoy. For the hundredth time Sam regretted the choice of a pedigree cat; he had a family tree longer than their own, bought from the most reputable breeders specializing in the Siamese variety. Mr. Green was as wantonly capricious as any blue-blooded human was capable of being.

"Hasn't he been fed?" he asked Kirsty irritably.

"He didn't fancy canned food today, and Mummy said not to give him any of the roast chicken 'cause it spoils him."

"Crafty devil," Sam tried to ignore his tantrum.

Mr. Green kept up his annoying whine weaving his way between vases, books, and Samuel Jennings's much-prized collection of Egyptian bronze and porcelain curios and replicas, with a restless elegance typical of his kind. His eyes greener than ever in his pointed face, his spare coat bristling with righteous protest. He looked at him, beige-into-burnished-gold . . . burnished gold . . . the phrase resonated with an Egyptian memory . . . and he decided to take on Mr. Green.

"Well, we'll see who gives in first," Sam said to Kirsty, firmly turning his back on the creature he had "spoilt rotten" according to Penny. The memory of that afternoon's defeat lined his resolve with steel now. "I'll show him who's the boss here. And I'll show her too, Ms. Dossa, wherever she comes from. Show her next time that I can be determined, too." His thoughts returned to the meeting again.

"Come on, Dad! What happened next?" Kirsty drew him back into the present.

"Sorry, darling! Where was I? Oh, yes . . ." he returned to the page in a lazy drawl and Kirsty lay back on the pillow to summon up the pictures in her head as his voice droned on:

" . . . Then Thoth cast a spell over the palace so that every living thing slumbered. Only the Pharaoh, King Thutmose himself, seemed to be awake . . . and yet it seemed that it was only his body which did not sleep. For, as if he were already dead, his three spiritual parts: The *Bai* or soul; the *Ka* or double; and the *Khou* or spirit left his body, and gathered about it where it lay on the royal bed as they would in the days to come. . . ."

It was their favorite. They called it the Egyptian Sleeping Beauty story. Sebastian was dozing already. Kirsty's eyes grew heavy well before the end. It was as if Amen-Ra himself had walked through the house to lull all living creatures in it by some mysterious process. Even Mr. Green had quietened and as Sam's eyes drooped, the dog-eared paperback slipped down to his chest.

He stood in the desert gazing at the pyramids, his neck bent back painfully as far as it would go, his eyes blinded by the glaring sun, treacherous silver sands shimmering around him. Against the twinkling sand, tucked among the gigantic pyramids of polished stone, he could see a majestic sphinx roughly hewn out of yellow sandstone. His eyes were riveted to the image: short, straight hair parted in the middle, unblinking stone eyes, strangely green, yet familiar . . . and dark full lips. He drew closer to the creature. Sand coated his polished black shoes with an abrasive film as he inched forward, ploughing heavily through the troughs and furrows that sucked him in, right up beside her stone paws spread out flat in steady defiance. As he drew closer his head leveled with hers, his chin jerked up, and his eyes locked into the mystery of the challenge. A challenge! His heart beat faster.

Tentative fingers shot out to touch the sphinx's face, but the stone felt rough and grainy, hot in the midday sun. His fingers trailed down along the yellowing stone cheek, the hair, and then stopped tremulously on the curve of her left breast. Miraculously, stone waxed into flesh, yielding, warm and soft to his touch. A vein throbbed beneath his ring finger, startling him out of his dream. He woke suddenly and completely and sat upright in one movement, sucking in the fine thread of spittle trickling down the corner of his lower lip.

He looked at the children peacefully asleep, at Mr. Green in a pose of resigned slumber on the window sill, and rose with a sigh, feeling vaguely uneasy about the tactile quality of his dream, its irritating disregard for historical reality. A sphinx with a recognizable twentieth-century face and real breasts! As mad as the goon show! The memory of the sexual innuendo embarrassed and discomfited him. It was unworthy of him—it made him feel unprofessional and low in a way only she knew how to: Ms. Happy Dossa from nowhere special, with her crystal green eyes and her metallic voice.

Happy stood near the entrance to the Redgrave Theater, straining her eyes to see what exactly was going on inside. A pall of darkness hung over the entire auditorium, with the exception of the tiny stage, faintly lit with a yellowish glow. The theater was far from being full but the energy of the crowd ballooned with a manic intensity in the shadows, threatening to erupt into the glare-filled corridors outside. She tried to concentrate on what was being said—she had promised the Dean a detailed report back. The speaker was a short man with soft rubbery cheeks, dark curly hair, possibly a young Greek-Cypriot. She noticed the admirable ease with which he commanded and held their attention.

"Enough is enough! We'll not stand by and allow the cancer of fascism to spread once again. If evil forces are allowed to grow unchecked, they mushroom and refuse to be contained again. If the university continues its policy of appeasement and indulgence in the name of free speech then we have no choice but to fight with whatever weapons we can muster. We must take action. The publication of *The Green Dragon* cannot be allowed to continue!" Forceful thumps punctuated his last sentence. Cheers and warm applause followed.

He took a deep breath and raised his right arm, "Those

among the staff who insist on defending the right of the Green Dragon Club to organize and publish a paper as obnoxious and offensive as this take on a villainous role. They are helping to nurture hatred and treachery in the guise of virtue. Those who shield fascism cannot be trusted. We must regard them as our enemies!" More cheers and cries of joyous approval.

"Friends and comrades, we need your support and encouragement. Our cause is just. *The Green Dragon* must die. As many of you may know, two of our office bearers have been on hunger strike for the past week. A big hand for both of them. Peter Gold and Youseff al Saki are heroes. They're determined to pursue this action until all our demands are met. They're willing to court death to ensure the success of our campaign. The Green Dragon Club must be closed down and its organizers expelled from this campus and banned for a minimum period of five years!

"I thank all of you once again for being here. Please continue your sit-in in support of this campaign. United, we are a force to reckon with. We'll paralyze this institution, take over this campus, and run it ourselves if necessary!"

The clapping and cheering grew louder. A group of women in a corner had already started humming songs of resistance, spreading blankets and themselves out on the floor. Happy could hear the buzz of excitement and energy rise and waft through the room like a palpable force. Goose pimples bristled on her arms. Her stomach tightened with a strange feeling of embattled excitement.

She tried to catch a glimpse of the heroes at the center of the campaign but they were stretched out on mats on the floor of the stage, surrounded by admirers and sympathy. Was the angel of death standing by, too, to watch this contest, she wondered? Driven by a mildly morbid curiosity she decided to make her way toward the dais where they lay to have a closer look.

Both of them were fairly young men, almost boys, one white, the other a deeply tanned brown with strong African features and hair. She guessed he was Youseff, remembering the story of the handsome Joseph from her grandmother's retelling of it. The smell of starvation hung about them already. Their eyes did not reflect the sparkling energy of their curly-haired leader. She wondered what filled their hearts and minds most at this moment: fear or hope?

As if she had spoken her question aloud, Youseff looked up and caught her glance. If, at any point, there had been fear in him his hunger had feasted on it, devoured it long since. His eyes smiled cheerfully, knowingly into hers. *Hope! Hope! Hope!* They sang a fearless song. She filled her lungs deeply with reassurance and turned around to leave. Her feet reluctant and heavy, she made her way slowly back to the Dean's office in the administration block thinking about what she would tell him.

"I tell you what I'll do, Sam, I'll fax this through to you now. I suggest that you read the piece carefully, think of what you'd like to say, make notes, then come around to the press office and we'll help you draft your response."

Sam heaved a long sigh, wondering if there was an alternative. "Well, what do you say?" Caroline's voice, clear as a crystal bell, bore down on him again.

There was subtle pressure in the suggestion, an insistence that would brook no argument. Perhaps not all that subtle, come to think of it! No point in trying to fight it, he concluded. "They've blown this out of all proportion, you know." His voice sounded like a whine even to himself.

"I absolutely agree with you. That's why it's important to deal with it as professionally as we can! Damage limitation, it's the only sensible thing to do."

"Sure." His voice was devoid of conviction although he would be the first to accept that he was no good at thinking on his feet. Caroline was right: The press office was trained to deal with problems like this. Perhaps he needed to put himself in their hands. He could always study the article and change his mind, if necessary.

He lit a cigarette and sat down to watch the fax machine as if it were a fiend from hell, programmed to exhale brimstone and fire on his head. Before his cigarette was out the telephone bell rang and the monster whirred, revving up dutifully to churn out the faxed story as told to the *Daily Mail* by the striking students. He pulled up each page as it rolled off the machine. Caroline had underlined the sections of the interview which referred to him.

Youseff al Saki—he remembered the name but realized with a shock that he could hardly recognize the face. The boy had lost three and a half stones in the two weeks of starvation, the article informed him. His eyes had sunk deep into their sockets, his plump dimpled cheeks were hollow pits, his lips scabbed. The sit-in and hunger strike had effectively disrupted classes in the humanities block this last fortnight, steadily gaining the support from more and more students. Prior to that the university had been able to ignore protests surrounding the Green Dragon Club and its infamous rag. Coverage in national dailies was bound to boost student morale.

"Fools! What a waste of time and energy!" His temper rose steadily as he read the article. It was an interview with Youseff who was still resisting pressure to give up the hunger strike. The Dean had taken a stand in favor of the Green Dragon Club. The student body was all up in arms now. Peter Gold had collapsed the day before and been admitted to the hospital.

Nowhere did the article expound his own position accurately. Instead all references to him had been made in the context of his "rigid views" on the origins of the Egyptian civilization. Youseff had identified him as one of the biased academics at the university who denied Africans their rightful Egyptian heritage by crediting its glory instead to the Aryans, the Greeks, the Arabs, the Mesopotamians, *anyone but black Africans!*

A racist! So now I am to be branded a *racist!* The trouble with mud is . . . it sticks. He lit another cigarette and paced up and down the office, a part of him anxious that Caroline would ring any minute now asking for his statement. She would not give him more than an hour to think his position through. "Damage limitation," she had said. What does that mean, exactly? Accept a reduced charge, negotiate the degree of guilt? But why?

He remembered the boy's face the day he had challenged him on this issue in class. He kept repeating something about the Pharaohs' curly hair, he had gone on and on about it. "But sir, they've never found 'bracelets of bright hair about the bone!' " he had smirked. "It's always been dark hair, black, wiry, and curly like mine, hasn't it?" He had perhaps read and investigated the subject in his own limited way, prepared his onslaught. He remembered feeling pushed into momentary silence by the boy's logic that day.

"It is easy to oversimplify these things," Sam had begun, slightly defensively. Defiant little idiot. Why do people blow things out of all proportion? Curly hair or straight, dark or blond, does it really matter? Does it? And if it doesn't, then why have I been arguing about it?

He rummaged for an ashtray among the papers on the desk and fished it out of the chaos. A glazed blue porcelain sphinx held a shallow bowl in its paws with exaggerated solemnity. He stared at the creature: She seemed unperturbed by the crisis of the day. His eyes slid down its glazed throat to where the human breast turned into beast.

If only the meaning of events did not elude us as they unroll through our lives . . . he thought, desperate for some spark of wisdom or inspiration. Penny smiled at him, at his confusion perhaps, from across his desk, a calm sepia image in a silver frame.

Objectivity is the cardinal principle of my trade, that's the principle I must follow. I know that more clearly than ever before. I must draw as far away as possible from the personal emotion attached to all this and . . . and try to read the article from beginning to end, without reference to myself. I need to honor my own integrity as a professional and not be driven by the university's need for a politically correct image. My statement mustn't undermine my own professionalism, or my future here as a teacher. After all, I'm the one who faces this rabble in the classroom, eye to eye.

He decided to ignore the messenger of death hovering behind Youseff's image, visible even in the photograph as if through an x-ray machine. His raw statements had taken on a strange poignancy in the interview. Was it the power of the saint, the martyr, the mystic, that added layers to his message? Or was it the same wisdom that routinely pours out of the mouths of babes into deaf old ears unable to recognize it? The interview read extremely well. He came over convincingly as an idealist, a Utopian who remembered earlier blueprints in every detail.

He had quoted Thomas More—clearly he was a hero and a model for his own conduct in the dispute:

Now am I like to Plato's city,
Whose fame flieth the world thorough;
Yea, like, or rather more likely
Plato's plat to excel and pass.

Here was someone who dreamed of perfection though the dream had fallen out of fashion long ago. He was still dreaming of justice when almost the entire world had decided to concur in its acceptance of the failure of that dream. Here was someone who was willing to make the supreme sacrifice when sacrifice was no longer in currency, no longer a virtue. His idealism, his saintliness were so unblemished, so visceral that they hefted Sam toward an imperative he may otherwise have been able to constrain—at least in these circumstances. Instead, he too felt obliged to take a strong and absolute stand for what he believed in. He could not be less than honest in this situation. He could not compromise, not faced with this.

His telephone rang, a fraught screech of anxiety from the press office. He sounded vague speaking patiently, as if to a very slow child: He had to issue a denial, some kind of refutation. After all, he was not a racist! *Was he?*

"I'm not so sure what I would be denying! As a scholar in my own discipline I know I cannot, in all honesty, change my stance. I have not been misquoted on the subject. I don't really know what I need to deny, Caroline! I wish I knew." Sam felt curiously liberated by this uncertainty. "As I see it, there isn't enough evidence to support the position he wanted me to take about the ancestry of the Egyptians."

"There's the broader issue, though. Let me write up something and send it to you." Caroline could not believe the size of the problem on their hands.

"The fucking idiot!" she swore to her personal assistant as she put the phone down on him. "Bloody academics! So irresponsible! I wish they lived in the real bloody world! Do you think he realizes the meaning of what he's saying?"

"What's he saying then?" Wendy responded with minimal interest, filing away at a chip on her nail.

"Some mumbo jumbo about the truth of his discipline. In effect, that he's not really bothered about denying the charge of racism. Would you believe it? Honestly! This is the climate we live in!"

"Maybe it's more useful to be on the wrong side these days?"

"Oh, Wendy," Caroline sighed, "you do have a way of hitting the nail on the head sometimes! Meanwhile, as they say in the business, this university has a bit of an image problem on its hands."

Happy had never met the chaplain before. She looked up as he came to sit down beside her with their two cups of coffee and a plate of digestive biscuits. His parlor was predictably olde worlde, as were the bone china teacups (Minton? English country garden?) though his language was refreshingly unworthy of his role in the college.

"I don't know what else to suggest. Only the Vice Chancellor has the power to sort out this blasted mess. Real dog's dinner, isn't it?" his biscuit crumbled untidily into his armchair.

"But there's no time to wait. Three days! He's sinking fast, I shudder to think what might happen in that time. Have you seen the hostility and anger that's getting pumped up in the students by the minute?"

"I know what you're saying, Happy. Here's a situation that doesn't make sense. Bloody meaningless confrontation, if you ask me!"

"I'm not one to believe in conspiracy theories, but the way events have shaped up on this campus is really strange. Both sides are so deeply entrenched, so dogmatic."

"We'll know if someone at the top gets nominated for a knighthood next year, won't we?" he winked.

"Might be too late for some." She put down the empty cup and rose. His unconditional sympathy for the students had been heartening. She had spent the last three days trying to push staff opinion in their favor, just to defuse the crisis. She was terrified lest something irrevocable like death bring them all to a point of no return. On a personal level the staff were all flexible, even sympathetic, but as a group, as a warring faction, they were as intransigent as the most hotheaded of students. The heads of faculties and the dean all sheltered behind the Vice Chancellor, and now that this young man's life was seriously at risk, he was away, out of reach on a week's holiday.

The Chaplain stood up to see her to the door. He had promised to try to contact the VC for her. She felt cold and numb as she stepped out of his cosy parlor into the dark winter evening. The students had mounted a candlelight vigil outside the Redgrave Theater. She stood near the heavy wooden entrance doors, watching. It was a moving spectacle, a fearful, breathless, hushed moment. She could feel the tension and bitterness in that subdued hum almost brushing against her skin.

Police had cordoned off two lanes on each side of the A class road, which ran between the blocks and buildings of the university. The quieter late-evening traffic, forced to slow down through the bottleneck, was less noisy than usual. She wondered what to do next. A part of her wanted to light a candle and stay with them but she resisted the temptation.

The door opened gently and Sam Jennings appeared on the pavement beside her. She tried to avoid his eyes but he had seen her. Somehow, he had managed to put himself in the opposite camp. He noticed her anxiety and drew up closer to say hello, forcing her to respond.

To an extent he had been prepared for the ostracism: He was aware of her anger and that of some other staff members, but he wondered why. Perhaps because the world at large oversimplifies solutions to problems. Black and white. Far too simplistic when the real world is overwhelmingly gray.

"Shall we go for a drink?" he asked hastily as he saw her turning to leave.

"Can't, I'm afraid . . . I'm booked to see a play," she improvised.

"It's early yet. A quick one . . . ?" he insisted.

"All right, then. It'll have to be very quick, though," she gave in with bad grace.

They walked around to The Jolly Beggar, which seemed unusually deserted for that time of evening, and he managed to get their drinks in record time. She was wondering what they could talk about to avoid the obvious, but he clearly didn't want to.

He took a deep breath and launched into an explanation of his own position. "All this was unnecessary. It's only giving free publicity and attention to a stupid, small-minded, parochial group! An insignificant loopy lot on the fringe, that's all, the Green Dragons! Sometimes it's best to tolerate rather than suppress things that act like a steam vent. They should've been ignored."

"It's too late to go back to that option," her voice sounded cold even to her own ears. She felt angry with him, extremely angry.

"How is he?" he asked.

"Seriously ill."

"Get him to stop. Talk to them," he urged.

"Didn't you hear me, Sam? It's too late! He's dying."

"I'll talk to the Vice Chancellor. I can get him to change his mind: I know."

"You? You'll talk to the VC?" Contempt accentuated the surprise in her voice. "Why *should* you? You've just said you don't believe in what the students are saying!"

"It would still be quite insane to carry on this conflict on these terms, that's why."

"I wish you'd changed your mind earlier, Sam. The VC is away for three more days and I don't think Youseff will last that long."

His face blanched. Then he opened his brief case and took out a blank sheet of headed notepaper. He wrote down a statement and handed it to her.

I, the Vice Chancellor of the City University of London, do hereby agree to all the demands of the Students' Union pertaining to the Green Dragon Club and its publication. I also agree to undertake appropriate measures to curb these activities within the campus as soon as possible.

Sincerely,

E.L. Whitton

He had signed the VC's name in a manner only vaguely resembling the real thing, but they wouldn't know. She shook her head in disbelief.

"Just give it to them. They'll accept it as real," he urged in a whisper.

"But that would be cheating! You could get into so much trouble, Sam. What if the VC doesn't agree to abide by this?"

"He will. I could claim that he asked me to write this on his

145

behalf. But even if he doesn't, at least the boy would be saved by then, wouldn't he?"

She sat staring at the note for a long moment. He was right. The students would accept it as a victory. It would be virtually impossible for the VC to fight against a fait accompli, an action for which a senior member of his staff, and a very close friend, had taken personal responsibility.

"Why are you doing this, Sam?" she couldn't help wondering about his motives.

"I haven't worked that out yet. . . . But you better take it and go before I change my mind."

"Right! All right, then. Great!" She looked into his eyes and smiled. Warm and effusive. Suddenly her usually somber and intense face was transformed. Her eyes glowed with a mellow hazel light, no longer that cold, stony green. She picked up his coat and held it up for him as he craned down gratefully to slip his frozen shoulder into the sleeve.

"If only one could solve all the riddles the sphinx keeps hidden under those stone paws. . . ." he was thinking. "If only . . ."

# RUBIES
# FOR A DOG:
# A FABLE

☙

# Shahrukh Husain

Shahrukh Husain (1950– ) was born
in Karachi and educated at the Convent of Jesus and Mary there. She
published her first stories in the children's section of the magazine *Woman's World* when she was eight years
old. She migrated to Britain in 1970
and has lived there since.

Husain writes fiction and nonfiction for adults and children, and
is particularly interested in folklore,
myths, and women's studies. She is

also a translator, a screenwriter, and a practicing psychothera-
pist dealing with intercultural issues. Husain coauthored *Urdu
Literature* with David Matthews and her husband, Christo-
pher Shackle (Third World Publications, 1985). Her books for
children include *Mecca* (Evan Brothers, 1993) and *Tales from
the Opera* (Barefoot, 1999). Her adult fiction series, originally
published by Virago Press and translated into many languages,
contains myths that she has reworked for modern audiences,
including *The Virago Book of Witches* (Virago, 1993; later published as *Daughters of the Moon*, Faber, 1994), *Women Who Wear
the Breeches* (Virago, 1995; later published as *Handsome Heroines*,
Anchor Doubleday, 1996). She has also written a nonfiction
work, *The Goddess: Power, Sexuality, and the Feminine Divine*
(University of Michigan Press, 2003).

Husain cowrote the screenplay for Ismail Merchant's 1993
film, *In Custody*, adapted from Anita Desai's novel, which was
nominated for an Oscar and a BAFTA award, and received the
President of India Gold Medal.

"Rubies for a Dog: A Fable" first appeared in *Women Who
Wear the Breeches* and provides a fascinating example of a woman's assertion of equality through cross-dressing. Husain's version was developed from an English adaptation that appeared
in *The Everland Storybook* edited by Oliver Brown (1931) but the
original story dates back to medieval times and is based on "The
Tale of Azad Bakht" from the great Urdu classic, *Bagh-o-Bahar*
(A Tale of Four Dervishes) by Mir Amman Dehlavi (1803), the
first book of Urdu literary prose. Although a reconstruction of
Turkish, Persian, and early Urdu tales, *Bagh-o-Bahar* portrays
the Indo-Muslim culture of the early nineteenth century. The
story provides an excellent example of how texts mutate across
countries, cultures, languages, and continents.

In the Urdu original, the King, Azad Bakht, is the narrator and tells a series of tales within tales, in which the coura-
geous but nameless "Wazir's daughter" is an important catalyst.
In Hussain's story, the Wazir's daughter is called Samira. She is
the central character and has a strong sense of self worth, as a
woman and an equal, and she sets out to prove it, admirably.

• • •

Once there was an Emperor, much loved and much respected, but when he put his faithful old advisor, the Grand Wazir, into prison, and worst of all, told nobody the reason why, people wondered about his sense of fair play. Still, everyone accepted that emperors can be erratic at times and that the Wazir had probably said something so offensive that it did not bear repetition. So everyone in the kingdom looked the other way. Everyone that is, except the Wazir's daughter, Samira. She refused to sit idle in the halls of her father's sumptuous mansion while he, the provider of all this luxury, languished in a dank cell with chains locking both his limbs and his lips. But try as she might, she could not get her father to tell her anything, and without the facts she could do nothing. "You are my child," the old Wazir said sadly, "and I thank God for you. I will not risk your life by telling you what happened. If I had a son he would do what is necessary to clear my name. But I cannot send a daughter."

When Samira's father refused her help because she was a woman, she felt humiliated and useless. She crept back to her castle and wept, and cursed the narrow vision of men who bound women in their homes, then considered them incapable of achieving anything outside.

"If I visit my father," she thought miserably, "I will only remind him that he has no son while I, his wretched daughter, incapable of helping him, remain ensconced in his mansion, swathed in silk, decking myself in gold and jewels and always in danger of jeopardizing his reputation. As far as he's concerned, the only good I can do is to live a blame-free life so that people call him a man of noble birth and without character."

A few days later, Samira received a message from her father. Was all well with her? He was grateful for the food she had sent and he did not wish to impose a visit on her, but he needed to know she was safe and well. A message would be enough.

Samira longed to see her father—but how could she? Her woman's body, her long hair, her feminine attire would be anathema to him. To see in her what could have been, but was definitely not, must be unbearable for him. She stood staring at herself in the mirror—exquisite as a *pari*, tall and straight as a cypress tree, rosy cheeked, from head to toe the essence of beauty. Yet she hated every part of herself. In a rage, she picked up a small dagger and began to rip away her clothes. Then she looked with pleasure at the velvets and chiffons and beaded silks lying in fragments on the floor. But when she looked up, her reflection still mocked her.

*"I'm still here,"* it taunted. *"Still beautiful and still female. Now what will you do to deny me?"*

Samira put the sharp blade to her head and long silken strands of hair slithered lifeless to the floor. For a moment she fancied she saw a woman reflected in the soft heap of her tresses—her mother. *"You are right,"* she seemed to say. *"I approve of your plan."*

Reassured, Samira ran to her father's bedchamber and began looking in his wardrobe. She searched and foraged amid the brocades and velvet until at last she found a small bundle of starched pink muslin, sparkling with silver mica from the sea. She undid the knot that tied it, and there it was! The outfit her father wore when he went wandering amid the crowds of Constantinople to learn what the people of his great Emperor Azad Bakht were thinking. It was useful for a Wazir to know whether people were content or discontent, what pleased them about their sovereign and what made them unhappy, whether they thought him wise or whether they decried a folly or two that had crept into his character. Then the Wazir would act on it. Cleverly and diplomatically, he would reshape the criticism and filter the contents of his findings into the Emperor's ear to mould him into an even better ruler, just as he had done for his father before him. No fool was our worthy Wazir—until this last time. What had gone wrong? For he had made a mistake that he would probably never have the chance to rectify. That is if Azad Bakht and the Wazir had their secretive way. But Samira had her own ideas in the matter.

Carefully she dressed herself in the flowing overcoat and baggy trousers her father wore to go out among the people. They were of plainer cloth and not so highly embroidered; a little duller, because the thread of the embroidery was dyed in the colors of flowers and vegetables rather than gold and silver; clothes that would not set her apart from the average merchant or businessman.

"Apart from the turban," she thought, "it's all much the same. I fit these clothes as well as my own. But the turban feels cumbersome on my head just as a father's duties must weigh him down."

Then Samira made her way to the dungeon.

"Your daughter has sent me," she said, deepening her voice. "I am her sworn brother and therefore your son. I am to be your champion and free you from this odious place. I beg you, tell me why Emperor Azad Bakht imprisoned you and how you can make amends."

The Wazir looked perplexed. He could not confide in a stranger, even if that stranger was sworn to be his champion. What if he was the Emperor's agent provocateur and not Samira's ambassador at all? He shook his head sadly. He felt a father's warmth for the boy, but barely knew him.

"There is something about you that I feel I can trust, but I cannot betray my Emperor," he said firmly. "He has commanded me to say nothing."

"Father!" cried Samira, removing her turban. "Don't you recognize me? I am your daughter! Please let me help you."

The old Wazir's eyes filled with tears. Tears of sadness, tears of love, tears of pride. And for a while he could not bring himself to speak.

"My child," he said eventually, clutching her to him, "you have cut your beautiful hair, the legacy of your mother, and you've given it up for me. It must have broken your heart."

Samira nodded. "Yes, but I would rather serve the living than the dead," she replied. "I have lost my mother, I am desperate to keep my father. So please, tell me why you are here."

The Wazir sighed. He was bursting with pride at his daughter's bravery and quite overcome by her devotion and determination.

"Then listen," he began. "One day some merchants from Badakshan visited our court with gifts for the Emperor. Among them was a wonderful ruby. It seemed to hold the depth of an ocean, an ocean at sunset when it is red and luminous because it has sucked the fire from the sun itself. And every time Azad Bakht looked at it, he forgot everything else. There is no doubt this was a rare gem. It captivated everyone who saw it.

"You know how it is with emperors—they often lose the distinction between the important and the less important. They are easily diverted by games and women and trinkets. Then it is up to their servants to remind them of the important things. And we tried, many of us, to point out to Azad Bakht that the ruby was excessively distracting—but would he listen? He began to suspect that we had our eyes on the ruby, that we wanted it for ourselves. Even that we were jealous of this inanimate stone. It was almost as if—God forgive me and cast dust in my mouth, but it must be said—it was almost as if Azad Bakht had begun to worship it. He could not bear to be without it. He would abandon meetings with important emissaries in order to have a quick peep at the stone. He would hold up vital proceedings to show off the gem to state visitors. Inevitably, one day matters went too far.

"A neighboring king was visiting to ask for Azad Bakht's support in a war against another king. The battle was a personal one and Azad Bakht would never have agreed in the normal course of affairs because this third king has always been faithful to us. But the visiting king saw his chance and seized it when Azad Bakht flaunted the ruby to him, and in tones at once awed and arrogant, demanded, 'Tell me, have you such a jewel in your possession?' Well, from then on they talked of nothing but the great gems of the world and how this ruby must be among the greatest. Before the meeting had ended, the clever visitor had procured Azad Bakht's help to fight his personal battle—our forces for his battle against a king who had never done us harm. Well, it was too much to stand by and accept. The king left, knowing he had outmaneuvered our young Emperor. It would be terrible for his reputation.

"That night when I went into the streets, the story had already got around. The people are forgiving, Samira, but not when their lives and their beloved country are at stake. They talked that night; talk to shame the bones of an old servant like me. Azad Bakht may be young, they said, but we've had boy-emperors before now who have brought great glory to the land. Little do they know, a boy-emperor is more likely to achieve glory than a young man, for his ego is not yet full blown and his ears more open to the wisdom of older men.

"I knew that night that I must tell the Emperor as bluntly as possible how the ruby was affecting him, that he must put his passion in perspective or he would do himself and his empire dreadful harm. That night, alone with Azad Bakht in his bed-chamber and after all the courtiers had left, I had my chance to speak.

"I admit I was nervous, but the Wazir is the servant of the Emperor, and the Emperor of the State, and the State of the people, and the people of God. So you see, I was at the bottom of a long chain. Soft words and gentle advice had no effect on Azad Bakht and, I don't know—I suppose it was partly the anger of hearing my Emperor criticized, partly the humiliation of withdrawing our word to the visiting king, partly my own earlier failure—but my blood was boiling and nothing drives a man to greater risk than simmering rage. Well, whatever it was that night it drove me to an action that has reduced me to this.

"I stood by the elbow of Azad Bakht and I said in as firm a voice as I could muster, 'Your Majesty, Shadow of the Eternal, Refuge of the World, Recipient of the Wisdom of the Almighty,

I have something important to tell you, but it will fall heavy on your gracious ear.'

"'What is it?' said Azad Bakht, growing a little crabby, for it was late at night. He rubbed the great ruby against his cheek, then reached out and placed it in a niche directly above his bed. I noticed that the exquisitely inscribed calligraphy of a verse from the Quran had been removed to make room for the wretched stone. It saddened me.

"'I will tell you,' I said, 'if you promise to spare my life.'

"'Yes, yes,' replied Azad Bakht, getting impatient, 'Your life is safe. Now get on with it.'

"Well, you can imagine how I felt. Clearly the Emperor was in no mood to hear criticism—and then not as harshly as I meant to put it—but I had no option because I had decided carefully on my words and methods.

"'Well, Your Majesty,' I said, looking boldly into the Emperor's eyes, 'it is about the ruby.'

"Quite unselfconsciously, Azad Bakht reached out and clutched the stone, holding it defensively to his heart.

"'Oh, you're not still complaining about my fabulous ruby, are you?'

"'It does not become a great Emperor like you to give such importance to a mere stone,' I continued.

"'A mere stone?' shouted the Emperor, holding up the ruby for me to see. 'Look how it sparkles and casts its light! It is sublime, it is supernatural. How can anyone but an idiot describe it as a "mere stone"? The like of it was never encountered anywhere else.'

"'Not so, my liege,' I quaked to hear my voice clipped and curt, but say it I had to, 'for I have heard tales that a merchant of Nishapur has a dog whose collar is studded with twelve rubies, each one as large and as perfect as this one.'

"Azad Bakht gasped and clutched his throat. Horrified, I rushed up to help him. I thought he was going to choke. It was as if my words had knocked the breath from him. But he pushed me away. He spluttered and turned the color of the luscious quinces of Lebanon. Then quite suddenly he regained control.

"'You have insulted me and that makes you a traitor,' he said in a voice that was quiet and very deadly. I have never seen my Emperor so cold and so terrifying as he was at that moment. 'Traitors die a hideous death, but you have served my family faithfully and wisely for many years and I have given you my word. Therefore, you will live out the rest of your life in the dungeons of the old fort.'

"'My liege,' I whispered, throwing myself to my knees, 'your wish is my command. But will my daughter be safe?'

"'Your daughter is my sister,' the Emperor told me. His words were spoken like a true monarch. 'She will be under my protection and may, if she chooses, move into the royal palace for her own security. If she prefers, however, she may stay in your mansion and I will pronounce her a ward of the Emperor.'

"Thankfully, I rose and opened the doors. At my own command, the Royal Guard escorted me to the prison where I am today. And if it were not for the graciousness of my Emperor, my punishment could have been horrendous. I could have had my eyes gouged out with hot pokers, been subjected to several hundred strokes of the lash, had my tongue amputated. . . ."

Samira shuddered and put her hands to her father's lips.

"Please, Father," she begged, "we need not dwell on such horrors now."

The Wazir shook his head. "It is important for us both to acknowledge how lucky I am. The Emperor has been merciful. My body is whole though I am growing weak, and a life in this cell is no great hardship when you send me wonderful food each day and all the parts of my body are intact. I haven't many years of life left—those I can eke out in relative peace, praying and repenting and nourishing my soul."

Samira stood up and walked back and forth for a while, building up the courage to put her question to her father. She could feel his eyes watching her, alert for her request. No, her father had not lost any of his faculties, physical or mental.

"Father," she said at last, "I want your blessings."

"You have those always," cut in the wily Wazir, before she could proceed with her request.

Samira began to lose her nerve, but recovered and spoke with greater determination than before. "I want to go to Nishapur to find the dog with the ruby collar. I want your permission and your blessings."

"Do you know what you're asking?" demanded the Wazir. "The city of Nishapur is far, far away, in Khorasan. You have to cross tracts of desert and face fighting hordes who know as little of mercy as they do of palaces. Only an army has any chance of getting past them."

"Two strangers stand more chance than an army," retorted Samira. "An army would put them on their guard. A caravan would alert them to infinitely greater treasures than one body can carry. But a single young man with an old attendant will pose no threat to warrior tribes. Besides, we know from the stories of the great minstrels that wit wins many a battle before it is ever fought."

"Ah, Samira, Samira," lamented the Wazir, "the lack of a mother has done you more harm than I ever imagined. You read books on battles and look deep into the Mirror of Princes and you talk back to your father. Well, I brought you up so I must take the blame. It would have been wiser to hand you over to my sister, then perhaps I would not be in this dilemma today."

"Father, you have given me everything I ever needed. You have nurtured in me the creativity and determination of a woman and a heart as brave as a she-lion's. In archery and swordsmanship I was the best among my companions. But people think a woman's body is frail and vulnerable—I concede that. That is why I have to dress like this. Isn't it ironic that I have to dress like a man in order to discover my potential?"

The Wazir looked at his daughter with new eyes. He could not deny this young woman, this brave and wise young woman, the chance of self-discovery. He sighed so deeply that his frail frame shuddered with the force of it. He would probably never see the girl again. Flesh of his flesh, fruit of his loins, beloved gift of his dead wife.

"But," he thought, "the greatest gift a parent can give a child is the approval to do what she must. Yet how difficult it is to give. Yes, and I bless her efforts—how hard it is to say those words. Yet I must say them because it is quite obvious Samira has thought a lot about the matter and I have no wish to stop my daughter from fulfilling herself."

The Wazir raised his hand and laid it on Samira's head.

"Go with my blessings," he said, "and never forget who you are and why you go."

Samira threw her arms around her father. Tears filled her eyes and, promising him she would remember all the advice he had given her over the years, she left the dungeon.

Up in her castle she made ready for the journey. She would need a few spare sets of clothes. A trusted servant was sent out to acquire these. She would need provisions, merchandise for trade, gifts to pacify the nomad robbers and other brigands. And gold coins and gems, which she had sewn into the stiffened hems of her coat and other robes. Finally, accompanied by the faithful servant, she set off on her journey.

The road was long and arduous and there were nights when they slept between the vast skies and the shifting desert sands, as huge, radiant stars hung in clustering branches above them, bright as the torches that lit the richest mansions of Constantinople. Occasionally, they would hear the tinkle of a hospitable camel bell and a kindly tribesman would raise them from their sandy bed and take them to his home. Then there were the easier nights in plush and humble caravansery, travelers' inns built along the trunk roads. Finally they arrived in Khorasan, traveling on, frequently asking for directions until they reached the city of Nishapur where they took rooms in a modest but comfortable inn. At breakfast on the very first day, Samira spoke to the landlord.

"Is there a particular quarter in this town where the jewelers have their shops?"

"There might be and there might not be," replied the dour fellow. "What is it that you seek? To sell or to buy?"

"To look, at first," responded Samira jauntily, "and then, if I find your Nishapuri goods worthwhile, perhaps to trade. A little buying, a little selling. That's where the fun of business lies."

"Oh, the arrogance of the young," grumbled the innkeeper. "Don't be so proud of your wealth and your youth, for the colors of such garments fade soon enough. As to your cheeky remarks—you'll not find better jewelers anywhere than in our Nishapur bazaars."

"What!' exclaimed Samira, enjoying the man's irritation. "Are you claiming that your jewelers have better gems than the ones from Badakshan, finer gold than the Arabian isles, diamonds more exquisite than the ones from India?"

"I do," insisted the innkeeper. "Our jewelers cast their nets far and wide and haul in treasures from the deepest, most obscure places. You have only to see their caravans when they return, twenty guards in front and back, horses and camels creaking with the weight of it all."

"I've seen many caravans in my day," laughed Samira, "and I have no wish to see any more. But I will take a stroll around your market to see if your boasts are true."

And so saying, she set off in search of the merchant with the dog. She walked the streets of the city all day, asking questions openly, making inquiries but learning nothing until, on the fourth day, she came across a large shop displaying such fabulous jewels that she was quite overwhelmed by their beauty. There were fat emeralds, winking, blinking pools of green; rubies like luminous roses and hibiscus; diamonds so large they were like mounds of white light; sapphires bluer than the sky after a rainstorm; topazes like sunbursts; aquamarines as clear as the turquoise seas; lapis lazuli, veined and speckled in gold; amethysts, jet, turquoise, amber. . . .

"The Emperor Azad Bakht would go mad here," she thought wickedly. "He would transport the entire shop and its contents to Constantinople."

She closed her eyes and placed her fingers on the lids to shut out the harsh glare of the stones. When she opened them again, they focused on a low bed on which slept a large hound. An attendant smoothed its beautiful red tresses while another fanned it, waving away the flies. A third stood a little way behind the others, watchful that the dog's dishes of food and drink were fresh and full. And around the neck of this elegant, pampered hound of Afghanistan was a large collar of velvet studded with twelve enormous rubies. She had found him! Her father's savior! Now she could prove to Azad Bakht that her father's words were the truth and not an idle insult. But first, she must ask the dog's owner why he had made a collar of rubies for a dog.

"I am curious," said Samira when the pleasantries were over, "to find out more about your dog. Why does he wear a collar of rubies?"

"The dog is called Wafadar—Loyal One," began the merchant of Nishapur. "The best friend man can ever have."

Then the merchant told Samira that during his travels as a boy he had encountered seven misfortunes. Each time Wafadar had saved his life, or befriended him.

"When I lay ill and hungry by the wayside, the dog guarded me from man and beast; when I was set upon by brigands and my companions abandoned me, he fought by my side. When, twice, I lost my fortune and suddenly had no friends in the world, Wafadar stayed by me, finding food for himself and for me by hunting fowl and wild deer. When finally, at the age of twenty-six, I made a fortune so vast that ten lifetimes could not make a dent in it, nothing was so precious to me as Wafadar.

"My old friend's traveling days were over. He was tired and deserved to rest. I decided to settle down once and for all and resolved to give my faithful old companion every luxury in my power, so ostentatiously that people would come to see the dog

159

and ask me to tell his story. Then I would have the chance to extol his virtues and pay him homage."

Samira was moved to tears by the merchant's tale.

"His story has spread far and wide," she said when she managed to collect herself. "It is because of him that my father, the Wazir of Constantinople, is languishing in the dungeons of Emperor Azad Bakht." Then Samira told the merchant who she was and why she had come in search of him, dressed in men's clothes.

"I am sorry that your father suffered as a result of telling Wafadar's story," the merchant said quietly, "and I would like to help in any way that I can."

The dog was awake now and lifted his head, then rose to his noble feet and ambled over to his master.

Immediately the merchant took a fine piece of meat from his jeweled plate and fed it to Wafadar. The dog picked up the offering and looked at his owner with love in his eyes, and Samira saw his love reflected in the eyes of the merchant. Quietly, she looked on as the merchant stroked and fondled his dog and the dog rested his long, graceful muzzle on the merchant's knee.

"I would like to help you," said the merchant, "because I admire your effort. You combine wisdom and courage with a soft heart and single-minded dedication. I didn't know women like you existed."

"Perhaps," murmured Samira, "They are not often given the chance."

But the merchant was too preoccupied with his next thought to hear her. "Come and stay with me in my humble home," he said, "and let us discuss your next step." He looked at Wafadar. "And you, old friend, would you be willing to go on another journey for your master's sake?"

Wafadar licked his master's hand and stood up, suddenly playful.

"He agrees," smiled the merchant. "He agrees to accompany Samira to Constantinople to plead her father's case. You have lived up to your name, Samira—a true friend and companion. In my country poets write of a little white dove called Samira who proved her friendship by traveling far and wide to repay a human who once saved her life. It strikes me that you have done the same." That night, in the halls of the merchant's manor, Samira fell in love and when the merchant proposed marriage, she accepted.

"But only on condition that you agree to come and live in Constantinople," she said.

The merchant agreed and the next day they embarked on the return journey, which this time was far more comfortable than Samira had imagined possible.

On her return, Samira's first visit was to her father.

"I am back, Father, and I have with me the dog with the collar of twelve rubies and the man who owns him. What will the Emperor say to that?"

The old Wazir fell on his daughter's neck and wept with gratitude for her safe return.

"My days were hell and my night hellfire while you were away," he confessed. "I imagined that you had been attacked by every evil and besieged by every conceivable misfortune. I felt sure I would never see you again. I would have thanked God a million times every moment of the day for the rest of my life, even if you had returned alone and without the means to free me."

"Shame, Father," laughed Samira. "You have very little faith in your daughter."

Then Samira sought an audience with the Emperor and requested permission to bring a companion. The audience was granted and Samira and the merchant told Azad Bakht the whole story. He described how Samira had left home dressed as a man to redeem her father's honor.

"And now that you know the facts, Your Majesty, we beg a reprieve for Samira's father, the Grand Wazir."

"I have never heard such an incredible story!" exclaimed

Azad Bakht. "And I thank God that I did not harm my Wazir or put him to death."

The Emperor immediately ordered the release of the Wazir, and in the presence of his family and his courtiers, he begged his forgiveness.

"And all this," concluded the Emperor, "has been achieved through the efforts of a devoted daughter."

"A daughter," thought Samira alone in her chamber that night, smoothing her soft fabrics to her skin, inhaling the perfumed atmosphere of her room, slipping between the silk of her bedclothes, "who is very happy to be a woman now that she has shown what womankind can achieve."

# EXCELLENT THINGS IN WOMEN

ॐ

## Sara Suleri
## Goodyear

Sara Suleri Goodyear (1953– )
is an academic, critic, and writer.
She grew up in Lahore and earned
degrees there from Kinnaird College
and Punjab University, and a doctorate from Indiana University in the
United States.

Suleri Goodyear is currently a
professor of English at Yale University, the founding editor of *The Yale
Journal of Criticism*, and on the editorial board of *The Yale Review* and

*Transition.* She is the author of the critical work, *The Rhetoric of English India* (University of Chicago Press, 1992), and two much-acclaimed creative memoirs, *Meatless Days* (University of Chicago Press, 1989) and *Boys Will Be Boys* (University of Chicago Press, 2003). Together with her friend, Azra Raza, an oncologist in New York, she has translated into English a collection of *ghazals* by the great Urdu poet Mirza Asadullah Khan Ghalib, *Epistomologies of Elegance* (Oxford University Press, forthcoming).

Suleri Goodyear originally wrote "Excellent Things in Women" as an essay that won a Pushcart Prize in 1987. The story became the first chapter of her creative memoir, *Meatless Days* (published under the name Sara Suleri). Suleri Goodyear contemplates the women in her family, and the differences not only among them, but between them and the women she knows in the United States. She makes the point that women in Pakistan think of themselves not as members of a group that may or may not exhibit solidarity, but define themselves according to the role and rank that they occupy within a home. Dadi, Suleri Goodyear's widowed grandmother, is the family matriarch. She continues to find ways to assert her will, even when thwarted—and she knows how to strike back—yet she is hardly the mean-spirited, harsh mother-in-law of both Eastern and Western stereotypes. Suleri Goodyear's vivid portrayals of her are juxtaposed with the portrait of Suleri Goodyear's Welsh-born mother, who quietly finds her way as an insightful daughter-in-law with the rare ability to skilfully blend East and West within the household.

• • •

Leaving Pakistan was, of course, tantamount to giving up the company of women. I can tell this only to someone like Anita, in all the faith that she will understand, as we go perambulating through the grimness of New Haven and feed on the pleasures of our conversational way. Dale, who lives in Boston, would also understand. She will one day write a book about the stern and secretive life of breastfeeding and is partial to fantasies that culminate in an abundance of resolution. And Fawzi, with a grimace of recognition, knows because she knows the impulse to forget.

To a stranger or an acquaintance, however, some vesitigial remoteness obliges me to explain that my reference is to a place where the concept of woman was not really part of an available vocabulary: We were too busy for that, just living, and conducting precise negotiations with what it meant to be a sister or a child or a wife or a mother or a servant. By this point admittedly I am damned by my own discourse, and doubly damned when I add, yes, once in a while, we naturally thought of ourselves as women, but only in some perfunctory biological way that we happened on perchance. Or else it was a hugely practical joke, we thought, hidden somewhere among our clothes. But formulating that definition is about as impossible as attempting to locate the luminous qualities of an Islamic landscape, which can on occasion generate such aesthetically pleasing moments of life. My audience is lost, and angry to be lost, and both of us must find some token of exchange for this failed conversation. I try to lay the subject down and change its clothes, but before I know it, it has sprinted off evilly in the direction of ocular evidence. It goads me into saying, with the defiance of a plea, "You did not deal with Dadi."

Dadi, my father's mother, was born in Meerut toward the end of the last century. She was married at sixteen and widowed in her thirties, and by her latter decades could never exactly recall how many children she had borne. When India was partitioned, in August of 1947, she moved her thin pure Urdu into the Punjab of Pakistan and waited for the return of her eldest son, my father. He had gone careening off to a place called Inglestan, or England, fired by one of the several enthusiasms made available by the proliferating talk of independence. Dadi was peeved. She had long since dispensed with any loyalties larger than the pitiless give-and-take of people who are forced to live together in the same place, and she resented independence for the distances it made. She was not among those who, on the fourteenth of August, unfurled flags and festivities against the backdrop of people running and cities burning. About that era she would only say, looking up sour and cryptic over the edge of her Quran, "And I was also burned." She was, but that came years later.

By the time I knew her, Dadi with her flair for drama had allowed life to sit so heavily upon her back that her spine wilted and froze into a perfect curve, and so it was in the posture of a shrimp that she went scuttling through the day. She either scuttled or did not: It all depended on the nature of her fight with the Devil. There were days when she so hated him that all she could do was stretch herself out straight and tiny on her bed, uttering most awful imprecation. Sometimes, to my mother's great distress, Dadi could berate Satan in full eloquence only after she had clambered on top of the dining-room table and lain there like a little molding centerpiece. Satan was to blame: He had after all made her older son linger long enough in Inglestan to give up his rightful wife, a cousin, and take up instead with a white-legged woman. Satan had stolen away her only daughter Ayesha when Ayesha lay in childbirth. And he'd sent her youngest son to Swaziland, or Switzerland; her thin hand waved away such sophistries of name.

God she loved, and she understood him better than anyone. Her favorite days were those when she could circumnavigate both the gardener and my father, all in the solemn service of her God. With a pilfered knife, she'd wheedle her way to the nearest sapling in the garden, some sprightly poplar or a newly planted eucalyptus. She'd squat, she'd hack it down, and then she'd peel its bark away until she had a walking stick, all white and virgin and her own. It drove my father into tears of rage. He must have bought her a dozen walking sticks, one for each of our trips to the mountains, but it was like assembling a row of briar pipes for one who will not smoke: Dadi had different aims. Armed with implements of her own creation, she would creep down the driveway unperceived to stop cars and people on the street and give them all the gossip that she had on God.

Food, too, could move her to intensities. Her eyesight always took a sharp turn for the worse over meals—she could point hazily at a perfectly ordinary potato and murmur with Adamic reverence "What *is* it, what *is* it called?" With some shortness of manner one of us would describe and catalog the items on the table. *"Alu ka bhartha,"* Dadi repeated with wonderment and joy; "Yes, Saira Begum, you can put some here." "Not too much," she'd add pleadingly. For ritual had it that the more she demurred, the more she expected her plate to be piled with an amplitude her own politeness would never allow. The ritual happened three times a day.

We pondered it but never quite determined whether food or God constituted her most profound delight. Obvious problems, however, occurred whenever the two converged. One such occasion was the Muslim festival called Eid—not the one that ends the month of fasting, but the second Eid, which celebrates the seductions of the Abraham story in a remarkably literal way. In Pakistan, at least, people buy sheeps or goats beforehand and fatten them up for weeks with delectables. Then, on the appointed day, the animals are chopped, in place of sons, and neighbors graciously exchange silver trays heaped with raw and quivering meat. Following Eid prayers the men come home, and the animal is killed, and shortly thereafter rush out of the kitchen steaming plates of grilled lung and liver, of a freshness quite superlative.

It was a freshness to which my Welsh mother did not immediately take. She observed the custom but discerned in it a conundrum that allowed no ready solution. Liberal to an extravagant degree on thoughts abstract, she found herself to be remarkably squeamish about particular things. Chopping up animals for God was one. She could not locate the metaphor and was uneasy when obeisance played such a truant to the metaphoric realm. My father the writer quite agreed: He was so civilized in those days.

Dadi didn't agree. She pined for choppable things. Once

she made the mistake of buying a baby goat and bringing him home months in advance of Eid. She wanted to guarantee the texture of his festive flesh by a daily feeding of tender peas and clarified butter. Ifat, Shahid, and I greeted a goat into the family with boisterous rapture, and, soon after, he ravished us completely when we found him at the washingline nonchalantly eating Shahid's pajamas. Of course there was no argument: The little goat was our delight, and even Dadi knew there was no killing him. He became my brother's and my sister's and my first pet, and he grew huge, a big and grinning thing.

Years after, Dadi had her will. We were old enough, she must have thought, to set the house sprawling, abstracted, into a multitude of secrets. This was true, but still we all noticed one another's secretive ways. When, the day before Eid, our Dadi disappeared, my brothers and sisters and I just shook our heads. We hid the fact from my father, who at this time of life had begun to equate petulance with extreme vociferation. So we went about our jobs and tried to be Islamic for a day. We waited to sight moons on the wrong occasion, and watched the food come into lavishment. Dried dates change shape when they are soaked in milk, and carrots rich and strange turn magically sweet when deftly covered with green nutty shavings and smatterings of silver. Dusk was sweet as we sat out, the day's work done, in an evening garden. Lahore spread like peace around us. My father spoke, and when Papa talked, it was of Pakistan. But we were glad, then, at being audience to that familiar conversation, till his voice looked up, and failed. There was Dadi making her return, and she was prodigal. Like a question mark interested only in its own conclusions, her body crawled through the gates. Our guests were spellbound, then they looked away. Dadi, moving in her eerie crab formations, ignored the hangman's rope she firmly held as behind her in the gloaming minced, hugely affable, a goat.

That goat was still smiling the following day when Dadi's victory brought the butcher, who came and went just as he should on Eid. The goat was killed and cooked: A scrawny beast that required much cooking and never melted into succulence, he winked and glistened on our plates as we sat eating him on Eid. Dadi ate, that is: Papa had taken his mortification to some distant corner of the house; Ifat refused to chew on hemp; Tillat and Irfan gulped their baby sobs over such a slaughter. "Honestly," said Mamma, "honestly." For Dadi had successfully cut through tissues of festivity just as the butcher slit the goat, but there was something else that she was eating with that meat. I saw it in her concentration; I know that she was making God talk to her as to Abraham and was showing him what she could do—for him—to sons. God didn't dare, and she ate on alone.

Of those middle years it is hard to say whether Dadi was literally left alone or whether her bodily presence always emanated a quality of being apart and absorbed. In the winter I see her alone, painstakingly dragging her straw mat out to the courtyard at the back of the house and following the rich course of the afternoon sun. With her would go her Quran, a metal basin in which she could wash her hands, and her ridiculously heavy spouted waterpot, that was made of brass. None of us, according to Dadi, were quite pure enough to transport these particular items, but the rest of her paraphernalia we were allowed to carry out. There were baskets of her writing and sewing materials and her bottle of pungent and Dadi-like bitter oils, with which she'd coat the papery skin that held her brittle bones. And in the summer, when the night created an illusion of possible coolness and everyone held their breath while waiting for a thin and intermittent breeze, Dadi would be on the roof, alone. Her summer bed was a wooden frame latticed with a sweet-smelling rope, much aerated at its foot. She'd lie there all night until the wild monsoons would wake the lightest and the soundest sleeper into a rapturous welcome of rain.

In Pakistan, of course, there is no spring but only a rapid elision from winter into summer, which is analogous to the absence of a recognizable loneliness from the behavior of that climate. In a similar fashion it was hard to distinguish between Dadi with people and Dadi alone: She was merely impossibly unable to remain unnoticed. In the winter, when she was not writing or reading, she would sew for her delight tiny and magical reticules out of old silks and fragments she had saved, palm-sized cloth bags that would unravel into the precision of secret and more secret pockets. But none such pockets did she ever need to hide, since something of Dadi always remained intact, however much we sought to open her. Her discourse, for example, was impervious to penetration, so that when one or two of us remonstrated with her in a single hour, she never bothered to distinguish her replies. Instead she would pronounce generically and prophetically, "The world takes on a single face." "Must you, Dadi . . ." I'd begin, to be halted then by her great complaint: "The world takes on a single face."

It did. And often it was a countenance of some delight, for Dadi also loved the accidental jostle with things belligerent. As she went perambulating through the house, suddenly she'd hear Shahid, her first grandson, telling me or one of my sisters we were vile, we were disgusting women. And Dadi, who never addressed any one of us girls without first conferring the title of lady—so we were "Teellatt Begum," "Nuzhat Begum," "Iffatt Begum," "Saira Begum"—would halt in reprimand and tell her grandson never to call her granddaughters women. "What else shall I call them, men?" Shahid yelled. "Men!" said Dadi. "Men! There is more goodness in a woman's little finger than in the benighted mind of a man." "Hear, hear, Dadi! *Hanh, hanh, Dadi!*" my sisters cried. "For men," said Dadi, shaking the name off her fingertips like some unwanted water, "live as though they were unsuckled things." "And heaven," she grimly added, "is the thing Muhummad says (peace be upon him) lies beneath the feet of women!" "But he was a man," Shahid still would rage, if he weren't laughing, as all of us were laughing, while Dadi sat among us as a belle or a May queen.

Toward the end of the middle years my father stopped

speaking to his mother, and the atmosphere at home appreciably improved. They secretly hit upon a novel histrionics that took the place of their daily battle. They chose the curious way of silent things: Twice a day Dadi would leave her room and walk the long length of the corridor to my father's room. There she merely peered around the door, as though to see if he were real. Each time she peered, my father would interrupt whatever adult thing he might be doing in order to enact a silent paroxysm, an elaborate facial pantomime of revulsion and affront. At teatime in particular, when Papa would want the world to congregate in his room, Dadi came to peer her ghostly peer. Shortly thereafter conversation was bound to fracture, for we could not drown the fact that Dadi, invigorated by an outcast's strength, was sitting alone in the dining room, chanting an appeal: "God give me tea, God give me tea."

At about this time Dadi stopped smelling old and smelled instead of something equivalent to death. It would have been easy to notice if she had been dying, but instead she conducted the change as a refinement, a subtle gradation, just as her annoying little stove could shift its hanging odors away from smoke and into ash. During the middle years there had been something more defined about her being, which sat in the world as solely its own context. But Pakistan increasingly complicated the question of context, as though history, like a pestilence, forbid any definition outside relations to its fevered sleep. So it was simple for my father to ignore the letters that Dadi had begun to write to him every other day in her fine wavering script, letters of advice about the house or the children or the servants. Or she transcribed her complaint: "Oh my son, Zia. Do you think your son, Shahid, upon whom God bestow a thousand blessings, should be permitted to lift up his grandmother's chair and carry it into the courtyard when his grandmother is seated in it?" She had cackled in a combination of delight and virgin joy when Shahid had so transported her, but that little crackling sound she omitted from her letter. She ended it, and all her notes, with her single endearment. It was a phrase to halt and arrest when Dadi actually uttered it: Her solitary piece of tenderness was an injunction, really, to her world—"Keep on living," she would say.

Between that phrase and the great Dadi conflagration comes the era of the trying times. They began in the winter war of 1971, when East Pakistan became Bangladesh and Indira Gandhi hailed the demise of the two-nation theory. Ifat's husband was off fighting, and we spent the war together with her father-in-law, the brigadier, in the pink house on the hill. It was an ideal location for antiaircraft guns, so there was a bevy of soldiers and weaponry installed upon our roof. During each air raid the brigadier would stride purposefully into the garden and bark commands at them, as though the crux of the war rested upon his stiff upper lip. Then Dacca fell, and General Yahya came on television to resign the presidency and concede defeat. "Drunk, by God!" barked the brigadier as we sat watching, "Drunk!"

The following morning General Yahya's mistress came to mourn with us over breakfast, lumbering in draped with swathes of overscented silk. The brigadier lit an English cigarette—he was frequently known to avow that Pakistani cigarettes gave him a cuff—and bit on his mustache. "Yes," he barked, "these are trying times." "Oh yes, Gul," Yahya's mistress wailed, "These are such trying times." She gulped on her own eloquence, her breakfast bosom quaked, and then resumed authority over that dangling sentence: "It is so trying," she continued, "I find it so trying, it is trying to us all, to live in these trying, trying times." Ifat's eyes met mine in complete accord: Mistress transmogrified to muse; Bhutto returned from the UN to put Yahya under house arrest and became the first elected president of Pakistan; Ifat's husband went to India as a prisoner of war for two years; my father lost his newspaper. We had entered the era of the trying times.

Dadi didn't notice the war, just as she didn't really notice the proliferation of her great-grandchildren, for Ifat and Nuzzi conceived at the drop of a hat and kept popping babies out for our delight. Tillat and I felt favored at this vicarious taste of motherhood: We learned to become that enviable personage, a *khala*, mother's sister, and when our married sisters came to visit with their entourage, we reveled in the exercise of *khala*-love. I once asked Dadi how many sisters she had had. She looked up through the oceanic gray of her cataracted eyes and answered, "I forget."

The children helped, because we needed distraction, there being then in Pakistan a musty taste of defeat to all our activities. The children gave us something, but they also took something away—they initiated a slight displacement of my mother. Because her grandchildren would not speak any English, she could not read stories as of old. Urdu always remained a shyness on her tongue, and as the babies came and went she let something of her influence imperceptibly recede, as though she occupied an increasingly private space. Her eldest son was in England by then, so Mamma found herself assuming the classic posture of an Indian woman who sends away her sons and runs the risk of seeing them succumb to the great alternatives represented by the West. It was a position that preoccupied her; and without my really noticing what was happening, she quietly handed over many of her wifely duties to her two remaining daughters—to Tillat and to me. In the summer, once the ferocity of the afternoon sun had died down, it was her pleasure to go out into the garden on her own. There she would stand, absorbed and abstracted, watering the driveway and breathing in the heady smell of water on hot dust. I'd watch her often, from my room upstairs. She looked like a girl.

We were aware of something, of a reconfiguration in the air, but could not exactly tell where it would lead us. Dadi now spoke mainly to herself; even the audience provided by the deity had dropped away. Somehow there wasn't a proper balance between the way things came and the way they went, as Halima the cleaning woman knew full well when she looked at me intently, asking a question that had no question in it: "Do I grieve, or do I celebrate?" Halima had given birth to her latest son the night her older child died in screams of meningitis; once heard, never to be forgotten. She came back to work a week later, and we were talking as we put away the family's winter clothes into vast metal trunks. For in England, they would call it spring.

We felt a quickening urgency of change drown our sense of regular direction, as though something were bound to happen soon but not knowing what it would be was making history nervous. And so we were not really that surprised, then, to find ourselves living through the summer of the trials by fire. It climaxed when Dadi went up in a little ball of flames, but somehow sequentially related were my mother's trip to England to tend her dying mother, and the night I beat up Tillat, and the evening I nearly castrated my little brother, runt of the litter, serious-eyed Irfan.

It was an accident on both our parts. I was in the kitchen, so it must have been a Sunday, when Allah Ditta the cook took the evenings off. He was a mean-spirited man with an incongruously delicate touch when it came to making food. On Sunday at midday he would bluster one of us into the kitchen and show us what he had prepared for the evening meal, leaving strict and belligerent instructions about what would happen if we overheated this or dared brown that. So I was in the kitchen heating up some food when Farni came back from playing hockey, an ominous asthmatic rattle in his throat. He, the youngest, had been my parents' gravest infant: In adolescence he remained a gentle invalid. Of course he pretended otherwise, and was loud and raucous, but it never worked.

Tillat and I immediately turned on him with the bullying litany that actually can be quite soothing, the invariable female reproach to the returning male. He was to do what he hated— stave off his disease by sitting over a bowl of camphor and boiling water and inhaling its acrid fumes. I insisted that he sit on the cook's little stool in the kitchen, holding the bowl of medicated water on his lap, so that I could cook, and Farni could not cheat, and I could time each minute he should sit there thus confined. We seated him and flounced a towel on his reluctant head. The kitchen reeked jointly of cumin and camphor, and he sat skinny and penitent and swathed for half a minute, and then was begging to be done. I slammed down the carving knife and screamed "Irfan!" with such ferocity that he jumped, figuratively and literally, right out of his skin. The bowl of water emptied onto him, and with a gurgling cry Irfan leaped up, tearing at his steaming clothes. He clutched at his groin, and everywhere he touched, the skin slid off, so that between his fingers his penis easily unsheathed, a blanched and fiery grape. "What's happening?" screamed Papa from his room; "What's happening?" echoed Dadi's wail from the opposite end of the house. What was happening was that I was holding Farni's shoulders, trying to stop him from jumping up and down, but I was jumping too, while Tillat just stood there frozen, frowning at his poor, ravaged grapes.

This was June, and the white heat of summer. We spent the next few days laying ice on Farni's wounds: Half the time I was allowed to stay with him, until the doctors suddenly remembered I was a woman and hurried me out when his body made crazy spastic reactions to its burns. Once things grew calmer and we were alone, Irfan looked away and said, "I hope I didn't shock you, Sara." I was so taken by tenderness for his bony convalescent body that it took me years to realize yes, something female in me had been deeply shocked.

Mamma knew nothing of this, of course. We kept it from her so she could concentrate on what had taken her back to the rocky coastline of Wales, to places she had not really revisited since she was a girl. She was waiting with her mother, who was blind now and of a fine translucency, and both of them knew that they were waiting for her death. It was a peculiar posture for Mamma to maintain, but her quiet letter spoke mainly of the sharp astringent light that made the sea wind feel so brisk in Wales and so many worlds away from the deadly omnipresent weight of summer in Lahore. There in Wales one afternoon, walking childless among the brambles and the furze, Mamma realized that her childhood was distinctly lost. "It was not that I wanted to feel more familiar," she later told me, "or that I was more used to feeling unfamiliar in Lahore. It's just that familiarity isn't important, really," she murmured absently, "it really doesn't matter at all."

When Mamma was ready to return, she wired us her plans, and my father read the cable, kissed it, then put it in his pocket. I watched him and felt startled, as we all did on the occasions when our parents' lives seemed to drop away before our eyes, leaving them youthfully engrossed in the illusion of knowledge conferred by love. We were so used to conceiving of them as parents moving in and out of hectic days that it always amused us, and touched us secretly, when they made quaint and punctilious returns to the amorous bond that had initiated their unlikely life together.

That summer while my mother was away, Tillat and I experienced a new bond of powerlessness, the white and shaking rage of sexual jealousy in parenthood. I had always behaved toward her as a contentious surrogate parent, but she had been growing beyond that scope and in her girlhood asking me for a formal acknowledgment of equality that I was loath to give. My reluctance was rooted in a helpless fear of what the world might do to her, for I was young and ignorant enough not to see that what I might do was worse. She went out one evening when my father was off on one of his many trips. The house was gaping emptily, and Tillat was very late. Allah Ditta had gone home, and Dadi and Irfan were sleeping; I read, and thought, and walked up and down the garden, and Tillat was very, very late. When she came back she wore that strange sheath of complacency and guilt which pleasure puts on faces very young. It smote an outrage in my heart until despite all resolutions to the contrary I heard myself hiss: "And where were you?" Her returning look was fearful and preening at the same time, and the next thing to be smitten was her face. "Don't, Sara," Tillat said in her superior way, "physical violence is so degrading." "To you, maybe," I answered, and hit her once again.

It set a sorrowful bond between us, for we both felt complicit in the shamefulness that had made me seem righteous whereas I had felt simply jealous, which we tacitly agreed was a more legitimate thing to be. But we had lost something, a certain protective aura, some unspoken myth asserting that love between sisters at least was sexually innocent. Now we had to fold that vain belief away and stand in more naked relation to our affection. Till then we had associated such violence with all that was outside us, as though somehow the more history fractured, the more whole we would be. But we began to lose that sense of the differentiated identities of history and ourselves and became guiltily aware that we had known it all along, our part in the construction of unreality.

By this time, Dadi's burns were slowly learning how to heal. It was she who had given the summer its strange pace by nearly burning herself alive at its inception. On an early April night Dadi awoke, seized by a desperate need for tea. It was three in the morning, the household was asleep, so she was free to do the great forbidden thing of creeping into Allah Ditta's kitchen and taking charge, like a pixie in the night. As all of us had grown bored of predicting, one of her many cotton garments took to fire that truant night. Dadi, however, deserves credit for her resourceful voice, which wavered out for witness to her burning death. By the time Tillat awoke and found her, she was a little flaming ball: "Dadi!" cried Tillat in the reproach of sleep, and beat her quiet with a blanket. In the morning we discovered that Dadi's torso had been almost consumed and little recognizable remained from collarbone to groin. The doctors bade us to some decent mourning.

But Dadi had different plans. She lived through her sojourn

at the hospital; she weathered her return. Then, after six weeks at home, she angrily refused to be lugged like a chunk of meat to the doctor's for her daily change of dressings: "Saira Begum will do it," she announced. Thus developed my great intimacy with the fluid properties of human flesh. By the time Mamma left for England, Dadi's left breast was still coagulate and raw. Later, when Irfan got his burns, Dadi was growing pink and livid tightropes, strung from hip to hip in a flaming advertisement of life. And in the days when Tillat and I were wrestling, Dadi's vanished nipples started to congeal and convex their cavities into triumphant little love knots.

I learned about the specialization of beauty through that body. There were times, as with love, when I felt only disappointment, carefully easing off the dressings and finding again a piece of flesh that would not knit, happier in the texture of stubborn glue. But then on more exhilarating days I'd peel like an onion all her bandages away and suddenly discover I was looking down at some literal tenacity and was bemused at all the freshly withered shapes she could create. Each new striation was a victory to itself, and when Dadi's hairless groin solidified again and sent firm signals that her abdomen must do the same, I could have wept with glee.

After her immolation, Dadi's diet underwent some curious changes. At first her consciousness teetered too much for her to pray, but then as she grew stronger it took us a while to notice what was missing: She had forgotten prayer. It left her life as firmly as tobacco can leave the lives of only the most passionate smokers, and I don't know if she ever prayed again. At about this time, however, with the heavy-handed inevitability that characterized his relation to his mother, my father took to prayer. I came home one afternoon and looked for him in all the usual places, but he wasn't to be found. Finally I came across Tillat and asked her where Papa was. "Praying," she said. "*Praying?*" I said. "Praying," she said, and I felt most embarrassed. For us it was rather as though we had come upon the children playing some forbidden titillating game and decided it was wisest to ignore it calmly. In an unspoken way, though, I think we dimly knew we were about to witness Islam's departure from the land of Pakistan. The men would take it to the streets and make it vociferate, but the great romance between religion and the populace, the embrace that engendered Pakistan, was done. So Papa prayed, with the desperate ardor of a lover trying to converse life back into a finished love.

That was a change, when Dadi patched herself together again and forgot to put prayer back into its proper pocket, for God could now leave the home and soon would join the government. Papa prayed and fasted and went on pilgrimage and read the Quran aloud with most peculiar locutions. Occasionally we also caught him in nocturnal altercations that made him sound suspiciously like Dadi: We looked askance, but didn't say a thing. My mother was altogether admirable: She behaved as though she'd always known that she'd wed a swaying, chanting thing and that to register surprise now would be an impoliteness to existence. Her expression reminded me somewhat of the time when Ifat was eight and Mamma was urging her recalcitrance into some goodly task. Ifat postponed, and Mamma, always nifty with appropriate fables, quoted meaningfully: "'I'll do it myself,' said the little red hen." Ifat looked up with bright affection. "Good little red hen," she murmured. Then a glance crossed my mother's face, a look between a slight smile and a quick rejection of the eloquent response, like a woman looking down and then away.

She looked like that at my father's sudden hungering for God, which was added to the growing number of subjects about which we, my mother and her daughters, silently decided we had no conversation. We knew there was something other than trying times ahead and would far rather hold our breath than speculate about what other surprises the era held up its capacious sleeve. Tillat and I decided to quash our dread of waiting around for change by changing for ourselves, before destiny took the time to come our way. I would move to the United States, and Tillat to Kuwait and marriage. To both declarations of intention my mother said, "I see," and helped us in our preparations: She knew by then her elder son would not return, and was prepared to extend the courtesy of change to her daughters, too. We left, and Islam predictably took to the streets, shaking Bhutto's empire. Mamma and Dadi remained the only women in the house, the one untalking, the other unpraying.

Dadi behaved abysmally at my mother's funeral, they told me, and made them all annoyed. She set up loud and unnecessary lamentations in the dining room, somewhat like an heir apparent, as though this death had reinstated her as mother of the house. While Ifat and Nuzzi and Tillat wandered frozen-eyed, dealing with the roses and the ice, Dadi demanded an irritating amount of attention, stretching out supine and crying out, "Your mother has betrayed your father; she left him; she has gone." Food from respectful mourners poured in, cauldron after cauldron, and Dadi relocated a voracious appetite.

Years later, I was somewhat sorry that I had heard this tale, because it made me take affront. When I returned to Pakistan, I was too peeved with Dadi to find out how she was. Instead I listened to Ifat tell me about standing there in the hospital, watching the doctors suddenly pump upon my mother's heart—"I'd seen it on television," she gravely said, "I knew it was the end." Mamma's students from the university had tracked down the rickshaw driver who had knocked her down: They'd pummeled him nearly to death and then camped out in our garden, sobbing wildly, all in hordes.

By this time Bhutto was in prison and awaiting trial, and General Zulu was presiding over the Islamization of Pakistan. But we had no time to notice. My mother was buried at the nerve center of Lahore, an unruly and dusty place, and my father immediately made arrangements to buy the plot of land next to her grave: "We're ready when you are," Shahid sang. Her tombstone bore some pretty Urdu poetry and a completely fictitious place of birth, because some details my father tended to forget.

&

"Honestly," it would have moved his wife to say.

So I was angry with Dadi at that time and didn't stop to see her. I saw my mother's grave and then came back to the United States, hardly noticing when, six months later, my father called from London and mentioned Dadi was now dead. It happened in the same week that Bhutto finally was hanged, and our imaginations were consumed by that public and historical dying. Pakistan made rapid provisions not to talk about the thing that had been done, and somehow, accidently, Dadi must have been mislaid into that larger decision, because she too ceased being a mentioned thing. My father tried to get back in time for the funeral, but he was so busy talking Bhutto-talk in England that he missed his flight and thus did not return. Luckily, Irfani was at home, and he saw Dadi to her grave.

Bhutto's hanging had the effect of making Pakistan feel unreliable, particularly to itself. Its landscape learned a new secretiveness, unusual for a formerly loquacious people. This may account for the fact that I have never seen my grandmother's grave and neither have my sisters. I think we would have tried, had we been together, despite the free-floating anarchy in the air that—like the heroin trade—made the world suspicious and afraid. There was no longer any need to wait for change, because change was all there was, and we had quite forgotten the flavor of an era that stayed in place long enough to gain a name. One morning I awoke to find that, during the course of the night, my mind had completely ejected the names of all the streets in Pakistan, as though to assure that I could not return, or that if I did, it would be returning to a loss. Overnight the country had grown absentminded, and patches of amnesia hung over the hollows of the land like fog.

I think we could have mourned Dadi in our belated way, but the coming year saw Ifat killed in the consuming rush of change and disbanded the company of women for all time. It was a curious day in March, two years after my mother died, when the weight of that anniversary made us all disconsolate for her quietude. "I'll speak to Ifat, though," I thought to myself in the United States. But in Pakistan someone had different ideas for that sister of mine and thwarted all my plans. When she went walking out that warm March night, a car came by and trampled her into the ground, and then it vanished strangely. By the time I reached Lahore, a tall and slender mound had usurped the grave-space where my father had hoped to lie, next to the more moderate shape that was his wife. Children take over everything.

So, worn by repetition, we stood by Ifat's grave, and took note of the narcissi, still alive, that she must have placed upon my mother on the day that she was killed. It made us impatient, in a way, as though we had to decide that there was nothing so farcical as grief and that it had to be eliminated from our diets for good. It cut away, of course, our intimacy with Pakistan, where history is synonymous with grief and always most at home in the attitudes of grieving. Our congregation in Lahore was brief, and then we swiftly returned to a more geographic reality. "We are lost, Sara," Shahid said to me on the phone from England. "Yes, Shahid," I firmly said, "We're lost."

Today, I'd be less emphatic. Ifat and Mamma must have honeycombed and crumbled now, in the comfortable way that overtakes bedfellows. And somehow it seems apt and heartening that Dadi, being what she was, never suffered the pomposities that enter the most well-meaning of farewells and seeped instead into the nooks and crannies of our forgetfulness. She fell between two stools of grief, which is appropriate, since she was greatest when her life was at its most unreal. Anyway she was always outside our ken, an anecdotal thing, neither more nor less. So some sweet reassurance of reality accompanies my discourse when I claim that when Dadi died, we all forgot to grieve.

For to be lost is just a minute's respite, after all, like a train that cannot help but stop between the stations of its proper destination in order to stage a pretend version of the end. Dying, we saw, was simply change taken to points of mocking extremity, and wasn't a thing to lose us but to find us out, to catch us where we least wanted to be caught. In Pakistan, Bhutto rapidly became obsolete after a succession of bumper harvests, and none of us can fight the ways that the names Mamma and Ifat have been archaisms, quaintnesses on our lips.

Now I live in New Haven and feel quite happy with my life. I miss, of course, the absence of women and grow increasingly nostalgic for a world where the modulations of age are as recognized and welcomed as the shift from season into season. But that's a hazard that has to come along, since I have made myself inhabitant of a population which democratically insists that everyone from twenty-nine to fifty-six occupies roughly the same space of age. When I teach topics in third-world literature, much time is lost in trying to explain that the third world is locatable only as a discourse of convenience. Trying to find it is like pretending that history or home is real and not located precisely where you're sitting, I hear my voice quite idiotically say. And then it happens. A face, puzzled and attentive and belonging to my gender, raises its intelligence to question why, since I am teaching third-world writing, I haven't given equal space to women writers on my syllabus. I look up, the horse's mouth, a foolish thing to be. Unequal images battle in my mind for precedence—there's imperial Ifat, there's Mamma in the garden, and Halima the cleaning woman is there too, there's uncanny Dadi with her goat. Against all my own odds I know what I must say. Because, I'll answer slowly, there are no women in the third world.

# A PAIR
# OF JEANS

&

## Qaisra Shahraz

Qaisra Shahraz (1958– ) is a novelist, script writer, and educator. She was born in Pakistan and moved to Britain at age nine and has lived there with her family ever since. She studied English and European literature and scriptwriting at the Universities of Manchester and Salford, earning two masters degrees. She is an education consultant, an international teacher trainer, a college inspector, a fellow of the Royal Society of Arts, and a member of the Royal Society of Literature.

Shahraz's publications include two novels: *The Holy Woman* (Black Amber, 2001), winner of the Golden Jubilee Award; and *Typhoon* (Black Amber, 2003). Both have been translated into several languages. Her fourteen-episode television drama, *The Heart Is It*, won two TV Awards in Pakistan. Her award-winning short stories are taught in schools and colleges; "A Pair of Jeans," her very first work of fiction, was first published in the British text book *Holding Out: Short Stories by British Women Writers* (Crocus, 1988). Since 1990 it has been taught in Germany from literary texts aimed for schools and in 2006 was among the stories chosen by the German Education Ministry of the Federal State of Baden Wurttemberg as compulsory required reading from 2007 to 2012 for the Abitur (higher level) English Literature exam for all the gymnasium schools for seventeen- to eighteen-year-old students.

"A Pair of Jeans" puts the symbolism of clothing at the center of the culture conflict in the lives of Asians in Britain. The jeans that Mariam wears for a normal, innocuous hiking trip put undue stress on her engagement. They become a symbol of all that her fiancé's parents fear: the loss of identity and cultural moorings in an alien land, and their loss of power over their son.

• • •

Miriam slid off the bus seat and glanced quickly at her watch. They were coming! And she was very late. Murmuring her goodbye to her two university friends, she made her way to the door and waited for her bus stop. Once there she got off and hurriedly waved goodbye to her friends again. She pulled her jacket close, suddenly conscious of her jean-clad legs and the short vest underneath her jacket. The vest had shrunk in the wash. All day she had kept pulling it down to cover her midriff. Strange, she felt odd in her clothing now, though they were just the type of clothes she needed to wear today, for hill walking in the Peak District in the north west of England. Somehow here, in the vicinity of her home, she felt different. As she crossed the road and headed for her own street she was acutely aware of her appearance and hoped she would not meet anyone she knew. She tugged at the hemline of her vest; it had ridden up yet again. With the other hand she held onto the jacket front as it had no buttons.

Her mind turned to the outing. It had been a wonderful day, and though her legs ached after climbing all those green hills, still it was worth it. Her eye on her watch, she hastened her pace. It was much later than she had anticipated. She remembered the phone call of yesterday evening. They said they were coming today. What if they had already arrived? She glanced down at her tight jeans. As soon as she reached home, she must discreetly make her way to her room and change quickly.

Just as Miriam reached the gate of her semidetached house she heard a car pull up behind her. Nervously she turned around to see who it was. On spotting the color of the car and the person behind the wheel, her step faltered; color ebbed from her face. On the pretence of opening the gate, she tried to collect her wits. Too late! They were already here. Her heart was now rocking madly against her chest. The clothes burned her. She wanted to rush inside and peel them off. She clutched at her jacket front, covering her waist.

She braced herself. She could not scurry inside. That was not the way things were done, no matter what. Calmly, she let go of the gate. She turned to greet the two people who had stepped out of the car and were surveying her. She didn't realize that she had let go of her jacket: It flew wide open, revealing the short vest underneath. Their eyes fell straight to the inch of bare waist flesh. The woman was her future mother-in-law, a slightly frail woman dressed in *shalwar kameez* with a chador around her shoulders. The elderly man was the woman's husband. He towered behind his wife.

Miriam was unable to look either of them in the eye. A watery, hesitant smile played around her mouth. She did not know what to do. Her cheeks burned with embarrassment. These were the very people she had wanted to impress. All she

was aware of now were the surreptitious glances they darted—
not at her as Miriam, but at the figure she presented in a pair of
Levis and skimpy leather jacket. This was not the Miriam they
knew but a stranger, a Western version of Miriam. She sensed
their awkwardness. They too were caught off guard and did not
know what to do. The father-in-law was bent on avoiding eye
contact by studiously looking above her head.

He pushed the gate open and in two strides had crossed
the driveway and was now solidly knocking on the front door.
Miriam stepped aside to let the woman, silently walking behind
her husband, pass. Miriam followed them in a semidaze. As she
closed the gate behind her, she remembered with mortification
that while the woman had accepted her mumbled greeting by
her reply, "*Wa laikum Assalam*," the father-in-law had ignored
it.

Miriam's mother, Fatima, opened the door to her guests,
beaming with pleasure and warmth. She had not expected Miriam to arrive with them. She got a shock seeing her daughter
hovering behind. Never before had Miriam seen such a dramatic change in her mother's face. Normally she wouldn't have
batted an eyelid if her daughter had turned up at 11 o'clock at
night, as long as she knew where she was and with whom, and
at what time she was returning home. Today, she was viewing
her daughter's arrival and appearance through a different pair of
lenses: those of Miriam's future in-laws.

The jeans, which wouldn't have aroused her interest normally, today stood out brazenly on Miriam's body, tightly
moulded against her full legs. Fatima gaped at Miriam's midriff showing through. Heat was now rushing through Fatima's
cheeks. An inch of her daughter's flesh was visible! Her mind
reeling, Fatima communicated her displeasure and signaled her
daughter with her eyebrows to go up and change into something
more respectable. Miriam was only too glad to oblige.

Squeezing past her mother and out of sight of their guests,
Miriam almost ran up the stairs to her bedroom, shut the door

behind her, and breathed deeply. The tiredness and exhilaration from the hill walking had vanished—discontent had taken its place. Two steps into her home had led to another world. The other she had left behind with her friends on the bus. What mattered now were the two people downstairs. And they mattered! Her future lay with them.

She peeled off her jacket, vest, and tight jeans and let them fall, lying in a clutter on the woollen carpet. She looked at them with distaste. Her mouth twisted into a cynical smile. "Damn it!" her mind shouted, rebelling. "They're only clothes. I'm still the same young woman they visited regularly—the person they have happily chosen as a bride for their son."

"Deny it as much as you like, Miriam," her heart whispered back.

"It's no use. They have seen another side of you—your other persona."

The other "persona" had, by accident or contrivance, remained hidden from them. When they first saw her at a party she was dressed in a maroon chiffon sari. Later, on each occasion, she was always smartly but discreetly and respectably dressed in a traditional *shalwar kameez*. Now they were seeing her as a young college woman under the sway of Western fashion and, by extension, its moral values. Muslim girls did not go outdoors dressed like that, especially in a short jacket which hardly covered the hips—and a skimpy vest! She had heard of stories about in-laws who were prejudiced against such girls because they weren't the docile, obedient, and sweet daughters-in-law that they preferred. On the contrary, they were seen as a threat, as rebellious hoydens who did not respect either their husbands or their in-laws. Miriam was all too familiar with such stereotypes.

She pulled off a blue crêpe *shalwar kameez* from a hanger. As she put it on her rebellious spirit reared its head again. "They're only clothes!" her mind hissed in anger.

She could not deny that by putting them on she had

embraced a new set of values: in fact, a new personality. Her body was now modestly swathed in an elegant long tunic and baggy trousers. The curvy contours of her female body were discreetly draped. With a quick glance in the mirror she left her room, a confident woman gliding down the stairs. Her poise was back. Her long *dupatta* was draped around her shoulders and its edge covered her head.

Once downstairs in the hallway, outside the sitting room door, she halted, her hypocrisy galling her. She was acting out a role, the one that her future in-laws preferred: that of a demure and elegant bride and daughter-in-law. Yet she was the same person who had earlier traipsed the Pennine countryside in a tight pair of jeans and Wellingtons, and who was now dressed in the height of Pakistani fashion. Or was she the same person? She didn't know. Perhaps it was true that there were two sides to her character. A person who spontaneously switched from one setting to another, from one mode of dress into another—in short, swapping one identity for another. Ensconced in the other home ground her thoughts, actions and feelings had seamlessly altered accordingly.

Her head held high, Miriam entered the living room. Four pairs of eyes turned in her direction. She stared ahead knowing instinctively that, apart from her father's, those eyes were busy comparing her present appearance with her earlier one. It was amazing how she was able to move around the room at ease in her s*halwar kameez* suit, in a manner that she could never have done in her earlier clothes. She sat down beside her mother, acutely aware of her mother-in-law's eyes discreetly appraising both her appearance and her movements.

After a while the conversation flagged. Fatima was doing her very best to revive a number of topics of interest to the other couple. The two guests, however, seemed to shy away, particularly from the one concerning their children's marriage in six months' time. Miriam noticed that they had made no direct eye contact with her. This was quite unlike their usual behavior.

There were moments too, when husband and wife exchanged surreptitious glances. Fatima was now quite anxious. From the moment her guests had stepped inside, her instincts told her that something was wrong. She was ready to discuss the subject with them, but first she requested her daughter to bring in some refreshments. The dinner had already been prepared and laid out on the dining table in the kitchen.

Miriam was only too happy to leave the room; behind her a hushed silence reigned. She puttered around the kitchen, collecting bits and pieces of crockery from the cupboards. Her own hunger had vanished. She was arranging the plates and glasses on a tray when she heard their voices in the hallway. They sounded as if were saying goodbye to her parents. Surprised, Miriam picked up the tray. Were they going already? They hadn't eaten anything! The table was laid for dinner. She called out, "Auntie," addressing her future mother-in-law. She turned and smiled. They were in a hurry to get home, she explained, because they had guests staying over.

"That is a lousy excuse," Miriam thought. If they had guests at home why did they bother to come? She returned to the kitchen and put the tray back on the table.

What a waste of time!

The two future parents-in-law walked to their car in a silence that continued during their journey. There was no need for communication. Each could guess what the other was thinking. On reaching home the so-called guests whom Begum had referred to earlier, had apparently gone. Their elder son, Farook, was not yet in. The younger one was upstairs, studying for his GCSE examinations. They could hear the music from the CD disc blaring away. He loved listening to songs as he revised.

Ayub shed his jacket and hung it in the hallway, then went straight to the living room. Begum followed, also taking off her coat and outdoor shawl. Switching on the television Ayub sat down in his armchair. Begum hovered listlessly near him a minute, looking down at her husband—waiting. Then, mechanically folding her woollen shawl into its customary neat folds, she left the room and went upstairs to her bedroom to place it in her drawer. For a few moments she stood lost in thought, looking out of the bedroom window: Her neighbor Mrs. Williams had another car. This was the third in six months. What did she do with them? Then she heard her husband call her name, his voice supremely autocratic.

Mrs. Williams and her love of cars put aside, Begum returned to the living room and sat down on the sofa opposite her husband, waiting for him to begin. Her heartbeat had automatically quickened. Seconds were ticking away into minutes. Her husband had made no move to say anything, his gaze on the newscaster. She picked up the Urdu national newspaper, *Daily Jang*, from the coffee table and began to read. More precisely she was pretending to read: The words were a blur in front of her eyes.

At last Ayub stood up, stretching his legs. Striding across the room he switched off the television. Returning to his chair his pointed gaze now fell on his wife.

"Well!" he began softly.

Now it was her turn to play; she pretended not to hear him or understand the implication of his exclamation. Absurdly, now that the moment of reckoning had come, she wanted to prevaricate, to put the off discussion.

"Well, what?" she responded coldly, buying time, peeping at her unsmiling husband over the edge of the newspaper.

"You know very well what I mean! Don't pretend to misunderstand me, Begum," he rasped. He was not amused by her manner, tone, or words.

Begum calmly examined the harsh outlines of her husband's unsmiling face. She was lost. She did not know what to say or how to say it, although she knew the subject he was referring to. Her lips would not open. She simply stared at him.

"Well, what do you think of your future daughter-in-law?

I thought you told me that she was a very sharif, a very modest girl. Was that naked waist what you call modest?" His voice lanced her.

"I am sure she is," Begum volunteered defensively. After all, she was the one who had originally taken a liking to Miriam.

"Huh!" Ayub grunted. "Sharif! Dressed like that! God knows who has seen her. Would you like any of your friends and relatives to have seen her as she appeared today? Would you, Begum?" The voice was cutting.

"But she's a college student—college students do dress like that. Haven't you yourself joked about tatty jean-clad university students?" Begum persisted boldly.

She wanted to excuse Miriam's attire to herself and to him. She knew she was not going to make a success of it because, in her heart, she agreed with her husband.

"Tell me, in those clothes of hers, would you be proud to have her as your daughter-in-law? I know I would not. You talk about her being a university student. Well, have you any idea what sort of company she might be keeping? You've only seen her at odd times, and always at home. Do you know what she's really like? Have you thought of the effect she could have in your household? With her lifestyle, such girls also want a lot of freedom. In fact, they want to lead their lives the way their English college friends do. Did you notice what time she came in? She knew we were coming yet that made no difference to her. Do you expect her to change overnight in order to suit us? People form habits, Begum, do you understand? Are you prepared for a daughter-in-law who goes in and out of the house whenever she feels like it, dressed like that, and returns home late? Don't your cheeks burn at the thought of that bit of flesh you saw? Imagine how our son will feel about her! Shame, I hope! And what if she has a boyfriend already—have you thought of that? *What if she has a boyfriend already?* What if she takes drugs? So many questions to ask ourselves! Do you know, we do not know this girl at all, Begum! Can you guarantee that she will make our son happy?"

He paused strategically, waiting for her to say something. Begum had nothing to add.

He continued, "You know of a number of cases where these educated, so-called modern girls have twined their husbands around their little fingers and expected them to dance to their tunes. Are you prepared for that to happen to your beloved son? To lose him to such a daughter-in-law? Have you the heart for that?"

Begum just stared, listening quietly to her husband's angry lecture. After twenty-five years of marriage she could read him like a book. His words, their nuance, the tilt of his eyebrow, the authoritative swing of his hand, the thin line of his mouth spelled only one message. With a sinking heart she guessed the outcome of this discussion. She did not know how to react even though she didn't disagree with him. Not one jot. When she saw Miriam standing near the garden gate with her jacket open similar thoughts had whizzed through her mind, although she would not have voiced them in such a harsh way. Her perception of what her daughter-in-law should be did not quite tally with the picture that Miriam presented to them, or with the clear picture that Ayub's words had conjured up. Why did that stupid girl have to wear those jeans and that vest, today of all days? And why did Ayub have to see her like that?

She had always reckoned on a conventional daughter-in-law—the epitome of tradition. Definitely not one who was so strongly influenced by Western forms of dress, culture and probably feminist ideas as Miriam. The mad girl had no qualms about blatantly showing a part of her body in a public place. Begum shuddered.

What about Farook, their son? How would they deal with him? Luckily, it was not Farook who had initially befriended Miriam but she herself. A glimpse of Miriam at a *mehndi* party had tugged at Begum's heart. From the first moment she had fit the image of what her future daughter-in-law should be like—young, beautiful, and well educated. She had just obtained three A levels and was now doing geography at university.

Begum had liked the way Miriam behaved—ever so correctly and gracefully. Above all, she had liked the way she dressed. How ironic that assumption was after today. It was the way the black chiffon sari had hugged her slender figure, and how her hair was elegantly wound up in a knot at the top of her head—just perfect. She was neither overdressed nor overdecked in jewels, nor over made-up as some of her peers were; nor was she overboisterous. In short, Begum had viewed Miriam as the epitome of perfection, everything that was correct and appealing. She had stood out among other girls. Looking back now, two years later, Begum was sure that, not her son, but she herself had fallen in love with Miriam at first sight. And not just that. Her name, Miriam, wove a magic spell around her. It had a special ring to it and she had loved using it.

There was more—Begum had taken a real liking to Miriam's parents too, especially her mother. And liking future in-laws, particularly the mother, was an important part of the equation. She knew of mothers-in-law who hated each other. Begum and Miriam's mother, Fatima, met for the first time at the *mehndi* party. After that they became warm friends and were soon in and out of each other's homes. With the subject of their growing children's futures looming in their domestic horizons the two mothers had, as a matter of course, discussed and dwelt at length on their children's marriage prospects.

Farook and Miriam had also met each other soon afterward. Often accompanied by their parents they, too, took a liking to each other. They found they were very compatible in their interests and personalities and had a lot to laugh about, often giggling together. When their parents suggested the idea of marriage both heartily agreed. Farook just couldn't help grinning all over. Miriam was struck with sudden shyness, her cheeks burning. Soon afterward an engagement party was held for the two. In order to let them complete their respective courses, the wedding was to be postponed for a year or so.

That was a year ago. Today Farook's parents had gone to meet Miriam's in order to discuss the arrangements for the forthcoming wedding. Instead they had returned home without even mentioning the word. Yet their thoughts were very much centered on that subject. But more importantly, on Miriam herself—her clothes and her body!

"Well?" Ayub's cold prompting brought his wife back to the present.

Begum turned to look at her husband once more and waited for him to finish what he was going to say.

"What are you going to do?" he rasped.

This time she could not pretend to misunderstand him.

She faced him squarely, poised for a battle. Yet, as she was about to utter the words, her heart sank. For she saw her Miriam fast disappearing from the horizon. As she tried to clutch onto her image in her mind, there arose the one of her in that silly pair of faded jeans and that ridiculously short vest. Her heart sank. It had to be. It was better to face the matter now than regret it later. The problem was how she, Begum, was going to deal with it. She had neither the heart nor the courage to play the role demanded of her, or the one she inevitably had to play in this drama. Knowing her husband she knew for sure that he would leave it to her—to sort out the situation with her son, and with Miriam and her family.

Once again she looked her husband directly in the eye.

"You truly don't want the wedding to take place, then?" she asked tentatively, still desperate to hold onto Miriam.

"I thought I had already made myself obvious!" He was enraged.

"I suppose I agree with what you say, but how are we going to go about it?" Begum stammered, the boldness gone, now very much resigned to her fate and Miriam's.

"I leave that entirely to you—especially as you were the one so hot on the girl. I am sure we can find lots of other women for our son, women who have a more discreet taste in clothing and a good understanding of female modesty. Similarly, I am sure, her parents will find a man more suited to her lifestyle than our son, a man who has the capacity to tolerate her particular mode of dressing, for want of a better word."

They heard the front door open. That must be Farook. They stopped talking and stared at each other. Begum's heart was thumping away, dreading talking to him about Miriam. She felt like a traitor. Getting up quickly she went into the kitchen to get his dinner, hoping he would go straight to his room first. Ayub picked up the newspaper and began to read.

Miriam had just got in from the university when she heard the phone ringing. She dashed down from her room to answer it. She faltered—it was Aunt Begum. She quickly obliged Begum's request to speak to her mother, then went into the living room and sat down to watch television.

Fatima left the meal she was preparing and went to speak to Begum. There were several moments of awkward pauses on either side of the telephone, and by the time the conversation ended a pinched look had settled around Fatima's mouth.

Begum nervously said her "Salaam." Fatima forgot to return the greeting and silently put down the receiver. She stared at the wall.

At the other end, her head bent over her legs, Begum thanked Allah that it was over and done with. She sank down against the banisters. She felt bad, oh God, terribly bad. She had hated herself every minute of that conversation, hated the role she had been forced to play. Putting herself in Fatima's position she realized how painful it must be for her. How would she feel if she were to find out that her daughter had been jilted at the last minute?

Mechanically, as if in a daze, and with her hand held against her temple, Fatima went into the living room. She sat down on the sofa, pushing the cushion aside absentmindedly, staring at the fireplace in front of her.

Miriam did not notice anything unusual about her mother until she realized that she hadn't said a word since entering the room. "What did Aunt Begum say?" she asked quietly. For some reason her heart's rhythm had altered.

"I—I," Fatima stalled. She was still reeling from the shock, not yet ready to divulge what she had learned. What would it do to her daughter? She turned away.

"What is it, Mother?" Miriam's heart had now gained a steady sharp beat. Dread entered. "What did Aunt Begum say?" she asked again.

Unable to control herself Fatima burst out bitterly, "She said that your engagement had to be broken off!"

Miriam paled. Her heart sank to the pit of her stomach. "Why, Mother?" she said quietly. She was amazed at how clearly her mind was functioning, although a buzzing sound was hammering in her head.

"She said that they came yesterday to inform us, but found it impossible to get around to doing so. Begum says that her sister insists that her daughter was betrothed to Farook. That they are well-matched. She says she is very sorry and apologizes, but apparently her sister comes first."

"Liars! What a lousy excuse!" Miriam's mind screamed, but she uttered not a word. Instead she left the room.

She ran upstairs to her bedroom and closed the door behind her. Standing in the middle, she drew in a deep breath. Where did this sister come from? Why was it she had never been heard of before?

"Not marry Farook?" Miriam said loudly. Why, only yesterday she had been planning how they would lead their lives together. In fact, deciding in which area they were going to purchase their house after they got married and had jobs.

Her mouth twisted into a cynical line. In her heart she knew. From that first moment she saw them that night, in her jeans and short vest, she had had a dreadful premonition. She had known, although she had denied it emphatically to herself, that something was bound to go wrong. Their faces, their body language had told the whole story.

The buzzing sound was still hammering in her head. Going to her wardrobe she pulled it open and looked inside. Her eyes sought wildly and her hands rummaged through the clothes and hangers until she found what she was looking for.

She pulled off the repugnant-looking article from the hanger and threw it on the floor, as if it burned her. She stared at it, mesmerized. Then she gave it a vicious kick with her foot. Her friends would never believe her if she told them.

The shabby and much-worn pair of jeans lay at the foot of the bed, blissfully unaware of the havoc it had created in the life of its wearer.

# BLOODY MONDAY

&

## Fawzia Afzal Khan

Fawzia Afzal Khan (1958–  ) was born in Lahore, educated at Kinnaird College, Lahore, and earned her Ph.D. in the United States from Tufts University.

Afzal Khan is currently a professor of English at Montclair State University in New Jersey. She is the author of *Cultural Imperialism and the Indo-English Novel* (Penn State University Press, 1993) and *A Critical Stage: Secular Alternative Theatre in Pakistan* (Seagull, 2005), editor of *Shattering the Stereotypes: Muslim Women Speak Out* (Olive Branch, 2005), and coeditor of *The Pre-Occupation of Post-Colonial Studies* (Duke University Press, 2000). She is a frequent contributor to *Counterpunch* and a contributing editor to *The Drama Review.*

Afzal Khan is a trained singer in the North Indian Classical tradition; she performs with her band, Neither East Nor West. She is a founding member of the international experimental theater collective, Compagnie Faim de Siecle. She currently splits her time between Montclair and Lahore, and has been invited to teach and develop university curricula in Pakistan.

"Bloody Monday" an extract from Afzal Khan's work-in-progress, a book-length memoir, *Sahelian: Growing Up with Girlfriends Pakistani-Style.* In this excerpt, despite protests from her Sunni mother, Afzal Khan attends the Shia, male-dominated Moharrum mourning procession, which commemorates the martyrdom of the Prophet's grandson, Hussain, at the Battle of Karbala (in what is now Iraq) and also recalls the sorrow of the surviving women, including the Prophet's granddaughter, Zainab. The combination of masculine curses and courtesy that accompany the safe passage of women through the Muharram crowds amid the rhythmic sound of men beating their chests in lamentation merges with Afzal Khan's memories of Spain and the bullfights she attended in Pamplona during the week-long fiesta to commemorate the martyrdom of San Fermin. In Spain, the Portateri carry statues of the Black Madonna and other emblems during Easter processionals; in Lahore, the *alam bardars* (standard bearers) carry the banners of Shia Islam in the Moharrum processions.

Afzal Khan superimposes on all of this an inner dialogue with U.S. cultural hegemony in which she compares Lahore's Hollywood fantasies of "America" with the mundane realities of American life. Her memoir culminates with a reference to Urdu's great poet Ghalib and, his *saqi*—his metaphorical cup-bearer/muse—to challenge the traditional role assigned to women in literature.

• • •

It is the tenth of Ashura in the Christian year 1997, the day the frenzied mourning of Hussain's martyrdom fourteen centuries ago reaches its annual peak for Shia Muslims the world over. I am visiting "home"—Lahore—on a research trip funded by my adoptive land, the United States. In the middle of Shalmi, the working-class inner sanctum of Lahori Shiadom, I find myself swept along a tide of sweat, blood, and tears at four in the morning. *"Behen-chod, madar-chod—arrey, arrey—*don't you have mothers and sisters, you fucking sons-of-bitches—*hai, hai,"* even the counter curses are couched in antifemale rhetoric. But tonight, or should I say early morning, as the city pulsates under cover of darkness, throbbing in passionate movement as if awaiting climax at the moment when the sun's first rays rend its black shroud, melting into the shrieks and moans and moans and shrieks emitted at hoarse intervals from the crowds of mourners, men receiving the sacrament, letting the blood flow freely between their gashes, in a strange reversal of roles . . . so it is that this morning Aunty and I are objects of veneration, Zainabs to their Hussain. "Let the women pass—*araam-say, bhai, yeh hamari behenain hain . . ."* the clanging of knives-on-chains hook and tear manly flesh punctuated with hypnotic dirges sung in honor of *Bibi* Zainab. . . .

Santa Maria, the Black Madonna, Holy Mother of Christ, Jesus, Jesus, *Ya* Ali! *Ya* Ali! *Ya* Hussain, *Ya* Hussain. . . .

July 5, 1999, crossing the border back into Spain—Pays Basque, to be exact—is an adventure. Zeba and I are stopped by the guards in a performance of power which we counter with the actors' power of performance—turning on female charm full throttle, keep the motor running, *behen-chod, ma di . . . yaar,* why are you cursing so much, fuck it, *meri jaan,* it's your bad influence of yesteryear . . . yours and Soori's—all his fucking and swearing, Holy Mother of Jesus, how many women did he hump at UVA . . . fucking asshole, he's still at it, tits and asses await him at every port, while the wife-who-won't-give-him-any raises their kids back home in Lahore.

So then, finally, the guards are apologetic, all that show of male authority comes to nought. . . . *Amusez-vous bien avec* Ay-meeng-way . . . clever man-in-blue, at least he'd heard of the great man. . . . I nod and wink and off we go, still in possession of our packets of Paki *charas* (courtesy of Soori) as our victory charms.

First stop, San Sebastian. As Hania drives around looking for the P sign, I am looking for signs of my own—the cathedral, for one. I head straight for it once we've emerged from the subterranean depths of the parking lot—it amazes me how efficiently Hania is able to figure out the parking protocol in foreign cities, never mind navigating the always menacing traffic. Anyhow, while she smokes her sixth Marlboro Light of the day, having expressed her distaste for cathedrals and bullfights in the same raspy breath—I enter the hallowed hall, its cool darkness a welcome shroud in which to lay at rest a spirit in constant, exhausting flight. . . . Minutes later that thought, too, goes the way of all other delusional fancies, spiraling up with the smoke of the Marlboro Lights, and after downing, rather speedily, the ubiquitous *café con leche* available at every Spanish street corner—we take some obligatory snaps and are on our way to the high point of my pilgrimage: Pamplona, where the sun is setting on the eve of Hemingway's centennial and the start of seven days of unabashed libidinal energy unleashed in honor of the fiesta of San Fermin, that ever-so-saintly bishop of Pamplona.

*Na ro Zainab, na ro* . . . don't cry for your brother, martyred in the cause of a just faith—always just, of course, but no, there is no room for the questioning impulse—justly silenced when confronted with the sheer magic of the Sanfermines, where popular religion and bullfighting have come together, conjoined for centuries. I want to feel the madness, lose myself running the *encierra*, wear white at the bullfights and drink till I don't know my name, chanting, *Ya* Ali! *Ya* Fatima! *Ya* Abbas! Beat that breast, baby, skin on skin.

You have become exotic
to yourself
grinned the professor in the ponytail
peeking through the lenses
the diamond in my nose
glittered in the sun
my blond streak
fittingly flamboyant
she's become
a damned liberal
living among them so long
his rage
foams on his lips
spewing forth
frightening
venom
those freaks those shias
shiites to your friends
he sneers
wallowing in their blood
i was entranced
by the beautiful boys
singing their songs
moving me to frenzy
in that climactic moment
between life and death
when all I could hear was the
clanging of the chains
before the blood burst forth
splattering my white *kameez*
and i thought
so this is ecstasy
remembering the dead
remembering the martyred

excess of memory
surfeit of pain
camera in hand
i beat my breast
so this is what it means
to be a stranger to my s/kin

Sylvie, our Spanish hostess married to a rich sheikh of Abu
Dhabi with a keen interest in falcon-hunting—at whose
stunning villa atop a cliff overlooking the Mediterranean we
spend our first two nights in royal splendor—is horrified at my
obsession with the Corrida. Do you know they make young
boys run in front of the bulls, and so many die each year? And
what about the bulls? Such cruelty to animals! I am campaigning
to ban this primitive custom . . . this, to the cheers of the other
women, Hania, her two cousins Bari Apa and Billi, and the
freshyoungthing, Aliya Merchant (no relation to Ismail
Merchant). I guess I'm lucky Hania has agreed to drive me to
Pamplona at all—1500 miles, no less—to honor an old
friendship and mock my literary fetishism, she says. But don't
dare talk to me about bulls, okay?? Meanwhile, grateful though
I am to have her road skills at my disposal, I can't help thinking,
what a bunch of—well, women, excuse me—I'm surrounded
with, now that I've discovered the machismo upon which my
feminism is built. . . .

My mother is horrified when I announce my intention of
spending the night running with the mourners in the inner city
on the Shia holy night of Ashura. Do you realize how dangerous
this is? People are killed every year! How can you be so enamored of something as uncivilized as self-mutilation in the name
of religion? You can't go! Tell your husband (spitting venom
in my face) to take responsibility for your behavior—what will
we do with your kids if you're killed in those mobs? Are you
mad? The hysterical reproach from mother's Ava Gardner eyes
is almost too much of a cross to bear, especially when she con-

fides to me in what has suddenly become a very pragmatic, no-nonsense tone of voice, that Shia Muslims (*if they can even be called Muslims!!*) are known to pollute the town's water supply following this primitive ritual with blood from their bodies. . . . What is a poor, rational Sunni to do??

> *Na ro, Zainab, na ro . . .*
> bleeding
> something awful
> This is a pragmatic poem
> about a pragmatic woman
> my mother
> she teaches me
> never to be free
> of surfaces
> smooth
> sailing
> like a pumice stone
> on my sole
> rough skin sloughs off
> as it appears
> the seams mustn't show
> this is Morrison's art
> and mummy lives a/part
> so well
> down syndrome baby and all
> never upset her
> nor daddy's tumor
> and subsequent disfigurement
>
> You came, then You left
> accuses the supplicant
> Look at my passport
> no entries no departures
> i was home

tending to my babies
it is common to
hallucinate
after a major operation
I had bad dreams
as a child
bad men
rough-bearded
breaking open our
house
my heart led away
Beautiful and Elegant
in a white cotton
sari
jasmine in her hair
She looks over her
shoulder
with those Ava Gardner
Eyes
as if to say
it's okay

II
So I see her
with that man
purring sleekly like a cat
his whiskers dipped
in mother's milk
it seems ages
have gone by
then I hear her
banging on the door
hysteria masked
practically
underground

you didn't see anything
there was nothing
to see
now i must go and
pick up your
da-ddy

The night is young at 10:30 p.m. The big ball of fire had barely disappeared as my girlfriend and I stepped lively out of our hotel, confronted immediately with the variegated odors of human and canine flesh all mixed up, with the pretence of perfume unable to mask the peculiar aroma of rich, raw sex . . . sex was definitely, unmistakeably in the air, pungent as an onion. . . . Without warning the crowd gave way and the choked-up lane that couldn't possibly go anywhere opened into the mise-en-scene of a passion play. My eyes locked into handsome uncle-by-default, intensely focussed in his stiff white kurta pajama, and reassured, I slipped into the trance of the men, elbowing my way into their wavelength, banging, hammering, wanting to be let into the magical performance (for my husband the engineer, the hinted orgasmic state in hindsight is yet another in an endless series of betrayals, deserving only a venomous spit I must accept both outside and in) fair flesh, dark flesh, thin flesh, fat flesh, young flesh, old flesh, hairy flesh, smooth flesh, taut flesh, sagging bellies, pounds and pounds of masculine meat so near and yet so far, I want to put my hands down under the skin beaten raw and red so the haze spreads all across the broad manly chests and the boyish ones, I want to take I want to take I want to take my fingers and dip them deep inside the redhot liquid and sign my name in blood, Fawzia was here. . . .

I see him on St. Nicholas Street first, then later inside one of those bars we danced and drank in, and I kept thinking, *Hai Allah*, I hope he isn't a Paki, what will he make of the two of us, hard-drinking Muslim girls (okay, okay, so we're both 40-plus, one rather stocky and short, the other tall and struggling against the middle-age spread) and would you believe it, here comes another one, same doleful eyes, older, pock-marked face that makes him look rather like Om Puri playing the fanatic's father in this year's hot new Hanif Kureishi film. I wonder if they are father and son selling flowers to pretty ladies, or perhaps to men in search of some.

I see him again, later—much later, a fish without water in a place with so much to drink, silently silhouetted against the pane of glass made hazy with so much heavy breathing. Tall-ish, but not too much. Rather slightly built, like someone not given to rich fatty foods, or to drink either. And then I laugh at myself, why, of course not, he couldn't, he has only flowers, red roses at that . . . or perhaps, now waxing lyrical, that is a great deal to have, who needs food and wine or a roof over one's head? Still, he is an uneasy reminder—of what exactly I couldn't say—rather unaware of my/our existence, it seems; though the smile, which wasn't quite one, flits about the corners of his lips, I can see those lips even in the darkness of the bar, white shirt open at the neck, black pants hanging rather loosely on bony hips, a bunch of red roses and sleek black—and I mean Black—hair, falling, falling, and ohmygod, are those . . . *chappals*??? Why yes, indeed, open-toed, scissor-style—I never did like them, so typical of Urdu-wallahs. I'd always joined my friends in mocking them (poetic justice that I ended up marrying one!). Through the mist I see him and then I don't. He is gone. Just like that. I could have sworn I saw him again from the balcony of my hotel room where Hania drags me back, unwillingly exhausted, at 3:00 in the morning. I go to hang my dripping bra and panties out on the railing above the bull-run path and there he is, red, white, and black, turning the corner, just ever so slightly out of reach. . . .

*She was a very strange woman. So strange that they called her Madame Sin, not knowing what else to trace her infernal energy to. But that was in the before days . . . when evil consisted of setting fire*

*to a poor bastard's peanut fields without really meaning to, and the
thrill of the chase was a black man racing behind with a scythe in his
powerful arms, and danger was climbing into jamun-heavy trees
pregnant with plump, purple fruit, afraid Papa would wake up and
discover us gone, and who would be blamed, the leader of the pack,
Madame Sin herself, tearing around, even in the scorching heat of a
120-degree Lahore afternoon, disturbing the peace on the outskirts of
Bathurst, in a little enclave of erstwhile colonizers. The thirst for
adventure, even then, was unquenchable . . . why did they call her
Madame Sin???*

I do not know him yet but can feel his interest, his passion for
detail, his reporter's eye watching it all, drinking it in. A dark-
complexioned man, slightly pocked-mark, with straight dark
hair that keeps falling into his face, making me want to clip it
back. The tonga ride back to Aunty's home on Temple Road
where we would try and sleep for a few hours before heading
back at dawn, just before *fajr* prayers, is incomparable to anything else I've ever done. It doesn't remind me of anything
except itself. The byways and alleyways brimming over with per-
spiring hordes even late into the night are, finally, deserted,
except for the odd mangy dog or cat. Clip-hoppity-clop go the
horse's hooves, poor beast of burden, no rest for you, not tonight
. . . Samir blowing smoke-rings while I scanned the sky above
me for a sign of light, a little silver moonbeam to add the right
touch to the surroundings, something to remember. Then,
suddenly, there we were at the old house peopled with our
girlish laughter from convent days, oddly silent now, and that's
when the spell is broken. No money for the tonga-wallah. The
reporter's *jaib* has been cut, the no-longer-so-stiff white kurta
has a big gaping hole, wallet gone. What is he going to tell his
brandnew wife, waiting expectantly for the first-of-the-month
delivery? Lost the money running with the Portateri alongside
Madame Sin?

## II

The drive to D.C. is painful. I mean the heat, and the traffic, lordylord, enough to drive a saint crazy, and being merely a sinner I arrive at Moina's in a state of barely suppressed rage. Poor kids, they had to endure the brunt of Mama's anger although, come to think of it, they're probably rather used to it by now, since just about anything and everything ticks off their mama (last night A said he might be forced to leave, he couldn't stand the rage anymore, festering festering, like storm clouds looming forever threateningly on the horizon. . . . I'm scared, he said, poor man, and I, secure in the knowledge of a permanent love I mistrusted, made purring noises, meant to be comforting, which somehow came out sounding insincere even to my prejudiced-in-favor-of-self ears).

Anyhow, where was I . . . ah yes, my friend Moina, a *mynah-bird* to me . . . well, it isn't exactly her house, not in the same way that the Lahore house had been hers, just as the residence at Temple Road is indelibly marked as her mother's place now that her father is gone. Moina's house in Gulberg, despite Mashuq's presence, really was hers, quite without a doubt. From the fragrance of the *chameli* flowers adorning both front and back lawns, to the gold-filigreed cushion-covers against ornately carved chair backs to, of course, the signs of music everywhere . . . and that is the first thing I notice as I walk into the spotlessly white-walled, white-carpeted duplex on Windmill Court—her organ, on its stand, black keys in stark relief against the all-white background. Thank God some signs of her past life have made it into the new world she has entered of her own free will, emancipated woman that she is.

*Hai, hai,* do you know, she had that affair going all those years . . . *haan, haan, bhai,* I'm telling you *na yaar,* she's married that Richard Gere of hers. (A always marvels at the fact that all my family—and, it would seem, the fantasy lovers of my near and dear ones, too—resemble Hollywood stars; all white ones at that: Zahid Mamoo is Gregory Peck, Mum's Ava Gardner,

Dad, despite his facial paralysis, is, who else, Clint Eastwood of course, and Farhan, my brother, looks just like Travolta, especially after he shaved off his terroristic mustache). So then it is disturbing that there are so many tears at each and every reminder of the way things were, maybe the sense of loss (*quelle gaspillage!* sobbed the insensitive husband one couldn't help feeling bad for at the end of *Entre Nous*, one of my all-time favorite movies, when his wife finally divorces him and sets up house with her shell-shocked girlfriend), cultural and familial pressures are harder to endure than she imagined.

I sing and drink a great deal, each sip of Bailey's Irish Cream, each note of Raga Malkauns, each silly little jingle of an Indian film song transforms into droplets of memory's perspiration, leaking out of the pores of our bodies and souls, our most blessedly confused happysad selves, skin resting on skin, salty tears and beads of sweat mixing with peals of girlish laughter gigglygalote . . . and white-haired, white-bearded Richard Gere himself, playing quite the knight-in-shining armor, clearly chagrined by his perceived betrayal of King Arthur, nevertheless sits down to meals served by his Guinevere. I am a bit nonplussed to see her playing this role, I must confess . . . and yet . . . when I sing again that night, David the son-in-law strumming away madly on his electric guitar in passionate accompaniment, it comes to me in the darkness of Darbari that Khayyam had gotten something right: *nor all thy tears nor words, e'er erase a word of It.*

The drive home is a real drag.

## III

Monday morning I scream and shout the kids into submission, and when I finally arrive at the doctor's office she wants to know if my wearing red means something. I tell her I've just recently returned from Spain where bulls and blood took over my consciousness. She tells me to get that kitchen done and stay home for the next few years. "Your teenage daughter needs you to stop running with the bulls," she advises, wagging the proverbial finger at me. "But I haven't really done that yet," I begin to protest, silenced suddenly by an image of Moina wearing red, twenty-two years ago. Honey and I are the only friends from school who make it to her wedding with a Sunni man, angrily shunned by her father. She is the first of our intimate circle to get married, exactly nine months after the Nepali has shamed her into a silence I still cannot penetrate, lacking perhaps the ability to love that way. . . .

I could have sworn I felt Khawar's eyes on me, boring through my rib cage at the precise moment when the matador locked his bull in a gaze to die for, and plunged the sword deep, deep into the enraged beast's wildly thumping heart, silencing it forever. Greek Tragedy in Government College this was not, though neither is it the quick, graceful movement Hemingway had so admired. No, this one is rather agonizing to watch. The bull writhes in misery, spurting blood and foam from its mouth, fixing its gaze on the lover's intent being, who then resorts to a second thrust, after which the creature continues to shudder convulsively for what seems an eternity until, finally, all movement ceases and the eyes glaze over.

Needless to say, the matador does not get his ear to toss into the adoring hands of the most beautiful woman in the crowd. Her disappointment is almost too much to bear.

> There you stand
> on those steps
> on that hot summer's day
> Such a dream come true
> Ghalib's *saqi*, my muse
> With a toss of your head
> and a swing of your hips
> how you hiss, stomping off
> oh my love
> sweet young love

what's the matter with you
has the cat got your tongue?
I wished then that the earth
would swallow me whole
chador, beard, passion
All
I'd rather BE Ghalib
and/not his damned *saqi*
Writing those poems
yes inspiring those rhyme schemes
I don't want to give up
my power you see
so I'll be my own
slave, thank you, pretty please
but remember
dear departed
there always shall be
that question to consider
when our souls clash again
what shall we both do
having written our *ghazals*
always already
so hopeless, so silly
Imagining Forever
being Mad about Me.

# KUCHA
# MIRAN SHAH

૪૦

*Feryal Ali Gauhar*

Feryal Ali Gauhar (1959– ) is a novelist, columnist, filmmaker, actor, and a development worker. She was born and brought up in Lahore and educated at the Lahore American School. She studied abroad at McGill University, Canada, and the University of London, UK, and studied film and television at the University of Southern California, the United States. She has worked for fifteen years in development communication, focusing on marginalization, poverty, and the nexus between women and the environment. From 1999 to 2005 she was a Goodwill Ambassador for the United Nations Population Fund.

Currently, Ali Gauhar teaches the history, theory, and technology of film at Pakistan's National College of Arts, and lectures on women and development at other institutes. She is working toward a Ph.D. in cultural conservation and management. She is a contributor to *Dawn*, and wrote the screenplays for her two films, *Pezwaan* (1994) and *Tibbi Galli* (1997). She developed the latter into her first novel *The Scent of Wet Earth in August* (Penguin Books India, 2002). Her second novel, *No Space for Further Burials* (Women Unlimited, 2007), has been translated into French and is being translated into other European languages, Persian, and Pashto.

"Kucha Miran Shah" is an extract from *The Scent of Wet Earth in August*, a novel set in a red-light district in Lahore. It is the love story of two powerless people: Fatima, the mute daughter of a prostitute, and Shabbir, a young man who has been apprenticed since childhood to a *maulvi* who sexually abuses him. "Kucha Miran Shah" is a pivotal chapter that reveals a traumatic moment in Shabbir's childhood when his uncle becomes the victim of an "honor killing" by the powerful landowner. Ali Gauhar presents a feudal society where a woman is regarded as her husband's possession, as are the people employed by him or living on his lands.

The framing of the story of the killing against the simple decency of Shabbir and Fatima's love story shows how the violence of honor killing reverberates through future generations. Ali Gauhar draws out the complicity of feudal lords, *maulvis*, and even an ordinary stall holder, in the exercise of male cruelty and power. Embedded in this episode is the obvious question: What happens to "honor" when it comes to the prostitution of women and the sexual abuse of defenseless young boys?

. . .

"Yes, that's the one. It's Super Hashmi Surma, isn't it?" Shabbir asked. He stood at the edge of Dilawar's vending cart. In the time between one death and another many humiliations had been forgotten, or forgiven. Ever since the wordless one had started sending him cards with pictures of hearts and birds and lovers exchanging gleaming gold rings, Shabbir had put away the hollowness of his past.

"How much is it, *Bhai* Dilawar?"

"Hey, Maulvi, you've been buying stuff from me for a whole year and you still don't know what things cost? What's the problem, Maulvi? You seem distracted these days. Did the summer's heat melt your brain?" Dilawar teased. He was the same. He was the same, despite the fact that prices had doubled and tripled in a year. His business was still booming and his manner was as mocking as always.

"Please accept my apologies, *Bhai* Dilawar. It's just that sometimes I forget, that's all. There's really nothing else."

"Well, it's good you don't forget to buy stuff from me," Dilawar said.

"How can I, *Bhai* Dilawar? Your stuff is good, and inexpensive as well."

"Of course, my stuff is good and the price is even better! Just five rupees for anything on this cart! Five rupees! You can't buy a needle for five rupees these days, Maulvi. I'm telling you, everything on my cart is cheap."

But Shabbir wasn't listening to Dilawar any more. His eyes had caught the dusty pink edge of Fatimah's chador as she turned the corner. In the past year she had become even more beautiful. Now, as she walked, her eyes were lowered in the manner of virtuous, decent women.

Fatimah stopped at the edge of the cart, her eyes averted, pretending not to have noticed that the man she had come to love stood right across from her. Shabbir, too, looked everywhere except at her, his eyes scanning the cheap merchandise on Dilawar's cart, his ears listening for the sound of wordless declaration.

Fatimah reached out for the bottles of lip gloss.

"Welcome, pretty one—what can I get for you today?"

Dilawar stretched his hairy hand toward the bottles and picked one out. Holding a mirror up to Fatimah, he murmured softly into her ear.

"Here, let me hold this one for you while you try on the lip gloss. Try the pink one—it will match your chador and your rosy cheeks!"

Shabbir shifted restlessly. His feet began to sweat in his Sandak *chappals*. He was outraged. *Women have to be treated with respect, comments about their person have to be restrained.*

"Go on, go ahead. I want to see how the gloss shines on your ruby red lips."

Shabbir fidgeted. Fatimah stood still, her eyes still averted.

"Here, let me do it for you. Let me show you how to make your lips look as if they've just been—"

"*Jenab*, I'm getting late and I would like you to take the money for this before I leave," Shabbir hissed.

"*Ik minit, yaar*, hang on. Let me finish with the girl—"

Dilawar turned toward Shabbir and then back again. Fatimah was walking away, one end of her chador trailing in the dust.

"Oye, don't you want the lip gloss? I've got some really nice rouge for your rose-petal cheeks! And some scented hair oil, Oil of Jasmine too—" Dilawar called out to Fatimah, but it was too late. The girl had turned the corner. Dilawar turned back toward Shabbir and spat the words at him:

"See what you did? You upset the girl and now she's gone! Why do you always have to say the wrong thing at the wrong time, Maulvi?"

"*Jenab*, it is not I who annoyed the young lady, it is your rudeness, the familiarity of your behavior that has upset her. You must not behave in this manner with girls from good families. That is like insulting the wives of our Holy Prophet, May Peace Be Upon Him. It is like defiling the names of Our Ladies, Khadija and Fatimah and Ayesha, May Allah Rest Their Souls in Peace. You are letting the devil take over, *Jenab*. You must not address young women from respectable homes as if they were—"

"Go to hell, Maulvi. Respectable, my prick! What do you know about this girl? Do you know that the old hags raising her used to be Shahi Mohalla's best known courtesans? Bloody whores! That's what they are, and that's what her mother still is! Good family indeed! You know nothing about these two-bit *randis.*"

"*Astakhfarullah!* God forbid, Sir! You should wash out your mouth with soap, otherwise the angels will urinate on your tongue," Shabbir said.

"Piss on my tongue, eh? It's more likely that they'll piss on you, Maulvi! Everyone knows the *haraam-kari* you've been up to with Maulvi Basharat! Everyone knows what he's been doing to you ever since you came here as a sniveling little kid!"

Shabbir stood immobile for a while. And then, when the tears stung his eyes, he began to walk away, an ocean roaring in his ears.

"The angels will piss on you, Maulvi! They'll defecate on you, they'll piss on your mother who left you here. They'll shit in your father's beard, that bastard who sired you and then decided to dump you with Basharat! That's who the angels will piss on."

As Shabbir turned the corner, trembling violently, he heard Dilawar through a haze of other sounds, nagging, whispering, hissing.

*In the dark, the soft sighs of regret rose from the cracked earth of their home like mist on a winter morning. His father wept, head bent in submission, fists clenched with rage, nails digging into unfeeling flesh. That night Chaudhry Sultan had sent his henchmen to attack their two-roomed home in Chak Naurang and avenge his sullied honor.* Chacha *Rab Nawaz had died of the head wound inflicted by the butt of Chaudhry Sultan's double-barrel shotgun. The body lay wrapped in a bloodied sheet, an armless body, the amputation had taken place in the back room of the* haveli *earlier that day. He had understood nothing of this kind of punishment until he heard that his uncle, Rab Nawaz, had embraced Chaudhry Sultan's wife with those arms; those powerful carpenter's arms had embraced a woman who could be touched by no man other than the one who had wed her, who had the right to bruise that body with unrelenting passion, who could drag her by the hair in midnight's drunken fits, kick her in her spine, twist her arms, and then pound her with his swollen manhood until she swooned with the pain of his ceaseless, breathless thrusting. Rab Nawaz had only held her, putting his sinewy arms around her slender shoulders as she sobbed, her body heaving with hurt, her mouth forming senseless words of anguish. He had held her because she had picked up the razor-sharp cutter he would use to shape delicate bits of wood into toys for Chaudhry Sultan's children. She had held out her arm and had started to work the thin blade into the soft flesh of her wrist. He had not even noticed her presence until she moaned softly as pain invaded her as yet unbruised parts. She had entered the back room where he had always worked, her feet wrapped in satin slippers, her young body wrapped in yards of muslin. There was a thick layer of sawdust on the brick floor of that room, golden shavings from the wood of the* diyar *tree, a gold carpet cushioning her fall from respectability.*

*Rab Nawaz smelled her presence in the room before he heard her. She had come into this room on other occasions, at other times. Once she had asked him to design a cradle for the baby, her first son after several unnecessary daughters. One time she had wanted him to repair the hinge on her jewelry box. And sometimes she would just come into the room and watch him as he worked, the muscles in his arms rippling as he leveled the uneven surfaces of the wood, shaving off layers that would curl and then drop silently onto the floor. The smell of flaked wood mixed with the aroma of her closeness, with the musk of unspent desire. Rab Nawaz had only made farm implements before being discovered by Chaudhry Sultan, and now he was fashioning cabinets and tables with lions' paws for legs. So much had changed for him since coming into the Haveli of Nagar Lal, also known as Sukhera House; he had no idea that along with the privileges would come the privation, the gnawing knowledge that desire was dangerous, that it would chip away at his resolve, whittling him down to a naked, unprotected core. That day, when she had tried to spill the blood that otherwise oozed out of every orifice every time Chaudhry Sultan flung her against the wall or bit her breasts or clawed her back, Rab Nawaz had grabbed her, pulled the cutter out of her hands and flung it onto the pile of sawdust. And then he had held her, desperate to repair the damage done to her, desperately fighting desire.*

*She had wept, her body wracked with unrelenting remembrance. He had held her in his arms. Chaudhry Sultan's patwari had discovered them like that, and taking advantage of the opportunity to destroy an old enemy, rushed to the haveli to report this unforgiveable transgression. Rab Nawaz was tied down to the planing table he had built himself, his arms were hacked off with the axe he would use to chop bits of wood for the children's toys, his throat was slashed with his saw, the serrated edge leaving jagged scraps of flesh just above the protective silver amulet he had worn around his neck since birth. Rab Nawaz died in the room with the golden carpet. In the evening when the light outside turned from lilac to peach to vermilion, the patwari and his men removed the armless body and dumped it in the field Rab Nawaz had held onto for years, refusing to succumb to the patwari's threats of ejection. As for Chaudhry Sultan's wife, it was said that she was found on the sawdust floor of the back room the next day, her wrists slashed to the bone.*

Shabbir turned the corner, all but blinded by the memory of the bloody misfortune that had ruined his family and brought him to his fate.

It was nearly evening and the crowds in the bazaar would soon swell, spilling over into the narrow lanes of Kucha Miran Shah. Shabbir waited outside *Apa* Nisar's newly constructed room, taking refuge behind the mound of rubble that had once been walls and fireplaces and home and hearth for some long-forgotten courtesan. He could still make out the name and date carved in relief on the battered wooden door which must have adorned the entrance to this house: *Raeesa Begum, Daughter of Budhan Bai, 1928.* This was where drunken men would trip and fall, picking themselves up from the effluent-soaked lane, stumbling into the bazaar, cursing all mothers, abusing all sisters, as if venting their fury against women would change their destiny and make them better men. Other than that, no one trespassed into this lane. Even the dogs in the neighborhood stayed away from this unlit cul-de-sac, sniffing at the pungent mix of urine and vomit and then turning away. Only *Apa* Nisar had braved the shameless men pissing into the collapsed structure of Raeesa Begum's boudoir. She had set herself down in one corner years ago. She was then nineteen years old, running from the gambling, drunken pimp who had bought her in Bombay, and then brought her across the border when faithlessness ripped open the seams of a shared history, when faith became the rallying cry for carnage. She was a Muslim, and like the lunatics in the asylum, prostitutes too were divided up according to the religion they professed. She had jumped off the truck bringing Muslim courtesans across the border, fleeing with nothing except the sari she had draped around her body.

Here, Shabbir waited for Fatimah with the patience of a man used to absences.

When she came, he gave her the box of Super Hashmi Surma and explained to her that it would cleanse her eyes much as her smile cleansed his heart of so much anguish. She smiled at him. Then placing her lips on the pistachio-green cardboard box, she kissed it. She laughed, and her joy eased Shabbir's pain.

# IMPOSSIBLE SHADE OF HOME BREW

&

# Maniza Naqvi

Maniza Naqvi (1960– ) was born in Lahore and has lived in Mangla, Tarbela, and Karachi, Pakistan. She has studied at the Lahore American School and Kinnaird College, Lahore. Abroad, she earned degrees at Mount Holyoke College in the United States, and at the Asian Institute of Management in the Philippines. She currently lives in Washington, D.C., where she works on poverty reduction and post-conflict reconstruction.

Naqvi is the author of four novels, *Mass Transit* (Oxford University Press, 1998), *On Air* (Oxford University Press, 2000), *Stay With Me* (Sama, 2004), and *A Matter of Detail* (Sama, 2008). Her short stories, poems, and essays have been published in various anthologies, including *Shattering the Stereotypes* (Olive Branch, 2005) and *Neither Night nor Day* (HarperCollins, 2007). Currently, she is working on a book of short stories set in Sarajevo.

"Impossible Shade of Home Brew" explores identity and sexuality, gender roles, parenthood, exile, and the blending of East and West across the centuries. The narrator vividly recreates the vitality and living fabric of Lahore, the city whose rich pleasures he avidly shared with his beloved son. The death of his son in a rickshaw road accident due to the neglect of rich passersby sets up Naqvi's concern with a universe, marred by prejudice, indifference, and artificial divisions, such as that of class.

The reference to Moharrum not only recalls the dramatic procession he enjoyed with his son, but the dirges recited at Moharrums, which lament the sons slain at the Battle of Karbala as well as the grief of their mothers, including the Prophet's daughter, Fatima and her daughter Zainab. The son's needlework, a piece of vibrantly colored embroidery that the narrator carries as a memento, also symbolizes the many hues of love and the conscious choice that the narrator and his wife made when they entered into their pragmatic, unconventional marriage, where she wanted a child, and he needed a face-saving social cover since his parents could not accept his sexuality. Perceiving himself as both a man and a woman, the narrator continues to develop the themes of duality with metaphorical references that reflect this, such as the choice of Ephesus, which is in modern Turkey, but was associated in antiquity with the Greek Goddess, Artemis, who was the twin of Apollo and was a compulsive hunter.

• • •

Tucked away in the frenzy of Lahore's traffic-congested Mozang Chungi, a framer's shop, narrow, dark, and dusty, bears on its back wall a minor conceit from history. A slight, which made the freshly formed impressions of a newcomer, even a tough customer like me, obsolete. At least it does in my memory, an old and faded letter dated some time in the late nineteenth century and attesting to the fine quality of the shop's work, signed John Lockwood Kipling. Curator of the Lahore Museum and Principal of the Mayo School of Arts. Perhaps it's all gone now, what with newer buildings encroaching that old downtown area—I don't know. It used to be there when I was there way back in the Eighties. "Le' go! Le' go!" I hear his voice. Tonight, as usual, a smattering of tiny twinkling mirrors wink and cover me, cautioning that the past is for the willing but it seems the only way to divine sleep.

The letter always caught my eye and was framed behind the tea-and-grime stained cloth-covered counter. Must have been around the same time as when his young son was in Lahore working as an assistant editor at the *Civil and Military Gazette*.

Such a long time ago I was there, visiting routinely the emaciated and chain-smoking septuagenarian owner of a framer's shop, as delivery dates on orders placed were rescheduled over and over again. The shop's dark interior, open to the street, smelled of everyday ordinariness: Car fumes tinged with the fragrance of *chameli* flowers that lay on the shop counter, strung in garlands; their scent folded into the smell of a mosquito repellant coil and the stale smoke of cigarette butts and an incense stick; all of them mingled with the smell of the antiseptic floor-wash, phenyl. Ordinary, normal, comforting. We would make our way there, my son and I, after I had picked him up from school. We'd stop at the dry cleaner's or the shoemaker's or tend to some other need of mine, to pick up seemingly endless additions to my treasured and admittedly flamboyant wardrobe. A pair of shoes here, a shirt there, a belt I could not resist. Inevitably, at every stop, I'd run into someone I knew. One knew, it seemed, everyone, and of course immediately a ritual would ensue: of exchanges, of perceived slights and complaints, disappointments, letdowns, and clarifications of a phone call not returned, an invitation not honored or reciprocated, a rebuke, a rebuttal followed by mutual admirations of haircuts and various other personal effects and, of course, always the weight gain or weight loss of each other duly noted.

"Great shirt! Egyptian cotton?"

"No, pure *khadi*, a new supplier down in Shalmi!"

"Very nice. Putting on a bit of weight, eh?"

"Am I? No! I don't think so! Do I seem to have?"

"Don't see you around the courts much anymore!"

"No, it's far too hot for me now! We'll see after the rains."

An encounter was incomplete without an opening salvo or a parting shot aimed at weight. All this time, from the corner of my eye, I could see my restive son's rising frustration as I kept delaying our final destination. On one such occasion, chewing through clenched teeth the plastic straw in his empty fruit juice pack, Sher had shouted at me, "Le' go! Please, le' go!"

"Le' go?" I had inquired in his direction, winking indulgently at my chance encounter acquaintance of the moment.

"Yes! Le' go, now!"

"I'm not holding on to you!"

"I said, 'Let's go!' " Sher had roared back at me.

"Oh!" I said, thoroughly amused, "that's better, *beta*, enunciate, enunciate!"

Off we went, finally. Even as we moved through the traffic, I'd constantly nod or wave to someone or the other. It seemed everyone knew us and we knew everyone. In such a manner we would make it to the framer's. For Sher such visits were always full of promise, first the expectation of delivery, to see his creation framed, then the frustration of a promise not kept, followed by the framer's apologies and excuses in between his hacking cough, and finally his plying of consolation in the form of a cup of *karak chai* or a *lassi*. Sher always chose the *lassi*, grasping the glass eagerly with his small hands as I looked on in consternation, anxious about the possibility of his contracting jaundice from drinking *lassi* in the bazaar. But I never stopped him; it was good for him, it helped create antibodies, made a man out of him. I always accepted the cup of tea.

To the framer's shop we had brought a piece of embroidery. It was a large piece, one square yard of red damask with tiny mirrors worked in with yellow thread. It had been completed by Sher in home economics class, perhaps the largest in his portfolio, of which he was very proud, for it included his entire repertoire of stitches ranging from chain to cross to mirror work. Twenty years later the piece travels with me: red, mirror worked, covered in swirls of needlepoint. Back then I had thought it quite hideous, but it was rendered by my son and deemed by Mrs. Moinuddin, Sher's teacher, fit for framing. I agreed wholeheartedly. Mrs. Moinuddin was a great source of solace and joy for Sher, each Friday afternoon in her classroom located in the basement of the school building, accessed through what seemed like a secret stairway. Here, taught by her, in her comfortable, narrow, elongated, parlor-like room, my son reclaimed through needlework his sense of poise and grace, which had recently been lost to the dance teacher, a great maestro of classical dance.

Sher had appeared at the audition for the dance class dripping with sweat, right after soccer practice in soccer cleats and shorts. Attempting to strap on to his bare ankles a heavy pair of *ghungroos*, the wide leather swatches covered with tiny metal bells, he had giggled at the maestro's head and eye movements. With this, Sher had sealed his fate and that of several others who had been inclined to giggle along with him. "Your deportment has all the beauty of a flat-footed elephant!" judged the great, but affronted, maestro.

"An elephant!" an indignant Sher had protested.

"Yes, an elephant," the great maestro elaborated serenely and with graceful employment of eye, neck, and hand movements, "an elephant listlessly wandering down the Mall toward Kim's gun, after having escaped from the Lahore Zoo on a late afternoon in the month of June."

My son had been inconsolable that afternoon when he

plunked himself on the seat next to me in the car on the way back home. "An elephant, a lazy bum! That's what he thinks!" Sher had complained quite brokenheartedly that the great maestro of dance had not even left him wiggle room for redemption, by at least caricaturing him as an energetic or enthusiastic elephant. And so Sher was not to be found charging toward Kim's gun, down the tree-canopied, shaded, and gracious Mall road; no, he was just wandering like an elephant. And a listless one at that. There was to be no consolation commentary, as in the school report card, where the failed Maths grade was offset with the comment, "Displays tremendous esprit de corps." Sher had always displayed plenty of esprit de corps. I had considered having a word with the dance teacher but thought better of it. Life's knocks; not all a bowl of cherries, y'know; can't always have it your way; good with the bad; good for the boy, makes a man of him.

I had always been overly protective and keenly felt my child's bewilderment at the slightest of rebukes. The framed embroidery with dozens of twinkling mirrors, with yellow chain stitches laboriously worked by Sher hunched over it for hours, tongue sticking out in concentration, had in some measure restored his pride. But watching his peers twirling across the stage in a blur of turquoise, mustard, and fuchsia, *peshwazes* and saris, while he sat in the darkened audience, plainly awestruck, had naturally left my Sher subdued and grumpy. Neither Kathak, nor Bharat Natyam, nor the Dhamal were to be performed by *jungli* brutes like him, as the maestro seemed to have implied. And I could do nothing to make up for it, except to frame his embroideries.

On rainy afternoons when the weather was fine and the monsoon was at its height, I'd take Sher to the outskirts of the city, to the dense mango grove at Niaz Baig, it was our special hidden place. We'd drink steaming cups of thick, heavily sugared, milky tea at a truck stall, then make our way into the thicket to sit by the canal and watch the rain come down. Submerged this way in every shade of green, the grass alongside the canal, the mango trees, the surrounding fields of rice, *koels* and wild parrots fluttering through the foliage overhead, we'd sniff till intoxicated the smell of sweet wet mud. Sher had discovered a water well with an inscription inside dated 1898. It read *"prem kuwan,"* well of love. I hadn't understood it then, when I visited the framer's shop almost a century apart from that curator of long ago, this sense of belonging, because it was mine to be had in such abundance.

Tonight there is no more of that—but more to blame for the state I'm in, there is for one, the breeze. It carries a train's whoa-whoa cautioning over to where I am about to fall asleep, transporting me back. Back to a house on Upper Mall where, around about the same hour, every night, perhaps at midnight, a passenger train, the Tez Gam or the Shalimar Express or perhaps another with a different name and purpose—cargo, perhaps— would go rattling by, trundling onward through the sprawl of the dead and the living crammed up against each other. Mian Mir, a human and concrete tapestry, just beyond the high walls of the serene compound where I lived. A densely packed grave-yard competed with squatters' settlements of multi-layered, illegal, overnight constructions housing refugees: those fleeing riots at Partition; then war-ravaged border villages during '65 and '71; and more recently from the deprivation of the country-side. The graveyard's existence was assured, having been there for centuries; it had history on its side while the squatters did not enjoy this luxury of permanence, newly arrived in compari-son and without leases to the land.

Tonight for me, it's the shores of the Aegean Sea, at a hotel called Kismet where, on the wall in the lobby, there are dozens of photographs. I peer at the one with two sun-tanned young people wearing white holiday gear who lean into each other as they pose with their backs against the balustrade on the terrace of the hotel. The caption tells me that they are the King and Queen of Denmark on their honeymoon back in 1966, having stayed in rooms 201 and 202. "Not separate rooms, surely," I muse out loud. "Presumably a suite, but then who knows what arrangements lead to a marriage." The bellboy is unsure of my joke but laughs anyway. He stands beside me and gives me his unhurried attention since there are only a handful of guests in the hotel this evening. He knows his job well: He is there to please. I look at him. He must be my Sher's age. Just shy of thirty? My eyes may have lingered too long on his face. I note self-consciously that he moves closer to me as he points out another photograph. There is something about my manner that always brings on such unsolicited attention. I am at a loss to figure out what it is.

Two other testimonies to the hotel's excellence and as a choice of destination catch my attention: a photograph of the Nizam of Hyderabad, and another of a lady called Kenize Mourad, Princess of Kutwara. I remember her from a copy of a society magazine I read not too long ago. The story of a woman, an Indian princess by birth, born in Paris to a Turkish mother on the eve of World War II and the Nazi invasion, born to a mother who escaped from an unhappy marriage into wealth in Kutwara. I imagine marigolds, *ittar*, rubies, diamonds, peacocks, and elephants. Listless elephants from which escape was sought. Turbulent times those, of war and uncertainty, of high romance and history.

The bellboy, having shown me to my room and placed my bags on the table, throws open the doors leading to the balcony and steps out. I follow. The fragrance of lemon blossoms just below in the garden mingles with the sea air. He points out the view of the open sea, the Greek island on the horizon and the nightclubs along the shore, then he turns and looks into my eyes. Perhaps you would like to visit one tonight? I realize, half-dismayed, half-flattered, that he senses an old and lonely soul in me, perhaps after my earlier comment on the nuptial attitudes of Danish royals and the far too long gaze upon his face. Or perhaps there is the less complex economic explanation, tipping me off to tip generously. The tourist season, it seems, will be slow this year. And the horn of a cruise liner in the distance, just as I am falling asleep, disorients me completely as she glides into the night. I have my piece of red embroidery with its winking and smiling mirrors spread out as a cover over the light wool hotel blanket that covers me inadequately. Outside, above the lemon-aided breeze, as a crescent moon rents open with its light, a sliver in the indigo sky, and rises steadily over the sea, it seems to whisper a rebuke to me. It's the first of Muharram and I've postponed a trip back home to Lahore yet again. Would it not have been the occasion to return? To watch the Zuljana make its way to Karbala Gamey Shah; watch the procession in Shalmi, enter the Lal Haveli inner courtyard from a latticed balcony for the *maatam* on the night of the ninth? To listen to the beating of hands against chests keeping time with the dirges of the believers, the powerful, frightening rhythm of sweet sorrow. To weep for atonement, to merge sorrow into an eternity of grief. And I am forever postponing return because too many things, too many places, always seem to get in the way. "It's nice to have you stay but go away, moon," I mumble in a traveler's weary whisper, "stop chasing me relentlessly with the same refrain wherever I venture." It's Ephesus this time. Revisiting history instead of mourning it. And yet, there it is, I am back. With you. A sardonic grin; a swagger in my walk, a *khais* memorably slung over one *boski*-swathed shoulder. Eyes that impossible shade of home brew. Wearing an expression hard to decipher, just a little bemused, a little amused, a little tired. I lean my body against the wall, cross those polo-playing, horse-riding legs of mine and shoot you that look, like I'm firing. I don't get it. That look. I-couldn't-give-a-shit look. A little bit like, "Fuck it, let's blow this joint" look. And you're thrilled. I've thrown you that look, you're the chosen one tonight for that fuck-it look. We were the very best, weren't we? The best kind that can ever be, deciding to live our lives together. So simple, that decision, between you and me. You and me. You, beloved, my perfect accomplice, my escape hatch, my haven from a match made by parents. We had saved each other it seemed.

"Well, why not?" you had said of her, that very lovely pick of the crop chosen by everyone for me. Everyone, but me.

"She's beautiful!" you had said.

"She's stupid-dull. What more do you want me to say?"

"C'mon! She's gorgeous!" you said.

"So is the cover of a girlie magazine. Only thing is, I could use a magazine to light a fire to keep me warm or as shade from the sun. She, on the other hand, is a total waste of space."

"God, you are mean. You do have a point though, she is rather chilly," you giggled.

"Tundra-atic! She just has to come into a room and the temperature drops by at least ten degrees. She could be Lahore's answer to load shedding as a substitute for air conditioning."

"Ouch!"

"What?" I protested. "It's true. And boring as hell!"

"She is pretty!" you teased.

"Stop going on like a jammed CD. She is pretty, there's no doubt about that, but beyond that there's not much else. I mean she's gorgeous, I want to be her, I mean I want to be her body, I don't want it!"

"She's a beauty! Look at her eyes—gorgeous!" you persisted.

"Sure, nice shape, but where's the light in 'em, where's the cheer? I tell you, if it weren't for those rocks, those huge two-point-five-carat diamond studs punctuating either side of her face, she'd be lacking any redeeming sparkle."

"Ouch!" you laughed.

"And her conversation, oh my gawd!" I continued, "Her conversation is mainly to refute any of my ideas or concepts with her standard, 'That is not the way it should be!' "

"Listen, don't you think it would be a good idea to let your parents know that you're not interested in getting married, at least not to a woman?" you suggested.

"Are you crazy?" I screeched.

"They are your parents. How long do you expect to continue lying to them?"

"Forever, just like they have to each other." I was firm.

"What?"

"No one needs to know about what really goes on in one's head," I said impatiently.

"Would you consider marrying me?" you had suggested softly.

"You don't want that!" I was floored.

"I'd like to have a baby!" You were so matter-of-fact, simple.

"Right. Let's get hitched." I was simple too.

"Thanks. Love you."

"Love you."

But we got fucked, didn't we? We made a mess of it. I blame them all for it, for our child. The entire city. How can it be that no one stopped? For godssake, a car accident, a child lying on the side of the road, a busy street at the busiest hour, and no one stopped. At the corner of Zafar Ali Road and Upper Mall, and no one stopped. How could they not have stopped? Because it wasn't one of them? Not one of theirs? They didn't think it could be Sher? Everyone knew us. Everyone! It's my fault. How could I have let him go in a rickshaw with the ayah to school that morning. I was in a hurry, had to get to work, needed the car to pick up clients on the way to the Kutchery, the High Court. How could I have done that? And when I finally got to the hospital you were there, leaning against the wall. You wouldn't look at me. Sher was gone. That was it. You wouldn't look at me.

And life went on. If Sher had been in our car instead of a rickshaw would they have stopped to help? How many of them were our friends who passed by that day, without a second look at a child bleeding to death as a frantic woman tried to stop a car, any car, for help? It took her an hour before someone stopped. An hour! How did that happen? But you look away, not from all of them, only from me. My best friend, the keeper of my being. The one who ran to me for all things to be escaped from, the one

I escaped with. I ran. Because this was not about you, this was not about me. This was about all the goodness we could ever be. An impossible shade of home brew, that I could not safekeep. That look away from me said all this to me. How could I have let this happen? My needs were the sole reason for Sher to be in a rickshaw that morning. Life goes on and I spend it, rescuing each day and running as far away as possible from the look that you will not look at me.

And you have not tried to reach me though I have sent you a postcard from each place. One today. At this time of the year it's unseasonably quiet. But even then, for so long now things have been my companions. Winking, whispering, cautioning, rebuking, smiling, soothing. I've spent the day gazing at the cerulean landscape from a canvas chair. From time to time I glance at others around me. As outsiders, barring conversation on history, what else can we say for this place that we find our-selves in for a short interlude? With no sense of the place and its people, its daily rituals, the other guests and I are left with banal commentary.

"Glorious sunshine!"

"Isn't it?"

"Pity the lack of tourists!"

"I know! I worry! The coast is almost free of tourists."

"Yes. The people here worry they may not come this year, the tourists, what with September 11 and now the threat that Iraq may be bombed. The bellboy said as much in the lobby earlier and so did the taxi driver!"

"Yes, our guide mentioned it as well!"

"Such things would damage the tourist industry, the hotel industry could collapse."

"But Ephesus would still stand."

"Ah yes, well thank God for that!"

"The Gods!"

"Yes, yes, indeed!"

It's not clear why it declined and ended, everyone says it's because the harbor silted up and it lost its port. All economic reasons. But surely life is more than economy, more than that? More than news? It's about the favors of gods and goddesses. It's about mothers and their grief. Artemis, Nike, Mary, Mary Magdalene, Fatima, Zainab. The same story over and over again. Though my grief runs far too deep, I concede it is also about fathers and sons.

At Ephesus there are the clay pipes still intact underneath the marbled streets. Evidence of a water and sewage system, a direct connection between the longevity of empire and the availability of public utilities, this I quip to a well-paid and appreciative guide. With you in mind, I think of having a photograph of me in front of the pile of excavated clay pipes with the senate in the background, you would appreciate the significance. But of course I don't, there's no point. Then there is the positioning of the grand library opposite the town brothel. Legend has it that there was an underground passageway connecting the two. I can just hear it now, old Marcus Maximillinus calling out, "Darling, I'm off to the library!" Sher would have said that, wouldn't he? And we would have stood there laughing with our beautiful young man.

The longing has been so intense, so intense that I can't seem to ever get back. Difficult this, to imagine a place that exists without me, and exists with me somewhere else. Indispensable to me. If I go back, what if it might not be there? The there, where I was. So I carry it with me, intact, the way I left it. Only thing is that I've taken the embroidery out of the frame, it travels easier. Perhaps tonight over dinner, where I will be asked to be joined by another guest, equally alone, I can make up a story about who I am. A lie is so much easier as a way to tell the truth. With all the photographs in the lobby serving as subliminal props, I will build a story about a drawing room, a well-appointed one, redolent with perfume, cigar smoke, and whiskey fumes, its sofas spilling over with guests who've known each other over generations, smug, at ease, exclusive, and

excluding, and at home. Here, women battling bulge and bore-
dom with their anorexia-induced stick bodies and big heads,
looking much like giant lollipops, strike poses of gaiety. They
try to ignore the dizzying amounts of food around them, taking
note only of each others' blow-dried and uniformly tinted hair,
glittering bijoux, forms, and fashions. Here, their men, bloated
with self-indulgence and marinated in liquor, swollen faced and
pot-bellied, congregate in corners nursing whiskies, trying to
forget their existence.

"And so you see, from there, from that cocoon of ennui and
self-satisfaction I have banished myself!"

"So you live here?"

"For the moment, yes, finding refuge in this hotel, a runaway from a faraway unhappy situation."

"If you don't mind my asking, it sounds intrusive, but may
I ask why?"

"No, not at all! Not intrusive at all, I assure you. But the fact
is that I just couldn't fit in, you see."

"You couldn't fit in?"

"Yes, I was the wrong type, if you know what I mean. But
my darling mother, God rest her soul in peace, had the foresight
to save me, her only child, from the stigma of her profession."

"The wrong type? What was your mother's profession?"

"You see, I am the child of a courtesan." I pretend to ignore
the change of emotions on my listener's wide-eyed face. I shrug
my shoulders for effect, "Perhaps I am the wrong type."

"How did she save you?" I am asked breathlessly as the listener with rapt attention moves closer across the dining table.

"Well, you see, she was very progressive and forward thinking. It is often the case. She sent me to a boarding school in
the hills. To a hill station embedded with Catholic missionary
boarding schools. From there I would have returned to Lahore,
but society there is unforgiving, though such things as courtesans and their children are an integral part of their culture."

"Boy, that's unfair!"

"Indeed, it is. Quite. It is, shall we say, a tradition of self-congratulation, of feeling one's importance by having someone at one's mercy. I can buy you, therefore I am. That collective sense of superiority. If you know what I mean. We can watch you being humiliated, therefore we are respectable. And so I have rebelled. I have chosen to run."

"You are brave, a very brave person! I am pleased to meet you. You should come live in America, we aren't prejudiced against people that way!" And with that I would need to endure a lecture on civil liberties.

Or I could say that I am looking into the possibility of joining the monastery at the house of Mary up on the hill at Selcuk. For I too, am mourning a son. No, it won't work, not for me.

Or perhaps the story is to be of a murder.

"Murder?" That would make them sit up and listen. The murder would be of a woman who, having married a rich and doddering feudal landlord, miraculously produces a child who she claims is his, of course. The sons of the patriarch from previous marriages are seething with fury. A courtesan's progeny to inherit a portion of their wealth? *Never.* And then one night, when the child has come of age, they send assassins to do away with the mother and her child as they lie sleeping in their large and darkened bungalow in Lahore's snug, well-appointed, verdant residential enclave and military cantonment called Chowni, a few miles away from the yellowing squat structure of Rahat bakery, at the hour when the bakers have just begun cracking eggs for the pound cakes for the day, and the beggars who work at this busy and lucrative locale are finally beginning to call it a night, curling up to sleep on the floors in its verandahs, on their burlap bedding kept in the crevices of walls and the branches of trees in the bakery's compound. The mother is stabbed and strangled brutally, the child escapes. "I am, of course, that escapee!" Admiration all around, plenty of sympathy. Yes, and would you please pass the gravy. *Boy, the folks back home will never believe it, we're so lucky to have met you.* Having thus established myself as *interesting and colorful*, there would naturally be a photo opportunity, insisted upon, at the customary balustrade out front, to be mounted later with the others in the lobby after I am gone. No, for now it won't come to me. A storyline that is authentic for a city so beloved, belonging to so many and to so many times. And a story about traveling the world and running out of time seems too mundane for consideration, somehow, too unattractive for a dinner conversation. A conversation that keeps a stranger interested, yet at bay.

I hear that huge cruise ships call into the port every day here. Up to six a day during the peak season. I cannot bear the thought of it. The air itself shakes with the noise of a ship when it comes into port as it blares instructions to its passengers multilingually—Japanese, American, French, and German. The air shakes with the engines rumbling, the horns blaring, and the smaller shuttle boats disgorging passengers from the ship to the shore for day trips. Here in Kusadasi, a cruise liner calling into port must dwarf the surrounding shore. Everything changes when strangers arrive and the residents are forced to sit out an invasion.

And here it is finally, I feel it coming. I can hear her call in the distance as she glides on the water tonight. Just one more chance, let me have this, this moment to dance with you, and you agree, dragging me through the bar tonight, holding my hand firmly, gently, saying, don't worry, I've got you, follow me, come through. And I, slightly intoxicated by you, slightly by the wine, knowing right place, right time, but more by my own sense of happiness and knowledge. Just thirty years shy? Wall to wall men pressed against each other, bodies pressed against each other, loving each other. And I in my black leather jacket, naked underneath, long, longed for a full-flowing, claret-red taffeta beaded skirt to my ankles, high-heeled pumps, being dragged gently through, squeezing, oozing my way through the pressed bodies, feeling them against me, legs, torsos, backs, hips, feeling hands on my hips, feeling hands against me, shutting my eyes, not caring, let them touch me, there is no harm meant here. Are all of them loving each other, yes, perhaps, they just want to make sure, perhaps they think I'm a woman, perhaps they know I too am a man. What if I am, I don't care, for them I can be, I'm here and this is all I want. And now I feel this, it's you dragging me through, shining me, reflecting you to me, so many images coming at me, of myself refracted back to me, for the first time me, not them, not their blinding light blinding me, taking you away from me.

# STAYING

&

## Sorayya Khan

Sorayya Khan (1962– ) is a novelist
who was born in Europe and moved
to Islamabad in 1972 with her parents, where she graduated from the
International School. She received
degrees in the United States from
Allegheny College and the Graduate
School of International Studies, Colorado. Khan has received a Fulbright
award and a Constance Saltonstall
Foundation Artist Grant.

Her story, "In the Shadows

of the Margalla Hills," won the 1995 Malahat Review First Novella prize. The daughter of a Pakistani father and Dutch mother, the idea of the world's interconnectedness is central to her novels, *Noor* (Alhamra, 2003) and *Five Queen's Road* (Penguin Books India, 2008). The latter weaves together a family saga and national history. The house built by an Englishman is shared after Partition among a Hindu landlord, a Muslim tenant and his family, and eventually, the latter's Dutch daughter-in-law. The novel, which revolves around memory, traverses several countries and examines how people survived the traumas of World War II and Partition.

"Staying" is an extract from *Five Queen's Road*, in which Khan reconstructs events in Lahore during Partition: The main protagonists cannot quite grasp that they have been overtaken by history. As Khan notes, Pakistan—a word coined in the 1930s to include the initials of the country's proposed provinces, and which also means "land of the pure"—suffered the most traumatic of births.

• • •

Dina Lal wasn't moving. He wasn't going to be pulled toward make-believe lines on a tonga. He wasn't climbing on board a train heading for the other side. He wasn't joining villagers taking step after tired step toward a make-believe border. He was staying put, and everyone who knew him thought him mad because of it. He made only one concession that summer. He moved from his childhood home inside the old city of Lahore to the house of an Englishman. He'd pretended that the majesty of the house, flowers, gardens everywhere was a gift for his wife. Or so he told her. Later, when he looked back on his life knowing full well the price, in family members, that his decision to stay in Lahore extracted from him, he knew it could not have been different. Lahore, in flames or not, was his. In stillness, rare in a city bursting with life and now death, the city was his. Walking the seething city that summer of Partition, Dina Lal moved slowly. His feet were heavy with conviction, as if loath to part with the dry and cracking earth beneath. Watching jagged flames claim snatches of still black sky from the rooftop of 5, Queen's Road, he scuffed his sandals on the cement. Hindu or not, he wasn't, goddammit, going anywhere.

It was an outrage, Dina Lal thought, this business of imposing lines where there had been none. Who were the British to draw imaginary—crooked, even—lines across his land and proclaim a random date when it would break (like a biscuit, for God's sake!) into two countries? He'd grown up a subject of the empire, as everyone else, Kings and Queens in his school books, the Empire spread like its railway tracks up and down the immensity of what wasn't theirs. Living in the midst of this had always seemed unjust, but not enough for Dina Lal to raise his voice and make a fuss. He'd profited from the railway lines expanding across his village land. But when the rumors became truth, when vague etchings became borders, he'd had enough. He would teach them all a lesson. On this side of the lines.

Dina Lal's wife, Janoo, short and sprightly like him, was of a different mind. She feared for her life the minute Partition became real. During temple visits across the city she collected stories. "What's wrong with you?" Dina Lal once shouted at her while she tried to share one with him. "Are you a sponge? Plug your ears against all that rubbish."

It didn't stop her. She brought home an endless assortment of Lahore's incidents: knifings, robberies, murders, and things far worse that she didn't quite know how to put into words in the presence of her husband. By the time she heard about the rapes she could barely speak. For weeks, every time she saw her husband, she would draw her open palm like a knife across her neck as if to impress upon him the horror swallowing the city.

At times like this, Dina Lal reflected on the woman he'd married. They had married when Janoo was very young, and had two children, two boys, almost immediately. She'd been so young then that her pregnancies had scarcely left marks on her belly or her breasts, and her youthful skin tightened up again as if it had never been stretched. His wife had once been lovely,

before the day-to-day worries of her small children put prema-
ture circles under her eyes and an edge in her tone that set Dina
Lal looking elsewhere for happiness. He'd found it in the arms
of another woman, a dancing girl, who gave him what he needed
and asked for very little in return. The arrangement satisfied
Dina Lal. In a perverse way, Dina Lal concluded, it was not
unlike the most successful relationship in his life, the one he'd
had with his father. Before his father died and left his fortune
to Dina Lal, their relationship had been marked by a satisfy-
ing mix of distance and intimacy, a balance that the familiarity
of marriage, among other things, could never afford. Twenty
years into his marriage, while Janoo went about her days drawing knives across her slender throat, Dina Lal recognized that,
children or not, their lives were no longer woven into one.

Janoo did not demand much of her husband. Recently, she
had only one requirement, that his driver be at her beck and
call to take her to her visits to various temples. At first annoyed
with the expectation (after all, why should he resort to getting
around the city like any common man?), Dina Lal discovered
that he enjoyed walking the streets of Lahore, something he
hadn't done since he was a child, and he had learned his way
around the labyrinth of alleyways inside Lahore's Old City.
Even as the city took on an anger and urgency all its own during the summer of Partition, Dina Lal wandered the streets
with little fear of vigilante groups who, for the moment, ignored
him in their quest to set things right. He didn't cower from the
streets even after he witnessed a neighbor dragged into a busy
thoroughfare and pummeled to near death with a child's cricket
bat. He spilled a perfect cup of sweet, milky tea in his lap when
he watched it happen from a nearby tea shop, but (remarkably,
he later thought) he didn't expect that such misfortune might
one day find him. Instead, Dina Lal wondered what his neighbor had done to deserve such a fate. He wasn't heartless, as he'd
overheard Janoo describe him to her last friend before she, too,
fled for the border; he was merely honest. His best protection

against the rage overtaking the city was that he hadn't done anything wrong. He believed this would be enough to keep him safe.

One evening, when Janoo returned from a trip to the temple where she prayed to the gods for protection, she recounted a story she'd heard about a crazy Englishman. More often than not, Dina Lal tuned out her recitations and left it to one of their now grown sons to do the listening. Not this time. Everyone in Lahore knew the man, if only by his house, which sat on a slight hill close to the important intersection of Lawrence and Queen's Roads. Dina Lal immediately pictured the tall, wrought-iron gates at the bottom of the property, the uniformed men who stood guard, and the troupe of *malis* who walked the lawns in the evening, sprinkling water on the grass from the bursting *mashaks* on their shoulders. Goddamn English, was Dina Lal's thought whenever he happened to pass the manicured grounds on his way back home, in time to see the *malis* traveling predestined routes on their nighttime duties. What was it about the island left behind that made this strange breed of Englishman insist on green grass, while all around the parched ground made nothing but dust?

The Englishman was John Smithson, Chief of North West Railways. Dina Lal had made his acquaintance some years earlier. The two had met at one of Dina Lal's famous Lahori parties where champagne flowed as easily as women. Janoo hadn't been able to bear her husband's excesses and, often, she'd retire to her upstairs bedroom, a wool cap pulled over her ears, while the party roared on below. Dina Lal realized that Janoo must have done exactly that the night he met Smithson, otherwise she would have put a face and a name to the *Angrez* she was now describing.

"He's lily white," she was saying, "Yellow hair. The donkey who makes an offer on his place will be cursed. Nothing good can come of anything they leave behind."

Shortly before Dina Lal's party, Dina Lal recalled, Smithson had returned from Murree, the famous hill station from which naked Himalayan peaks could be glimpsed on a clear day. Dina Lal loved Murree, the snow scattered on the distant mountains, the roads built on the edges of cliffs and the bazaar that wound back and forth with the sway of the hills. Smithson slapped Dina Lal on the shoulder when the two men discovered that Dina Lal's favorite place to stay was a short walk from Smithson's summer retreat. A few weeks later he received Smithson in his office, when the land in the vicinity of his ancestral village was needed for the possible extension of a railway line. When Dina Lal accepted payment in exchange for the land, he'd had in mind that he would invest the money for his sons. Much to his dismay, his sons did not turn out to be serious students. They played far more than they studied, so he had put the proceeds from the Railways sale in a bank to wait for a day when the two boys might calm down long enough to find their way in life. With that day yet to come, Dina Lal still had a big pot of money in the bank.

"What's he asking for it?" Dina Lal said suddenly, interrupting Janoo. The amount that Janoo mentioned was identical to the sum set aside in the bank. Although Dina Lal was not a religious man, the coincidence had him thinking that the gods were at work. Much later he thought the gods, whether it was one grand one or limitless smaller ones, were responsible for his next words.

"Let's buy it," he declared. When Janoo stopped speaking in midsentence and her mouth opened so wide that he could see the sinking gap where her largest molar had been pulled out, he added, "For you. A gift for you," as if this clarification would somehow help mitigate his wife's astonishment.

Dina Lal's decision not to leave for India had Janoo questioning her husband's sanity. But when he spoke of buying a big yellow house far too grand for its own good, owned by an Englishman in a city being ravished, she thought him completely mad. For her own peace of mind she resolved to think of him as yet another victim—albeit a different kind—of the Partition that was breaking her land and heart into two.

"No, thank you. Nothing good can come of anything they leave behind," she said, repeating her earlier words a little less gruffly. "Don't say that," Dina Lal added in irritation. "Good riddance to them. Besides, they're leaving us behind. You think nothing good can come of that? Why, we'll be free!"

But Janoo wasn't listening. She'd turned to leave the living room of the spacious home that had been theirs for twenty years. A few months earlier she wouldn't have heeded her husband's words. But each day news from the temples rattled her further. They'd entered a new age, the times were different, unlike any other, and nothing, absolutely nothing, was the same. Including the man standing behind her, going on about the wisdom of his proposition. She needed to find her sons. Even if they pulled away from her when she tried to touch them, she would know there was something she had made that was still true.

A few days later, based on Janoo's information, Dina Lal called on John Smithson. Unknown to him, John Smithson had already compiled a list of prospective owners of 5, Queen's Road, and respectable man that Dina Lal was, he was on the list. Before Dina Lal could bring it up on his own, Smithson revealed his hopes.

"My house, 5, Queen's Road," Smithson started, "I'd like to sell it."

"I see," Dina Lal replied, caught only slightly off guard and feigning ignorance. "The Railways are selling it?"

"Right," Smithson responded. "But we're looking for someone very special indeed to take the place. Someone, you understand, who would know enough to value what they'd got."

Smithson paused, then, as Dina Lal, schooled in showing the kind of modesty the English appreciated, answered, "Certainly, certainly. Such a lovely house you have."

"I wonder," Smithson asked, "whether I could interest you in my house?"

"I have one," Dina Lal replied, the bargaining side of his landlord character surfacing through no fault of his own. Then he clarified himself, remembering all his properties. "Plenty of them, I mean."

"It's a good price," Smithson countered.

"Real estate . . . it's in quite a slump these days," Dina Lal replied consolingly.

"The price is very, very fair." After revealing the exact amount ("nonnegotiable, you understand," Smithson had added), he went on to list all the items inside the house that would be included. The billiards table, the dining table that sat twenty-four guests with plenty of leg room, the Railway crockery, sofa sets and beds, chandeliers bought in the most prestigious London stores, the verandah furniture. "Bloody hell," Smithson finally said, sweeping his arms wide. "You'd have everything left behind."

Strangely, because Dina Lal knew nothing about gardening and had never cared to learn, it wasn't until Smithson arrived at a description of his garden that Dina Lal leveled his undivided attention to the details being described. The longer he listened, the more fantastic and alarming Smithson's account became. Unless he'd gone to see it for himself the next day, he might have thought the brandy was at work in Smithson's rendering. On and on, Smithson went. Much of the garden was imported. The bulbs, for example, the plant food, and the original grass seed from Bengal bred to withstand the heat of the tropics. Smithson had each variety of bougainvillea, hibiscus, sage, periwinkle, lilies, and other plants of which Dina Lal had never heard, at the tip of his tongue. But he was fascinated not only by the account, which might have been drawn from the fantastic fairy tales his wife once narrated to their young sons, but also with what appeared to be desperation. It had majesty and grandeur at its command, but it was desperation all the same. Dina Lal had an inkling that Smithson feared returning to his faraway country. He could think of no other explanation for a grown man to be entirely wedded to details that couldn't reasonably be expected to survive his departure. Against his better instincts, ones that had recently taken to blaming each and every white man he saw for what was fast becoming the horror of Partition, Dina Lal felt sorry for Smithson.

"Johnny, Johnny," he said, confident that their early afternoon brandy would forgive his leap into familiarity. Dina Lal studied Smithson's eyes, a strained blue, before speaking. If only he'd been teasing Janoo with the prospect of the house, he cast away the joke with a deep sigh. "Let's settle it, then," he said firmly to Smithson. The next afternoon, coming up the winding driveway for the first time, Dina Lal thought it was obvious that 5, Queen's Road belonged to the British. The grandeur of the house, the colonial architecture and the stream of servants made this clear. Halfway up the drive, Dina Lal received further confirmation. In Lahore, city of infinite smells, it was the absence of any smell at all that made the house unmistakably British. Bloody bastards, he thought, how did they do it?

Inside, Smithson gave Dina Lal a tour, hardly pausing for breath. He pointed out the woodwork on the verandah, the elaborate fireplace mantles, the room with only a billiards table in it, the doorways framed with arches. Dina Lal was shown bathrooms large enough to be bedrooms, with porcelain sinks deep enough for a child's bath. The oversized living and dining rooms could be divided by intricately crafted French doors. Smithson informed him that before construction on the house had even been completed, the locks on the doors and the decorative fixtures had arrived from England. Dina Lal pretended to listen attentively. Strangely, Smithson reminded him of a new father presenting his child to someone else, drawing attention to the round kneecaps, a neck buried in soft folds of skin, things Dina Lal might have missed about his own children had Janoo not tirelessly pointed them out to him.

"You're not married?" Dina Lal asked, interrupting. Smithson shook his head and when he returned to the description of the house, his enthusiasm wasn't quite the same. In a duller tone Smithson further clarified the offer. Within earshot of his servants he offered Dina Lal not just the house and most of its contents, but the domestic help, including the man who was sweeping the verandah nearby as they spoke. His name was Yunis and he was a smart man, very loyal. When they finally spoke of the price, Dina Lal knew it was more than reasonable but he couldn't help trying his hand at negotiating. Dina Lal was met with unexpected stubbornness.

"Not negotiable," Smithson repeated.

"This is India! Why, everything is negotiable here!" Dina Lal responded.

In the end, Dina Lal was insulted because Smithson refused to budge by even one rupee from his price, if only as a measure of good faith. He didn't recall Smithson being as rigid in other business dealings the two had had. He was exasperated enough to almost point this out to Smithson, but last minute apprehensions of losing the deal curbed his tongue. Eventually, he agreed to Smithson's strange figure.

Smithson, however, was not satisfied.

While Dina Lal listened in disbelief, Smithson outlined his conditions for the sale. Dina Lal could only own 5, Queen's Road if he promised to retain the crew of *malis* Smithson had hired and trained, and who would continue to care for the garden according to the schedule Smithson had devised. For example, the rose bushes would be pruned early in October so that they would bloom one more time in December. The miniature waterways that irrigated the garden were to be redug after the annual monsoon season, but not too soon after the rains. The last thing Dina Lal heard before he stopped listening was that Smithson was planning to move a model of the railway route into 5, Queen's Road, where it was to become a permanent fixture.

Excessive as this and the numerous other conditions were, Dina Lal vigorously nodded his head.

"Huh, huh, huh, huh, *jee*," he said, agreeing to all of Smithson's conditions, impatient to expedite the sale.

Finally, the two men shook each other's cool, damp hands to finalize the deal. Soon! Dina Lal thought as he descended the long driveway where green grass was groomed to grow between bricks laid in a careful zigzagging pattern. *Soon you will be far, far away, Johnny, in your own country—nothing but an island!—and I will live in your house any damn way I please.*

The first time Dina Lal walked into 5, Queen's Road after it became his, Smithson's ship was sailing the Indian Ocean. If Lahore had been seething before then, it was exploding now. Days earlier, the first trainloads of massacred bodies had rumbled down the intricate tracks of Smithson's railway system from one side of the border to the other and back again. As far as Dina Lal was concerned, there was only one way to explain it. Madness had descended when the line of Partition, inexact and incomplete, was penciled in on the Englishmen's maps. Any hope of it lifting had all but faded.

Standing in full view of the spectacular garden Smithson had left behind, framed by purple bougainvilleas climbing their own way into the astonishingly cloudless sky, Dina Lal's wife tugged at her husband's shirt. Only barely out of earshot of their two sons, almost grown men already, she spoke.

"But we don't need this!" she pleaded, as if she could still change her husband's mind, despite the deed already signed and transferred to her husband. "Where we live—it's fine. Please, my love, please."

Dina Lal loosened himself from her grasp and paid her no mind.

Upon entering the house, Dina Lal was annoyed to see that Smithson had done as he'd promised and placed his railway model on a table in the front parlor. He recalled what Smithson had said about the delicacy of the model, but Dina Lal didn't stop his servants from pushing it to one side and piling boxes on it, as if the slopes and ridges of the topographical model comprised a flat surface. Late that night, as he walked by the table on his way to bolting the front door, Dina Lal noticed an envelope taped to the corner of the table. In the dim yellow light he recognized his name on the crisp stationery. Squinting, Dina Lal slit the envelope with his thumbnail and began to read Smithson's first letter to him.

Dina Lal, my friend, I've entrusted you with my house and, grand as it is, it will require a bit of work to maintain. We've gone over the specifics and I needn't, I'm certain, trouble you with them again.

But even more than this house, I hold dear my model of the Empire. (If you look closely, you will see Murree, the dot painted in red near the upper right. No lines lead to it as the Railways—which in my opinion was our largest failing—could never figure out a way to reach the quaint town we both love at the bottom of the sky.) I had hoped to donate the model to a museum, but the chaps at Lahore Museum couldn't find the time to look at it. I will continue to pursue finding a permanent home for it from England, but until then I ask you to care for it. (If it develops a slight crack, you can mend it with the gypsum powder I've left in the bag below. Dab it with a bit of water and rub the powder into it, that ought to solve the problem.) Should you be interested, the various colors of lines denote different routes: The green one shows the places I visited during my years in British India. I request you to leave the model in the front parlor of 5, Queen's Road. It will be safe there, and when I find a place where it can be properly exhibited, it will be easy to move through the front door.

I do hope you enjoy this house as much as I have. One day (if things ever return to normal), I might visit. We'll be in touch, and may God bless you.

Dina Lal was ready to dismiss the letter as a poorly conceived (filthy, even) joke until he read the last line. Had Smithson no respect? As if it were the Englishman's goddamned God who watched over 5, Queen's Road and not the abundance of other ones whom Janoo had already made a mantel for, that heard his prayers and blessed him instead. Idiot, Dina Lal thought as he crumpled the letter and dropped it on the floor for Yunis to sweep the following morning.

It was only the first of a stream of letters. But already then, the onion parchment on the floor crumpled into a wad smaller than his fist, Dina Lal suspected greater powers at play. In the years ahead, he often wondered if the gods on his side of the lines had made it their mission to keep ill will flowing into the house he'd bought from the Englishman. His city in shambles, it was hard to imagine that he'd once enjoyed Smithson's need. As if exploiting it could have set anything right. With more land and houses than he knew how to use, he'd bought 5, Queen's Road—because he could. Still, if only his father could have seen him in those early days! He'd stood on the roof surrounded by row upon row of planters spilling with endlessly blooming flowers he never learned to name. From above, the city spread out like a map, he'd pretended that his life, already full, was only beginning. Like the country, land of the pure, just born.

# SOOT

ॐ

## *Sehba Sarwar*

Sehba Sarwar (1964– ) is a novelist, essayist, and poet, and her work has been published in anthologies and magazines in Pakistan, India, and the United States. She was born and raised in Pakistan and earned degrees in the United States from Mount Holyoke College and the University of Texas at Austin.

Her first novel, *Black Wings*, was published in 2004 (Alhamra). Presently based in Houston, Texas, she is working on numerous writing projects, including a second novel. She also serves as the director of a Houston-based arts organization, Voices Breaking Boundaries, and returns regularly to Pakistan to write and spend time with family.

"Soot" looks at a younger generation in India and Pakistan who have been separated from each other since Partition, with the gulf widening with each subsequent conflict. Curiosity and then the discovery of common interests and the similar problems that South Asian countries share, draws them to each other. Running through the narrative is the echo of East Pakistan, the majority province that became Bangladesh following a civil war, and which, the protagonist realizes, has been virtually erased from public discourse in Pakistan.

• • •

"You must eat our milky *rasmalai*," the taxi driver said in perfect English, shaking his head continuously, as if in full agreement with himself. "It is the best dessert in all of India."

Tired from a day of travel, Zahra leaned into the back seat, barely acknowledging the driver's comments with her nods.

"There is much to see here: the Marble Palace, Nakhoda Mosque, Eden Garden, and all our temples." Intrigued to learn that Zahra was from Pakistan via Chicago, he had travel advice for her. "My recommendation to you, do not talk about the '71 war. People are passionate about Bangladesh, so it will be a difficult topic for you. If you stay away from talk of wars between our countries, you should feel very welcome."

Karachi to Kolkata was not far, but delayed flight, late connections, and airport security checks had made Zahra's travel excruciatingly long. Exhausted, she had little energy for the driver's running commentary. As they entered the city, she stared out at the yellowed buildings, which looked older than the ones she knew in Karachi. The streets, packed with moving bodies, were different too, filled with cars of all shapes and sizes, buses, and two-wheeled rickshaws pulled by thin, muscled men.

After scribbling down his mobile number for her, the driver dropped her at the youth hostel off Ballygunge Circle. "Yes, if you need tours of our city of joy, please telephone me and I will show you around." He winked and drove away.

Tucking her hair behind her ears, Zahra made a mental note to toss the paper as soon as the taxi turned the corner. She rang the bell and the door clicked open. She clutched her heavy canvas suitcase with both hands and clambered up the dark stairwell. In the hallway upstairs, Raj and Shoma, a husband and wife team who managed the hostel, greeted her with smiles. Shoma patted Zahra's hand, then disappeared through a doorway; Raj silently ushered Zahra to her room. It didn't take long for Zahra to figure out that he spoke mostly Bengali. He didn't understand much Hindi, which she could speak since it was so close to the Urdu used in Pakistan.

After freshening up, Zahra walked up to the third floor balcony, where sunshine trickled in through bamboo mats. In the serene space, far removed from the commotion of the streets down below, two American students settled into cane chairs and sipped tea. Through the introductions that followed, Zahra learned that Melanie and James were doing research for anthropology doctorate degrees at their respective institutions in the United States. They too, like the taxi driver, like the hostel managers, and anyone else Zahra met on the journey from Karachi to Kolkata, asked: "What are you doing *here*? You're from Pakistan, you're studying in the States, and *you're* doing an internship in India?"

Zahra tried to find a parallel for them. "Well, it's like Americans doing internships in Cuba." To bolster her comparison, she pointed out some similarities between being a Pakistani in Kolkata and being an American in Havana. There was a history of war, different languages were spoken, and it was almost as difficult to travel between the United States and Cuba as it was between Pakistan and India. James and Melanie's furrowed their eyebrows; giving up trying to explain her reasons for being there—which she herself didn't fully understand—Zahra listened to their stories about Kolkata.

"This is an exciting city," Melanie said. "So much art, and there's always political demonstrations going on at the university. But you know all that, right?"

Zahra nodded, though she didn't. She already recognized that no matter how different she might feel in Kolkata, people would assume she knew more because she looked similar to those around her. Her family was from north India, and all her relatives had been excited when they learned she would be doing a three-month internship in Kolkata. "It is far from our home, but you will learn so much," her mother had said, getting teary-eyed as she always did when someone discussed travel to India. She had been born in New Delhi three days before Partition and had never returned to her city of birth.

After tea, Zahra wandered through the streets of southern Kolkata. She soaked in the old buildings with latticed hallways, round verandahs, and high walls. She stepped carefully around the broken sidewalks, nearly tripping on banyan tree roots. She had to wind her *dupatta* around her nose to filter the smoke billowing out of trucks, buses, and cars. Over the chaos of horns beeping and people shouting for buses, she tried to use her mobile to call her mother to tell her she had arrived safely, but the street sounds were too loud.

Finally, she ducked into a dusty low-ceilinged Internet café in the Esplanade. She shot emails to her parents, and to Juana and Rathna, her roommates in Chicago. The connection was slow. She waited for images to solidify on the screen and glanced around at the young men dressed in kurtas and jeans who camped out in groups of three or more in front of derelict machines. In the States, where she had done her undergrad and was now enrolled in a master's program, everyone worked on personal laptops. In Karachi, Zahra knew there were similar Internet shops, though she had never needed to visit one. This shop could have been located in the heart of Karachi, but the sounds around her were different. Bengali was a soft and lyrical language. Listening to the inflections, Zahra was reminded of Roohi who was from what used to be East Pakistan and who worked as a maid at her aunt's house. Roohi's entire family had once been in West Pakistan, but after the civil war of 1971 when East Pakistan broke away and became Bangladesh, they returned to Dhaka. Roohi stayed on but she always talked of feeling alone in Karachi. Now, sitting in the heart of Bengal, on the other side of the border from Dhaka—but close—Zahra could understand why Roohi felt isolated and angry. No one in Pakistan talked about Bangladesh or the atrocities the Pakistani army had committed there.

On her way back to the hostel, Zahra followed Melanie's advice and took the subway, Kolkata's quiet and saner method of transportation. The hostel was silent when she entered. Holding out her hands in the dark hallway, she felt her way to her bathroom. Beneath the naked bulb, she noticed dirt streaked across her cheeks. When she blew her nose, she was surprised to find black sticky soot, city pollution, covering the tissue paper. Finally, exhausted from a day of travel, she lay down on the twin bed, marveling, once again, at how an afternoon conversation with Rathna and Juana had brought her to Kolkata.

"I had so much fun," Rathna said, rocking back and forth in a rocking chair without arms. Rathna was from India. She was sharing her experiences of interning with a social services nonprofit in Bangkok. "All I had to do was to write and ask for a grant and my trip was funded."

"Maybe I can do something like that with Shirkat Gah in Karachi?" Zahra wondered out loud. "It's a great women's organization."

Rathna laughed. "Didn't you come here so you could get away from home? Go somewhere else. There are so many cool cities. Go to Kolkata! There's always a lot going on there—art, culture, politics. And it's not that far from Pakistan. You can always stop off in Karachi. I spent a month in Mumbai with my family."

"Well, now I need a break from life in the States," grimaced Zahra. After completing her undergraduate, she had returned to Karachi and worked for two years in women's development, and then had joined the master's program in Chicago. "This country's different from when I was at Pomona," she added. "The moment I say where I'm from, they look at me like I'm going to detonate a suicide bomb. And if I don't say anything, they think I'm Mexican and start telling me to go back. I can't finish this program."

Juana, their older roommate from Mexico, nodded. "Take some time off, *amiga*," Juana said. "Then come back and finish. We've put in too much time to quit. You only have another year. Once you get out, you can do real work. We can't quit." She turned the page of her textbook. The fluorescent light flattened her features. "I'm sick of being here, too. My home's on the other side and they want to make walls to push us out. But you know we're going to win, right? We're reproducing at a faster rate than they can throw us out!"

By the end of the conversation, Zahra checked out the website of an organization in Kolkata, City Streets, that provided free healthcare. Rathna had filled her in on the director of the program, an older man, Sohan Roy, who looked like a Bollywood movie star.

"I've heard he's a flirt, but a wonderful host," Rathna said. "You'll have a great time."

Rathna's voice resonated in Zahra's ears as she entered the City Streets building. An attendant escorted her to Sandhya Sengupta, a senior woman in a sari, who held out her hand for a shake, but then changed her mind and offered her cheek for a kiss. "It is unusual for us to get a Pakistani intern, but we can certainly use your help," she said. "You could work on our newsletter and our website. That way, you can learn about what we do, and we can use your technology skills."

Zahra nodded in agreement. "That sounds fine."

Sandhya brushed her hands together, as though she were

cleaning away a layer of dust. "Excellent. We'll get you started." Sandhya led her to a small cubby that would serve as Zahra's office. "Mr. Roy was looking forward to having you as our guest. But he won't be here for a few months. He's teaching a course in England. He told us to take care of you."

Zahra nodded, feeling like a little girl whose helium balloon had been released into the smoky sky. She shook away her feeling of disappointment and sifted through the small stack of stories to edit. When she finished, she sipped tea and read through City Streets's publicity materials. In the hallway, she heard two men discussing the rise of HIV cases in the city and the outbreak of cholera and typhoid. From what she'd gathered, City Streets hired at least twenty other employees, but Zahra felt too shy to walk out of her cubby and introduce herself. Her day lightened up a little when Amita, another young woman who worked on marketing, joined her in the small room.

One of Zahra's first off-site jobs was a visit to City Streets's mobile nursing station at the Tannery, Kolkata's old leather-processing neighborhood. She got into a van with two nurses and Amita; the nurses were going to do patient checkups, while Zahra and Amita were instructed to collect stories.

Once in Tangra, the City Streets's crew situated itself in a makeshift clinic packed with more than fifty women sitting on benches and on the floor. An arid smell of sweat rose up Zahra's nostrils; flies floated through open doorways. The nurses set up instruments and began to collect blood, take temperatures, and document symptoms. Amita deposited herself on a bench to record stories, while Zahra hesitantly opened the camera case. She fiddled with the aperture. When she was in college in California she had taken a photography class, but had not practiced since. She tested the light. She held the camera in her right palm to test its weight.

To her left, an older woman was sharing her story with Amita: "They closed the factories, and I had a stroke. Now I have no money, and my son is dead. What do I do?" Feeling her own breath change, Zahra picked up her camera, focused the lens for a close-up of the woman's face and clicked. Turning around, she captured images of another woman, who was talking about her husband's lung cancer and her own miscarriages. "We can't have children here," she said. "They don't even want to be born."

Having spent many childhood afternoons at her mother's clinic where women struggled with daily health problems, Zahra had always been committed to making a difference back home in Karachi. But, as she squinted her eyes behind the camera lens, she grappled with how she could return to Chicago where problems seemed simpler, and the solutions presented could not be applied to the world in front of her. Pushing away her thoughts, she stepped into the narrow street and photographed a group of boys and girls splashing in rancid street water.

A week later, Sandhya summoned Zahra to her office. "These are fabulous," Sandhya said, pointing to a contact sheet with black-and-white photographs. "I didn't know you were a photographer?"

Zahra flushed. "I'm not . . . I mean, I haven't been trained."

"Maybe you should be." Sandhya held out a sheet that showed two boys throwing water at each other. "We'll use this in our brochure. Of course, we will give you credit. I'm going to email these to Sohan right now."

To celebrate Zahra's work, Amita invited her out for a drink at a bar on Park Street. As soon as they slid into their chairs, Amita blurted out: "So why are you doing this internship? You could've read about the work we do. There're no Pakistanis here." From the rush in her voice, it was clear she'd been wanting to ask the question for some time.

The bar was filled with men and women who had stopped in for drinks after work, and there was laughter in the air. Relaxed, Zahra shared Rathna's stories about City Streets. "I'm kind of disappointed Mr. Roy isn't here. . . ."

Even before Zahra finished her sentence, Amita threw her head back and laughed so hard that the group at the next table turned around to look at her. "Oh, forget him. He's a player," Amita said.

Zahra joined in Amita's laughter. "You know, I haven't said this to anyone, but I'm not very impressed with Mr. Roy. He gets paid a lot, but he's never here. That's why some NGOs have a bad reputation in Pakistan, too."

Amita smiled tersely. "We do good work. But we could do better. We need to dedicate more money to treatments for lung cancer, HIV, or just plain healthcare for pregnant women. You've seen how much the city needs."

Moving on to her second gin and tonic, Amita confessed that she, too, had left her parents' home in Mumbai after hearing about Sohan Roy and the work he did. "But honestly, I'm disillusioned. And I'm only twenty-three. I'm telling you, the best thing about coming to Kolkata is getting to know this city—and living alone." Amita rented an upstairs flat through a family that lived on the ground floor. "My mother feels better knowing there're older people watching over me. And my landlords don't report on my boyfriend, or how often he comes over. Thank goodness for cell phones and email . . . that way my mother feels she can be connected with me, but she doesn't need to know everything."

"I wish I could live like that in Karachi," Zahra said. "Pakistan's a difficult place for single women. When I'm home, I live with my parents."

By the time the two women exited the bar, Amita had invited Zahra to move out of the hostel—where Zahra had to report in before ten o'clock each night—and, instead, rent the empty room in her apartment.

"My roommate moved out a month ago," Amita explained. "I've been looking for someone else. You'd be perfect!"

Through Amita, Zahra experienced another Kolkata. One of

the first shows Zahra saw with her new friend was an improvisational comedy performance at a small theater. Even though Zahra couldn't understand Bengali, the performers were strong; she was able to comprehend their jokes through their expressions and body movements. Another night, they listened to rock music in Amita's friend's backyard. As the evening progressed, Zahra learned that the drummer, Manik, who worked as a graphic design artist by day and was a musician at night, was Amita's boyfriend. Once Zahra moved into Amita's, she became accustomed to Manik dropping by at all hours, often armed with beer or vodka. The three stayed up through the night talking.

On one such evening, Zahra told her new friends: "I emailed my ex today in Karachi and told him I don't want anything to do with him. Just because he was the first guy I was with doesn't mean he should be the last. And when I go back to Karachi, I'm going to take a photography class. It's all I want to do." She took a swig of beer. "I left Karachi for graduate school to get away from the life I was living, but it's not like Chicago's been any better. Cheers to Kolkata."

The three clinked their beer bottles. Manik strummed his fingers against Amita's calves. "Our government told us to hate you because of what your people did in Bangladesh. I might be drunk but I know you're not the enemy. You didn't support the military. There you are, from the other side of the border . . . and we're not that different."

Zahra nodded. "At least now more and more people are speaking out about the violence that took place. But they don't teach it in history books. You need to visit Karachi one day. It's strange how we can be neighbors, and still be so distant. Our governments make it hard for us to cross the border, so we fly over each other's countries."

The three stayed up late making plans about starting up a twin organization in Kolkata and Karachi. "Our organization will give power to street kids," Amita said. "We'll teach them photography and filmmaking. And we'll collect money to send them to school."

Zahra's internship ended as quickly as it began. Her suitcase open, she folded her new stack of saris—pink, bright purple, green, colors she'd never thought she could wear—along with hand-stitched blouses. Another stack was a pile of books by Tagore (in translation), DVDs of Satyajit Ray films, and anthologies, films, and music she'd collected during her stay. She was leaving in a different manner from the way she had arrived three months ago. Her friends were driving her to the airport and her phone book was filled with names of artists, teachers, health workers, and activists that she'd met during her three-month internship.

At the airport, Amita gave Zahra a tight hug. "Take good care of yourself. I know we'll be friends for a long time."

"I want to come back and start that organization with you," Zahra replied. Her heart felt heavy, as if her suitcase were strapped against her chest. She had plans to be in Karachi during the summer before she returned to Chicago. She knew that when she wrote a report for her internship, she would be able to record her experiences at City Streets, but there would be no place to write about the education she had gleaned from her friendship with Amita.

On the airplane, a worn-out bead bracelet that Amita gave Zahra snagged against the arm of her airplane seat and broke away. Zahra tucked the beads into her pocket. Feeling tears rise up, she concentrated on staring out the window at the smoky sky and at airport workers who shoved swollen bags into the airplane's belly. She cleaned her nose and noticed that her tissue came away with streaks of soot that she had wiped away every night for the past three months. The thought made her eyes tear up even more.

The air at dawn in Karachi was tepid. Morning rays had touched all edges of the city and, slowly, heat was rising. Undeterred by city violence, Karachi Airport was brimming with tired mothers and their children from Dubai, England, and the States who poured in for the summer holidays. As Zahra emerged from inside the airport lobby into the shaded waiting area, her eyes fell on her mother and her older brother who pressed against the rail, waiting for her. She hurled herself in her mother's arms and stayed there for some time. Until that moment, Zahra hadn't realized how much she had missed her—not just in Kolkata, but also in Chicago.

Her mother stroked Zahra's hair. "You look more grownup after this trip," she said. "I want to hear *all* your stories."

As her brother drove down Shara-e-Faisal toward their house in Defence Housing Society, Zahra's new eyes absorbed the decorated trucks, the putt-putting rickshaws, and the men and women chasing after minibuses. The sky that stretched over Karachi's low landscape seemed whiter and larger than before, and though there was traffic on the road, the city seemed to be almost empty compared to the density that filled Kolkata's streets at all hours.

"There's so much exciting stuff happening in Kolkata," she said, as she shared stories of Kolkata's theater, community groups, and bars. "We should learn from it."

Once they pulled up at the house, Zahra inhaled deeply. She stood under the bougainvillea, appreciating its violet shade.

Tired from all the movement and action in Kolkata—and Chicago—where she had to look after herself every minute, Zahra relished being back in Karachi. In her parents' house, she didn't have to take public transportation, or worry about meals and rent. Most of her friends were away for the summer. With time on her hands, Zahra spent much of her time reading and sending emails to her friends in Kolkata and Chicago, regaling them with stories about Karachi's mangoes, her photography class, and her daily walks by the sea.

One morning, three days before her departure—shortly after calling Emirates Airlines to reconfirm her seat back to

Chicago—Zahra set out for Seaview, where she walked every morning. She parked the car, strapped her camera to her side, and began to briskly walk along the seawall. As always, she found herself remembering her morning tea with Amita, their races to the subway station, and their evening walks through Kolkata's Horticultural Gardens. Now that her break from Chicago, a city almost halfway on the other side of the world, was coming to an end, she thought of the long cold nights in the library with Juana and Rathna as they struggled to complete courses that seemed so distant from their respective homes in India, Pakistan, Mexico, and the escape they sought by exploring the city beyond their campus.

The monsoon wind increased and she braced herself against the spray that hit her body. It was high tide and rough waves covered almost all the silver gray sand. In less stormy seasons, Seaview looked different: In the evenings, the beach was filled with families who rode camels or horses, enjoyed tea, or simply watched the surf. But Karachi waters during monsoon season were always turbulent.

Zahra slowed down a little, toying with her aperture. She focused her camera lens on a little girl who sat cross-legged on the seawall. The girl had ratty hair and no slippers; as she stood up on the wall to balance herself against the wind and spray, Zahra clicked. Then, she put the camera in its case and turned around to greet the strong breeze herself.

As she walked along, Zahra drew out her mobile phone and texted Juana words she'd been repeating to herself ever since she had landed in Kolkata: *Not coming back to States. Need to sit still longer. Will call you.* With a deep sigh, she deposited the phone in her pocket, continuing to walk, at a slower pace.

She decided that later that evening, she would phone Juana and explain her decision. Juana would probably disagree and say: "Once you start something, you owe it to yourself to finish." But maybe after Zahra explained to her about taking pictures, Juana might understand. Maybe then Juana would say, "It's important to know yourself and your neighbors." For Juana, from Mexico, knew all about her roots, closed borders, and neighboring countries at war. Zahra was certain that Juana would continue to fight for the rights of the undocumented, and that the protests against sending U.S. forces to Iraq would only increase. As for her graduate program, Zahra knew that there was nothing there that she hadn't already learned in Kolkata or could not learn in Karachi.

As she watched the cresting waves of the Arabian Sea, three seagulls floated above her without moving their wings. Every now and then, when a gust pushed them in a different direction, they flapped their wings ever so gently to redirect themselves, then rested, floating again.

# LOOK,
# BUT WITH
# LOVE

ଔ

## *Uzma Aslam Khan*

Uzma Aslam Khan (1969–    ), a
novelist, was born in Lahore, grew
up in Karachi, and was educated at
St. Joseph's College and St. Patrick's
School. She earned degrees in the
United States from Hobart and
William Smith College and the
University of Arizona. She has lived in
Lahore since 1998 with her American
husband, the novelist David Maine.
She has taught literature and creative
writing at the Beaconhouse National

University in Lahore, and at The University of Arizona in Tucson, and has been a distinguished visiting writer at the University of Hawai'i at Manoa in Honolulu.

Khan is the author of *The Story of Noble Rot* (Penguin Books India, 2001), and *Trespassing* (Penguin Books India, 2003), which was short listed for a Commonwealth Prize and tells of a brutal murder during Karachi's ethnic violence in the 1990s. Her third novel, published in 2008, is entitled, *The Geometry of God* (Rupa). Her books have been translated into several languages, and she has written articles for various newspapers and journals worldwide, including *Drawbridge*, *Counterpunch*, and *Dawn*.

An extract from *Trespassing*, "Look, but with Love" points out the gradual destruction of age-old coastal communities in Karachi—a new breed of trawlers has destroyed the livelihood of traditional fisherman, including the protagonist, Salaamat. His search for survival leads him to Karachi's bus workshops, which, together with the country's trucks and buses, are largely owned by Pathans—tough, light-skinned migrants from the poor, northern, landlocked areas of Pakistan that border Afghanistan. At the workshops, the Pathans mock Salaamat as a dark-skinned man and as a foreigner. The excerpt lays bare Pakistan's complicated national dialogue about migration and notions of homeland; and the ethnic conflicts that have beset overcrowded cities like Karachi, where every community fights for space.

The hub of an all male-underworld, the bus workshops of Karachi are made up of men who have left their families behind in villages. They express their memories, desires, and aspirations by painting the exterior of trucks and vehicles with vivid images of natural beauty, mythic characters, and complex calligraphy, including the words *"Dekh, Magar Pyar Sey"* (Look, but with Love), which gives the story its title and also becomes a metaphor for Salaamat's obsession with a provocative dream woman painted on one of the buses who becomes a substitute for romance and desire in his real life.

• • •

## APRIL–JUNE 1984

In Karachi, Salaamat learned new words fast. The sand of his village was replaced by granite, mud with cement, fish with scraps of rubbery mutton, and that too on good days. He smelled no salt in the air, only smoke and gases that made his chest burn. The moon was dimmed by lights a thousand times brighter than those the trawlers had burned. The brightest were for weddings: little colored bulbs strung from trees and rooftops. An entire house could light up like a private galaxy. Women did not sit outside homes, wedding or not, smoking. At first, he barely saw any at all. And there were ways to cross the rivers of asphalt without being hit by wheels.

For days after entering the city Salaamat sat on roadsides watching, stunned by the variety of wheels. On the beach, he'd seen weekend visitors ride down the shoreline on motorcycles, but he'd never known how many kinds of vehicles there could be. Now here they were, whizzing by him, vehicles each with names he longed to know. At a *paan* and tea stall (the tea was wretched but he learned to drink it) that hired him, he asked regulars to teach him. While painting the *paan* leaves with betel juice, he timidly repeated: Nissan, Honda, Suzuki, Toyota. It helped him forget how differently those around him spoke. Here he was not merely half-deaf but half-dumb. Avoiding speech, he quietly studied how the car models changed depending on the year, and formed opinions on which color best suited each style.

But what he loved most were the buses. He accidentally said so one day. The customers laughed, sucking on *supari*. "Every man dreams of having a car and you dream of buses!"

He explained his tastes to no one.

The buses were decorated as lavishly as boats for the annual fair at his village. They were boats that rocked on a solid sea. He studied the designs, drank in the rich colors, memorized the names of the shops that made them, all in Qaddafi Town. He learned this was near the eastern outskirts of the city, and as soon as he'd saved enough money Salaamat hopped onto one such bus.

The interior was pink and gold, and in each corner was a different picture: fish dancing; storks wading; a lofty crown; parrots with girlish eyes, preening. The tranquility of each scene contrasted with the activities of the commuters who spat *paan* juice everywhere, extinguished cigarettes on fish fins, blew their noses on crown jewels. The sea salt he'd been unable to smell since coming here ate into the paint and left the interior crusted with rust. The bus shook with its load; five men hung from each of its doors and many more stood on the fenders, thumping the bus when it was time to jump off. Salaamat kept asking the conductor for Qaddafi Town. Finally, the man grabbed his kurta cuff and pushed him out.

Knees wobbling, Salaamat entered the first bus workshop he passed. It was called: Handsome Body Maker.

Seven buses were parked inside, in various stages of construction. A large man stepped out of an office, gruffly asking what he wanted.

"I . . . I want work," Salaamat replied.

The man turned toward the office, shouting something incomprehensible. Two others appeared. The mighty one who was Handsome, opened his palm and shook it rudely under Salaamat's chin. "*Wah!* We should thank the Almighty the foreigner has come to us!"

Only one of the others, bald as an egg, laughed. Touching Salaamat's locks he said in a high-pitched voice, "A pretty boy like you should have no problem finding work." He turned to Handsome, adding, "You are Handsome but he is Pretty."

"But he's so dark," protested the rose-cheeked Handsome between chuckles.

"It'll rub off!" said the bald man.

The third man was the smallest. He had a thin mustache and heavily oiled hair, and as yet had not cracked a smile. He squinted, "Where are you from?"

Salaamat tossed his head proudly and named his village.

"A *machera*!" the skinny man sneered. "No wonder he's black."

"There are no fish here, *meri jaan*," said the bald man, wagging a finger. "Of course, if you're clever, you can catch other things."

Salaamat cleared his throat. "I'm clever and can learn a new trade. I ask only for food and lodging and will work as many hours as you need me to."

The men looked at each other. Handsome said, "For an *ajnabi* you speak confidently."

The bald man again fondled Salaamat's locks. "Keep him. He speaks well."

Handsome smacked his back and declared, "Then, Chikna, I'll let you decide what to do with him."

The skinny man interjected. "We can't allow an *ajnabi* in here."

"Since when have you owned this place?" Handsome retorted.

The skinny man said nothing, but Salaamat understood his gaze. This was the one to watch.

There were four doors behind the buses. Toward these Chikna now led him. Pointing to the small bundle in Salaamat's hand, he asked, "Is that all you have?"

Salaamat nodded, looking closely for the first time at the seven buses. He stared, trying to understand their progression from one stage to the next. The first was just a skeleton—a brown mass of metal plates with four wheels. But the last was a glinting gem.

"That's called a chassis," Chikna pointed to the first. "The bus owner gives us that and we do the rest." After a pause, he added, "How old are you?"

"About seventeen."

Chikna shrugged. "I've been working here since I was seven. Maybe it's too late for you." He pushed open a door to a storeroom. The floor was strewn with painted strips of steel, chains, wires, paint cans, stickers, hubs, brushes, lights, a pile of crowns, and lopsided, childlike sculptures of eagles and airplanes. "You can sleep here."

Salaamat dropped his bundle inside.

"There's a toilet at the back," Chikna continued. "Our families live in there," he pointed two doors down. "You can eat with us, but we've had our lunch. Can you wait for dinner?"

Salaamat nodded. He hadn't eaten but wasn't going to say so.

Outside, more workers were arriving. "What can I do now?" asked Salaamat.

"Today, just watch. Tomorrow you'll start with me." He walked away.

Salaamat shut the store's door and moved toward the buses. He wound his way around each, coming finally to the last. He then stood and took every detail in.

The exterior was painted a glittering magenta. Along the sides were nailed the strips of metal with garish floral patterns that he'd seen in the storeroom. The bottom edge of the bus was ringed around with chains ending in hearts. Wings figured elaborately everywhere: There were flying horses painted near the headlights and a sculpture of an eagle with a foot-long wingspan attached to the fender. The top wore a sort of palanquin, a bed of intricately worked metal, with the front decked in one of the airplane structures also in the store. The plane looked like a ship's figurehead. Attached to one wing was a national flag, while on the other a sign read: PIA. Whoever painted the bus had not simply wanted it driven but sailed, and not simply sailed but flown.

But the best awaited him at the back. Here was the most beautiful woman Salaamat had ever seen. She had eyes the size of his palm, a sensuous nose, and plum-like lips half hidden behind a flimsy cloth held in a henna-dipped hand. On her right side was written, "Look. But with Love." She did exactly that to him.

Salaamat was spellbound. The harder he stared the more certain he felt that she blinked, then blinked again. Her lips twitched in a smile she attempted to restrain, but failing that, she covered more of her face with the transparent *dupatta*.

"Ah, I see you've met Rani," said a voice. Salaamat forced himself away from the picture. It was Chikna. "She's a naughty one, I'd be careful. And don't let Hero see you get too close. He's very jealous."

"Hero?"

"Him," Chikna pointed to the skinny man who was painting two buses down. "You two already started on the wrong foot. And now Rani seems to find you as pretty as I do." He tilted his head and raised a brow saucily.

"What does Hero do here?" asked Salaamat.

"He's our painter. He made Rani. He loves everything he does. He's in love with himself." Chikna tweaked Rani's cheek roughly.

Salaamat had to stop himself from fighting him for he could see Rani wince. "I want to make a bus just like this one," he blurted. "I want to learn to make all these things. Including her." Rani hid behind her cloth and Chikna threw his bald head back and laughed.

# THE PRICE
# OF HUBRIS

&

## *Humera Afridi*

Humera Afridi (1971–   ) is a New
York-based writer of Pakistani origin. She was born in Lahore, spent
her early years in Karachi, and left
Pakistan at twelve with her parents
for the United Arab Emirates. She
earned her degrees in the United
States at Mount Holyoke College
and Carnegie Mellon University,
and was the recipient of a New York
Times Fellowship at New York University where she earned an MFA in

creative writing. Her work has appeared in the *New York Times* and several anthologies, including *Leaving Home* (Oxford University Press, 2001), *110 Stories: New York Writes after September 11* (NYU Press, 2003), and *Shattering the Stereotypes* (Olive Branch, 2005). Currently, she is finishing her first novel and teaching at Western Connecticut State University.

She says that she "endeavors to capture the dissonance that arises from the incommensurable worlds" her characters inhabit. As a woman belonging to the Pathan Afridi tribe, she carries with her the consciousness that she, "a northern Pakistani tribal outcaste walks the streets of New York" while her ancestral home on the borders of Pakistan and Afghanistan is often described as the "world's most dangerous place."

Set in New York a few days after 9/11, "The Price of Hubris," a version of which first appeared as "Circumference" in *110 Stories: New York Writes After September 11*, welds the crisis of the bombed city with the pain of a young Pakistani American woman who finds herself abandoned by her lover and regarded as an enemy in New York. In the story, the young woman is confronted with the post-9/11 prejudices that blame all Muslims for the attack on New York and consider all dark-skinned foreigners Muslims. Alienated from distant Pakistan, she makes an attempt to bond with fellow New York Muslims and faces yet another exclusion, this time in the mosque, where Muslim women are not allowed to participate in congregational prayers.

• • •

The woman has trained herself to wake up to precise images: aquamarine sea, limestone villas, sand the color of caramel custard, and a canteen crackling with newspapers and conversation. For a week now, she has awakened to this collage of all the beaches she has known.

Each morning the dream fills the barren plain that has been her mind since he left exactly one week ago; each morning the dream dissipates more quickly. She uncurls herself from her *ajrak* duvet. The yellow of pomegranate rinds and the warm reds of madder that had thrilled her when she bought the block-print comforter from a handicraft store are invisible now. She reaches for the remote and turns on her radio. She has no television; she is still new here.

Less than a mile from where she lives there is a world destroyed, mangled, spitting fumes of burned steel, flesh, and plastic. *The price of hubris*, the radio announcer posits, based on a comment made by a right-wing televangelist. The woman slides her feet out of bed but keeps her head on her pillow and listens. Today has been declared a national day of prayer and mourning. The barricade north of Houston Street has been lifted. She is free to roam beyond the circumference of the five square blocks where she has been zoned for the last four days since the attack. Anxiety prickles at her, anxiety about this strange new freedom.

She has three tea bags left—she has been conserving her rations as there have been no deliveries below 14th Street—and she steeps one now in a white mug and slips on her jeans and prepares to venture beyond the frontier. She will buy her first newspaper; she will buy sugar. She searches for her ID card, removes the stud from her nose.

Her lover—though after this last time, could he really be called that?—said: *We should leave it at the level of skin. No telephone calls, no email.* This woman who had moved alone to the city three weeks ago cannot get her lover's words out of her head. She mutters them, remembering the breadth of him against her, wishing she'd said them first. She slings her surgical mask around her neck, rummages in her closet for a *dupatta*. She is not devout, nor one to carry the baggage of tradition, yet she gropes around for a scarf to cover her hair.

She thinks of her husband. He will call soon from the home they had shared till three weeks ago. She will miss the call. On the fourth day after this world was sabotaged, she knows that the other man, the one with whom she has this arrangement, this mutual exercising of lust, will not telephone. Each time, in the days following his visit, the sensation of his presence dissipates, but now she does not let him out of her head. To do so will mean creating space for the horror outside.

Three people on her street—all Caucasian. Smoke belches and curdles from the site, subsumes the neighborhood in an acrid haze. She positions her mask over her face and walks north. Two people pass her and glare. Is she imagining it? On the first afternoon, a woman outside the deli said, *These fucking Arabs! I don't understand them.* Then, looking at her closely, said, *You're not Arab, are you? I mean, you're not Palestinian?*

At Houston Street she shows her ID to a South Asian police officer, forces a pinched smile. People cluster on either side of the blockade. As she crosses the street it feels as though she has left a country behind. Four men shove past her; one of them mutters something loud and incoherent.

Earnestness is not what the city is about and she wears her sin too close to her skin. She flags a cab, *11th Street and 1st Avenue, please.* She does not say Madina Masjid. The driver peers at her through the rearview mirror. He is brown and complicit. It is Friday, the day of communal prayer.

The woman feels she is driving through a palimpsest. A new city, an altered reality has layered the streets on which she has not been permitted to walk for the past few days. The few people out of doors cluster around posters of the missing, reading their lives, learning the maps of their bodies, the birthmarks and tattoos that render them unique. She wonders about the people alive, the ones putting up the posters, going from wall to wall with tape, watching the sky for rain.

The car stops at a red light. She cannot believe that the man who fucked her seven days ago hasn't bothered to email, to call. She cannot believe she is thinking of him still and that she has thought more about him than at any other time, in any other year. She cannot believe she is becoming this sort of woman, the sort of woman who baffles her.

A voice rasps through the window: *I'm going to fucking kill Osama. I want you to know I'm going to get him.*

*Okay, okay, very good*, the driver says like he's soothing a colicky baby.

The man at the window looks at her, says: *I'm telling this cabbie here I'm going to kill Osama.* He has a scruffy orange beard, a thin pasty face. The light turns, the tires screech, the driver swears under his breath in Punjabi.

Once out of the cab she wraps her hair in her *dupatta*. There are three photographers and two white journalists in denim skirts and bright stockings. There are no Muslim women in sight. But it is Friday, she thinks, they must be inside. She approaches a man in a mustard kurta-pajama, asks for the women's entrance. He looks over the length of her body, tilts his head. *Why? Do you want to pray?* She disregards him and walks into the squat building. There is office carpeting, sheetrock walls; it smells like someone's cooking. There are only men. One says, Yes? as if she were a foreigner. It is evident to them she is not a mosque-goer; she lacks the protocol.

*Where are the women, please?*

*No women here*, he says abruptly and opens the door to let her out.

Standing in front of this mosque she feels stripped to the bone. Shameless; adulteress; wine-drinker: Her jeans seem to say this to the men, as do her boots and the fact that she is here alone on a day when the women are secure at home.

You are here, she thinks, in this city, among things and people, vehicles and street vendors, but you cannot say a word. The sins of this life seem as flat as copper pennies ground under heeled boots, worthless as vanity, lost in dirt. There is a sudden newness to the street, there is a sudden stark separation of the soul from the world that sifts around and through the body. You are here, she thinks. When you awake tomorrow, and the day after, and the day after that, this is where you will be.

# RUNAWAY
# TRUCK RAMP

༄

## *Soniah Kamal*

Soniah Kamal (1972– ) was
born in Karachi and grew up
in Britain, Pakistan, and Saudi
Arabia. At sixteen, she moved
to Lahore with her family and
was educated at The Lahore
Grammar School and The
Lahore College of Arts and Sci-
ences. She graduated with honors in the United States from
St. John's College in Maryland
and received the Susan Irene

Roberts award for her thesis, "On Prince Charmings, Frogs, Love Marriages, and Arranged Ones," based on Vikram Seth's novel, *A Suitable Boy*. Kamal's short stories and essays have been published in the United States, Canada, and Pakistan, and in the anthologies *Voices of Resistance: Muslim Women on War, Faith and Sexuality* (Seal Press, 2006), *Letter from India* (Penguin Books India, 2006), and *Neither Night nor Day* (HarperCollins, 2007). She writes a weekly column, "My Foot," in the Pakistani newspaper *The Daily Times*. She lives in the United States, has traveled extensively across the country, and has long wanted to write a road-trip story.

"Runaway Truck Ramp" explores both the sensitivities and misunderstandings of cross-cultural communication and how preconceived ideas of The Other are both challenged by and can percolate into a relationship. The title evolved from Kamal's fascination on the U.S. highways with the steep, runaway truck ramps by the side of roads that appear to her as if they were leading to the heavens, although, of course, the truck goes up, slowly slides back, and ultimately comes to a stop. Kamal equates the ramps with life itself, "which seems promising in the beginning but slowly one realizes that more and more one is living in the past, i.e. has reached the zenith of the ramp, and is now falling back into memory and what might have been."

• • •

I was in the hospital's chapel when he came in, said, "Excuse me, thought this was the smoking room," and would have left had I perhaps not been howling, my blue mascara measled over my reddened face, a million crumpled tissues spilling out of my lap.

"Are you," he said, "okay?"

I managed to nod and he insisted on getting me a cup of water, which I downed.

"I can go or . . ." He sat next to me on the wooden pew right in front of the pale green-gowned Mary cradling a baby Jesus.

"My mother just died." I doubled over with fresh sticky tears. "Oh God, it's sounds so dreadful, just saying it."

"I'm so sorry."

"Three years coma-ridden," I tried to focus on Mary's gown chipped by her little toe, "but once we bury her there's no hope of ever seeing her again and that's what makes death, death and shit, it's all too much." I blew my nose and wiped my cheeks with the back of my hand. "I keep feeling like I'm going to fall down and what if I can't get up again?"

"Smoke?" He held a hard pack between incredibly long fingers.

"Under the circumstances," I said and lit up.

"Name's Sulaiman." He held the paper cup for me to ash in. "But if you can't pronounce it just call me Sully."

"Michelle," I said and because my mother had always maintained displaying polite interest in other people no matter what, I asked, "Doesn't it offend you, having to change your name so it isn't mispronounced?"

"Offend no, feel sorry, yes," Sully paused, glancing at the altar, "because there are so many names you people cannot pronounce."

We should have never met again, Sully and I, except that I'd left my *Memoirs of a Geisha* in the chapel (I'd been expecting to go on reading to Mom, not for her to die) and the front page was inscribed with my name and address and Sully, being a conscientious individual, decided to return it.

I invited him into the kitchen where he sat on an orange bar stool, his long legs dangling on either side, his thighs spread wide. "A complete stranger could have gotten hold of it," he said. I told him about my heart attack when I found out my Dad was cheating on my comatose Mom and that, after two hours of deliberation, I'd decided to allow Dad to be human and to regress into childhood myself.

"I used to inscribe books in the sixth grade and somewhere that habit, along with jump rope, got lost and so I'm trying to reenact nice bits of my life before my heart takes off with it completely." I pulled a pineapple magnet off the fridge door. "I want to stop being the girl who feels guilty laughing because her mother can't. I want to learn to skate a perfect figure eight. I want to drive through . . . oh, Africa."

"I'm going to be driving to California."

Dad was not happy with my plans.

"You're going on a three-day, possibly longer, trip with a complete stranger?"

"Not complete."

Sully and I had been meeting almost daily for three months. When Mom fell ill I'd dropped out of college to be with her as much as possible and Sully, from Pakistan, had just graduated from UC Boulder and was waiting to hear back from job interviews. We both had plenty of free time to indulge in coffee or curries, matinees at a dollar cinema he hadn't known was a block away from him, or tossing a Frisbee around in the park, or walking through Scandinavian Designs, pretending we were furnishing our house.

He prefers bamboo. I like faux fur in oranges and greens. He likes tall porcelain vases. I like intricate crystal. He likes tea in a fine china cup with a saucer. I like good-sized mugs that weigh down my wrists. He could live in the ocean. I'm not that fond of water.

He tells me that I unnerve him, the way I watch him, as if he were a bird so intent on following a worm that it doesn't know there's a cat waiting to pounce. And why do I stare at his fingers so?

Because I'm in love with them—so long, so delicate, like white opera gloves—but I don't say so. Instead I tell him I'm a writer and so I stare at everything for research purposes.

I tell Erin, my best friend, he's so interested in my work and always reads immediately what I give him and says it's nice, but when Erin tells me reading is not the equivalent of caring, I just roll my eyes and remind her that she has yet to read what I gave her ages ago.

Erin and Sully had met at a sport's bar where we were

watching the Denver Nuggets take on the Minnesota Timber-wolves and were, as far as I was concerned, enjoying pitchers of beer and chips and salsa, watching the halftime game filler of *America's Stupidest Criminals*, when Sully said, "I guess all Americans are good, but why are so many so stupid?"

I laughed, and laughter was good for me but Erin, her hands curling around her beer mug as if it were a cross, said, "How can you just generalize like that?" She jabbed her tortoise shells up the bridge of her nose. "I mean, how do you dare?"

"Don't worry," Sully said signaling the waitress for another pitcher. "My people—we're all cunning and competitive and class and color conscious like crazy."

"I don't care what—"

"The whole world," I said, kicking Erin under the table to shut up, "is fucked up," but Erin didn't shut up and, in fact, proceeded to gang up with Dad over my not going on any trip with Sully.

That I lived at home still didn't change the fact that I was old enough to do what I wanted, and anyway I told Dad that he'd be glad to have me out of his and his new wife's hair. Though he said, "No, no," I could see that I'd scored, and in the end the only condition I agreed to was that we'd take my car, since Sully had been planning to sell his in California anyway and could just as well do so here.

So it's Tuesday morning. Bright, sunny, crisp. I pick up Sully. He takes a look at the large moving trailer attached to my Jetta and claps. I glance at his one backpack and clap back.

We stop for gas and munchies. I get cheese dip, ruffled potato chips, and a Dr. Pepper. Sully indulges in a pack of mild cigarettes and a bag of assorted suckers. By the time we hit the interstate he's licked through a blueberry and a sour apple.

"Are you going to miss Denver?" I ask.

"No," he says with purple lips and tongue.

"Not even your friends?"

"You asked about Denver."

"What's the difference?"

"One's a place," he rips the wrapper off a cherry sucker, "the other are people."

"Don't people make the place?"

"They make it tolerable, I suppose." He bites off a chunk the sucker. "My fiancée's the romantic one."

Whenever he mentions his fiancée I feel a sudden sadness, like when I picture lynching trees or the unsinkable Titanic doing just that.

"She sends me taped passages from books she's read. And letters. Lots of letters." He tapped his T-shirt pocket where I could make out the outline of a folded envelope.

"She's learning to bake an orange chiffon cake and plans to take Chinese cooking classes next. She's—"

"A cook?"

Sully frowned. "Why do you women always put each other down?"

I want to lean over and kiss him.

"Do you like her?"

"She's demure. I like that." He lights a cigarette. "Women here are . . . as if asking them to sew a button on my shirt is insulting their very integrity."

"Hey! Sew your own damn buttons."

"See."

"But why wouldn't you sew?"

"Why wouldn't you?" He takes a long drag, the long cigarette a mere stub between his straw-long fingers. "And I do sew my own buttons."

"Bet your fiancée can't wait to sew for you."

"She won't have to. Tell me," he glanced at me, "what do you like? In a man."

"Shit!" I swerved.

"Yeah?"

"No, I mean, did you see that roadkill? I couldn't even tell what it was."

Sully craned his neck out of the window, we'd left it far behind, whatever it had been, lying there in the middle of the highway, a fat, furry carcass, jumbled up.

"It just makes me so sad," I said as we left Colorado and entered Wyoming. "A hit and run no one could care less about."

I didn't tell him that I liked in a man what I'd seen in him: glasses of water and book returns and sewing himself and his fiancée not having to, his swan-wing fingers, his profile, smooth curve after curve, not like some men with protruding foreheads, huge noses, or receding chins.

He was engaged to be married.

After the carcass we drove through Wyoming in silence, broken occasionally for a comment or two about how flat it all was and ugly, I said, and Sully expounded on beauty and the beholder, and I told him to stop being so righteous, ugly was ugly, had he ever had a heart attack?

"How did you have yours?"

I wanted to be harsh and unrelenting. I wanted to see black and white and fuck the gray . . . something about the animal, the way it just lay there helpless, dead, beyond help, like a coma, a child with cancer, or a teenager trying on a pair of Adidas and suddenly clutching her friend and saying, as I had to Erin, "Something's wrong. My arm's killing me, and my chest—I know my boobs aren't growing"—even in pain and panic the need to be witty, funny, anything but a garbled mess.

Only when we got to the ER and I was rushed past patients nursing hurts yet to be seen did it occur to me that I could die, that I could die before Mom, and that I didn't want to die a virgin.

Erin, who was going to be a virgin till marriage, took it quite well. She had one condition though. "You have to tell me every detail," she said.

I lost my virginity to Tyler Harris, Literature 101, as taken with Jackson's "The Lottery" as I was. My, it felt good to kick him out the next morning from my dorm room. Tyler was peeved, perhaps because he hadn't gotten to it first.

"Damn, girl," he said, "relationship's supposed to last more than one night," but my heart was too weak to take anything longer or stronger.

Essence said I could walk into a room, take a survey, hone in, chat up, take the boy, and dispose of him afterward like well-chewed gum, we the women of the millennium, and that's what I did: Take Charge. That's the type I fell under in a *Marie Claire* quiz. No mooning around and pining for a guy for me, and so here was Sully, I found him attractive, and so why not, except I just couldn't do my routine—pull him over, fondle him, or just say, "Wanna fuck?"

I wondered if Sully had ever been sick a day in his life, wondered what he would do if a car smashed into him on a road and he lay there, fresh and shiny, his cockiness leaking out and people just passing by.

Just passing by.

In between chatter and silences we listened to tapes. I played everything by Tori Amos, and Sully, songs, he said, by back-home bands like Junoon and Vital Signs.

He could understand Amos, but I couldn't tell what his were on about and somehow it seemed unfair that, of the two of us, he of the third world should be the bilingual one. I told him so and he gave me a talk about identity, culture, bi-, tri- and multi-. That's a well-rehearsed lecture, Erin would say, I said, but when Sully rolled his eyes I decided not to bring up Erin again because I didn't want anyone rolling their eyes at her, no matter what.

We stopped after seven hours of driving at a Best Western in Wyoming since Sully had run out of cigarettes.

"Separate rooms," he told the desk clerk, a young woman with bushels of brown hair streaming stiffly from her nostrils.

I stood outside Sully's bedroom door for a minute, then entered mine.

We breakfast on burgers. According to Sully there is no other way. He eats with a plastic knife and fork, dipping the bite-sized bun, meat, lettuce, and tomato into a puddle of ketchup in a cardboard tub.

I take a bite out of mine. Ketchup drips down my fingers. I lick the wedge between my thumb and index finger.

"That's very attractive," Sully says. "Very sexy."

He looks at me as if I were a morsel to chew and spit out, or swallow and eventually expel anyway.

"What's wrong? You're blushing."

I cannot lean over and kiss this guy *this guy* because *dammit* dammit he makes me shy.

I call Erin from the restroom. This can hardly, she says, be love. Are you rolling your eyes, I ask. She says, why yes. I switch my cell phone off after that. I don't want her calling to make sure that I'm not falling.

Today Sully's behind the wheel. His slinky fingers sink into the steering covered in fur. Sunshine glints off the length of his fingernails. I twine my hands around the headrest, yawn, and stretch. He whistles, looking at my straining shirt and denim skirt riding up over the tan lines on my thighs.

"Hey," I say whacking him on his upper arm, "what would your fiancée say!"

"That I'm engaged to her but not blind."

I whack him again, this time on his forearm, another whack forward and I can grab those fingers in my short, chubby ones, the fingernails chewed to nubs, but he turns the key in the ignition and the grabbing moment is gone.

"My fiancée," he says, adjusting the rearview mirror and backing out smoothly, "believes in dreams." He glances at me. "I had a dream about the two of you last night." He exits for the interstate. "You were both playing chess."

"Who won?"

"No one. It was fucked up."

He switches his tape on again. There's this one Pakistani song that sounds like Black Sabbath but it's not. It's a warning to copycats, Sully says, and rather tongue in cheek since its music is hardly original itself. He begins to tell me tidbits about the band but I'm not interested and inquire instead, "Why do you like demure women?"

"I like women who know they're women," he rocks his head to the music, "like you."

"I'm demure?"

"What do you think?"

"Define demure."

Another song comes on, he sings a few lyrics—he's got a terrible voice, but he's so confident—and says, "the opposite of bold."

The opposite of bold. Why not? Why couldn't it be me? Hadn't I not knocked on Sully's door last night? I'd gotten up twice to go to his room, but hadn't I ended up in my own bed? Damn right, I was demure.

"How demure is your fiancée?"

"So demure I'm going to ravish her behind and she won't know why the hell she's not getting pregnant."

"Sully!"

"What?"

But he's laughing and I laugh too, because of course he's joking, joking about demure being so important, and behinds, and all the U.S. girls, two a week if possible, he's going to have sunny side up. But between the laughter there's a savageness that supposes his fiancée may as well be blind and deaf, because what she can't see or isn't told never happened.

We're still laughing when we leave Wyoming and enter Utah. Still laughing when flatlands turn greener and greener and the bushes turn into trees. Laughing when we stop at a gas station where we use a unisex restroom, the seat piss-splattered and stinking. Laughing as we buy cheddar sandwiches, laughing coming out to the car surrounded by seagulls, five, ten, fifteen large creatures pecking the tarmac and others swooping so close they could land on my hair.

Not laughing I rush into the car, glad the windows are up and mouth to Sully, "The Birds," and Sully says, "they just want to be fed." He walks amidst them boldly. I think: How modest of me to retire to the car, how demure, is it feminine the fear I felt or just unique to me?

I open the car door, gingerly step out, again laughing. How simple explanations are—it's not a horror movie, it's hunger or greed if I go by the way the gulls are gulping our sandwiches as if they were meant for them all along.

We are still laughing when we get to Salt Lake City. Laughing as we drive on sprawling spider-leg flyovers and guessing which exit to take. Laughing when we take a wrong one and laughing when we take the right one and get to Holiday Inn.

We park, enter the lobby, there are rooms available, we get a room, go back to the parking lot, disengage the trailer, go back inside, decide to freshen up and then find a nice French restaurant because we want meat, meat, glorious meat—we are giddy over nothing in particular and everything in general— over demure and bold and everything in between, but when we get to the room the curtains are drawn and the bed beckons. For a second I feel bad for a fiancée baking chiffon cakes and then decide that she's not my problem, she's his, and that I can take her place and, because I won't be busy baking, will make sure no one takes mine—and we find ourselves naked on the bed, in it, off it, back on, and now he's on, I'm off, my knees pinned against the rough brown carpet and when I look up for a moment in the mirror adjacent to us, I see Sully's head cradled in his hands, eyes shut, mouth pursed, and I finish it off, swallow, swallow, he says and I do and then come up and say, "My turn" and sit up, brusquely, when he says, "No, no, I can't do that."

And he doesn't. He just won't. I cajole at first. Then discuss. Then argue. Then yell. And finally say please, and when that doesn't work I hobble into my clothes, grab my bag, and storm out.

Clad in a towel he follows me into the elevator, seizes my arm, the elevator door shuts.

"I know it's not fair," he says. "I know and I'm sorry."

"Then why did you let me?" I press LOBBY.

He shrugs.

"What if your demure virgin of a wife expects you to?"

His shoulders are on the narrower side, there's a fat, flat red mole on the left one. His legs, I see now, are thinner than mine.

"If it comes down to this or her leaving me."

He lets go of my arm and bangs a fist in a palm and this strong reaction over my leaving pleases me enough to return to the room.

I decide to show patience in this matter and lean over to kiss him and he rears back.

"What!"

"Umm . . . can you wash your mouth first? Please."

"It's you in my mouth, you can't kiss me, but I'm expected to swallow."

When I leave this time he doesn't follow.


Thursday. I don't know what Sully did for breakfast but I ate the donuts and black coffee provided in the lobby where he was waiting for me.

"Hello," he said.

"Drop dead," I said and again when he tried to help me hitch the trailer to the car.

We drove out of Utah with the radio on at the first audible frequency. The DJ was announcing a contest to win free Bette Midler concert tickets.

I drove upon a straight highway with a lake on both sides that increasingly became whiter and whiter until finally they were nothing but immense, vast stretches of salt. If I didn't know I'd swear it was snow.

"I'm sorry," Sully said. His arms were crossed, his hands

tucked into his armpits. He looked tired. As if he hadn't slept.

"There's nothing to be sorry about," I said. "You're an asshole and now I know."

The radio station is coming on garbled. I turn it off. Sully turns on his tape. Today it's not sounding so hot. Fucking band copying Black Sabbath—who the hell did they think they were, third-world wannabes. I switch it off.

Sully turns toward his window and stares out and is still staring when Nevada comes upon us in the guise of huge billboards with women wearing frilly dresses, advertising casinos voted, by people whose tastes we don't know, for having the best food around.

I'm thinking dark thoughts about love and demureness and beginning to wonder if I'm an insensitive creature—the man finds genitals dirty, not just mine but, for God's sake his own, he couldn't even kiss me, all he did was ask me to rinse my mouth, and what had I done? acted like dirt was no issue at all. I want to apologize, but I can't. I just can't get over the hump of me on my knees and he not.

But when he finally speaks hours later, "I have to go to the restroom," I'm ready to begin anew and so I stop.

The women's restroom at Ernie's Country Store in Oasis, Nevada, could do with a touch-up. When Sully emerges from the men's I ask him if there was any toilet paper in there.

He looks at me and I think it'll be him now who won't answer. "Plenty," he says.

It's a relatively big store selling food and drinks and gifts like ponchos and glass dolphin wind chimes. There are a few video poker and Pilot Peak's slot machines by the entrance, all occupied.

Sully grabs some beef jerky. I get a Dr. Pepper. There's a long line at the checkout counter held up by a girl of four or five. She's hugging an armload of candy and screaming at her mother who is trying to yank the goods away from her.

The man emerges like a charging bull. I think he's crippled, the way he's bouncing up and down, his thin, blond braid wafting like a wisp of smoke, then he begins to grunt, "ooo ooo aaa aaa ooo ooo." He's scratching his armpits like a chimp and he is a chimp, a damn fine one too, because the little girl, enthralled by the monkeying of a grown man with a light brown full beard in Birkenstocks and khaki shorts, drops her candy to copy him and the mother swoops down, picks her up, nods a thanks, and hurries out, leaving everyone behind clapping as the man takes a bow.

When we leave the Oasis, minding the black beetles doddering through the sand, Sully shakes his head.

"What an idiot," he says getting into the car. "How could he just do that without a care about looking like a complete fool?"

"Because he's bold and demure all at once and not pretending to be one or the other. Something some people just can't see or get. He's just a stupid American, I guess."

Sully's breathing quickens but he doesn't say a word. In the car he turns on his tape. I don't switch it off. Pettiness brings no one closer. Nor does it create distance.

When we get to Reno I ask for separate rooms but it is Sully who shakes his head, says "Just wait," and as soon as we enter the suite in La Quinta Inn, tumbles me onto the queen size bed.

"Are you sure?" I say, alarmed at the ferocity. "Are you sure?"

Without an answer he dives down; he's clueless. Twice he gags, but before I can say anything he takes a deep breath and is back at it.

I'm getting a bit sore. I wonder if helping him out would indeed be the complete opposite of demure. His fingers uselessly clutch the beige bedspread on either side of me. If this is how he performs do I want to be his wife?

I brush aside doubts because of course he'll get better. He's a novice and there is no such thing as a natural. But for now I faked and did a great job because he came up beaming, gasping for air, and I leaned over to kiss him, to let him know I appreciated this done *for me* but he shoved me aside and hurtled into the bathroom and I could hear him gargling. He gargled for at least an hour, it seemed.

When he came out we shared a cigarette. I kept smiling and he kept saying, "What? What?" and not looking me in the eye. After the smoke I spread him out on the bed, longing to tell him that I loved him. I whispered, "I thought you were only going to do that with your wife."

I'm sitting on top of him, stretching, triumphant, my fingers locked, arms thrown back, proud, arching my lower back, breasts and belly button—one smart, continuous treble clef.

"I was practicing," he says.

It should not sting—practice—but it does. Cheap. Trashy. Whore. For. Someone. Who. Will. Marry. A. Virgin. And. Do. Her. Backside. Until. He. Decides. To. Flip. Her. Over.

I lower my arms, slide off him, grab a cigarette as nonchalantly as possible, trying to still my shaking fingers.

"Hey," Sully says, sitting up on one elbow, "what's wrong?"

"Nothing." I light it, take a puff, decide no aggravation is worth damaging my heart any further, and offer it to him.

I watch him suck on the cigarette butt, run his tongue over where my lips were a moment ago, and wish I'd just put it out.

"I'm taking a shower."

I melt into the scalding water, which doesn't go deep enough into my ears to scour out hearing that I am a practice session—not the real thing—not that I want to be the real thing, of course not, *but what if I did*, so damn it don't point it out. I feel indignation for the land of "America."

"Can I join?" Sully's turning the knob but I've locked the door—he must think I'm a silly, sweet American to be sharing a bed but showering in private.

I call out I'm done, turn off the water, and then realize that, in my hurry to get away, I've forgotten to bring any clothes.

"Can you hand me my clothes?"

"Are you kidding?"

He must think I'm mad, and to keep some sanity intact I emerge bundled up in towels, open my suitcase, turn my back, let the towels fall, remember he's a butt man, turn around, and see him smoking again, looking at me, one brow raised.

"What's wrong?"

"Nothing."

"Yeah?"

"Yeah."

"Wasn't I any good?"

"It's not that."

When I'm fully clothed, it comes out. "I didn't like being 'practiced' upon."

"Thought that would get you."

"I don't like being played mind games with, either."

"Why are you so upset?" He ashes on the tourist guide to Reno.

In the dim lamplight his fingers look like old, discolored wooden chopsticks.

"I don't," I say, "like calling a fuck a fuck."

"It's not just . . . a fuck . . . It's . . . we're friends."

I roll my eyes.

"Michelle?"

I turn away.

"Again not talking?" He shrugs, takes a last long drag of the cigarette, swishes it under the tap in the sink built into the room, then tosses it into the garbage can. The room smells of wet smoke, a maggot-infested carcass slowly burning.

In Reno and not going to a casino. I feigned sleep while Sully got ready and left. I talked to Mom and then to God. I could have called Erin or Dad but they would have gotten worried, thought I'd been raped, but how: *I just couldn't put my finger on it.*

I wanted to get a separate room but there was a Bette Midler concert and apparently we were darned lucky to get any room at all.

When Sully came back I was watching a *Beverly Hills 90210* rerun. He crawled in next to me—to forgive is divine—but when his fingers crept up my knee I stiffened, pushed them off, and lay down with my back to him.

What does he know about me: that I like onion dip with ruffled potato chips, that I only drink Dr. Pepper, that my mother's dead, that my father had an affair and remarried, and that I've had a heart attack that cranked open my legs.

What do I know about him: nothing I care to recall.

"Do you mind if I change the channel?"

I don't answer, and after a second he flips through and finally settles on Leno. I hear Leno taking digs at Kevin Eubanks, mocking Donald Trump, and then making a fool out of a couple in the audience on account of them dressed in identical jeans, T-shirts, and hats.

Sully's tickled. The bed's shaking. He's laughing like his life depends on it: He sounds like I imagine a donkey being castrated would.

He's laughing and I wish we'd respect ourselves, us Americans—all of us and each other—and quit thinking that pointing out our mistakes is healthy and will endear us to the world, because here is this man come for an American education and planning to stay for an American job and making room in his plans to fuck an American girl or two per week, but first confuse her about demure or not demure, confuse this naïve American who thinks she's bold and brave and going about the world on her own terms.

He's in deep sleep, his eyelids jerking in the way that used to scare the life out of me when I was a kid. I pack my duffel bag. I leave.

I wonder what he'll think in the morning. Me gone, my car gone, and I hope he knows that this is me screwing him up his butt.

I think about him often those first few months and it keeps

coming down to "practice, practice, practice," but over the years as I relate my experience with a Pakistani man, he goes from being that fuck to that arrogant prick to that asshole (no pun intended), to that jerk, to that stupid guy, and to finally rest as this guy who made me feel like a slut, worse, an unpaid slut.

I push this matter into a cabinet, right into the blackest corner at the back.

Monday night preparing to watch TV.

The kettle whistles. I pour the boiling water into my favorite mug, a pink one Josh gave me saying, "I Have a Dream . . . for All Mankind . . . PMS." The instant vanilla cappuccino froths up. It smells, as my daughters would say, yummy. I turn on the TV to watch Ally McBeal but I cannot. I just cannot.

Tuesday afternoon in the garden.

I am loosening up soil. My beefsteak tomatoes are doing very well, but I don't think that my Russian roses will win anything this year. Leaves have fallen into the pool again. The soil is damp and smells of life and I may as well lay me down and die.

*Last Sunday morning at the BookWorm, browsing.*

There's no trick of the light upon the eye. I am not going mad or having a heart attack. I recognize him—Sully.

It is Sully.

Dark brown Sully in a white shirt, a little heavier in the jowl area, his hair thinner and much shorter.

Sully on the cover of *Writers Inc.*

Is he still making fun of us and being rewarded with fame and fortune?

I am an animal going on my perfectly normal way only to be run over and left there.

Many summers ago Josh and I met and married. Josh did good, and I'm a full-time Mom who shops from a farmer's market and buys only organic, cage-free eggs, and goes to lunches at the club, hosts a huge Christmas dinner annually, and sometimes doesn't mind wearing the same color T-shirt Josh is wearing.

Wednesday evening.

I visit Dad, taking him a big basket of home-cooked goodies. He outlived his second wife, too. I turn the key to his front door and find him watching *The Philadelphia Story*, chuckling away as if he'd never seen it before.

It's the first time that whole week, as I sit on the ottoman with Dad's feet in my lap, cutting his toenails, that I don't feel completely useless or totally empty and sad.

I am the proud founder of two successful book clubs. I read to the blind once a month. Josh and I vacation twice annually. Once with the kids and then without. Then there's always sex on Saturday night so as to keep ignited the eternal flame, followed by lazy Sunday mornings and BBQs with friends. I enjoy gardening, swimming, and taking Bundt, our dalmation, for walks in the park.

So why did I leave the bookstore as if my life were one very big joke?

Saturday, twenty to midnight.

I am not the spider woman I usually am in bed.

"What's up?" Josh says.

I tell him:

*The Maritime Warrior*: "Best novel of the year."

*Entertainment Weekly*: "A must read."

Author Jean Splice: "It's a beauty."

Amazon: "Four hundred and ninety-nine reviewers out of five hundred have given it four stars out of five."

It's about a foreign student from Pakistan and a guy, their chance meeting, which leads to a cross-country trip and love or something like it, and hate too, definitely hate.

Josh tells me not to fret, it will come, will my time.
He kisses me, turns over, and falls asleep.
I'm up all night.

Thursday afternoon.
I'm lunching with two girlfriends. We're low carbing this month and wondering if we dare have a caramel frappacino each. I laugh on cue, don't chew on my straw, lay my napkin out just right, but when they ask how my novel is coming along, I get tears in my eyes and it makes them really uncomfortable, which makes me feel worse.

I do write, yes, I contribute regularly to *Kitchen Cooks* and *The Four Walls Chronicles*, both stellar webzines, but I wish I'd never told anyone that I was working on a novel because it's been years, and is still a work in progress about a guy who leaves a girl asleep and carless in a motel after she inadvertently says something terribly offensive to him—but here is my book, my idea, *my life* stolen from right under me, and I'm still incomplete and he seems all done.

Friday, quarter after four p.m.
Why do I stare at Bundt thumping his tail faster now, a sure sign that the kids are nearly home from school?
"Shit," I say. "Shit, shit, shit," and Bundt cocks his ears and raises his head off the floor to look at me.
"I'm okay," I say but it feels like I'm having a heart attack.
I breathe again when Judy and Nora rush in, toss their bags in the foyer, Bundt is barking his behind off, Nora's upper arm is bruised.
"I fell off the swing," she says, covering the yellow indentation on her golden skin with the opposite hand.
"Did not!" says Judy. "She thinks she's Laila Ali and got into another fight."
"At least I don't think I'm Beyonce."

"Judy, please take your hands off your hips," I say.

I place on the table slices of smoked turkey, honey mustard, crustless nine grain bread, two tall glasses of 2 percent milk, and they're still arguing about swings and fights and sneaks when I go up the stairs two at a time.

Last time I ran away from Sully and eventually from life, as I'd envisioned, it had turned me into a runaway truck up a dead-end ramp at an incomplete stop.

"Go," Josh told me when I began blubbering about wanting to ask Sully if he'd ever felt sorry and hadn't known where to reach me to apologize.

"Just put it away," Erin said.

But the past cannot be tucked into a cabinet behind the files of one's present. A snide remark, a betrayal, a mistake, an unrequited love, an insult: These are the one-night stands that determine the future of the rest of our nights.

I suppose I could read Sully's book for answers, but I wanted to get my heart down and dirty—I want to see if he meets me with open arms or asks who I am.

I wanted to know what became of his fiancée.

I would like to say that I just threw on anything to attend Sully's book reading, but it took me two hours to come up with an outfit, and even then I wasn't wholly satisfied.

# THE OPTIMIST

ಙ

## *Bina Shah*

Bina Shah (1972– ) is a short story
writer and novelist. Though born
in Karachi, she spent her first five
years in the United States, where
both her parents attended the University of Virginia's graduate school.
She was educated in Karachi and in
the United States at Wellesley College and at the Harvard Graduate
School of Education. She has lived in
Karachi since 1995, and contributes
columns to www.chowk.com, *Dawn*,

the *Friday Times* and a fashion glossy, *Libas*.

She has published two short story collections: *Animal Medicine* (Oxford University Press, 2001) and *Blessings* (Alhamra, 2007); and three novels: *Where They Dream in Blue* (Alhamra, 2002), *The 786 Cybercafe* (Alhamra, 2004), and *Slum Child* (published in Spanish; Random House Mondadori, forthcoming 2009). She is a coeditor of Pakistan's new English-language literary journal, *Alhamra Literary Review*.

"The Optimist" is the story of a family, divided between Pakistan and Britain, that has not been able to grasp the ramifications of migration and travel and modernity. In arranged marriages, couples often do not meet before the wedding—and sometimes a photograph is all that they have by way of introduction. Brides are expected to behave dutifully, submissively, obediently—to be the perfect mate—so their husbands might come to appreciate their qualities. Shah has taken these elements and transposed them into a modern family where arranged marriages are not mandatory but, where a rich young man in Pakistan falls in love with the photograph of his cousin in Britain. Shah reverses the misogynist notion that men are free spirits who have to be roped into marriage by women, and along with the male/female dichotomy, plays with the disjunction between generations, showing the longing of migrant parents for their "home," while their children regard the old country as alien, remote, and threatening.

• • •

## ADNAN

I know Raheela doesn't love me. She chose to tell me this on the day of our wedding in Karachi. The moment our *nikah* was signed she said that she hated me.

"You're a fool," she muttered under her voice, her barely moving lips painted scarlet to match the beautiful veil thrown over her head. There were so many people coming up to the stage to congratulate us and so much noise from the guests at the buffet that at first I thought I'd heard wrong. The lights of the video cameras were burning my eyes. I had to blink rapidly to keep them from watering with pain.

"What did you say?" I asked in a low tone. I thought I'd misunderstood her. She had a strong accent that always made me think of red double-decker buses, Cadbury's chocolate, and the BBC.

"I'm sorry, I didn't hear you."

She didn't move a muscle, not even to shift her forehead into furrows of disdain. Her eyes stayed perfectly blank but the lips still moved, whispering words that stung. "This will never work. You know I don't love you. I can't stand the sight of you, Adnan. I'm only doing this to make my parents happy. I'll be back in England before the year's out." She threw a glance my way. "Oh, my God, don't even try to make me feel sorry for you. I can't stand men who cry."

I tried to explain that it was only the intensity of the lights and that I have very sensitive eyes, but my father's brother and his wife approached us on the stage. I had to look up as they began to congratulate us. My aunt pressed an envelope of money into Raheela's small hands, which were decorated with intricate webs of henna. My new wife arranged her features into a smile; it astonishes me to this day how she has such command over her expressions. I can never keep my emotions off my face. That's the difference between a man and a woman.

As soon as my uncle and aunt stepped away, my aunt tottering down the steps on pencil-sharp heels, Raheela leaned toward me. Perhaps she'd make a joke about them: my aunt in her fussy sari, my uncle who stank of whiskey and had grown long wisps of hair that wrapped around his head to hide his bald spot. Instead, she told me what she thought of me: that I was stupid and ugly; that she had never wanted to marry me; and then she finished off with a string of creative curses in three different languages, English, Urdu, and Punjabi. My cheeks flushed crimson. Sweat broke out under my arms. I didn't think girls from England knew that kind of language.

But I was born in July, the sign of Leo the optimist. I knew things could change between us if she only would give me a chance. I've loved Raheela from the day I saw her photograph. I still remember all the details: a beautiful sea-green *shalwar kameez*, dark hair cascading down her shoulders, milky eyes looking straight into the lens, not dipped shyly away to portray innocence. It was her cousin's wedding, the way they have them in England, in some strange recreation center with a dirty pool. I'm sure those old English ladies who wanted to use the pool that evening must have cursed them all night long.

I saw her and knew she was the one. We Leos are extremely romantic people who always let our hearts dominate our heads. My aunt told me her date of birth and it turned out she was an Aries, another fire sign like me, so I knew we would get along well. Compatibility is important to me. The days our parents lived in are gone, where you'd take a stranger into your bed and get to know her only after you'd made her your wife.

My middle-aged parents despaired that I might never marry because I was already twenty-seven and still hadn't chosen someone to settle down with. It's not true that all the pressure is only on girls. Even men here have to hurry up or else people start thinking you're wild, you're gay, you aren't stable, you don't want to face up to your responsibilities. My mother sobbed her worries about me late at night or over the phone to her sisters, but she shouldn't have worried so much. I just hadn't felt that leap in my heart, that wild feeling that makes you think that if you jump off a cliff you'll sail with wings into the sky instead of crashing straight into the ground. I felt that way when I saw Raheela's picture.

So I sat down with my parents one evening after dinner. My mother had turned on the television to get her fill of Indian soap operas and my father had settled into his evening newspapers. This was the right time to speak. I cleared my throat.

"Amma, Abba, I've decided something."

"Yes, son?" My father's voice was indulgent. They looked up benignly at me, expecting me to tell them that I was going to the beach, or that I was traveling to Dubai next week on business.

"Well . . . I've decided I want to get married."

My father opened and shut his mouth a couple of times. "Son, *beta*, Adnan . . ." he croaked, then shook his head and gave up.

"Who is she?" asked my mother, her lips trembling. She always feared that I'd set my heart on someone unsuitable: a Shia, maybe, or a girl from a bad family background, someone too independent, a girl who was dark-skinned instead of fair.

"It's Raheela."

"Raheela? Farook and Amina's daughter? In England?"

"Yes, yes, Raheela. I want to marry her, Amma."

My father put down his newspaper and patted me on my arm and shoulder again and again, as if relieved of some weight that had been on his chest for a long time. My mother began to cry with joy and her words were rushed and jumbled in her excitement. "We can finalize the engagement by the end of this month. Oh, Adnan, I'm so happy, you've made me so happy. What made you decide?"

I was proud to tell them that I had seen her photograph and fallen in love with her. They accepted this without question. It didn't matter to any of us that Raheela lived in Leicester, a city somewhere in the north of England. No matter how many years her father had spent in that city, he was still one of us underneath.

He and his wife would have made sure to raise their daughters in proper Pakistani fashion, even if they lived in England.

My mother smiled radiantly, then took my face in both her hands and kissed me over and over again. "My son . . ." she said, still crying and smiling at the same time. "You've made me so, so happy. Thank you."

"When can we call them?"

"I'll call them tomorrow," she replied. "They'll be so happy to get our proposal. You know how hard it is to find good boys over there. I'm sure they won't object to a quick marriage—after all, Raheela's been out of school for some time. We can give them everything: stability, a good home, a good boy."

My mother rhapsodized about Raheela's beauty and good character, residence permits, and British passports. But I couldn't care less if Raheela had come from the moon. She would get used to the way we live over here—as long as I made her happy. My mother was already dreaming of having a daughter-in-law to boss over and train to help her in the kitchen, but Raheela would not easily adapt to our lifestyle without a lot of love and kindness. A marriage takes compromise, you see, and I'm nothing if not a reasonable man.

### RAHEELA

"Raheela, is that you, home already?"

"Yes, Mum, it's me." I had just come in from work, knackered. It was freezing outside, the wind whipped around my ears and stung them as I stood at the bus stop for ages and cursed myself for missing the number 72 again. The thought of a hot cup of tea and a seat in front of the fireplace kept me going the whole walk home. "God, it was so cold outside. My ears feel like blocks of ice. Why on God's earth did Dad decide to settle here, instead of some decent place like the Bahamas or Morocco?"

Mum was in the kitchen making *parathas* with spinach and potatoes, my favorite dish. I crept up and hugged her from behind, grabbing a bite of the *paratha* as I did so. "That tastes good, Mum. Is the water still hot? I'm dying for a cuppa . . ." I said, aping the broad Yorkshire accent that my mum hated. But today it evoked no reaction from her; she didn't even roll her eyes.

Instead, Mum turned around to face me. "Raheela. You take off your coat and sit down. Your father and I have something to tell you."

"Oh, God, Mum, not another story about Nahid. I can't deal with this today. She's my sister and I love her, but I just can't. You don't know what I've been through. There was this old crumbly who came in with ten-year-old coupons to pay for his food. These bloody rude boys were opening packages of stuff and eating them before they were paid for. And this blind man brought in his guard dog and it pissed all over the floor in front of my checkout line!"

I plopped myself down at the table and stretched out my legs. Mum brought me an unexpected cup of tea; she hadn't done that for me since my last year of school when I was studying for my leaving exams. "Thanks, Mum!" She smiled at me, but her eyes were always so tired. They were my eyes, thirty years on, and I dreaded the day that I'd look into my own daughter's eyes and recognize them in her face, but not in mine anymore.

"Farook!" called Mum. "Farook!"

Dad came in from the front room. He didn't sit down with me but stood at the kitchen door, waiting for Mum to put his cup of tea in his hands. I ate a few biscuits and sipped my tea until I realized that they hadn't said a word. I looked at both their faces. "So what's this all about?" I asked. "Are we moving to the Caribbean, then?"

"It's a bit complicated," said Mum.

"It's not," Dad put in from the doorway.

"Will you let me speak to her?"

"All right, all right." He shifted his heavy frame, then decided to join us. My eyes traveled from one face to the other. Maybe this wasn't about Nahid, after all. Had I done something wrong and they'd found out about it? Apart from the occasional cigarette in my room at night and a few times that I'd gotten drunk on gin and tonic at the club, I really wasn't a trouble-maker. Besides, at twenty-two, you've got to live a little and I wasn't harming anyone with my adventures.

"Raheela . . ."

"That's my name, don't wear it out."

Mum looked impatient, as if this were no time for jokes. I settled my features into a contrite expression. "Sorry, Mum. What were you saying?"

"Well, it's like this, Raheela. Your *chachi* called today from Karachi."

"Yeah? Is everything okay down there? That one doesn't like to waste the cost of a phone call on us every day of the week, does she?"

"Raheela, will you please listen to me?"

"Sorry, Mum."

"She called . . . she called because . . ."

Five minutes had already gone by and I still had no idea what Mum wanted to say. My tea had gone cold by now. I got up to fill my cup with more hot water.

"Sit down, Raheela." Dad's frown brought a momentary fear to my stomach. He never spoke to me in that tone of voice. In fact it wasn't very often that he spoke to me at all. "Raheela, your uncle and aunt called with a proposal for you. For their son, Adnan."

"That's very funny, Dad. April Fool's is months away. Can I go now? I've got to use the . . ."

"It's not a joke, Raheela. They proposed. And we accepted."

Suddenly the floor and the world beneath it fell away from me and left a red swirling storm in its place. Dad's voice echoed from far away as if across a distant valley, and the words weren't making any sense. He repeated himself, his lips moving, but no sound accompanied them. My mother was nodding, as pleased as if they were telling me I'd won the Lottery.

Then the moment passed and I could hear their voices again, telling me that Adnan, my twenty-seven-year-old cousin, wanted to marry me and take me to Pakistan to live with him and his family. How he was well settled in a good job in a travel agency. That he was a good boy and the only son, and would get "everything" after his parents were gone. "You'll have a good life over there, Raheela," said Mum. "It's much easier, you know, with servants and the weather and everyone with good values over there, not like this place where nobody knows whether they're coming or going."

I gripped the teacup so hard that it shattered right across

the table, sending a sudden spray of blood spattering on my face. My mother and father jumped up in alarm, my mother rushing around for towels and Dettol and plasters, while I screamed so loudly that the entire neighborhood would have been able to hear.

"How could you do this to me? What do you mean, you've accepted! It's not like I wanted to marry that fucking stupid bastard in the first place, but you didn't even have the courtesy to ask me!"

"*Raheela!*" shouted Dad, as Mum pressed the towels on my bleeding hand and swept the shards of china off the table. "How dare you use that kind of language! There's no question of asking you. Get those stupid Western ideas out of your head."

We argued back and forth for what seemed like hours, Mum crying, Dad shouting, and my voice becoming more and more shrill as I tried to explain to them that I didn't *want* to get married, that I loved England, that I didn't want to go to Pakistan and marry someone I didn't know.

"They're family," said Dad doggedly. "You have to do it, I've given my word now."

"Well, you'll have to drug me to get me over there. I don't care what you think. I'm not doing this." I flung aside the towels and the Dettol that Mum offered to me on the end of a cotton swab. The blood dripped from my hand as I went up the stairs, leaving a trail of red protest across the hall and all the way to my room.

But the power of Pakistani parental persuasion is far stronger than any drug they could come up with in a lab. Guilt, guilt, guilt, day in and day out. Nagging by day, sobbing by night. "Please, *beta*, try to understand this is the best thing for you. We wouldn't lead you wrong. We're your parents. We love you. We want the best for you."

And that was just my mother. My father threatened to lock me up, to force me to quit my job if I didn't listen to him. I shouted that sending me to Pakistan would be worse than any torture or house arrest they could devise for me. "It's like Ethiopia out there! They don't even have proper bathrooms! They'll make me wear *hijab*, for God's sake, and they'll never let me work!"

"But why should you work? Adnan is doing so well for himself. He is a partner in the travel agency. You can get tickets to come visit us any time you want. Don't throw this chance away, Raheela, or you'll regret it later when you're thirty and no one wants to marry you."

I didn't care. If I could have converted to Catholicism and become a nun, I would have. I refused to have anything to do with him, I wouldn't answer his emails or open his letters. I threw away any pictures my mother brought for me to see. I didn't want to know. Even if I saw his horrible face, his pathetic weak smile, his ridiculous clothes, it would only convince me further that I wanted nothing to do with him. His letters were like jokes to me. I opened one once, when my mother wasn't looking. He had horrible, careful, girlish handwriting.

My dearest Raheela, I know that we don't know each other very well, but that's something I'm hoping to change. I suppose I should begin by telling you something about myself. My birthday is July 25th, so I'm a Leo, the sign of the Lion. That means I'm an optimist by nature.

The saccharine stickiness nearly made me puke. This guy was twenty-seven years old, why the hell was he telling me about his star sign? I'd stopped reading the horoscopes in the paper when I was seventeen. Did he really think it would make a difference if we were astrologically compatible? Pakistanis, especially Pakistani men, are not exactly the epitome of charm and intelligence. They're so thick you could make a dining table out of all the wood that's between their ears. Not only that, they're chauvinistic and they live their lives according to their mothers' commands. This whole bollocks about getting married was probably his mother's little idea, come to think of it.

I couldn't take it anymore, so I started going out. A lot. I wouldn't bother coming home from work, I'd just go straight to my friend Nina's place where we'd smoke spliffs and then go out to a club. Before, I used to go just to have a good time and a few dances. Now I was looking for more: escape from a fate that was looming in front of me, bigger and bigger with each passing day. One night I picked up an English guy, took him back to Nina's place, woke up the next morning to find his jeans already gone from the chair he'd hung them up on the night before. It was the first time I'd ever done anything like that. It hurt like hell, but I looked down at the blood on the sheets and thought viciously to myself that they weren't going to get the little virgin they were expecting. That would show them.

My behavior got back to them through the grapevine, as it always does: "That Raheela, she's gone off the rails. She's gone completely mad. Her parents must be so ashamed." I didn't care how ashamed they were, they had to know that I was a grown British woman with rights and freedom, not a Pakistani village girl. My mother cried every night and begged me to listen to her. I kept my distance and my silence until the day that I came home on a Sunday morning and found Nahid, red eyed at the kitchen table, waiting for me.

"Dad's already at the hospital." She sniffled, wiped her hand across her nose. She refused the tissue I offered her, staring furiously at me. "Mum's had a heart attack. For God's sake, Raheela, you're going to kill her like this."

I kept the terror off my face, turning it into a smooth hard stone as we rode on the bus to Glenfield Hospital, while Nahid sobbed brokenheartedly all the way and made the nice old biddies on the bus turn around and stare at us and whisper to each other. I knew exactly what they were saying. *Poor, poor things* and *Asian families*, and *Tragedy, isn't it?* All the things they always say when they see us stupid Pakis making fools of ourselves in public.

Two months later I was on a plane to Pakistan with the rest of my family to become my cousin Adnan's unwilling bride. My mother had recovered enough from her ailment to accompany us on the flight, and even had enough energy to laugh and smile with my father and sister, while eight hours passed by and I didn't say a single word to anyone. I kept a magazine in front of me but the words blurred before my eyes and nothing I read registered in my brain.

## ADNAN

Raheela didn't let me touch her on our wedding night. "That's your bed over there," she said, pointing at the couch. She must have seen the naked disappointment on my face, because she laughed at me in a way that seemed totally at odds with the beauty of her clothes and jewelry, which she hadn't even bothered to remove yet.

"Did you actually think I'd have sex with you?" She threw off one golden sandal, then the other, revealing feet painted in the swirls and whorls of red *mehndi* that I found so irresistible. I wanted to clasp her feet in my hands and run my fingers up her legs. "If it weren't for my mother, I'd make you get another room. So don't get any stupid ideas or else you'll have to sleep outside in the hall."

I flinched at the shards of glass in her voice. "Raheela . . ." My throat was too dry to form any sensible words. I coughed and tried again. "Raheela, I love you." I was sweating openly now despite the air conditioning which she'd turned up to full blast.

She laughed again. "More fool you, then."

Instead of begging her I busied myself with going into the bathroom and changed into my pajamas, splashing cold water on my face. I stayed there for a good fifteen minutes, smoking a cigarette. If I gave her time she might change her mind and let me into her bed. I'd be gentle, I wouldn't rush her or hurt her for the world. But when I came out she was already asleep, or at least pretending to be, the light turned out, her breathing heavy and regular.

I stumbled my way across the room, stubbing my toe on the end of the heavy glass table, and lay down on the couch. She hadn't even left me a blanket to cover myself with and I shivered all night in the air conditioning. In the morning I awoke with a heavy cold, while Raheela laughed and talked at my parents' house and ate the *parathas* and eggs that my mother had prepared for our wedding breakfast. I drank tea and nursed my broken heart with two aspirins and a bottle of cough syrup.

In the week I'd taken off work we spent the days in a haze of dinners, lunches, visits with her family who were due to go back to England at the end of the week. During the day Raheela was everything I had fantasized her to be: talkative, charming, vivacious. She was beautiful in her pictures but looked even better in real life. I still couldn't believe my luck that this creature had agreed to marry me, and I tried so hard to show her how much I appreciated it with chocolates, flowers, teddy bears, not to mention the silk suits and heavy sets of jewelry my mother had had made for her before the wedding. She wore the jewelry and the clothes, and hid the bears on a high shelf inside the hotel cupboard.

The second and third nights after our wedding the couch was still my wedding bed, but on the fourth night Raheela was sitting on the bed dressed in a gown of some silken material that made my heart pound when I saw her limbs move beneath it. She glanced at me from time to time when she thought I wasn't looking.

"Adnan," she said, in a voice slightly less hostile than the one she'd used before. "Could you give me that box of chocolates on the table there, please?"

I sprang to the table, overjoyed to find a way to please her. She let me sit at the end of the bed and I opened the box for her. I chose one and held it out. To take it from me she had to touch my fingers with her hand. She reached out, and when she touched me I felt a jolt in the pit of my stomach. The chocolate fell from my fingers into her hands; she put it in her mouth and chewed it slowly.

"Give me another," she said in a husky voice. I gave it to her. "One more." This time she took my hand in hers and brought my fingers to her lips. She paused before allowing my fingers to rest on her lips for a moment. I thought I felt the touch of her tongue on my fingertips and I nearly died.

That was the night she took me into her arms and let me make love to her. And the next night, and the next. I knew what it meant to be in ecstasy. She was soft and tender and so brave, even that first night she didn't cry or make any noise that indicated I had hurt her, even though I've heard that most girls make a terrible fuss about their first time.

But even when I told her I loved her, holding on to her tightly and whispering urgently into her ear, she never said it back to me. Even though she wrapped her arms around me and let me stroke her hair and push my face into it as much as I liked, she wouldn't say those three words. Never mind, I told myself, it will come.

At the end of the week her family was ready to return to England. Raheela and I drove to the airport to drop them off. Uncle Farook was tense, Nahid seemed bored, and Raheela's mother was sobbing loudly in the back of the car. Raheela's eyes were bright, though, and she seemed strangely happy as we made our way to the terminal.

Her hand in mine was cool and firm as I squeezed it and held it tight. "Are you okay?"

"Fine," she whispered to me. "Let's hurry, we don't want to miss the flight."

I parked the car at the side of the road, in front of Departures, with the lights flashing so that they wouldn't tow it away. I helped to unload the luggage and my new in-laws were soon settled with three baggage trolleys, tickets and passports in hand.

"Do you mind waiting in the car?" Raheela asked me quietly, underneath the din of the jet planes landing and taking off, the noise of the departure area and the confusion of passengers saying goodbye to their loved ones. "I just need a moment alone with them."

"Of course." Inside the car I closed the windows and turned up the music to give them some privacy. I could see her dark head as Raheela hugged first her sister and then her parents hard, her delicate wrists locked around her mother and father's neck. An arrow of masculine pride pierced me, knowing that she was my wife and I was going to be the one to take care of her from now on. My mind slipped ahead to later that night when I would kiss those wrists, hold her hands in mine and tell her again how much I loved her.

Five minutes passed, then ten. The loud chime that announced the departure of the Emirates flight to Dubai and London woke me up from my daydreaming and I sat bolt upright with a jerk. Where had she gone? They wouldn't have let her go inside to see off her parents; that wasn't allowed anymore. Maybe she'd gone to find something to eat. When she got back I would take her upstairs to the top floor of the airport, where you could get McDonald's and see the passengers in the departure hall below through the fiberglass bridge.

Twenty minutes passed and my stomach began to sink. Beads of perspiration were running down my face. I began to imagine the worst: a kidnapping, an accident, perhaps she'd fainted and they had taken her to the airport infirmary. They'd page, any minute, I'd have to go running to find her and bring her home with me, put her to bed and let her rest.

When thirty minutes passed, I knew what she had done.

I couldn't bear to go back home. I parked the car in the car park, then walked back to Departures and slowly climbed up the stairs to the observation deck. It was a blisteringly hot day, the kind of day that burns your face and turns your skin into a living, crawling mess of sweat and dirt. The Emirates plane squatted on the runway in the distance, ready to take off. Within a few minutes it rumbled down the tarmac and swooped into the sky like a smooth giant albatross. I could feel my heart leaving my body and going away with it, back to England, across all those miles of desert and ocean.

But I don't believe in bad luck. In fact, if I do everything right, all of this could easily turn around. I could go to England, find her, not get angry with her for running away, promise to love her all my life. I'll tell her that I'll give up the travel agency here, move to Leicester to be with her, and start again there, even if I have to drive a taxi or work in a petrol pump. My parents won't understand, but I don't need them to. When she sees how much I love her, she'll accept me. Maybe then she'll tell me she loves me, and my life will be complete.

# SURFACE
# OF GLASS

&

# *Kamila Shamsie*

Kamila Shamsie (1973– ) is a novel-
ist who was born and brought up in
Pakistan and educated at The Karachi
Grammar School. She earned cre-
ative-writing degrees in the United
States from Hamilton College and
the University of Massachusetts at
Amherst and has taught at both.

Shamsie is the author of five
novels: *In the City by the Sea* (Granta,
1998), *Salt and Saffron* (Bloomsbury,
2000), *Kartography* (Bloomsbury,

2002; Harcourt, 2002), *Broken Verses* (Bloomsbury, 2005; Harcourt, 2005), and *Burnt Shadows* (Bloomsbury, forthcoming 2009; Doubleday, forthcoming 2009). Her books have been translated into several languages. She has won the Prime Minister's Award for Literature and the Patras Bokhari Award in Pakistan and has been short-listed for the Liberaturpreis in Germany and twice for the John Rhys Llewellyn Award in Britain. She has also received the British Council's 70th Anniversary Cultural Relations Award. She has written for many publications, including the *New York Times*, *The Guardian* (UK), *Dawn* (Pakistan), and *The Daily Star* (Bangladesh). After many years of living between upstate New York, London, and Karachi, Shamsie is now based in London.

"The Surface of Glass" tells of a maidservant in a rich household and draws attention to both the uncertainties and limited possibilities that life has to offer people disadvantaged by poverty. This portrayal of psychological trauma illuminates the harsh lives of the poor in Pakistan, but also says much about the human imagination, the power of belief, and the desperate reliance on holy men and superstition for cures when there are no other options.

• • •

The nights when the moon was full were when Razia felt closest to Allah. She wondered sometimes if He, too, felt closest to her on those nights, but then she felt it was wrong to wonder such a thing though she didn't know why. She also didn't know why the new cook hated her so much. But among all the not knowing there was this piece of knowing: that he did hate her.

However that had come to pass, she knew she wasn't to blame. She had given no cause for offense, and in the beginning she was actually glad he was there because he replaced the cook who was a drug addict and always sneezed into the food. Razia's feelings about eating someone else's sneeze were strong, stronger even than her gratitude to the drugged cook—Kamal, his name was Kamal—for always saving the biggest tomatoes for her.

When the new cook arrived he did not sneeze into the food. But he also did not save the biggest tomatoes for Razia. She determined right away that she would like him because it seemed too petty to hate a man for failing to give you the biggest tomatoes. When Razia decided something it was hard for her to undecide it. Many months went by like this, until the new cook was not the new cook any longer, he was merely the cook and he hated her. Why should he hate her? some might ask. It is not a bad question, unless a bad question is one that has no answer. It is obvious that he had nothing to fear from her, and she never turned the burner on high so that his korma burned— so that eliminates the two most obvious possibilities.

The first time Razia thought of turning the burner on high was when the elder daughter of the family said to her mother, "Why do I need an ayah now, at this age, when I am old enough for lipstick and even a little rouge." She did not, no would not, would not ever say, and why do I need a cook now? Razia knew this and the cook knew it, too—so why did the daughter have to say it when he was listening?

But she said it and what is said is said. So the cook knew— and Razia knew he knew—that cooks are for always and ayahs are for children. That same day—or maybe not, maybe some days after but at any rate soon enough—the thing happened that made Razia undecide what she had earlier decided about liking the cook. The thing that happened was this: Razia was praying and the mother was calling. Razia was trying to pray faster but the mother was calling louder so Razia left the prayer unfinished and went to answer the call. First, though, she turned down one corner of the prayer mat because of the devil. When Razia came back to the prayer mat it was flat—not a wrinkle, not a tassel turned. There was no one in the house except the mother and Razia and the cook. It could only have been him—that hoarder of large tomatoes—who smoothened the mat and let the devil sit on it. The devil was not lazy and he was not tired. He did not sit in order to rest his knees, no, he did not. He sat so that he could suck up the prayers from the mat before they went up to heaven. If Razia had only been praying for larger tomatoes that would have been one thing, but she had been praying for her son's promotion and that was another thing entirely.

Her son was not promoted.

Razia told the devil's helpmate that her son had not been promoted. He said, oh really, well, Allah's will, here have some *keema*. She took the *keema* and started to eat it, but then she stopped. There was another taste in there: not chilli, not cumin, not coriander, not clove, but something else. The elder daughter came into the kitchen and took a spoonful of *keema* straight out of the pan—she was wearing her new clothes that cost as much as Razia's son made in a month in his job without the promotion. Razia saw her put the *keema* into her mouth and thought of that taste—not cumin, not coriander, not clove, not chilli, but something else. Perhaps that something was poison.

A week later the moon was full. Razia blew prayers around the house, both outside and inside, and then twice around the bed of the younger daughter who didn't wear lipstick yet but one day would, and soon.

There! She had done what she could do, though no one listened to her when she said that when the poisoner chopped onions he was not thinking of onions but of necks. Then she left the house because her unpromoted son was the one person who listened to her and said, you must come away with me now.

But the poison had started working already so Razia was sick when she got to her village. Her son took her to a *hakim* who took the money her son held out to him and said, this is black magic. The *hakim* was short and his teeth were bad but he had many Qurans. There are tall men who cannot say as much. Razia took a Quran from the *hakim*. At first she could not choose which one to take so he pointed to one and she took it. He said, open to the first page. She did. There is a name written here, the *hakim* said, gesturing to a page that was blank save for a sinewy string of letters, indecipherable to her. He read it out loud and asked, do you know the name? It had been many weeks since she had used the name even in her own mind, and for a moment she didn't recognize it. But then she nodded—twice, to show the first hadn't just been an involuntary jerk of her head. The *hakim* pointed to the mirrors along the walls and she followed the lazy gesture of his hand and saw the Poisoner's face everywhere, all around her, pressing against each surface of glass.

When she stopped screaming the *hakim* said, There, we have captured the one who did this to you. You are free.

Freedom was tiring. Razia went home and lay down in bed, as she always did at this time. It was just after one in the afternoon. He was serving food and They were eating food. It was good, so good, to have those twenty-odd minutes of rest in the daytime hours with no one saying iron, sew, clean, carry. She lay down in bed as she always did for those twenty-odd minutes; but now it could be twenty more—why not twenty after that ?

Razia closed her eyes. She thought of Him in the kitchen with no one to watch him. She thought of Them at the dining table, their plates piled high. She stretched and smiled and imagined a taste. Not cumin not chilli not coriander not clove.

# THE OLD ITALIAN

❧

## *Bushra Rehman*

Bushra Rehman (1974– ) is a poet, essayist, and fiction writer. She was born in Brooklyn, New York, and grew up in Queens. She was educated at the College of New Rochelle, New York; Dominican University of California; and she earned her MFA from Brooklyn College. Her family is originally from the North-West Frontier Province of Pakistan but her father and his relatives lost their land and livelihood when the huge

Tarbela Dam was built. Her family moved to the United States, returning briefly and unsuccessfully to Pakistan when Rehman was in her teens.

Rehman is a coeditor of *Colonize This! Young Women of Color on Today's Feminism* (Seal Press, 2002), and her poetry has been collected in the chapbook *Marianna's Beauty Salon* (Vagabond Press, 2001). Her work has appeared in *ColorLines, Mizna, Curve, SAMAR, Voices of Resistance: Muslim Women on War, Faith and Sexuality* (Seal Press, 2006) and *Stories of Illness and Healing: Women Write Their Bodies* (Kent State University Press, 2007). She has been featured on BBC Radio 4 and in the *New York Times* and *NY Newsday.*

Currently, Rehman is at work on a book about a Muslim community in Queens; "The Old Italian" is an excerpt from an early part of the novel. The story depicts Razia Mirza, a Pakistani girl who is growing up in both the Muslim religion and the culture of a poor, urban neighborhood. Her father and uncles have just founded the first Sunni mosque in New York City. Rehman explores the way neighborhoods in New York City change with each new wave of immigrants and how the children of immigrants internalize the racism they confront in these evolving communities. Rehman shows how an immigrant community clings to age-old customs even though they are divorced from the living fabric of their homeland.

The sadistic acts of a Pakistani American mother and her son's brutal behavior become emblems of a culture; as does a poor immigrant Muslim community's inability to keep pets (albeit the Prophet's proverbial love of cats) or to grow plants in terrain so different than their homeland. The reference to their language, Pashto, defines them as Pathans and designates the region to which they belong, northern Pakistan. The story also brings out the natural ease with which children can cut through barriers imposed by adults and the gendered differences between childhood play initiated by girls and boys.

• • •

When Saima and I ran outside, a train was just passing. Saima's house was crammed up next to the train tracks, and every time one passed, it would blast through, blowing garbage and letting its long wild siren blow in the air. The houses were all by the railroad tracks like this:

railroadtracksrailroadtracksrailroadtracksrailroadtracks

Saima's house                           Farah's house

Lucy's house                           Old Italian's house

When Saima and I got outside, with the sound of her little brother Zia screaming behind us, we saw that Lucy and Farah were already hanging out in the frontyard, under the grapevines. Zia was screaming because his mother was forcing tablespoons of hot chili powder into his mouth. It was the way Saima and Zia's mother punished them.

It was hot hot hot. Lucy was sitting on a milk crate snapping her gum and her long dark hair. She was wearing short shorts. Her belly was chubby as cake. It pushed through her T-shirt.

Farah was lying out flat, hogging the entire sofa Lucy's mother had put out under the grapevines.

All over Corona, there were sofas like this, growing like mushrooms in our fronts yards, yellow, red, orange, brown. Who could get rid of a sofa after paying so much? This one was red vinyl, and I could hear Farah's skin unstick when she got up.

"I'm bored," Farah said when she saw us.

"I'm bored too," Lucy said.

"I'm bored three," Saima said. "Move over." She pushed Farah's skinny legs over to the side.

"Whaddayou want to do?" Farah asked. She must have been too hot to start a fight.

No one answered for a few minutes.

"We could go get some ices," I suggested.

"Anyone got money?" Lucy looked around, but we all shook our heads no. We were ten, so we didn't have jobs.

"We could go to the park," I said.

We heard the sound of Zia crying from one floor up.

Saima's eyes stayed looking at the window. "My mother's not going to let me," she said.

"You know when Aman crashed his bike in the fence?" Farah asked. Aman was Farah's brother whom no one liked.

"So?"

"So, there's a hole where we can look into the old Italian's yard."

The old Italian's yard was a field of sunflowers. He must have planted them years ago, crammed up each seed close to each other, and now the sunflowers grew so close together and so tall, we could see their heads bend over the fence. On warm days in the summer, the old Italian wandered through his garden, a floating head among the flowers. But mostly he leaned out from his second floor window, smoking his pipe and letting his belly hang out. He was always looking at whatever was going on in the neighborhood, at the new halal meat stores and Dominican mothers pushing wheelie carts.

Saima reached over her head and snapped some grapes off the vine. There were a few that had turned purple and sweet. Then she jumped up. "Let's go."

We were all experts at climbing fences. In a few minutes we were pushing against each other to press our eyes against the large crack. It was the size of a hand. I saw the old Italian. The knees of his pants were worn from bending down to water the flowers. He poured water and it caught the light. The sunflowers stiffened and straightened, and the light moved through the flowers like lions set loose in Queens.

Up close, the old Italian was a giant. There were puffs of white hair around his smooth bald head. His face was old and sun burned, cracked. He was wearing a white tank top, and it made his skin look older. He had a shoebox in his arms.

"Whaddya think's in that box?" Lucy whispered. She pressed her body against the fence.

"Maybe a dead baby," I said.

"Don't be stupid. It's a shoebox. He's probably got shoes in it. And stop hogging already." Farah pulled Lucy and me out of the way.

"It could be a really small baby," Saima said. Then, all of a sudden, she screamed and pushed back so fast, we fell over.

The old Italian's eye was pressed into the crack looking back at us. Just as quick as it had come, his eye disappeared.

"Great idea, Farah," Lucy said as she dusted off her legs. She was starting to grow hair on her calves. It was still light blond, but I could see it as her skin got darker in the summer.

Farah straightened her skinny body up. "Whatever. I'm not scared of him. Let him come over here."

"Oh yeah? What would you do?" Saima's *kameez* had also gotten dirt on it and she was quickly trying to rub it off. I knew her mother would not be happy about cleaning another dirty *shalwar*.

While we were arguing, the old Italian had walked around the corner and come in through Farah's fence. He walked slowly with a limp. His pants were blue and splattered with paint. He had a big belly as if he were pregnant.

He spoke with a thick accent. "Hallo."

"Hello," we mumbled as if we were in school.

The heat was pushing off the cement. I heard cicadas, and the sound of the train over them. He held the shoebox out to us.

We gathered around, and this time we didn't push. It was lined with newspaper, and in the center, there was a gray kitten. She was so tiny, she could've fit into my palm. Her fur puffed up all around her like a gray halo.

"I find her in the flowers," he said.

We looked up at him. We had all become mute with the kitten so close. I had never seen one in real life. I had only seen them on the Scholastic posters my family couldn't afford to buy. I reached out to touch her softness. She was gray as a cloud on a thundery day, as the balls of wool that settled under the furniture of Saima's house.

When I touched her, a spark of electricity flew in through my fingers and the world around me came into focus. I saw the chain links of the fence, the weeds that grew up and everywhere in Farah's and Saima's yard. Everything compared to the kitten felt harsh, dirty, brown, covered with graffiti.

Our neighborhood was left over from the Italians. When we moved in, most of them moved out. But some of the old ones hadn't left. They sat on stoops with milky white skin and let the sun drip over them, or they hid behind doorways, stacks of old newspapers, and cold salads. They watched us all the time, frowning.

They had spent a generation planting and creating gardens out of the hard rock soil of Queens. When mostly Italians lived there, gardenias and roses grew, cherry trees and magnolias burst from the ground. But in our hands, these same gardens filled up with weeds, old sofas, and rusty old cans.

It was the first time the old Italian had ever talked to us. "You wan' her?"

"Oh yes, yes, yes," we said.

He grunted, relieved we had finally spoken. And just like that, he became uncomfortable. He placed the box down under the grapevines. He walked out through the fence, back to his garden.

Like a pressure cooker bursting, everyone starting talking at once.

"Stop touching her!"

"You stop touching her!"

Soon we all were fighting.

"Stop! You're scaring her!" Lucy yelled, and the kitten jumped inside the box.

She was shivering. For all she knew, we could have been shouting about how to kill her.

I turned to Lucy. "Can you bring milk?" Only Lucy could

go into her fridge without her mother yelling at her.

Lucy hesitated, but then she said, "Only if one of you comes with me."

Saima and Farah both looked at me. Lucy was Dominican, and our mothers wouldn't let us into anyone's house who wasn't Pakistani, but I lived two blocks away, so my mother was the least likely to find out. Besides, Lucy was my friend.

There was a door that had once connected the two yards, maybe back in the day of the Italians. But it had rusted shut so we always had to climb the fence. My *shalwar* snagged and ripped on a chain link. My mother was definitely not going to be happy about that.

"They should figure out how to open this stupid door," I said.

Inside Lucy's house, everything was different than I imagined. The way Saima's mother described it, I would have thought there were fountains of beer and drugs everywhere. I didn't know what drugs looked like though, so while Lucy went into the kitchen, I looked around, looking for something that might look like drugs.

There was an old table fan going in the livingroom, blowing hot air around. There were orange sofas with plastic, an old TV with aluminum foil on the antenna, books, newspapers, and shoes scattered around the brown carpet. It could have been anyone's house. When I went into the kitchen behind Lucy, I saw they even had the same fridge as Saima. When Lucy opened it up, there was beer inside and for some reason I felt better.

"We better hurry, my mother's still in the bedroom putting her face on."

Before I could ask what that meant, I heard her mother call out, "Lucy?"

Lucy didn't answer, but she should've because just then her mother came in. She must have been getting ready to go out. Her hair was all in pink curlers and her makeup was half on, half off. Lucy was just about to pour some milk into a cracked cereal bowl. Her mother smiled at me; then looked at Lucy and said something in Spanish. Lucy started talking back to her mother. I didn't understand what she was saying.

I looked back and forth between them. From Lucy's hands, the way she moved them around, I could tell she was telling her mother about the kitten. Her mother's smile got tighter and tighter and then finally snapped and fell apart. She said something else. Lucy looked at me as if to say it's time to leave.

When we walked out, Lucy carried the bowl carefully. There was just a little milk in it, but it was enough for now.

I climbed over the fence first. Lucy passed the bowl to me and then climbed over too.

"What would it feel, do you think," I asked, "If you lost your mother?"

Lucy didn't answer at first. She concentrated on how to get her bare legs over the fence. When she was on the other side she said, "If I lost my mother that would be good 'cause then she wouldn't be yelling at me all the time."

I decided not to ask Lucy what her mother had said. Even with Saima and Zia's mother, I never asked. She was always yelling in Pashto, and I knew it wasn't good.

When we got back to Farah's yard, Saima and Farah were still playing with the kitten. Saima was saying, "Meow," trying to speak in the kitten's language.

There wasn't enough room in the shoebox for the bowl. Everyone else was too scared to do it, so I lifted her out of the box. I could feel her small bones in my hand. I put her under the grapevines. We watched as she explored the dirt and sticks scattered there. The kitten was still shivering, but when we put the bowl of milk next to her, her pink tongue came out like a snail. She started drinking.

I don't know how the whole day passed, but we couldn't feel the heat anymore. We spent the whole afternoon with the kitten. Saima, Farah, and I wanted to give her a Muslim name, but Lucy wanted to give her a Catholic name like Maria. We finally settled on Maria Perez Parvez Din, but since that was too long we just called her Miss Kitten.

We decided Lucy had to beg her mother to keep it. It had to be Lucy because we were Muslim and Lucy was Dominican and everyone knew Muslims didn't have pets. Lucy looked doubtful, but she said she'd ask.

The next morning, I was up early and after eating *nashta*, my mother gave me permission to go back to Saima's and Lucy's. I told my mother all about the kitten. She gave me a look but she let me run over right after breakfast.

When I got to Saima's and Lucy's, Lucy was under the grape trees. The front of her T-shirt was wet with her tears. By her feet was the box with the kitten, but I didn't hear any kitten sounds. I looked in the box. It was empty.

"What happened to Miss Kitten?"

Lucy didn't answer, she ran inside and slammed her door. I rang Saima's doorbell. No one answered there either.

I heard the sound of the train coming from the back alley next to the railroad tracks. I knew I shouldn't follow it, but I did.

At the end of the alley, there was a circle of kids. Saima's brother Zia and his friend Nelson were in the center. There was a circle of blood at his feet. Zia was holding what looked like a rat in his hands.

The children were yelling. "Throw it! Throw it!"

"Zia!" I was only a few years older than him, but in our families that still had some power. "Zia!"

He turned and looked at me. There was terror in his face. I must have sounded like his mother. But the crowd was pushing now. He turned his back on me, arched his arm back. I saw it was our kitten in his hands. Its body sailed through the air, and it landed on the railroad tracks.

It could have still been living when the train came.

"Zia!" I screamed and ran to grab him, but all the boys

scattered and ran down the alley laughing. "Zia! Zia!" But my voice sounded like nothing under the tracks of the screaming train.

When I walked back, my throat felt like it had a rope tied around it. The old Italian had limped out into the back alley and was looking at the ring of blood on the cement. The horrible feeling in my stomach felt like vomit. He looked at me, and the concern left his face. It became filled with the look I saw from all the other Italians. A look of hate.

Then I knew they were right. We were bad. We were as dirty as all the old Italians said. We didn't know how to take care of life. We didn't know how to grow anything, and when we touched the world it died.

# VARIATIONS:
# A STORY
# IN VOICES

ಬ

## Hima Raza

Hima F. Raza (1975–2003) was a poet, critic, and academic. She was born and brought up in Lahore and graduated from Kinnaird College, Lahore. Abroad she earned degrees from The University of New South Wales, Australia, and the University of Sussex, UK. Raza taught English literature and creative writing at universities in Lahore and London. She published two collections of experimental poetry: *Memory Stains*

(Minerva, 2000) and *Left-Hand-Speak* (Alhamra, 2002). The latter forged new directions in Pakistani English literature with the bilingual poems "Us in Two Tones" and "In Translation," which employ both English and Urdu as integral parts of the text. In 2003, she was killed in a car accident in London.

"Variations: A Story in Voices" is one of Raza's few short stories and develops the themes of duality, distances, and thwarted love, which run through her poetry collections. The use of three voices, as well as poetry and prose, accentuate the sense of a collage, built layer by layer. Raza's portrayal of unrequited love is intertwined with themes of exile and the idea of occupying "the spaces in-between": Even the *jamun* berries that she refers to have an indeterminate taste—neither sweet, salty, bitter, nor sour. She knits together Britain and Pakistan with ease, while acknowledging the ambiguities of identity. One character's muddled liberalism provides a humorous sidelight to the often painful dilemmas of Raza's immigrant characters.

• • •

## VOICE I: SUSCEPTIBLE

### THE FARAWAY FACTOR

A friend who lives far away from Lahore's brief winter calls me out of the blue to talk about homesickness. He does not miss that city of smog and choking sunsets per se; only the four walls that mark the compound of his parents' house. I am intrigued by this nostalgia and ask him to divulge more. The list is something like this. The sound of his two-year-old German Shepherd's scratching at the verandah door, the purple aftertaste of *jamuns*, the smell of August rain, his mother's voice. I point out that at least half his list is made up of generic items—the monsoon spreads its wings over most of the country and *jamuns* are not confined to his address—but he remains unimpressed, resolutely wistful. I ask whether he knows the English name for *jamuns*, oval shaped berries usually consumed with salt, which makes the insides of the mouth pucker and the salivary glands work overtime. He doesn't think there is an English translation for this fruit or the experience of eating it. We both agree it's better this way.

That night I repeat the conversation in my head and keep stumbling over the word "home" in two languages. Something broken, unhappy, to be kicked in the teeth and run away from, to miss from a distance, to dream about in black 'n' white. I cannot bring myself to image it any other way. At least not yet. Home wavers between silence and schizophrenia, holding back, biting tongues, locked doors, and the season of sad questions. I am a stranger here, a tentative observer of the stories that seep out from the edges of this frayed metropolis.

You shared a wise insight with me one night—"Never date someone who lives more than five miles away from you." The simple assurance of knowing that your lover's touch and smell is a short drive away is enough to keep you there, sometimes long after "the thrill is gone."

I watch you woo them, win them, and worship them. I watch the tables turn and see you left behind, licking your wounds while they mysteriously fall out of love, follow the urge to try other flavors, and transfer you into the new best friend. It would be nice if I could simply fall out of love with you.

Over the years I have cherished quite a few. Wrong ones, weak ones, well-intentioned but confused ones, and every time I've had to negotiate a man, he came with the distance tag attached. In fact the only instance when boy and girl lived in the same vicinity was at age seventeen. He was my first and least complicated love. I was bored senseless in six months.

I seek out these specimens. The ones who live at least an ocean away, the ones you can miss so beautifully without ever having to really know them. The ones who allow you to fantasize for a month, or even a year, and sometimes the wondering is worth it. Then there's you. I have imagined your smile from a different time zone, from next door, walking behind you, lying next to you . . . and you have no idea.

I know how distance becomes engraved in the hand and eats you up from the inside. The space between us—I can trace its structure with my eyes closed, can hum its tune while painting my toes, and then pretend it doesn't matter when you walk in the door. Just like that.

Masks.

She suffers from unreasonable expectations and operates in the hypothetical; creating alternate endings, erasing beginnings. A woman somewhere between young and old but age, like reason, is a relative thing. She has ten fingers and ten toes. The rest is a jumble of fluctuating dimensions. She's not good at keeping up with changes . . . they simply drag her along most times.

She talks about a hundred things, except the maddening beauty of a particular name that drowns in her eardrums and reemerges through her eyeballs, in a hopeful wetness.

It's not fear but foolishness that holds us down.
Us,
Just a collection of other peoples' words, stories,
Mostly incomplete, not thought through.
When will I stop measuring my life against you?
When will I hear your voice like a distant waterfall
But not move toward it?

Men find comfort in the familiar. I know you like Diet Coke better than most beverages. You take your whiskey with water, your coffee with sugar, chilli sauce with almost anything. I pay attention to the details and memorize them but I don't know any intimacies. Are you a good kisser? Do you hold your girlfriend's hand for no reason? Are you tender when it matters? The things I'll never know and can't properly imagine with you.

As a recurring symbol, the telephone suggests that you are holding an intimate confidant one step short of total trust . . . using a cellular phone implies that this problem travels with you (the online dream dictionary).

I was trying to call him but the signal kept breaking up. Later, in the same sequence, he materialized on my doorstep and we played with a dog. Can't find the interpretation of "oversized golden labrador" anywhere. Clearly there is a plan but I am not able to understand its workings. Clues come in the shape of coincidences, dreams, instincts, vague ideas that can mean everything and then only as much as we want them to mean.

## THE GAMES BEGIN

"I can't say no to you," he said earnestly enough, quite out of the blue. And with that single, simple declaration, undermined my oh-so-subtle attempt at being wondrous, flirtatious, mysterious under a blazing sky, the music of flies, the threat of watching eyes.

Not the most romantic setting, you understand.

Tried a different approach the following day. Tried to tell him about the positive and how he helped me accentuate it. About windfalls and him being one. That was so subtle, even I lost the point midway.

Hello, Mr. Congeniality.
Mr. Hook-me-up-with-a-jazz-CD,
a jog in the park, a shag in the dark,
the element of surprise backfired (again).
Did he get it?
Almost . . . but I helped him overlook it.

I've been waiting for a long time. Four failed relationships later I'm still waiting, except my patience is running thin, my temper is quick and I'm tired of having to explain it. At almost thirty, I'm left with pretty slim pickings—middle-aged males see me as "viable game" and even most of them want college girls . . . I have three words for you, pal: dirty old man.

I'm in a tight spot here and it's not going to get any easier as gravity does its thing on my body and cellulite appears in all the wrong places and suddenly people don't turn around to look when you walk past them.

Damn.

The things women do to impress men include the usual list of stupidities related to physical appearance: four-inch stilettos so he'll forget you're a borderline midget, and push-up bras that feel like the crucifixion and make you look like Pamela Anderson's almost-sister. But there are other idiocies also embraced by women in their attempt to "fit in," to make the men they covertly woo think that they are really "like one of the guys" (chilled out, laid back, generally unflappable) with the added bonus of possessing feminine wiles. . . .

I dated a skater when I was thirteen. It lasted two weeks because I got tired of scraped knees and bruised elbows. At that age similar interests simply equaled affection, and while we'd like to think that people outgrow this trait as they mature, our instinct remains to seek mates who are mirror images of ourselves in one way or another. In this particular case vanity got the better of me, and I decided that the sweat of trying to win the skater's affections was not worth the hassle. But most women display a lot more spunk than me in this regard.

Take Leila for instance, an old chum who has totally lost her marbles since becoming infatuated with a "biker boy" half her age. Last weekend I saw her hanging on for dear life, perched on the back of this young man's latest toy—a monstrously large red motorcycle that seemed capable of breaking the sound barrier. In all the years I've known her, Leila has never gelled with automobiles of any shape or size. After failing her driving test thrice she declared she was "not meant to drive but be driven, darling!" So imagine my shock at seeing Leila's attempt to descend from her beau's bike in the style of an action hero—except Leila's athleticism failed her at the worst possible moment and she almost cracked her skull on the pavement. Naturally she did not admit to injury at this point and leaped to her feet a little too quickly (she was seeing stars) to announce, "Absolutely fine, darling. Just lost my balance. When can we do this again?"

[What Leila really thought but would never say in front of the biker boys of this world is this: "I just broke a bloody nail and feel I cracked a couple of vertebrae as well! Time for tranquilizers and a back brace. Can I have this fool put away for reckless endangerment?!"]

## WO/MAN BLUES

My brother came by today to tell me his woman's left him. Again. It's the third time in as many months. Get a clue. He says he's not ready to let her go. I'm a little tired of providing tissues, tea, and sympathy. Last time he took to the bottle and ended up with liver damage. This time he's busted his kneecap. The correlation is dubious; unless self-loathing resides in the patella.

In my mind love is the talent of acceptance. When someone's annoying idiosyncrasies either suddenly or slowly turn endearing, then you arrive at a place that is bound to teach you a few unpleasant lessons in self-preservation.

Not that she's a slow learner, not that she lacks common sense or initiative, simply a sense of survival. That has to be it. The reason for this strange flippancy, her heart-on-sleeve behavior.

This is how she pictures it; a man, a woman, an undisclosed location, no sense of time or space to fill in the gaps, nothing but two people who say only this to each other.

Man: you know who I am?
Woman: the reason I am.
(But this is how it is)

He calls her his sister and his heart in one breath.
She wonders what it means, now that he's squeezed her heart dry.

(Just because it's unrequited, doesn't make it any easier to get over.)

Truth is
Overrated
Not sugar-coated
Inappropriate
Flippant
Transient
Matter-of-fact,
Takes a minute to swallow
And a lifetime to digest.

## VOICE II: SIMPLE

### DON'T TAKE IT PERSONALLY

Sara calls me late one evening as I plod through an unending pile of grading exams. I haven't heard from her in a few weeks and I presume it is because she's still trying to break up with Sameer, her boyfriend of three years.

"Next time around, I want to be able to say no without feeling guilty," Sara sounds weary, frustrated, in need of reinforcement. "To draw boundaries between his demands and my needs without feeling like I'm a bad person for having needs in the first place. It makes me a bad person, doesn't it?"

"No Sara, it just makes you real," I try not to sound as irritated as I feel—this is going to be a long phone call and I'm already behind schedule on marking. I figure it's best to let her vent and keep my advice to a minimum, since she never listens to it anyway.

In a nutshell, the reason for Sara's current melancholy is this: After having worked three weekends back to back, the girl finally managed to schedule a Sunday afternoon of serious pampering. A ninety-minute deep tissue massage with Rainbow

Light, the miracle masseur at Sara's health club, who appears once a week to tend to massage therapy addicts like my dear friend.

On her way home from this feast of lavender oil and the expert touch of Ms. Light, Sara got a call from Sameer asking her to drop by his place with much-needed nourishment. (Did I forget to mention that the boyfriend in question is also the laziest man on earth?)

You would think Sara's reply to this request would be, "I'm on the other side of town, Sameer. Why don't you order takeout or go to the deli around the corner? I've just had a long massage and want to go home and take a nap." Instead Sara finds herself taking a fifty minute detour to Drummond Street where she buys enough *biryani* to feed a *baraat* ("because he loves Indian food") and finally trudges to Sameer's apartment who receives this culinary gift without so much as a proper "thank you" (a grunt is meant to suffice) before getting down to the business of filling his belly.

I listen to Sara's narrative and roll my eyes at least half a dozen times during the span of this story. She'll never learn, he'll never know, and I'll remain stuck in the middle of this shit.

"But where are you from *originally*, mate?" Simon asks the mini-cab driver in a curious display of friendliness, and accompanies the question with a hearty laugh meant to suggest camaraderie. I cringe visibly at the remark but hold my tongue. Simon is a well-traveled Englishman, genuinely interested in "other" cultures (perhaps that's why he's dating me), but after a few pints on a Friday night his politics become skewed, his tone can be patronizing. If Simon were simple I'd let it go, brush it off, move on to the next remark, but somehow his inability to sense the cab driver's hesitation, his disregard for the man's indignation, make me feel like I've failed to sensitize Simon to anything other than his own pallor. I catch the cabby's expression in the rearview mirror and quickly look out of the window to avoid his gaze. I can hear him thinking, "Who are you to ask me where I'm from, *mate*? Acton, Lewisham, Brixton, High Barnet . . . but you want to hear that tone which creeps into my voice when I say the word Morocco, right?"

There are three kinds of migrants. The apparently assimilated who secretly yearn for lost home/s, the truly assimilated who deny their cultural origin to some extent, and, finally, the unassimilated migrants who recreate the most consumer friendly aspect of their estranged culture and market it as fried food or ethnic clothes on the local high street.

For now I dwell only upon the in-between subject. The assimilated migrant, also known as the bounty bar—brown on the outside, white on the inside—the man who looks like he should understand me but in effect has no clue about my position because his cultural values are entirely alien to mine. A particularly dangerous kind of man because he's unaware of his dual appeal; white girls go his way to score a piece of exotica, and brown girls make the effort because they think they're getting lucky with one of *their kind*. It's all very complicated, and you should ask me because I have fallen for many bounty bars in my time, only to see these relationships turn into a sticky mess in my hands.

### How It Is
Once the discrepancies slap you in the face
there isn't much left to do but walk on by,
to the next potential stimuli.

When Sam eventually got dumped he watched TV for thirty-two consecutive hours, drank too much beer, didn't shower all weekend, and lay on the couch like a beached whale. When Sara arrived at the brink of distraction, she did four loads of laundry back to back and scrubbed the bathroom until she could see her sobbing reflection in the floor tiles.

So many plans and change of plans; yes I will, no I won't, maybe I should . . . like a guinea pig stuck in a weird science of my invention, waiting for something big to happen.

I am alone because I fucked up. I am alone because I am too scared to change the pattern. I am alone because I don't know how to let go of imagined ideals.

I can convince myself of anything. Even things like I never really loved you. And here I am, without you; alive, around, dazed.

**VOICE III: SASSY**

**BACKGROUND GOSSIP**

More than I can handle at present. Maybe you'll call me bitter but the abominable colleague has just returned from his honeymoon, and despite having shut my office door I can hear him whistling through the wall. It would all be hunky-dory if he wasn't my least favorite human being; short-tempered, hormonally unbalanced, no sense of humor, balding to boot, so don't ask me how he has managed to bag this sweet, intelligent woman as a wife.

Maybe he's great in bed. Maybe deep deep down, he's an angel. Maybe the world makes no sense. See, I know I'm sounding jealous and I'm not. Not of him or her, or even the situation. I don't want marriage per se, but I want to walk into my office with a smile on my lips and a whistle in my throat, and I want it to be because I've found the closest thing to perfection in the opposite sex.

Instead, him and all the other egotistical-for-no-apparent-reason sort of men seem to get good women and I'm now left with the option of hooking up with the married ones, running after the gay ones, or building a meaningful relationship with my vibrator.

Don't do that eye-rolling thing please, because I can see

you—" such a drama queen, no wonder she can't get a man . . . poor thing."

Anyway, for what it's worth, I'll tell you my side and I'll tell you nicely so you understand.

On my last birthday I found out that the man I had wholly and solely given my heart to (when he obviously couldn't give a hoot), had decided to marry his ex-girlfriend. Call me crazy but I think I deserved a phone call. A little hint maybe, that he was planning on doing the wedding march with someone else while I fantasized about nuptials and puppies and beach resort vacations featuring him. But no. I had to hear the news from my best friend's man who heard it from his uncle who assured his nephew that this was "already old news, kid."

After having spent the past couple of months getting lots of good advice from my friends (who are either married or in "happy" relationships) on how to forget this piece of excrement and move on to better, brighter things, I'm thinking the whole concept is overrated. One only has to look at the current divorce rate to gauge just how successful this "until death do us part" thing really is.

Then there are couples who wisely stay away from the legalities but still end up operating as one entity. "We wish you . . . we are hoping . . . we are planning"—Jesus, I don't care about "we," I don't even really know your partner, I asked YOU because you are the one I've had the pleasure of knowing since WE were six. And when these two-in-one ladies start spewing advice my way about how I should "cherish my freedom," wait for something perfect to materialize instead of "settling for someone who doesn't appreciate you," it makes me want to scream!

{Aside}
#1

"God bless you please (Ms.) Robinson," can you cut the shit and quit looking at those twenty-year-old chicks with perky tits and a wide-eyed wonder that will be erased soon enough, that will compel them to compare their fading glow to other, fresher blossoms while you snigger from the sidelines.

#2

Maybe men become attractive only when they're unavailable and safely out of reach. . . .

Meanwhile Leila's temptress-like aspirations continue to fall short of the forbidden fruit because of poor stamina and mad expectations.

### Doing Your Head In
remains unaware of the consequences of his un-thought-
    out
actions,
my increasingly schoolgirl reactions
bound to be a drag in the end (like all good things are),
bound to make me roll my eyes and kick myself in the
    shins . . .
one woman's truth is another man's
funky kinda freaky shit     ("what the hell are you talking
    about?")
that your mama warned you about   ("where's this coming
    from?")
but you were too busy     (don't lose your balance in a
    blink, girl!)
chasing the slightest, silliest,    (don't ask me what
    she sees in him!)
bound to make you fall flat    (cloud in the sky).
on your face

She needs to be more matter-of-fact about this:
The unfolding of non sequiturs.
Matter-of-fact:
She's more confused than ever.
Matter:

Flesh is not the best measure of love.
Fact:
None of it means much beyond a moon or two.

He's a star in the making all right. Getting ready to break
unsuspecting hearts with a casual glance, that crazy smile before
walking home, the long way round to "the real thing."

Wide-eyed
Doe-eyed
Girl forever true,
Too green to know the worth of a good thing,
The punishments of indecision.

### It Takes Practice
"what you doing?"
"taking it easy."
"how, exactly?"
(that's for me to know and you to ponder
very, very slowly, in candlelight, well after midnight . . .)
I smile a little
"see you tomorrow?"
"maybe . . ."
(the boy next door just turned into a possibility)
Unravel this

He fumbles with clasps and even though it slows down the proceedings just a fraction, it's infinitely endearing. The last candi-
date could undo the tiniest, trickiest piece of metal and
simultaneously smoke a cigarette, answer the phone, do a few
push-ups. It was disconcerting; made me wonder how many
times that player had been around the block.
This one is sweet.
This one is promising.
"This one will bring out the prose in me," she thought,

looking at herself full length in the mirror and examining the details. Two eyes, two ears, a nose, passable lips, all in place (a growing double chin). She's complete as she stands.

What does she see in him?

(A vulnerability that seeps through his fingers and floats toward her outstretched palms, across the table that marks the safe distance between them.)

> Your lips lengthen my spine,
> catching the salt between my thighs,
> spoiling me in the best possible way.
> Don't Say It Out Loud
> How do I break it down further?
> You have the potential for becoming air;
> as still, as necessary, just there.
> Not a casual coming together of two
> but the sweat which spells unspoken togetherness,
> a contentment in the blood.
> Another time
> Another place
> I might have looked you in the face,
> dragged you by the hair to the nearest cave
> and kept you a week, a month, a year . . .
> but if touch hardly lasts, why ask silly questions?

Later she finds an old lover's letters tucked in the corner of her bedside drawer. There is no urge to read them but she holds them just the same; feels their weight press into her palm, the vision of off-white squares of paper torn from a lined notebook makes her smile. She remembers that time well, and now the prospect of a scrawled script winking at her in mirror fashion defines an image of him frozen in time, forever twenty-one, full of a self-assured loving, an unhurried laughter.

In spite of this nostalgia she realizes she does not have any "real" memento of him, even though he has been the possibility tugging at her insides all this while. Now as they become more jaded, thicker at the waistline, she wonders about him in silence, in a way more meaningful than common interests and surprise tokens of affection.

Contact as a cure for insomnia:

The right amount of pressure applied consistently across the shoulder and chest by a reasonably strong, willing, reassuring arm that materializes just behind your curled frame has been known to produce a soporific effect.

Better than counting sheep, cocoa cups, grinding teeth . . .

If she held herself any tighter, she'd choke the air supply.

# SCAR

&

# *Aamina Ahmad*

Aamina Ahmad (1975– ) grew up in London and earned degrees in London from University College and Goldsmith's College. She worked for the BBC World Service before becoming a television script editor. Her credits include a number of primetime shows in Britain including *Eastenders*, *The Bill*, and *Hustle*. She now lives in San Francisco.

"Scar" is an examination of Pakistan's class system and the

relationship between Kaakee, the daughter of a maidservant, and
Aaliya, her employer's daughter. As is quite common, these two
characters were playmates as children, which allowed Kaakee
to grow up with an imagined sense of equality. This gradually
changes as the two grow older and their worlds diverge, but
Kaakee still believes she is privileged within the household,
despite the drudgery of her daily life. With great sensitivity,
Ahmad describes how readily the family Kaakee has served and
even her relatives assume that Kaakee is guilty of theft.

• • •

"Kaakee!
  *"Kaakee-ee."*
  Kaakee could hear Baji calling her as she watched the water
from the tap flow across the floor of the bathroom toward her
feet. Crouching, she rubbed at the cracked skin, letting the cool
wetness collect between her toes. She turned off the tap and the
water shrank back, reluctantly, toward the drain. Kaakee began
sweeping the floor with her *jharoo*; the scratching sound slow
and methodical. She stopped for a second, expecting to hear
Baji call out to her again, but it was quiet.
  She looked around the dark bathroom, murky except for the
hazy sunshine coming in from the skylight above. How refresh-
ing to bathe in this dank room on a hot day, to feel your feet
squelching in rubber Bata *chappals*. Kaakee looked at the dry
wooden *chowki* sitting on the floor, covered by a film of water.
It didn't seem right; she filled the plastic mug with water from
the bucket under the tap anticipating the "clappp" of the water
smacking the wood—
  *"Kaakee!"*
  Kaakee stopped and turned to see Baji standing in the
doorway, holding up her *shalwar* so her feet wouldn't get wet;
her skinny ankles pointing outward.
  "I've been calling you. Didn't you hear me?"
  Kaakee said nothing; it wasn't a question.

"Thomas says something's wrong with the Suzuki again. Be a good girl for me and collect Aalia from college."

As Baji turned Kaakee straightened up and emptied the mug of water on the *chowki*; although it turned a satisfyingly deep woody red she didn't notice. A sudden sense of anxiety seemed to grip her. Her eyes moved to the clock just above the white tube light that ran along the side of one wall like a flash of lightning. It was already one; she would have to hurry if she didn't want to be late for Aalia.

Outside the tall college gates drivers stood in sweatless *shalwar kameezes* next to their sleek cars, while Kaakee hovered uneasily by a fuming blue rickshaw and its driver—the engine firecracking, ready to spring off as though it couldn't bear to be stationary for more than a few moments. She had crisp new notes that Baji had given her to pay for the rickshaw, and strict orders to make sure they drank a Pepsi before coming home. As she waited for Aalia a young driver noticed her. Although she ignored his gaze she found herself standing a little straighter and tucking her hair behind her ear though it needed no tucking. These were the kind of *rishtas* her mother hoped for: clean-looking men with six-weekly haircuts, a profession and Rs 2000 a month. She and Aalia didn't talk as they once used to so she couldn't mention the driver's unwavering attention, but perhaps Aalia would walk past him and notice that his eyes hadn't shifted from Kaakee's direction, perhaps she would mention it. They might discuss it, pore over it, even. Perhaps. She looked ahead, waiting for Aalia with some excitement.

Kaakee spotted Aalia emerging with her friends by her side, and waved. The surprise on Aalia's face, the thin smile, made Kaakee lower her hand uneasily. Aalia gestured to the group of girls that Kaakee was here to collect her today. Her friends looked over. Kaakee, suddenly self-conscious, tugged at her *kameez*, wiped the sweat from her upper lip with the edge of her *dupatta*. Aalia approached with a friend by her side, Kaakee looked on, a rising sense of tension. She swallowed as Aaalia introduced Maheen, and both girls stepped into the rickshaw. Kaakee squeezed in between them, suddenly aware of the thick smell of her own sweat; she held her arms tightly against her sides, asked politely after Aalia's day and then shyly relayed Baji's message about the Pepsi. Maheen wasn't bothered and Aalia looked unsure. Kaakee was aware that Aalia glanced at her before deciding that they should stop for a drink.

At the main market Aalia told Kaakee to get a drink for herself as well. She stood outside in the shade with her bottle while the girls sat inside the rickshaw with theirs. Kaakee sucked on the straw bobbing in the bottle; sloop, sloop, sloop and the dusty dark liquid was gone. She waited for the girls to finish. As they chatted Kaakee heard Aalia mention the name of her fiancé, but there was little else she could make out. She thought of the young driver, what it would be like to sit with Aalia and Maheen whispering and giggling about him. The hum of their voices continued. She looked away feeling bad, not wanting to eavesdrop.

Aalia handed her two half-drunk bottles to give back to the drinks stand.

"That was a good idea. I needed that, *hehna*?"

Kaakee saw Aalia glance at her empty bottle; she felt a surge of embarrassment as she turned toward the drinks stand. Kaakee wondered if that was why Aalia had agreed to stop, because she thought Kaakee wanted a bottle at their expense? Perhaps she thought Kaakee had suggested it for herself and not because Baji had told her to. Kaakee felt wounded—she handed over the money Baji had given her and discreetly pulled out two rupees of her own from her bra to contribute to the cost of the drink she'd consumed. She got back inside the rickshaw, perching on the seat to make more room for the girls. They sat close, engrossed in conversation. Kaakee could hear nothing but the loud buzzing of the rickshaw on her talk-less journey home.

Kaakee dipped the clothes deep inside the metal bucket; the

water surged up around the fabric against her wrists and hands. It was like being pulled by strong arms. The washed clothes, heavy with water, landed on the line with a thwack. Thwack—thwack; a tune. From somewhere, a melody came into her head, a Nayyara Noor *ghazal*. Without thinking she began to whisper the words to herself. Awkward, unused to the sound of her own voice, it felt strange to move her lips. In her head the tabla's beat zipped along and Nayyara's voice trilled firmly, confidently and, somehow, her own voice got a little louder. Suddenly Kaakee realized how good it felt stretching her face muscles, her tongue moving in her mouth. There was a change in tone; Nayyara was heading for a high note. Kaakee singing with her, felt ready, ready to hit the note that she and Nayyara were approaching when the clanging of a door silenced her.

Next door, their neighbor Khawar had come out onto the balcony. He stood with a cigarette in his mouth, buttoning up his starched shirt over a white vest, taking in the busy traffic on Durand Road. Kaakee remembered how, long ago, she and Aalia would walk here along the side of the house, trying to catch a glimpse of Khawar; Aalia desperately hoping he would come out on the terrace to fly his kite. Back and forth they'd walk, hour after hour. The sense of excitement was enormous. Every angle, every "in" to a conversation was planned on those back and forth walks, but when, on a rare occasion they did see Khawar, a sudden, profound sense of shock would lead to awkward, mostly silent, encounters. Despite this, each meeting, after intense discussion and dissection, always produced a sense of optimism. Encouraged, they'd phone Khawar and listen to his repeated Hellos? and Who's this? before playing a snatch of a *filmi* love song into the phone and hanging up. When they heard Khawar was getting engaged they both went into mourning for a few days. As well as Aalia's heartbreak there would be even less to do in the afternoons than usual.

Kaakee's hands reddened as she squeezed the water out of Baji's *kameez*. She busied herself, hoping Khawar would think her too busy to chat. But he greeted her politely and asked after her mother.

"Not long now," he said. Kaakee looked confused. "The wedding."

Oh yes, Kaakee nodded.

"And then it'll be your turn." Kaakee nodded again but she felt the muscles in her neck stiffen a little at the mention. She knew she ought to smile or offer up an "Inshallah," but she couldn't. Khawar fell silent. Kaakee realized he looked a little embarrassed, perhaps he'd expected a cheeky quip and was surprised that she'd said nothing, perhaps he had just remembered Kaakee's age and that girls like her should have been married a long time ago. Suddenly there seemed to be no easy way to end the conversation. The balcony door clanged again. Khawar's son toddled out and he picked him up; he looked relieved to see his boy.

"Say salaam to Kaakee *Baji*." Khawar lifted up his son's arm and made it wave to Kaakee; the little boy's fingers splayed out star-like for his ungainly wave. Khawar didn't look to see if Kaakee was waving back, she realized it didn't even matter if she were there. Khawar's handsome face, fascinated, charmed, was concentrated on his child. Kaakee looked at the boy's chubby legs curled around his father's waist and waved back.

The door was closed but you could just hear the tape of English songs from Aalia's room. Kaakee pressed the iron down firmly on Aalia's wrinkled turquoise *dupatta*. She remembered sitting in Aalia's room with her friends knowing, as she sat there, what a privilege it was to be included as they tried on nail polishes, squirted French perfume on their wrists, and sang along with songs she didn't understand. She would sit on the floor, a little apart, watching, smiling, ready to bring in the trolley with snacks for them or to relay a message to Baji from Aalia, justifying her presence by serving some purpose. Knowing she had to serve some purpose to be there at all. It didn't matter. She was there.

∞

Kaakee couldn't remember quite when things had changed, if it was sudden or slow, but they had. She had known they would; her mother would say at the start of each school year that Aalia was getting too grown up for Kaakee's company. Kaakee ignored the warnings but things did change. And once they had it seemed strange to think that they were ever any other way. Aalia and her friends would talk about exams, American movies, boys; but now it didn't matter how quiet Kaakee was or how tightly she tucked herself into a corner, trying to make herself invisible—she wasn't, and it made them uncomfortable. Even Aalia. She no longer stopped to translate a story or explain a joke, her manner was distant when she spoke to her. It seemed to Kaakee that no one else had even really noticed the change except for her. She wondered if Aalia ever thought about it.

"Where's Ammi?" Kaakee looked a little startled as Aalia spoke.

"The tailor's, near Station."

Aalia paused. Kaakee looked at Aalia, "What do you need, maybe . . . ?" Uneasily she continued, "maybe I can help."

Maheen was sprawled out on Aalia's bed, which was covered with material for outfits. Bored, she was flicking through an old copy of Baji's *Pakeezah* magazine. Aalia stood over the yards of cloth, anguished. Kaakee, uneasy, stood in the doorway as the red cassette player hissed away in the background.

"What should I do?" Aalia asked.

Kaakee looked puzzled.

"I can't have all of these made, I have to decide which will go best with my set. For the *nikah* lunch." Aalia held open an Emerald Jewelers' box.

The necklace and *tika* looked heavy; the gold was dark like honey. Aalia pulled out the *tika* and held it against her forehead. The metal looked as though it might be hot to the touch but Kaakee knew that it would be cold against Aalia's skin.

"So? What's your opinion?"

Maheen looked up from her magazine. Kaakee felt Aalia's eyes on her, inquiring. Her face felt hot. She looked across at the fabric in front of her. She felt under pressure; there must be an answer that Aalia was looking for. There was a tightness in her throat as though something was stuck there. She couldn't even make out the difference in the colors, the strange sensation in her throat was so distracting. She held out her arm unsteadily, not even sure what she was pointing at, "That one."

Aalia picked up an orange chiffon suit.

"That's got silver on the border, it won't work, " Maheen said. Kaakee's face burned, her throat felt dry. Aalia looked at the fabric, a little puzzled at the choice but interested. She held it up against herself and looked in the mirror. Kaakee faintly remembered herself and Aalia playing with Baji's jewelry and makeup, stuffing Baji's bras to dress up as *dulhans*. Soon Aalia would be getting ready for her own wedding. The fabric fell open; Kaakee took in the contrast of light fabric and heavy jewelry.

Occasionally, she would be asked to dig out some item of jewelry or old shawl for Baji or Aalia from some hiding place. To wear to a wedding perhaps, or just to remind themselves of what they actually owned. At the forefront of her mind was the task, there was never time to really feel the softness of the shawl she was carrying or to see how a pendant caught the light. She wondered what it was that made you want to touch things, shiny, bright things, even if just for a moment, and even if you knew that once you had them in your hand they didn't make you feel the way you expected to, or perhaps feel anything at all.

The *tika* swung off center as Aalia raised the fabric higher against her frame. Kaakee looked down, wanting desperately to get out of there.

Aalia looked at her, "I don't know. It might be nice."

Kaakee couldn't help laughing as she watched the cook, Hameeda's, youngest child lapping up tea from a saucer like a cat. Through the wire mesh on the kitchen door she could see her mother sitting on the charpoy, combing her hair. Kaakee started to look forward to the end of the day—she thought of watching the PTV drama with Baji, she might suggest to her mother that they visit her *khalas* after dinner instead. Kaakee felt as though she might really enjoy that today, she'd tell them about Aalia's dilemma, the mound of fabrics and colors, about helping Aalia choose her *jora* for the *nikah*. The thought made her smile a little and when Baji started calling for her, she moved quickly. Suddenly, there was a lightness in her movements. She straightened her *dupatta* as she entered the living room.

"Baji, you'll have to tell me what happens in *Tanhaiyan* tomorrow, I'm going to take Ammi to Khala's," she couldn't help grinning.

Baji's expression made her stop.

"That's fine. Just help Aalia will you, she can't find part of the set for the wedding. I don't know what she's done and I don't know what we'll say if we don't find it."

The search began. Baji held open the Emerald Jewelers' box; there were just velvet stubs where the earrings and *tika* should have been. It didn't matter if they had to turn the whole house upside down, Baji said; they had to find the missing items.

Aalia and Maheen looked on silently as Kaakee and Hameeda went through Aalia's room. They folded up the fabrics that lay across the bed and systematically went through the boxes, drawers, and shelves. There was nothing there. They looked through laundry bags, behind cupboards, under chairs and beds. Baji supervised as Aalia recounted her movements, what she had tried on, where she had walked, what she thought she had put away safely. Kaakee could hear the panic rising in Aalia's voice as she explained for the third time why she had taken the set out of the cupboard in the first place. She just wanted to try it on and look at the clothes along with it. Aalia tried to make it sound necessary. Baji's voice became more shrill as the search continued—these things weren't meant to be played with, if Aalia thought Baji could replace jewelry that her in-laws had paid for, she was mistaken.

Kaakee looked for a second time in places she had already searched. Baji stopped shouting and Aalia went to lie down once Maheen had left. They looked in the spare rooms that were locked and hadn't been opened in days, they searched the verandah, the Suzuki, places where the *tika* and earrings would never be. The strain on Baji's face increased. Hameeda gossiped about the shame of a broken engagement. Kaakee, sick at the thought, searched, resolute.

A terrible suspicious silence seemed to come over the house. As she unpacked and repacked cupboards, Kaakee kept thinking of the unfastened *tika* swinging gracelessly against Aalia's forehead, the dark heavy gold. Aalia emerged from her room, red-eyed. Kaakee looked at her and offered up a reassuring smile—she wanted to comfort her, tell her they would find the pieces. Aalia would wear the full set on her wedding day with the orange suit that Kaakee had picked out for her. Aalia looked away.

Kaakee walked into the passageway lined with trunks on both sides. She swallowed, there was really only one explanation now for why the jewelry hadn't been found. She thought she could hear Baji and Aalia talking softly to each other. She imagined Baji reassuring Aalia now, telling her they would find the culprit. The silence in the house would be a probing one, inquiring, waiting. They would have to go through all the comings and goings in the house today.

Kaakee sat down by one of the trunks; she knew this one had Baji's wedding saris in it. She knew what was in each trunk, each cupboard. She had grown up in this house, she had been cleaning it since she was eight when she had first started helping her mother here. At first it had felt like an adventure, leaving the drudgery of school to come up to the *kothi*. And Aalia. Her friend was here. They talked, they went to places Kaakee would never have been: department stores, beauty salons, restaurants. The friendship meant her position here was special, but that wasn't what was important—it was real, a real friendship that mattered. She thought of Aalia's tear-blotched face, mottled just as it had been when she lost at Carom or Ludo when they were girls. Kaakee stopped; Aalia had looked away just now. She wasn't sure, but as Aalia's eyes darted away did she see something, a flicker of something in them? Kaakee felt her chest tighten; perhaps Aalia was telling Baji that Kaakee had been in the room when she was trying on the set.

Kaakee-ee.

*Kaaaakeee.*

"Kaakee, *jaan*," Hameeda said softly, "Baji's calling you." Baji's eyes didn't move as Kaakee stood before her. As Baji talked, Kaakee couldn't think of anything but the searing pain in her chest. She found herself recalling the slow, scratching sound of her *jharoo* on the bathroom floor. She thought of water creeping up her arms as she washed clothes, like a person's hands touching her. She thought about her days here in the *kothi*. About how much things had changed in the *kothi*, everything but her life. Her hands were strong and hard now from wringing out sodden clothes, the muscles in her body were firm from stretching and bending as she swept the rooms in the house; but really, everything was the same. Years had gone by, years without talking to Aalia, without really talking to anyone. Soon Aalia would be gone, and there wouldn't even be the hope of a moment that reminded her of the time they had spent as friends. Now, under suspicion, there could never be the hope of anything. Kaakee wondered if things might have been different had she married. She thought of the *tika*, its weighty, thick color. She tried to imagine it against her own skin, to imagine the excitement of putting it on, knowing it was her own wedding day. Baji was waiting for an answer. Perhaps nothing would have been different, she would still have been here, day after day, her children helping her, their little hands folding and carrying, summoned to play with Aalia's children when she visited. And each time as she left to go back to her own home, Aalia would put a few notes in their hands. Kaakee wondered why Aalia wasn't there too, she thought of her waiting in her room, not wanting even to see Kaakee. Disgusted at the sight of her, perhaps.

Where had she hidden them? Where had she put them? Baji wanted to know.

Kaakee wanted to answer but the pain in her chest was so distracting. Where, where, where? Nowhere, she wanted to say, nowhere. But she couldn't. And as she looked at Baji, still waiting, she saw how things might be different, more than just a series of sounds, of claps and thwacks and rote movements that made up her life. Kaakee thought of Aalia, her friend. She thought of how she might change things. At last, at last, terrifying as it was. When Baji asked again, where and why, Kaakee looked at her and said nothing at all.

Kaakee approached the charpoy where her mother sat with Hameeda. Kaakee's mother puffed at a hookah, she didn't look up as Kaakee sat down with them.

"Are you all right, Kaakee?" Hameeda asked.

Kaakee nodded. She didn't know what to say.

"Baji's been good about things. They won't call the police," her mother said.

Kaakee felt tears in her eyes. She swallowed, blinking them back.

"Your *chacha's* found somewhere for you to go, in Cantt. It'll be better, you might even make a match there."

Kaakee felt cold right through to her insides. She wanted to sit by her mother and put her head on her mother's shoulder. She wanted to say something, to explain. But she couldn't. There was no way to explain.

Neither of them asked Kaakee what had happened, it didn't matter. They knew that it was only what Baji and Aalia thought had happened that mattered; the *kothi-wallahs'* conclusion meant there was no need for further investigation, whatever the truth, whatever the logic. There was nothing more to say. Kaakee got up and walked into the darkness.

She went around slowly to the side of the house and sat down on the steps outside the bathroom door. When she washed clothes in the bathroom she would open this door and look out beyond the steps where the soft light of the sun shone on the plants, on the old Suzuki, through the lattice work on Khawar's balcony. In and out of the ironwork the sunshine weaved, sloping down, extending upward, it went everywhere, freely, wantonly. She imagined it now as she sat in the darkness. She thought of the house that she would be going to. It was far from here. Aalia would never have to see her again. Kaakee had ended something that she had known all her life. She felt empty, drained, worse than she felt most days.

Kaakee tucked her legs beneath her and held them—and as she did, her hand felt something. She had forgotten all about it. She ran her hand up against the scar on her calf. Smooth and shiny, the shape of an incomplete 8, it stood raised on her skin, eager to be noticed, to be felt. Aalia had a scar too, from her appendectomy; she said she'd have it forever. Kaakee touched it again, remembering the fall from Aalia's bicycle as her fingers grazed the slippery mark. She had never shown it to Aalia or told her about it; Kaakee had taken the bicycle without asking.

That night, the night she took the bicycle, a *rishta* had come for Kaakee. She had waited in the bedroom as her mother and Hameeda met the scrawny young man and his parents. They didn't bother calling her out. Someone had told them the boy was an addict but it was too late to cancel the meeting. He said nothing as his mother babbled on. Kaakee emerged as the family left. She noted her mother's silence and gently stroked her mother's back. It didn't matter, she comforted her as she patted her mother's arm. Kaakee escaped outside. Another time she would have gone into the *kothi* and told Aalia about it, but they didn't talk like that any more.

She had wandered into the darkness around the house and sat on the bonnet of the Suzuki. There on the side was Aalia's bicycle. She looked at it, bent upon itself as though it was trying to curl up and sleep after a long day. Over the years she had watched Aalia become an expert cyclist—one hand, no hands, arms folded. Kaakee looked at the bicycle; suddenly she longed to ride it more than anything else. She looked up at the house, the television was on, they were still up but watching. She straightened out the bicycle and hopped on to the seat. She cycled up to the gate, unsteady. Back to the Suzuki, then again to the gate. With each trip, the ride got smoother. Kaakee started to cycle a little faster and as she did, she felt a breeze against her face, cooling her under her arms, her sticky back. Faster, faster she went and then like Aalia, she stood up on the pedals. She wished Aalia could see her. Suddenly, she felt her hair come loose from the *joora* she had tied, it took her by surprise and made her laugh, just to herself—her hair was flying behind her and the breeze felt stronger than ever. She looked down at the cobbled path, the plants, the black earth in the beds—it all seemed so far away, the view from here was lovely. But so high, so exciting. She felt like she was flying.

Now as she sat on the step, Kaakee ran her hand over the scar again. She would have this forever. I never showed you, she thought, you never knew. Kaakee remembered the breeze in her hair, just like flying.

It was like silk under her fingers. I wish you had seen it, she thought.

# AND THEN
# THE WORLD
# CHANGED

ൟ

## Sabyn Javeri-Jillani

Sabyn Javeri-Jillani (1977–  ) is a
poet and short story writer. She was
born in Karachi, educated there at
St. Joseph's College, and has lived
in England and North America.
Her fiction has been published in
*The World Audience* (USA), *Wasafiri* (UK), *Tresspass* (UK), and *The
London Magazine—A Review of
Literature and the Arts* (UK). As her
contribution to this anthology is also
the title story, so was her story the

title story in the HarperCollins anthology *Neither Night nor Day (2007)*. She lives in London and is earning her masters degree at Oxford University.

"And Then the World Changed" describes a lively multicultural neighborhood—a traditional *mohalla* with old houses and narrow lanes—in an older part of Karachi in the 1960s. The story evokes the heavy hand of martial law hanging over the country and its people, who thirst for news from sources other than the censored broadcasts of Radio Pakistan. Uncle Bobby's huge American car and its radio become symbols, not of modernity or Westernization, but of subversion—providing access to music, songs, and broadcasts beyond the reach of the censors. The story highlights how the sense of personal and national threat created by war—the 1965 conflict with India—leads to polarization and divisions that foreshadow the armed conflicts that broke out among Karachi's ethnic communities in the 1990s and the rise of violent religious extremists in Pakistan, with their parrot-green turbans as a symbol of Islam.

• • •

It wasn't easy, steering a car through the narrow streets of old Karachi. Tiny beads of sweat formed on Bobby Uncle's forehead as he craftily navigated the big-hooded vehicle. Much to the amusement of passersby who looked on with unabashed curiosity at the strange contraption making its way through the brick-paved alleys, he continued to struggle with the giant steering wheel. Short and thin, he seemed dwarfed by the car he drove. It was the kind of motorcar they had only seen in a cinema hall. Usually, a donkey cart or, if there was a special festival, a small taxi would occasionally grace their streets—but to see an actual bright and shiny motorcar make its way down the narrow paths of their neighborhood was not just cause for curiosity, but an actual thrill.

Some shouted at him to get the evil invention of the West out of their *mohalla* while others slapped the bonnet, screaming directions. "Here, here, take a left, back up a little, brother.

*Arrey*! Watch out for the pole!" The lads shouted advice while the children jumped up and down, trying to catch a glimpse of the interior.

Munna, Bobby Uncle's five-year-old nephew, ran out in the alley to see what all the commotion was about. He nearly fell into an open manhole in his excitement when he discovered that it was his very own uncle who was the owner of this glossy motorcar. He ran back inside the house, announcing at the top of his lungs to his deaf grandmother, his baby sister, his next door neighbor, and his mother, who was busy preparing the afternoon meal, the arrival of the shiny contraption into their family.

"A motorcar! A real motorcar, I've seen Bobby Uncle drive up in one."

"Are you making up stories again, Munna?" asked Munira, his ten-year-old neighbor who spent more time in their house than she did in her own.

"I swear on your dad's grave, he has a real live motorcar!" replied Munna.

"Oye! You son of the devil!" she screamed at him, "How many times have I told you not to do that. My father is alive, thank Allah."

"What are you shouting at my son for?" Munna's mother came to his rescue.

"Look at him, *Apa*! He does it deliberately to upset me, sending my Pa to the grave when he is alive!"

"Oh, come now. He probably picked it up from the rogues on the streets," she consoled. "Munna, stop disturbing the women and go and play outside." She shooed him out.

Outside, Bobby Uncle was still struggling with his Chevy.

Turning corners with a Chevy in the maze of narrow alleys that formed the old town was no joke. Bobby Uncle was half leaning out of the front window while well-wishers hung onto the sides, offering their expert advice. Suddenly the car lurched forward and then, with a grueling screech, it shuddered to a stop. Bobby Mama fell forward over the steering, knocking over a roadside seller's wares. The seller cursed him, but Bobby Mama was too embarrassed by the dead engine to care about the seller's loss. To save face Bobby Uncle announced to the neighbors that he had stopped the car there because it was the best parking spot in the neighborhood. The fact that it blocked old woman Hajjin's doorway and the turning into the next lane, seemed of little concern to him.

He tooted the car's shrill horn and Munna's Hindu neighbor, Luxmi, rushed out with a *pooja thali* to ward off the evil eye. Other neighbors like the deaf Jewish musician and short-sighted Parsi uncle also stepped out of their stooped doorways to look at the novelty in their neighborhood. When Munna's *amma* saw the motorcar she couldn't stop gushing to anyone who'd listen, what a success her brother was. She would go on for hours and Munna's poor father regularly bore the brunt of her praise for her brother and his motorcar. Especially when they had to travel by bus on the rare occasions that they left the neighborhood.

The car was grand—to that everyone agreed. Nobody seemed to care that it never started. It coughed and groaned but never ran. The rides by the sea that Munna and his mother had been looking forward to would have turned into haunting complaints had it not been for the car's sleek new radio. Every Saturday, Munna's mother and other women from the neighborhood would get into the car and tune in to All India Radio. They would listen to the gossip about movie stars, and sing along with Indian film songs banned by the strict Islamic regime. A stranger to the neighborhood would find it very odd and perhaps a little spooky to see a car bulging at the seams, its windows covered with *dupattas* in respect of the veil, shaking from side to side with music drifting out. But while the women held a weekly gathering in the car, the men met up at night. At nine p.m. sharp, the neighborhood men would gather around the car and Bobby Uncle would tune the radio to the World Service.

*Beep. Beep.* "This is BBC London," the announcer's voice would boom out, "You are listening to Muhammed Shafi with the latest news in Urdu." A silence would descend on the *mohalla* as the men concentrated on happenings around the world.

These were the days before television made its way to Karachi and radios were a luxury of the rich. But the dedication to the nightly news was due more to strict media control by the state. The country was under the grip of a Martial Law leader who edited the news himself. If it was a dry day and the President wanted it to be a wet one, you could be sure the announcer at Radio Pakistan would read out news of rain. With parched skin and dry throats people would curse the dictator and turn to other sources of information, like independent newspapers. But not everyone could read and this is where Bobby Uncle's radio came in.

He had a passion for gatherings, which he referred to as *mehfils.* Being an unmarried man with no family other than his sister, he would cling to company. These nightly gatherings with him in the driving seat made him feel very important.

Dressed in starched white kurtas the men would bathe, change, and hurriedly eat their dinner in time to get a good listening spot around the radio. Luxmi's husband would close his shop early and bring along his son who always dressed like heroes on the big screen, with slick hair and tight trousers. Parsi Uncle would also arrive early with his own chair as he didn't like to stand. Parsi Uncle had a radio in his house but the women in the neighborhood said it was an excuse to get away from his bossy wife, Munizeh.

Munna, too, would tag along with his father. Most of the children would be shooed off as they inevitably found some cause to make a noise. But Munna, being Bobby Uncle's nephew, would park himself on his lap and listen to the entire bulletin until he fell asleep. Munna found the announcer's voice very pleasant and soothing. He was too young to care about what Nixon said or how many people died in Gaza, but Mahpara, the female presenter's voice, would make him dreamy and transport him on faraway journeys to strange lands. Of course, he knew there really was no America or Ireland, at least that's what Munira had told him and Munira was older than him. Munira didn't go to school because she was a girl and had two older brothers who needed education more than her. They would make it up to her by giving her a grand wedding some day, her mother said, when Munira protested. But even without a proper education Munira was smart—she knew the names of all the prophets and most of the holy words.

Sometimes when her mother let her off kitchen duties before eight, she would sneak to the back wall and try to listen to the car radio. The next day she would show off her knowledge of the bulletin to Munna. "Do you know who stole the sewer lids off our alley?" Munna would shake his head and she would say wisely, "It was America. It comes in the dead of night and steals the lids of our sewers so disease and illness spreads and we drop off like flies."

"America is a country, not a person. Bobby Uncle told me so," Munna would say.

"Oh, you're such a child!" Munira would tease him and run off.

While Munira thought the West was behind all the evils in their neighborhood, thanks to the Ustani who taught her the Holy Book, the men at the nightly radio gathering seemed to think that India was behind all the trouble in their country. The Bulletin always had a few shift-the-blame stories, and most of the time the enemy next door was the root cause of evil.

But lately the gatherings around the car radio had grown more somber. Conflict with India was escalating and there was tension in the air. Men would gather around the car at eight and stick around after the bulletin to discuss matters. Intolerance seemed to be on the rise. Luxmi no longer came to Munna's house and her son Gopal did not attend the news sessions at night. There was a rumor that some overzealous religious fanatics had burned the temple by the sea.

Most of the uncles who didn't go to the mosque did not show up after that night. And the next day when the broadcaster with the sweet voice announced that Indian soldiers had killed Pakistani villagers along the border, Munna noticed that none of his Hindu and Christian friends came out to play.

Munna was too young to understand all this but he knew that he missed his friends and neighbors. The car radio that had brought them together seemed to have created an immeasurable distance between them. Even Munira seemed withdrawn. She had stopped blaming "America" for all that went wrong. Instead she blamed it on the religious minorities in the country. "It's all Luxmi's fault," she would say. "She could be an Indian spy, you know! She probably gets a commission to steal the sewer lids so there is disease and illness in the neighborhood and we all drop off like flies."

Munna listened with his head cocked to one side. He found it hard to believe that sweet, plump Luxmi who always gave him sweets when he passed by her door could be the enemy. But Munira was right. She did look different from the rest of the women in the *mohalla*. She wore a fiery red dot on her forehead and worshipped little dolls that Munna secretly longed to play with. She was different—so were the other people whom Abba and his friends referred to as "Minorities."

Still, Munna found it hard to hate them. It was easier to hate the men in parrot-green turbans who went around burning temples and churches and shouting slogans against white-skinned foreigners. But then Munna was only a little boy. He was too young to pick and choose whom to hate and whom to admire, but deep in his heart he knew one thing for sure—in the days to come when people had been divided into categories of Mohajirs, Masihs, and Sindhis by invisible lines and uncrossable borders, he would miss his old *mohalla* in the city by the sea, where difference did not mean distance.

# CLAY FISSURES

໐ຉ

# *Nayyara Rahman*

Nayyara Rahman (1984– ) is a free-
lance contributor to local magazines
and online forums. She was born and
brought up in Karachi and graduated
from the Institute of Business Management. As a student, she received
several creative-writing prizes,
including first prize in a national
essay competition held by National
Accountability Bureau (NAB), Pakistan. Her short story, "Clay Fissures,"
was one of five winning entries of a

nationwide British Council contest and published in a collection called *I Belong* (British Council, 2004). Her work has also appeared in *Neither Night nor Day* (HarperCollins, 2007).

"Clay Fissures" is another exploration of identity and belonging in Pakistan. The references to the singers Noor Jehan and Mehdi Hassan and the film star Waheed Murad reflect the admiration for popular performers and the role their art plays in defining a young country's self image. The narrator, Pradeep, is marked as different primarily because he is an albino, but also because he is not Muslim. The story makes an interesting comment on color—whiteness—as identity, particularly when Pradeep migrates to the United States, where white skin is commonplace and yet he remains an outsider. The reference to Mr. Ruknuddin, who chose to remain in West Pakistan after the 1971 civil war in which East Pakistan became the independent Bangladesh, presents the concept of nationality as a choice and a commitment, rather than a birthright.

• • •

"Pradeep, go sit on the bench."

I sighed and trudged toward the shady end where Sir Gul Muhammad had placed the benches. Watching the shining faces of my classmates as they ran after the football, I wondered, "Will I ever be like them?"

It wasn't just the game that made me ask that. My eleven-year-old self was an outsider in many ways. It was 1953 and patriotism was still a young, strong spirit in Pakistan. People were proud of being Pakistani. They were proud of being Muslim. They were proud of their brown skin, which reflected wheat—the lifeblood of Pakistan. And here was I: Pradeep Sehgal, the adopted albino son of a Hindu merchant and a Eurasian seamstress.

There was a long cheer. I looked wistfully at the field and then looked away again. Sir Gul meant well. But he didn't seem to realize that a fiercer sun shone down on me than the one he meant to protect me against.

I had never really known what it was like to be a part of anything; to belong anywhere. At seven, a quarrel with my brother had resulted in the discovery of my "adoption." I was also accustomed to being excluded from every game that is woven into the tapestry of childhood because of what my parents called my "colorless skin."

Even at school, I was different. Arithmetic was a general favorite at Rossmoor Academy. I hated it, for I had no patience with something everyone loved to do. After all, bullying "Sunflower Pradeep" was also the most popular sport there.

Thankfully, those were years when sport hadn't overtaken the appreciation of culture. The Beatles may have swung the rest of the world into the 1960s, but Pakistan had its own way of biting into that delicious slice of time. Waheed Murad was a rage. Mehdi Hasan and Noor Jehan were moving the nation with their beautiful music. It was an insane, ecstatic time.

For me, growing up was floating in the wind like a seed. It was fun, but it was fleeting. I needed solid ground to settle down and take root.

Besides, I was still different, still "apart." I still didn't know who my real family was. My foster father's marriage to a Christian had demoted his caste, which, in effect, confirmed my "outcaste" status. I resolved that I would never follow any belief that would make a man a stranger in his own land.

Land! I still marvel at fate for igniting this passion within me. The smell of loam, the dance of the monsoon, the gift of rain coursed inside me and gave me reason to grow, despite myself. I literally dug in. All my drive poured into my work. In 1966, I graduated second in a class of 250 with a double major in geography and geology.

I worked for the government after that. To my delight, my job made me tour the country frequently. To my dismay, I was treated as an outsider wherever I went. The partiality would have been unbearable if it hadn't been for Mr. Ruknuddin.

I always thought my boss was an intriguing fellow, partly

because he truly enjoyed his work in the geology department. In a year when Bangladesh was lauding itself for its independence and Pakistan was mourning the loss of its "Eastern" bloc, Mr. Ruknuddin's presence in a Pakistani government office stood out like a rock in a stream. It was ironic that he should have chosen to continue working in Karachi for his family lived in Dhaka. His younger brother had been killed in "the war," fighting on Bangladesh's side. No matter how I thought about this, I just couldn't understand why Mr. Ruknuddin still worked in Pakistan. I ventured into this daunting territory during lunch when I asked Mr. Ruknuddin how he felt about Pakistan after his brother's death.

Mr. Ruknuddin looked up. Apparently, this wasn't the first time he had been asked that. His half-empty *biryani* plate lay before him when he said the words I would remember in another age. "We all make our own identities. He was willing to die for his land and race. I choose to live for mine. This doesn't make him a martyr or me a traitor. It simply makes us who we are."

Time, I imagine, abrades all. In 1972, destiny veered my life again. Mr. Ruknuddin summoned me into his office one morning and handed me an envelope. With hands that shook like autumn leaves, I ripped it open.

It was an offer to join the American Geologists' Council! My work in exploiting the Karez, or salt lake system in Pakistan, had apparently made quite an impression on observers abroad. My academic credentials were impressive, Mr. Ruknuddin had already sent a most glowing reference, and so the letter went on.

For a moment I stared at Mr. Ruknuddin. Then I grabbed him in a bear hug. He returned it with a grandfatherly smile. "Yes! Yes! Yes!" I cheered, all thirty years of me jumping. "Allah bless you, sir!" At that moment, everything about the universe became insignificant. All that mattered was that I had received every Pakistani geologist's dream job.

Three months later I was working in the United States. My

work centerd on environmental hazards. Earthquakes took me to Los Angeles; the oil crisis took me to Texas. It was an exciting life and a happy one, too. Any racism against me was squashed merely because nobody could be too sure of my "Asian-ness." So, although my name and accent continued to raise eyebrows, I fitted in quite nicely in Every Man's Land.

A geologist will never say, "It's a small world," because for us the world grows more mysterious and challenging every day. I have seen more climatic disasters than any weather reporter can dream of. Indeed, there were so many that their horrors simply consigned themselves to a mental compartment labeled "Unfortunates" in my mind. Indeed, there was only one "horror file" that my thoughts consulted again and again.

In 1988, a drought struck the West Coast and was making its way to the Great Plains. It had decided that its final whiplash would be in the Mississippi River Basin. I was assigned to go there.

I regretted it.

There was something about the faces of the drought victims, a tired, defeated vulnerability that reminded me of a past I was eager to forget. I sighed, muttered expletives, and made no secret of the fact that I couldn't wait to escape. I regarded these people with a callous impatience I had never felt before. Yet, for some reason, I could not be resentful for long. Pity replaced contempt. I plunged into the rehabilitation work with a drive I didn't know I had and worked hard to alleviate their suffering.

Perhaps I was trying to make up for lost time. Perhaps I was trying to make up for lost loyalties.

Whatever it might have been, it was then that I realized that sometimes you learn to value things too late, and by the time you do it's best to just forget them.

Time passed quickly. Color fever was high in the 1980s. The United States had seen a new rival in Japan, Americans discovered new villains in the "yellow people" and recognized old slaves in the "black" ones. They had just begun to realize what it felt like to have Mexicans in their land, and considering how many of those there were the Americans weren't overly enthusiastic about the new brotherhood. Still, remembering their loyalty to their former "white" masters, brown people continued to take pride in subserving themselves in an alien land.

I know the worth of race; after all it is something that has tried hard to make my life worthless. I had been through stilted friendships. I had seen promotions sneak past me to glib, rakish subordinates. Perhaps one reason why I never married was that I always thought a potential wife would look at me in the same way as everyone else. For many years I blamed myself. I did all I could to be like everyone else, but the more I did the more unfamiliar I became to myself.

It took some time before I realized that people didn't react to who I was. All they saw were the pink eyes and flaxen hair. They heard the singsong voice, heard the foreign-sounding name, and decided that I deserved to be treated like an outsider. I had spent years blaming myself for something that didn't come close to being my fault. But the discrimination also taught me that the only place where color really matters is in a rainbow. Imagine those colors geometrically allotting themselves a square meter each of the sky, and you will know what I mean.

Speaking of skies, my American stars shone down on me one evening—or so I thought. I was in San Francisco when I received an unexpected phone call. It was from Mr. Ruknuddin. After an exchange of pleasantries he congratulated me for receiving the National Explorer's Award and a recent Fellowship Grant. Surprised at his acumen, I thanked him. He then mentioned that he'd kept abreast of my work and was wondering if I would be willing to offer my expertise to Pakistan.

"I can't tell you why right now, but we really need you here," he said.

"I'll come."

It was only after I hung up that I realized what I had just done.

The phenomenal stupidity of it! Was I supposed to leave my work and rush over to satisfy the whims of a former boss? Not everyone receives a Fellowship Grant—was I supposed to just forget it? What did Pakistan have for me, anyway? I hadn't returned to the country in years! Why had I said yes?

That was the problem: I knew why.

As Mr. Ruknuddin had requested, I took the first available flight to Pakistan, landing in Balochistan, the country's biggest and most wasted province. In my hotel suite, Mr. Ruknuddin explained: Foreign investors were interested in helping Pakistan establish a copper and gold refinery at Saindak. This was wonderful, except that the project had been stalled until it received security clearance.

"Pradeep," he said, his eyes grave. "We think that place is dangerous. We need your help to know for sure. A lot of people are counting on you."

"What's the problem at Saindak?"

"Oh, nothing's wrong there. But Koh-e-Sultan is showing signs of waking up again."

I stared at him. Koh-e-Sultan may have been a formidable volcano once, but it hadn't erupted in 800 years. "That's absurd!" I cried.

Quietly, Mr. Ruknuddin said, "We certainly hope so."

To appease all, the government insisted on keeping the investigation as low-key as possible. That meant limited research, limited funding, and big risk.

I thought nostalgically of the United States.

In any case, we submerged ourselves in the task. The seismograph spat out pages of data like the ECG reading of a coma patient. The prognosis wasn't exactly discouraging. Koh-e-Sultan would either erupt any time in the next fortnight, or remain dormant for at least another 52 years. At least we had time to prepare for the disaster.

Unfortunately, it was our preparation that gave us away. Although we had been discreet in our collection of mud samples and seismic information, we could not have been secretive about evacuating the locals and their cattle from the scene. "Soil testing" was quite a plausible reason. Or at least it had been until our delineation marks were discovered. The Chinese investors were the first to hear of it. Then came the locals. Next was a large array of reporters from all over Asia. Most annoying was a European diplomat who doubled as an amateur geographer.

We had tried our best to evacuate the place but the public's love for show prevailed. On what we imagined was Judgement Day, the outskirts of Takht-e-Sultan were a circus! The locals had gone through a lot of trouble. Thanks to them, the "spectators" in question could witness the entire event from an adjoining plateau, which, despite its awesome view, was safely several kilometers away. Heaven knows that I have seen nature at its most ruthless. I have worked myself through calamities without flinching, but that day I prayed. Every vein in my body quivered as I imagined lava licking off life.

Eventually restlessness got the better of me. Ignoring the incredulous glances of my teammates in the Research Office, I headed to the outskirts. The frenzy there was unnerving! I could sense the fear and the excitement. We all stood together and waited.

4:30, 5:30, 6:30 . . . The lion would continue to sleep! Relief flooded through us like an elixir. We hugged and shook hands and cheered. Europeans, Chinese, and Baluchis: Christians, Jews, Buddhists, Muslims, and a Hindu all brought together by circumstance. Fate had painted these disparate backgrounds into one picture.

I saw a Pakistani journalist help a Sikh one photograph the scene. An Indian journalist who had come up to cover the economic benefits of the refinery was discussing it with a Chinese businessman—no notebook in hand. Suddenly the sting of having once been "Sunflower Pradeep" dissipated. When I saw the diplomat hug a tribal chief, I remembered Mr. Ruknuddin's old words and they started to make new sense. The tribal chiefs, notorious for their love of war, posed for photographs and then went off together to offer Prayers of Thanks.

When one of the Chinese businessmen boomed: "Pakistan *zindabad!*" tears filled my eyes and I cheered, for I knew exactly what he meant.

At last, I had come home.

# GLOSSARY OF
# SOUTH ASIAN WORDS

ಹಲ

*Abba*: Father

*Achoot*: Untouchable; lowest caste of Hindu

*aiiay:* Enter! Welcome! Come in!

*ajnabi*: Stranger; foreigner

*ajrak*: Ancient hand-block–printed patterns associated with the province of Sindh

*alam bardar*: Standard bearer

*Allah-u-Akbar*: God is great

*Allah-wali*: A woman dedicated to God

*alu ka bhartha*: Mashed potatoes, spiced and fried

*Amma*: Mother

*Ammijee*: Mother

*amrit*: Nectar, water of life, ambrosia

*Angrez*: The British

*apa*: Appellation for elder sister

*araam*: Rest, calm, ease

*araam-say, bhai, yeh hamari behenain hain*: "Go easy, brother, these are our sisters"

*arrey*: An exclamation of familiarity with several connotations, for example, "Well!" or "Oh!" or "Hey!"

*Ashura*: The tenth day of Moharrum

*Astakhfarullah*: God forbid

*Ayat*: Quranic verse

*azaan*: Muslim call to prayer

*badmash*: Miscreant

*Baji*: Appellation for older sister

*baraat*: Marriage procession

*bari*: Larger, older

*batashas*: Crisp, fluffed white sweets that are made of boiled sugar

*behen*: Sister

*behen-chod*: Sister-fucker

*beta*: Son; also a non-gender-specific term of affection for a child

*beti*: Daughter

*bhabi*: Brother's wife—also used for wife of close friend

*bhai*: Brother

*Bharat Natyam*: Classical South Indian dance

*Bibi*: Lady

*biryani*: Rich festive dish of rice and meat/chicken

*boski*: A type of silk with a matte finish

*chacha*: Paternal uncle

*chachi*: Wife of paternal uncle

*chameli*: Sweet-smelling double jasmine whose fragrant buds are often strung together as personal ornaments for women, particularly for a young bride, but can also be used on other occasions

*chappals*: Thronged sandals (Bata *chappals* are *chappals* bought from the well-known shoe store chain, Bata)

*charas*: Hashish, hemp

*chowki*: Wooden platform

*chunri*: A gauzy head covering with colorful patterns created by tie-dyeing

*dadi*: Paternal grandmother

*desh*: Country, homeland

*desi*: Pertaining to the subcontinent; belonging to *desh*

*diyar*: Cedar tree

*Dhamal*: Sufi dance that embodies mystical ecstasy

*Dukhmo*: Towers of Silence, the area where Parsi funeral rites take place

*dulhan*: Bride

*dupatta*: Gauzy scarf-like covering

*Eid*: Religious festival; *Eid-ul-Azha* celebrates the end of Ramazan, the month of fasting; *Bakr-e-Eid* commemorates and emulates Abraham's sacrifice

*fajr*: Dawn, early morning

*filmi*: From a film

*gharara*: A pajama made so wide and flowing and with many gathers that it resembles a skirt; a *gharara* suit includes the knee-length shirt that is worn over the *gharara*; the large *dupatta*, which is draped over the shoulders and can be pulled up to cover the head, if need be

*ghazal*: An Urdu poem with clearly defined meter and form

*ghungroos*: Wide leather swatches covered with tiny metal bells

*goonda*: Thug

*gora*: White

*gullies*: Narrow lanes

*haan*: Yes

*hai*: A general exclamation of lament

*hakim*: Doctor; a practitioner of traditional medicine

*haleem*: A special dish created by cooking a mixture of wheat, spices, and meat for many hours

*hanh*: Yes

*Hanuman*: Hindu monkey god

*haraam*: Forbidden; sinful

*haraam-kari*: Sinful doings

*haveli*: House; large and spacious dwelling

*Hehna?*: "Is it not?"

*hijab*: Head covering that hides the hair

*iddat*: The mandatory four months and ten days of seclusion that a widow must observe after her husband's death to ensure that if she is pregnant, the child's paternity cannot be questioned

*Ik minit, yaar*: One minute, mate

*Inglestan*: England

*ittar*: Perfume or scent, usually oil based

*jaan*: Dear, darling

*jaib*: Pocket

*jamun*: Tree with large purple edible berries

*jee*: Yes; as an appellation, this is a term of respect

*jenab*: Sir

*jharoo*: A type of broom

*joora*: Coiled hair worn as a bun at the back of the head

*jora*: Two- or three-piece outfit

378

*jungli*: Uncivilized; wild; from the jungle

*kameez*: Shirt

*karak chai*: Strong tea, usually a specialty in bazaars, or road stalls

*Karbala*: One of the holy cities of Islam where the Battle of Karbala took place

*Karbala Gamey Shah*: Site in Lahore where the Muharram processions end

*Kathak*: A classic dance form in the northern areas of South Asia

*keema*: Mince

*khadi*: Handwoven cotton

*khais*: Large shawl worn by men

*khala*: Maternal aunt

*khas ki tatti*: Large matting of sweet-smelling reeds

*Kitni der laga di*: "It's taking so long"

*koel*: South Asian cuckoo

*kothi*: House

*kothi-wallah*: Owner of the house or property

*Kurukshetra*: The plain where the mythological Battle of Kurukshetra took place in the Hindu epic, *Mahabharata*

*kuwan*: A well

*lassi*: Cool drink made of diluted yoghurt and sugar or salt

*ma*: Mother

*Maajee*: Mother

*maatam*: The ritual and rythmic beating of the chest with the right hand in lamentation during the rites of Muharram

*machera*: Fisherman

*madar-chod*: Motherfucker

*Mahabharata*: Sacred Hindu text and epic

*maidaan*: Empty plot or open common land

*mali*: gardener

*mannat*: A religious supplication entailing a vow

*mashak*: A large leather pouch in which water is carried

*Mashallah*: By the grace of God

*Masih*: Christian

*masjid*: Mosque

*maulvi*: Muslim cleric; *maulvi* sahib is a respectful form of address

*mehfils*: Social or cultural gatherings

*mehndi*: A party with specific rituals, including songs and music, which is an intrinsic part of a wedding but takes place a night or two before the actual marriage ceremony

*meri*: My; mine; for example, *meri jaan* means, "my darling"

*Mia*: Lord, master; can also mean husband

*mohajir*: Refugee; terms used for ethnic communities that migrated to Pakistan at Partition from India

*mohalla*: Neighborhood

*momani:* Maternal uncle's wife; aunt

*mynah-bird*: A type of starling

*na*: "No," but depending on the context, if used as question, can also mean, "Isn't it so?" or, "Don't you agree?"

*Na ro Zainab*: "Don't cry, Zainab"; Zainab was the granddaughter of the Prophet and among the captives after the Battle of Karbala. Her lamentation for her kin, including her martyred brother, Hussein, and her sons killed at Karbala, is central to the poetry and elegies recited in Moharrum. In Shia Islam, both she and Fatima, her mother (the Prophet's daughter) are venerated in their own right.

*nani*: Maternal grandmother

*namaz*: Prayer

*nashta*: Breakfast

*nazrana*: Money given as a blessing or offering

*nikah*: Marriage ceremony

*nutfa*: Seed, sperm

*paan*: Leaf of the betel plant that is dressed with various condiments and chewed

*pani*: Water

*paratha*: Fried rounds of bread made from wheat flour

*parda/purdah*: A curtain; also indicates the segregation of the sexes in a traditional Muslim household, and women who observe the veil

*pari*: Fairy

*patwari*: Steward

*peshwaze*: A traditional dress worn by women since Mughal times that consists of a tightfitting, bodice-like shirt that flares out from the waist to the knees like a skirt. Worn over a type of pajama that clings to the legs.

*pooja*: Form of worship for Hindus

*prem*: Love

*Qul*: The reading of a Quranic surah at the conclusion of a *soyem*

*Ram*: Hindu God, hero of the *Ramayana* epic

*Ramazan*: The month Muslims fast from sunrise to sunset; Ramadan

*randis*: Prostitutes, whores

*rasmalai*: Light curd cheese balls soaked in cream and syrup

*rishta*: Marriage proposal

*sakhi/saheli*: Friend; a term used exclusively for women, indicating companionship and sorority

*saqi*: The cupbearer; beloved; an image used metaphorically in Urdu poetry

*shalwar*: Baggy, ankle-length trousers

*sheesham*: Rosewood

*shikar*: Hunt

*Sindhi*: Belonging to the province of Sindh

*sindhur*: Vermillion worn by Hindu women in the parting of the hair

*sola topi*: A sun helmet made from the pith of the *sola*, a swamp plant

*soyem*: The final mourning rite on the third day after the funeral

*supari*: Small chips of betel nut, coated with condiments, to be chewed; also used to dress paan

*Surah*: Chapter of the Quran

*surma*: Collyrium used to outline and beautify the eyes

*thali*: Tray, large plate

*thero*: Wait

*tika*: Jeweled ornament worn on the forehead—to adorn newly wed brides in particular

*tilak*: Red mark worn on the forehead by Hindu women

*vataan*: Country; homeland

*Wa laikum Assalam*: "Peace be upon you"; is said in response to the greeting "Salaam aleikum," which means the same thing

*wah:* Wow! Wonderful!

*Wazir*: Minister or counselor of state in a Muslim country, sometimes spelled "Vizier."

*Ya Ali! Ya Hussein*: Cries of lamentation in Muharram calling upon the names of Ali, the Prophet's son-in-law and his martyred son Hussein

*yaar*: Mate; pal

*zenana*: Women; the women's apartments in a segregated household
*zindabad*: Long live
*Zuljana*: The steed that Hussein rode at Kerbala; a white horse representing Zuljana is part of the processions of Muharram

# ACKNOWLEDGMENTS
# AND PERMISSIONS

ഇരു

## ACKNOWLEDGMENTS

I would like to thank Saba Gul Khattak and Kiran Ahmed of the Sustainable Development Institute in Islamabad for bringing Ritu Menon and me together; Ritu Menon and Women Unlimited for making this book possible and for their kindness and hospitality in Delhi; Ameena Saiyid and Ramik Akhund at Oxford University Press in Pakistan for their continuing support; Rukhsana Ahmad and Moazzam Sheikh for their help; Aamer Hussein and Anjoli Roy for introducing me to new writing; The Feminist Press, in particular Gloria Jacobs and my editor Anjoli Roy for their cooperation and painstaking care; and, as always, I owe a special thanks to my family: Saleem, Saman, and Kamila.

—from the Editor, Muneeza Shamsie

## PERMISSIONS

*The Women Unlimited edition of this volume included the following stories, whose copyright information follows:*

Talat Abbasi, first broadcast as a prize winner in the BBC World Service short story competition, 2000. Reprinted from *Bitter Gourd and Other*

*Stories* (Karachi: Oxford University Press, 2001) with the permission of the publisher and author.

Humera Afridi, first published as "Circumferece" in *110 Stories: New York Writes after September 11* (Ulrich Baer, Ed., New York: New York University Press, 2003). Revised version, "The Prince of Hubris," printed with the permission of the author.

Fawzia Afzal Khan, altered and abriged version first appeared in *Aizah Magazine,* volume 3, issue 2, December 2003, Atlanta, Georgia. This version a chapter of a memoir in progress, *Sahelian: Growing Up with Girlfriends Pakistani Style,* is published with the permission of the author.

Feryal Ali Gauhar, excerpt from chapter 9 from *The Scent of the Earth in August* (New Delhi: Penguin, 2002). Reprinted as "Kucha Miran Shah" with permission of the author and Penguin.

Uzma Aslam Khan, from *Trespassing* (New Dehli: Penguin, 2003). Reprinted with the permission of the author and Penguin.

Shahrukh Husain, first appeared as "Rubies for a Dog" in *Women Who Wear the Breeches: Delicious and Dangerous Tales* (London: Virago, 1995). Revised version, "Rubies for a Dog: A Fable," printed here with the permission of the author.

Sorayya Khan, from *Five Queen's Road* (New Delhi: Penguin Books India, 2008). Reprinted with the permission of the author.

Nayyarra Rahman, from *I Belong: A Collection of Short Stories* (Karachi: British Council, 2004). Reprinted with the permission of the author and the British Council.

Hima Raza, printed here with the permission of Anjana Raza and Begum Nasim F. Raza.

Roshni Rustomji, from *Asian Americans on War and Peace* (ed. Russell C. Leongand Don T. Nakanishi, Los Angeles: UCLA Asian-American Studies Center Press, 2002). Revised version reprinted with the permission of the author.

Qaisra Shahraz, to Prof. Liesel Hermes for the original publication of

*Photo Credits*

For Shahrukh Husain's photograph: Helen Pedersen

For Soniah Kamal's photograph: Mansoor Wasti

For Maniza Naqvi's photograph: Adnan Dumisic, photo studio, Sarajevo

For Tahira Naqvi's photograph: Jaishri Abichandani

For Sehba Sarwar's photograph: Dawn, a daily newspaper in Pakistan

For Bina Shah's photograph: Behrouz Hashim

For Kamila Shamsie's photograph: Salma Raza

For Muneeza Shamsie's photograph: Ayesha Vellani

For Sara Suleri Goodyear's photograph: Azra Raza

For Nayyara Rahman's photograph: Tahira Rahman

For Bushra Rehman's photograph: Jaishri Abichandani

For Qaisra Shahraz's photograph: Veronica Taylor

**The Feminist Press at The City University of New York**
is a nonprofit institution dedicated to publishing literary and educational works by and about women. We are the oldest continuing feminist publisher in the world; our existence is grounded in the knowledge that mainstream publishers seeking mass audiences often ignore important, pathbreaking works by women from the United States and throughout the world.

The Feminist Press was founded in 1970. In its early decades the Press launched the contemporary rediscovery of "lost" American women writers, and went on to diversify its list by publishing significant works by American women writers of color. More recently, the Press has added to its roster international women writers who are still far less likely to be translated than male writers. We also seek out nonfiction that explores contemporary issues affecting the lives of women around the world.

The Feminist Press has initiated two important long-term projects. Women Writing Africa is an unprecedented four-volume series that documents women's writing in Africa over thousands of years. The Women Writing Science project, funded by the National Science Foundation, celebrates the achievements of women scientists while frankly analyzing obstacles in their career paths. The series also promotes scientific literacy among the public at large, and encourages young women to choose careers in science.

Founded in an activist spirit, The Feminist Press is currently undertaking initiatives that will bring its books and educational resources to underserved populations, including community colleges, public high schools, literacy and ESL programs, and international libraries. As we move forward into the twenty-first century, we continue to expand our work to respond to women's silences wherever they are found.

For information about events and for a complete catalog of the Press's more than 300 books, please refer to our website: www.feministpress.org or call (212) 817-7915.